For Yael

My grandson and one of my youngest readers

This book is for you

Chapter One
When a Plan is Not Yet a Plan

"**I** have a plan."

That was what Alex Hawk *said* as he lay on his stomach on a bluff overlooking an armada that threatened the freedom the people of Kragdon-ah held so dear.

Beyond those brave words, he could admit only to himself that what he had was more like a vague outline of a plan. What he had was a concept: *Take the fight to them.* The what, when, and how of executing that remained elusive.

He felt the warm presence of his daughters, Sanda and Amy, lying on the grass beside him, and that gave him a belief he could solve this seemingly unsolvable puzzle. Many such puzzles had presented themselves to him over his lifetime. He had solved them all, no matter the sometimes-staggering odds against success.

Behind him, he heard the sound of the young warriors he had led on what they initially thought was a karak-ta egg hunt. That egg hunt was out of the question now. All access to the karak-ta nests—the mighty birds that laid the psychotropic eggs—were cut off by the massed army of invaders that were slowly loading the captured Kragdon-ah onto the gigantic sailing ships.

Alex scooted away from the edge and Sanda and Amy did the same. He pointed at three of the young warriors and said, "Belly crawl up and look down. It is a sight like you've never seen before."

The three dropped to their stomachs and crawled forward. When they saw the ships below, Alex heard them suck their breath in. When you live your whole life thinking a bow and arrow is the height of technology, huge three-masted sailing ships are not just surprising, but confounding. They wouldn't have been any more surprised if a spaceship had dropped from the skies and landed on the beach.

Alex made sure that each of the warriors got a chance to see the vista below, then gathered everyone well away from the edge. He couldn't have said why he was so bent on remaining unseen by the invaders. Theoretically, the Winten-ah had four more years of safety, the result of winning a Thundan against the invaders. Still, this was war, and in war, information is power.

Alex looked at the group assembled in front of him. "I would like to return to Winten-ah without them seeing us. I have a feeling we may run into more of the caravan approaching the beach if we return using our normal path across the domain of the ronit-ta." He was fully back in the mindset of Kragdon-ah now and thought of the dire wolves only by their Winten-ah name—ronit-ta. "Do any of you know another route home?"

Werda-ak the Younger stepped forward.

Of course it's you. So much like your uncle, you could be him made over.

"I know a way," Werda-ak the Younger said. "But it will take us two extra days to return home."

Alex considered, weighing safety versus how worried Sekun-ak would be if they didn't return by tomorrow.

"Werda-ak, I'm putting you in charge." He watched as the young man's chest puffed out visibly. "Lead the group back to Winten-ah by that route."

"Are you not coming with us?"

"I will return by the more direct route. One man can remain unseen in areas where a group will be spotted."

Monda-ak stood close to Alex, leaning against him slightly. The dog was confident that when he spoke of *one man*, he meant one man and his best friend. There was never a question of whether or not the 300-pound dog would accompany Alex. They were inseparable.

"Are you going to cross the plain alone? That has been death for many a creature."

Alex weighed that. "When we crossed earlier, the ronit-ta were nowhere in sight. I believe the caravan of the invaders scared them away. I will trust that is still the case."

Werda-ak the Younger gave Alex a skeptical expression that was half *it's been nice knowing you*, and half *it's your funeral*.

Amy took a half-step toward her father. Before she could speak, Alex held his hand up. "I'll be fine. You stay with the group. I don't know how dangerous this path will be, but they may need you and your sword, or Sanda and her bow."

Amy was a long-time veteran of arguing with her father and recognized when there was no path to success. She shrugged, stood on tiptoe, and brushed her lips against his cheek. Sanda did the same, whispering, "See you at the cliffside."

"Watch out for each other," Alex said to their retreating backs. Werda-ak the Younger was already leading them away. They were not big on formal goodbyes in Kragdon-ah.

Alex couldn't help himself. Instead of starting back toward Winten-ah, he once again crept to the edge of the bluff and stared down at the activity playing out below him. It appeared very organized.

If there was a guy walking around with a clipboard, it would look like one of my old units preparing to depart on a mission.

Finally, he crept away and stood, looking up at the sky. He laid a hand on Monda-ak's head. "We'll never make it home tonight, and we're not crazy enough to attempt to cross the plain in the dark, but we can make it to the edge of the clearing before we sleep."

Monda-ak stared at him, waiting for something resembling a real command. His trusting brown eyes didn't so much as blink.

"For now, go ahead and hunt. But stay close. We don't want to be discovered, understand?"

Monda-ak wasn't human. He was much better than that. The people of Winten-ah believed that his breed had the intelligence of a five-year-old child. Alex thought that was fine as far as it went, but knew that Monda-ak was smarter than that and understood most everything he said.

Alex followed the rough trail they had taken on their way to the bluff. Monda-ak managed to catch a few rodents by following his keen nose and digging down a few feet, chasing them. It wasn't near enough to be a meal for him, but it would keep him going for the moment.

When they reached a spot where Alex could look out over the plain, they stopped. As Alex had feared, the caravan of invaders and captured Kragdon-ah continued. Quietly, he said, "We'll stay here tonight. Go find your dinner, but go that way," Alex said, pointing away from the caravan's path. Monda-ak disappeared, on the hunt.

Alex found a likely tree and climbed up, looking down on the thread of people and horses that still stretched as far as he could see. He pulled a handful of jerky from his bag and chewed it as he watched and thought. There would be no fire on this night, but it was no hardship—the temperatures would be warm.

Alex had never managed to completely adapt to sleeping in the crook of branches in trees, and as he had gotten older, it had become worse. When he first dropped from the tree in the morning now, he walked like an old man for the first few steps. Even with the ten years the visitors had stripped away from him, he knew he was approaching that time when he wouldn't be able to just run over things any more. He would have to start using his head more.

Monda-ak returned with bits of fur attached to his muzzle—evidence that his hunt had gone well. He padded directly to the tree Alex was in and lay down silently next to its trunk. Soon, his snores wafted gently up to Alex, punctuated by the mighty farts his kind was justifiably famous for.

Alex leaned his head against the trunk of the tree and fell asleep with his own words—*I have a plan*—echoing in his ears.

He awoke a few hours later. It was still completely dark, but the movement of the birds in the trees told him that dawn wouldn't be far away.

He squinted into the darkness to see if the caravan was still passing, but it was too dark to see. He strained his ears, but couldn't hear a whisper of movement from below. He dropped as lightly as he could to the ground and yes, he walked with a crick in his back for a few steps.

Monda-ak raised his head and looked at Alex.

"No commentary from you, fur-face."

Alex relieved his bladder, being careful not to pee on any tree. This was the same forest where he had once irritated one of the giant cockroaches by splashing urine on the trunk. Seeing the terrifying creature skittering down toward him had taught him enough of a lesson that he had never made the same mistake again.

He stretched, rolled his shoulders, and did his best to bring life back to his limbs. As he expected, the first faint light showed in the east. He crept to the ridgeline and looked down at the plain.

He could see the path that the caravan had worn in the preceding days. It was empty as far as the eye could see. It had been empty when they had crossed the plain the day before, as well. That told him that the prisoners of Kragdon-ah were being shipped from various locations at different paces. There could be another group of them that would leave from the east. He had no interest in meeting them.

Alex laid a hand gently on Monda-ak's head and nuzzled his neck. He didn't even need to bend over to do that, which is why the mighty dog engendered such fear in those he attacked.

"We need to not be seen," Alex said to him. "Be as quiet and small as you can be."

Monda-ak wagged his tongue as though the idea that he could ever be small was comical.

"I said, 'As small as you *can be*.' Don't get too literal on me now."

Alex did not drop down to the trail they normally used. Something told him that it was possible there might be guards posted at various points along it. Nice little campsites that served as way stations as the caravan passed. If they were there, Alex did not want to run into them. The red pole that stood in front of Winten-ah offered them protection, but it was miles away and would do him no good here in the wild.

He dropped down the side of the hill where there was no path. He paid for that decision in flesh as various vines and thorns tore at his clothes and imbedded in his arms and legs. Monda-ak moved into the lead. His coat and skin were thick enough not to be bothered by such mundane challenges and he was able to break the trail for Alex.

In short order, they were out of the woods and on the plain. The sun still hadn't risen in the east, but the sky was pink and he felt he could see well enough to cross the plain.

This plain had once stood as his primary obstacle to getting home. When he had first been captured by the Winten-ah, his thoughts had only centered around escaping and making his way back to the door. It was this plain that had stopped him.

His friend and fellow time traveler, Dan Hadaller, had told him of his own escape attempt and how he had been treed by the ronit-ta for two nights before the Winten-ah had rescued him. That—and Alex's own encounter with the wolves—had dissuaded Alex from attempting the same crossing until it was too late and the original door had disappeared.

And now he was here—facing the same challenge of crossing the plains almost alone. *Almost* was key, though. As long as he had Monda-ak at his side, he knew he had a chance in any fight.

He set out dead east toward the sunrise, although he still avoided the well-worn path they had traversed the day before. Walking across the plain was not difficult. It was essentially a five-mile square of open field covered in tall Kragdon-ah grass. As long as you could walk in a straight line, you could make it from one side to the other—barring an interlude with the ronit-ta, of course.

Alex walked at a brisk pace, hoping to cross the open area before the heat of the day settled in. As always, he kept his head on a swivel and his ears open for the slightest whisper of sound from behind. Monda-ak stayed close, keeping pace precisely.

There were times that Alex wished he was as tall as the Winten-ah, or any of the tribes of Kragdon-ah. At six-foot-two, he had been on the tall side in twenty-first century Oregon. He was at least eight inches shorter than the average Winten-ah, however. He craned his neck and stretched upward as he walked, hoping to catch the first glimpse of the tree line that marked the end of the plains and the beginning of Winten-ah. Once he saw the leafy green tops of the trees, he would know he was within hailing distance of help from the guards who stood vigilant in their branches, undoubtedly sweeping the horizon for any sign of the returning party.

Alex thought he was getting close to the place where he should see the tree line when he spotted something much worse. Ahead and to his right, he saw the curved silver back of a ronit-ta.

Chapter Two
Face-off with a Ronit-ta

I t was still spring, and so the grass was only half-grown, which meant it only came to Alex's waist. The fact that he only saw the back of the dire wolf meant that it was crouched in a hunting posture. The only animals within likely hunting range were he and Monda-ak, so it was not hard to guess what was on the menu.

Alex knew that ronit-ta rarely hunted alone. They were pack animals.

He didn't stop completely, but he did slow his pace. He used a technique he had been taught long ago. He kept his eyes straight ahead, but focused on what he might see in his peripheral vision. He would spot any movement that should not be there.

No matter how alert he was, he didn't see any other sign of the pack.

Ronit-ta surround their prey and chase them in a direction where they can be set upon by multiple wolves. Alex had never seen a lone wolf hunting.

A thought occurred to him. It was likewise possible that this wolf had never seen a lone human try to cross its domain. Perhaps she was as puzzled to see Alex as he was to see her.

Alex gave Monda-ak a hand signal and stopped. Both man and dog automatically fell into a long-practiced fighting stance—legs spread wide, weight evenly distributed. Alex had his two-bladed ax in his right hand and his stabbing sword in his left.

If it did come down to a battle with the ronit-ta, Alex liked his odds with Monda-ak at his back.

For long seconds, a light breeze ruffled the fine gray hairs on the slightly curved back. Then she gave up the partial cover of the tall grass. She stood and looked at Alex and Monda-ak with her unblinking yellow eyes. She lowered her head slightly and took two, three, four backward steps before she turned and jogged away.

Alex laid a hand on Monda-ak's quivering shoulder. "Yes, you are a magnificent fighter. You would have torn that ronit-ta to shreds. But she knew that too and chose to live to fight another day."

Monda-ak's muscles relaxed and his posture changed. He took his eyes off the retreating ronit-ta and instead looked at Alex with his trusting gaze, letting his tongue loll comically.

Alex smiled and put one arm around his best friend. "Let's head for home."

Ten minutes later, the tree line came into view and Alex immediately heard the blast of a horn, sending the message on down the line and to the cliffside. He picked up his pace. When word reached the caves that Alex and Monda-ak were traveling alone, it would set off a wave of concern. Mothers would worry about sons and daughters. Sekun-ak would worry about all. As the chieftain of the Winten-ah, he carried responsibility for all on his broad shoulders.

As soon as Alex reached hailing distance, the guard in the tree shouted, "Gunta, Manta-ak. Is all well?"

"All is well," Alex said, answering to his Winten-ah name. "But I have a tale to tell. Please pass the word on that the others will be following."

The guard put the horn to his lips and blew two short blasts and one long. Then the second guard dropped to the ground and ran for the cliffs carrying the more complete message.

By the time Alex reached the path that ran alongside the trees and led to the open field in front of the caves, curious Winten-ah were approaching from the other direction. They peppered him with questions, but Alex held his hand up.

"Everyone is fine. There are no casualties. But, I want to only tell this story once, so it will have to wait until I see Sekun-ak."

The group accepted that and walked happily along with Alex, relieved that their brothers and sisters were safe.

By the time they reached the field where their crops were planted, much of Winten-ah had gathered to greet them. Children ran forward and clamored around Monda-ak, who, even after all this time, was irresistible to them. Torana stood at the back of the crowd, the tiny girl named Sista-eh perched on his shoulder. He towered over even the tallest Winten-ah by a good two feet. His misshapen face was split in a homely, welcoming grin.

At the front of the crowd was Sekun-ak. Alex stopped before him and the chieftain laid his hand on Alex's shoulder in the traditional Winten-ah greeting.

"Tell me," Sekun-ak said simply.

Alex took a deep breath and told the story of the karak-ta egg hunt that turned into something else altogether. He told how the open plain had been suspiciously devoid of ronit-ta, the endless caravan of prisoners, and, finally, the armada floating in the natural bay.

Sekun-ak listened carefully to the story, keeping his own counsel. When Alex finished speaking, he said, "This explains much, doesn't it?"

"Yes," Alex said, touching two fingers to his forehead in agreement.

"This is why they wanted to capture us all instead of simply killing us, which they could have done. They wanted to take us to their land and use us as slaves." His upper lip curled at that last word.

Sekun-ak had been a slave himself for a few brief weeks, and he had never forgotten.

"Did you know there were civilizations—large tribes—on the other side of the big water?"

Sekun-ak tilted his head at Alex. "You still ask the strangest questions, my brother. I did not *know* there were other tribes across the water, but I *believed* there were." He let a small smile touch his lips. "We are the Winten-ah—*the people*—but we have never thought we are the *only* people."

Sekun-ak fell silent, letting this new information sink in.

"I didn't want to be discovered by the invaders, so I sent everyone else by another route. Werda-ak said that way would take them an extra day to arrive. I knew everyone would worry about us and I was afraid that you might send a rescue party looking for us, so I hurried here with Monda-ak."

"You were right. If none of you had returned by apex, I would have been concerned. First thing tomorrow, I would have sent a scout team out to look for you."

"And they might have stumbled right into the caravan," Alex added. "I know we are protected from being captured by them, but I don't know if that applies to small bands in the wild."

Sekun-ak turned to a tall, well-built warrior. "Davin-ak, take six people with you and go to meet them. They are likely fine. That is not a dangerous path. But in case they have run into trouble, let us go and meet them."

"Do you know which path they are taking?"

Again, Sekun-ak looked at Alex, amused. "It is a path that crosses Winten-ah. Of course I know it."

Alex fell silent, committed to not asking any more silly questions for the next few minutes.

Sekun-ak raised his voice. "I think everyone knows the story now. They are all fine. Go about your business." The crowd dispersed.

Sekun-ak moved closer to Alex, lowered his voice, and said, "What do we do now?"

Alex had known the question was coming. "We have two choices. The safe path, which I believe will lead to our destruction. And, the risky path, which will also likely lead to our destruction."

"But we will go down fighting with the second choice."

"Yes."

"Let's go to the meeting room. I'd like to ask a few elders to join us."

Alex looked at Monda-ak and pointed at the children. "Go play with them."

Monda-ak woofed his agreement. He would always rather be playing in the field with the children, where they often rode him like he was a horse, than lying on the stone floor of the cave while people talked endlessly.

Alex called to Sekun-ak, "I'll meet you there. I want to find someone first."

Sekun-ak waved a hand as he walked toward the caves, his mind already on a dozen new problems.

Alex allowed himself a moment to stop and take in Winten-ah. The field where he stood had been wide open when he had first arrived. Now, large swaths of it were given over to raising krinta, the hearty corn-like vegetable that was the result of seeds gifted to the tribe years earlier. There was still plenty of open space for the children to run and play, and a long green stretch where Nanda-eh and her archers were able to practice their craft.

Workers still toiled at the ruined waterfall that had once run freely beside the cliffside. Its pristine beauty had been ruined by repeated cannon shots from the invaders. They had only been trying to destroy the Winten-ah water source, but had unknowingly also annihilated the only door back to twenty-first century Oregon in the process. Alex was sure it was still in there somewhere, just buried in the rubble.

Sitting next to where the waterfall had once been, was an odd-looking structure. It looked a bit like a rectangular shipping container turned on its end, with a peaked roof to give it protection from the rain. It was as tall as it was wide because it was Torana's home. He was too large to fit comfortably in the caves, so the Winten-ah built this home for him when he was banished by the invaders for losing the Thundan to Tinta-ak.

Just before Alex departed on the karak-ta egg hunt, he had stashed Darand, another exile from the invaders, in Torana's house. From the initial look on Darand's face, Alex hadn't been sure the forced roommates were going to work out. He seemed terrified of Torana, which was a reasonable reaction to any nine-and-a-half-foot tall giant.

Torana was still in the field, playing with the children and Monda-ak. Next to Torana, Monda-ak looked like a normal-sized dog.

Alex climbed to the lowest level of the cliffside and walked to Torana's house. He didn't bother to knock, but pushed inside, curious as to what Darand might be doing.

The former invader sat at the oversize kitchen table. He looked very much like a small child who had somehow managed to snare a seat at the adult table. He had a bowl in his lap and another at his feet. He was snapping peas vigorously and tossing them into the bottom bowl.

Alex couldn't help smiling. It appeared that even the fearsome invaders could be housebroken with a little effort.

Darand looked up from his labor, slightly embarrassed to have been caught doing something so mundane. When Alex had challenged Nekuna—one of the commanders of the invaders—to a contest for the freedom of the Garta-ah people and lost, Darand had been left in charge of the tribe. Now he was reduced to snapping peas while sitting on a ridiculously-too-large chair.

He reached up and set the bowl with the unsnapped peas onto the table, which was at eye level for him.

"Manta-ak," he acknowledged.

"Darand," Alex said. "We need to have a talk."

Darand took a deep breath, held it a moment, and let it out slowly. "I knew this was coming. I know my life depends on you."

"No, not me. Your life depends on the council of Winten-ah. They are meeting right now. I went to the big water yesterday and saw your ships."

"They are not my ships."

Alex closed his eyes for a beat, looking for patience.

"The ships of your people. I saw them loading the people they captured onto the ships."

Darand looked at him, not bothering to waste his breath in denial.

"We need to decide what to do," Alex continued. "You will have one chance to help yourself. If you tell us the complete truth about everything, you may have a chance to live. If I detect any falsehood, you will not live to see the next sunrise. If I later find out you have lied to us, I will make it my duty to kill you. Understood?"

Darand's eyes were wide and moist. "I will not lie. I want to live. I owe those who I was born with nothing. They made me an outcast, knowing they were sentencing me to death. I have no loyalty to them. Take me to your council. I have a story to tell."

Chapter Three
Darand's Story

"The voyage to this land that you call Kragdon-ah was awful," Darand said.

He stood in front of Alex, Sekun-ak. Darand's grasp of the universal language was still not ideal, but his months in the caves of Garta-ah had improved it. And the knowledge that his life depended on the outcome of this meeting gave him a passion that helped get his message across.

Sekun-ak held up a hand to stop him. "You say that we call this land Kragdon-ah, and that is correct, but what do you call it?"

Reverting back to his native tongue for a moment, Darand said, "Prindan Zand." He switched back to the language of Kragdon-ah. "It means The Lost Lands."

"We were never lost," Sekun-ak observed. "But go on. Start by telling us where your homeland is and what it is called."

Darand paused, gathering his thoughts, and grasping for particular words.

"Even that question isn't easily answered, but I will do my best. If it seems like I skip over things, it's not what I want."

Alex smiled at him, attempting to reassure him. If he got so nervous that he lost his already uncertain grip on the language, none of this would do them any good." Just start at the beginning, wherever you think that is."

Darand took a half-step back, considering.

"Our land, Drakana, was much like Kragdon-ah far back into lost memories. Then, two-hundred-and-twelve summer solstices ago, Makinta emerged from the wilderness, fully formed. He is our god, or so most think of him that way. His arrival changed everything. He led us out of the darkness and brought magic with him."

Alex nodded to himself. *Sounds like someone like me. But he didn't have much interest in conforming to the way things were.*

"Is this Makinta still alive?" Alex asked. "If he's a god, he should be able to live a couple of hundred years, right?"

"That depends."

"Does it?" Alex asked again.

"Makinta has moved his soul from his body to a new body—always one of his sons—six times. We still call him Makinta. Is he really the same person? I cannot say." Darand made a face that seemed to say, *that's above my pay grade.* "It doesn't really matter, because each Makinta, whether the same or one of his sons, still rules the land."

Darand closed his eyes for a moment, obviously trying to sort the story before telling it.

"I say they brought magic, and they did. They took us out of the caves and showed us how to build sturdy houses and walls that could not be easily broken through. They brought weapons, which you saw when we came here. When Makinta first came to Drakana, we were a small tribe ourselves—no bigger than Winten-ah. But Makinta showed us how to protect ourselves and trained us to use the weapons he brought. We spread out across the land, capturing other villages, and making them part of Drakana as well. Before the first Makinta moved into his son's body, our small tribe was a hundred times bigger."

Darand turned to Sekun-ak. "That is why it is hard for me to say where our homeland is. I know where the original Drakana is, but it was abandoned long ago and is nothing but ruins now. Drakana is everywhere within many days journey of where it started. Once Makinta took over our land, we built boats and moved to other lands. We were never beaten, but we didn't want to kill everyone, we wanted to make them part of us."

"Is that what you came here to Kragdon-ah to do? Make us part of this Drakana?" That last word did not slide easily off Sekun-ak's tongue and came out slightly garbled.

"Not on this trip, no, but next trip, yes. For this trip, our job was to weaken the villages and land by capturing as many as possible and taking them home to do the work no one else wants to do."

"Make them slaves," Sekun-ak said.

"Yes. That is the plan. You saw the ships. They are loading many of the people of Kragdon-ah to take them home and make them slaves in different parts of Drakana. Then the first captains will share information with Makinta and he will use this to plan their return to make this part of the world Drakana as well."

Silence filled the cave. Sekun-ak and Alex exchanged a long look, but neither spoke.

"I don't believe there is any way to stop them. For every one of you, there are a thousand of them. They have resources and weapons that you will never have. The only way for you to be safe from the Drakana is if they do not know you exist." He let his chin drop to his chest. "And now, they know you exist. You are as doomed as I am."

"From where I sit," Sekun-ak said, "I would rather be in my position than yours."

Alex couldn't help but smile to himself at the truth of that.

"How many men were on each of those ships?" Alex asked. He had been able to see that the ships were huge, but it had been hard for him to truly gauge what that meant from the bluff.

"It varied from ship to ship, depending on what else the ship was carrying. One ship was designed to carry the horses, and it only carried a few hundred men. Others had—" he paused, searching for the number in the unfamiliar language—"how do you say ten times one hundred?"

"A thousand."

"Yes. More than that."

Alex turned to Sekun-ak. "I counted eighteen ships. That means they might have landed with twenty-thousand or more soldiers. No wonder they were able to run over all of Kragdon-ah."

"And," Sekun-ak observed, "if that is what they sent to this *lost land*, think how many soldiers and weapons they have at home."

"How big is the army they left behind?" Alex asked Darand.

A look of panic crossed Darand's face. "I don't know how to answer that. It would be a bigger number than I have ever known."

Alex raised a hand. "Don't worry. That's fine. I didn't really think you would know. You can go back to the house you share with Torana. We will have more questions for you. Don't go far."

"Unless," Sekun-ak said stone-faced, "you want to try your hand in the wilds of this *lost land* again."

Darand paled and scurried from the cave.

When Alex turned to Sekun-ak, he saw that mischief lit his eyes. "I think you take pleasure in scaring him like that."

Sekun-ak did not deny it. "That is the problem with stama, I think. It makes you feel strong. Invincible, even. But when it is taken away, your weakness is revealed. When he held the upper hand in the cave in Garta-ah, he was impressed with himself. Now, stripped of his stama, he stands quivering before us."

"Which is your way of saying you take pleasure in scaring him like that."

Sekun-ak placed two fingers against his forehead, then his expression turned serious. "What do we know now that we did not know before?"

"I think that this god of theirs, this Makinta, is just someone like me. Someone who stepped through a door, but when he did, he ran into a tribe that did not have any aversion to stama. Instead, they embraced what he could do for them. He was not immortal. I think he just passed on what he knew and maybe the location of the door to his son who took his place and so on and so forth. No magic there."

"That leaves us in the same position we were in before. Live our next four years in peace, waiting for them to come back and attack us. Anything else seems impossible."

"I don't think so. We know a lot about them now, and I can find out more from Darand. I believe he was telling us the truth. I can get some useful particulars from him." Alex smiled at Sekun-ak. "Now I really do have a plan."

Chapter Four
Hatching the Plan

The next morning, Alex and Monda-ak caught Darand as he made his way to the krinta patch with a hoe over his shoulder. *He's doing his best to make himself useful. I'll give him that.*

"I have some more questions for you."

Darand dropped the hoe from his shoulder. If he had any hesitation about giving information out about his people, he didn't show it.

"Let's sit here on the ground and talk for a time. Those rows of weeds will still be there in a few minutes."

"Of course," Darand said. He wiped his forehead with his sleeve. It was still only late spring, but even in the morning, the sun was warm.

"It looked like it would take them a long time to load all the prisoners onto the boat. They were only using one small boat to transfer people back and forth. Is that all you had?"

"No. Each ship had at least two of those boats. If you only saw one, they were just beginning to load people."

"They could be ready to leave in just a few days, then."

"I can't say that I really know. It wasn't my job."

"But how long did it take to unload all the soldiers and horses when you arrived?"

"It took a little over a day. It was quite a process to unload the horses. That took the longest."

Alex mulled that over. "They could be gone already, then."

Darand said nothing. Alex got the idea that he wasn't particularly interested in speculating.

"Were you brought along to be a soldier?"

For the first time since he had been banished, Darand laughed. "No, no. You could probably tell that when you saw me try to command. I am no leader of men. I was raised in a seaport to be a sailor. As a boy, I could walk on the rolling deck of a ship as well as I could on dry land. But, when we arrived here, sailors were no longer of any use, so we were made soldiers." Darand looked a little embarrassed. "I am married to Nekuna's sister. So, even though he hated me, he gave me the cushy job watching over the Garta-ah."

"The cushy job that almost got you killed," Alex observed.

Darand squinted at Alex in the sunshine. "That's the way of it, isn't it?" He pulled some grass out of the ground and threw it back down. "I would like to see my wife and little girl again someday, but I know I never will."

"You never know what will happen. When the ships crossed from Drakana to here, did they travel together? Were you in sight of each other the whole way?"

"As much as possible. We didn't have enough navigators that were good enough to take readings from the sun and the stars, so we tried to stay together so the best ones could lead the way. Still, four of our ships drifted off course and were never seen again, and one was so badly damaged in a storm that it barely made it here."

"How long did the journey take?"

"Three full cycles of the moon."

"You weren't one of the good navigators were you?"

Darand laughed. "I was a deck hand. I said I was raised to be a sailor, not a captain or a navigator."

"I knew I couldn't be that lucky. If we had a ship, do you think you could help us find our way back to Drakana?"

Darand's eyes widened. "You're thinking of going there?" He gazed off into space for a long moment. "No, I would be of little help. If we landed somewhere, I could speak to the people there and interpret for you, but I could not help you find Drakana." He tapped a finger against his knee. "It's hard to miss Drakana though. Any island or piece of land big enough to support the smallest community has been overwhelmed. They either surrender and become part of Drakana, or we overrun them and replace them with loyal Drakana from other places."

"This Makinta is intent on taking over the world."

"The only people who could stop him are the barbarians. There has been a truce of sorts between Drakana and the barbarians for a long time, but it is constantly threatened. That Makinta was willing to take troops away from possibly fighting the barbarians shows me that he is confident. I believe his plan is to take over all of the rest of the world, surround the barbarians, then kill them. They will never surrender."

"I've known a number of men like Makinta who had similar plans."

That surprised Darand. "You have? Did they succeed?"

Alex wanted to wave his hand around him and say, *We're still breathing free air, aren't we?* But that seemed disingenuous since those people had existed back in his own time. Instead, he just said, "It did not end well for them. They found themselves dead in a bunker or otherwise dispatched, often by their own people."

"That will never happen in Drakana. No one would dare challenge Makinta. They believe he is too powerful."

Alex chose not to argue the point. He had never heard of Makinta until the day before, so he wasn't ready to form any solid opinions yet. He had seen his fair share of tinpot dictators and local warlords with the same reputation, who fell apart when a well-armed warrior stood in front of them with bad intentions.

Alex was beginning to get a picture of how Makinta had managed to take over as much of the world as he had. That understanding helped him to solidify the plan he was formulating.

Alex stood and said, "Thank you. You've been forthcoming. If you will continue to be so, Sekun-ak will allow you to live."

"Will he allow me to live somewhere other than in the hut of the giant?"

"If you want a roof over your head, that is your only choice. Feel free to grab a blanket and sleep under the stars, but when you were in the wild, you likely met a few of the bugs of Kragdon-ah. No doubt they will take pleasure in feeding on you while you sleep."

Darand unconsciously scratched at a still-healing bite on his shoulder. "I suppose if he hasn't killed and eaten me yet, he probably won't tonight."

"That's the spirit," Alex said, turning back toward the cliffside.

He found Sekun-ak meeting with the woman who was responsible for the tribe's food preparation. Alex waited until they had finished, then approached him.

"I spoke to Darand," Alex began.

"Did he ask to be removed from Torana's house again?"

"Oh, yes. I'm sure they will eventually become friends, but for now he is still scared to death of him. Even though Torana can't speak, I'm sure Darand will eventually realize that he can understand his native tongue."

The two men walked away from the smallish cave where the food was prepared for the tribe and stepped to the opening that looked out over the field below and the forest in the distance.

"I understand more about the invaders now. I need to go to Danta-ah and speak to Harta-ak and Versa-eh. If my plan is going to work, we will need help. I'll visit Rinta-ah, too."

"Of course. I will have our fastest horse brought up from the stables."

"One other thing," Alex said. "I think we need to send the hunting group back looking for Karak-ta eggs. I want them to report back to me. I need to know if the ships are still there, but I don't want them discovered. Maybe Werda-ak could lead them. He is stealthy. Have him take the way that leads to the bluff and look down. If the ships are gone, they can complete their hunt. If the ships are still there, I'd like them to return here and report back."

In another society, the idea of sending someone in their mid-teens to lead an important mission would never be considered. Winten-ah was entirely competence-based. If you could do a job, you were allowed to do it. That was how Werda-ak's namesake uncle had been picked to accompany Alex on his dangerous mission to rescue Lanta-eh.

"It will be done."

Sanda and Nanda-eh were walking by and caught the tail end of Alex's suggestions.

"I will gather my archers and we will go along again," Nanda-eh said.

Sekun-ak waved them away. He laid his hand on Alex's shoulder. "Good speed to you," and he was gone.

Chapter Five
Danta-ah

Alex and Monda-ak made the trip to Danta-ah in good time. Sekun-ak had been as good as his word and had indeed given Alex the finest horse in the stable. Even so, Alex had not wanted to push the horse too much to make it easier for Monda-ak to keep up.

Monda-ak was more than thirty years old now—an incredible age for any dog from the twenty-first century. It was not an unusual age for his breed in Kragdon-ah, however. There were reports of dogs like him living to see sixty summer solstices. Still, Alex knew that not unlike himself, Monda-ak was no longer the brash young pup he had once been, able to run at a good trot for hours and hours on end without a rest.

When Alex approached the area where he knew the first Danta-ah guard shack would be, he slowed to a walk. The shack was recessed off the well-traveled trail, but Alex had seen it often enough to know exactly where it was. The thing that surprised him was that there was now a nearly identical guard shack set on the opposite side of the trail.

Alex paused between the two. A guard emerged from the Danta-ah shack and recognized him immediately.

"Gunta, Manta-ak."

"Gunta. Who is this?"

The guard looked disdainfully at the other small shed, where two men emerged and looked at Alex. "The invaders."

"An uneasy peace then?"

"Versa-eh says we cannot kill them, so yes."

Continuing in the universal language, Alex turned to the two Drakana soldiers. "Gunta."

One of them said, "Gunta," softly.

Alex leaned toward the Danta-ah guard. "Do they know more of the language than that?"

"Yes. That seems to be their primary job here."

"Do they ever attack anyone who tries to pass?"

"They are as gentle as kittens," the guard answered. "They don't seem to want to cause any trouble at all, but I get a feeling they are keeping track of everything."

"Good enough," Alex answered. "Let Harta-ak know I'm coming."

"We did that before you ever spoke."

Alex waved, Monda-ak woofed just to make sure his vote was counted, and they continued on toward the city built inside the caldera.

When Alex approached the gate he was pleased to see that Danta-ah was once again the thriving trade community it had been before the Drakana army had appeared. The deposit of salt appeared to be only slightly diminished from when he had first laid eyes on it twenty years earlier. Versa-eh had an excellent head on her shoulders and understood that parsing out small amounts of the *danta*, or salt, made each pound of it more valuable. The eternal law of supply and demand was just as strong as ever and Versa-eh tightly controlled the supply.

Even so, a number of carts were pulled up to the salt deposit, where bags were weighed and the alecs-ta pulled the cart to wherever it was going.

Versa-eh and Harta-ak waited for Alex just inside the great gate. They followed his gaze to the salt.

"The invaders have been a huge challenge for us. But I will admit that the bridge they built has allowed us to open up more trading partners to the north."

"The village is flourishing," Alex observed.

The couple looked around at what they had built with pride. The streets were cobbled and neat, the houses all built with perfect right angles.

"The invaders have a name now," Alex confided. "They call the place they come from Drakana."

"Drakan-ah," Versa-eh said, letting the name roll around in her mouth.

"No, no *ah* on the end. Just Drakana." Alex paused and wondered if that distinction mattered at all with a people who still had very little written language. He shrugged.

"How did you finally learn the name?" Harta-ak asked. They had all puzzled over how to figure it out since the invaders had first shown up. At least, they had puzzled over it during the times they weren't actively defending themselves from being enslaved.

"From the man who was left to watch us in Garta-ah—Darand. When you defeated their champion, Versa-eh, Darand was banished. I found him a few days later, wandering in the wilderness. He has been happy to tell us whatever we wanted to know in exchange for giving him shelter."

He noticed that both of them swelled a bit at the mention of Versa-eh's defeat of the young girl named Nissina. It was pride. Well-earned and it had saved all of them.

Alex told him the rest of what he had learned from Darand, including his hunch that Makinta was someone who had come through a door just like he had, and how he had orchestrated the massive country and army he now controlled.

Alex cleared his throat, not really wanting to ask what he had come all this way for. "Sekun-ak and I have been thinking of a plan."

Versa-eh's eyes narrowed. She knew and loved Sekun-ak, but she also recognized that though he was a great chieftain, long-term planning was not at the top of his skill set. She allowed the slight disingenuousness to pass unremarked.

Alex fixed Harta-ak with a look. "I will need your help to carry it out."

"Of course. Name it and I will do it."

Alex held up a hand. "Don't be so hasty. It is not a simple task that can be accomplished in a few days or even a few months. It will take you away from Danta-ah for a very long time. Longer than several solstices."

The couple exchanged a glance. "Then we had better sit down and feed you before you ask and my husband agrees," Versa-eh said, acknowledging the likely answer no matter how terrible the ask.

They walked to the house Harta-ak and Versa-eh shared with their two children, who were outside, since it was not dark yet. No one in Danta-ah stayed indoors while there was still daylight in the springtime. There was too much work to do.

Versa-eh laid out bowls and utensils for the three of them and served a cabbage stew from a pot that had been simmering over a low fire. "If I'd known you were coming, I would have put some meat in it."

Alex breathed deeply and said, "Not necessary at all. It smells so good."

She ladled out three steaming bowls and set them on the table. Monda-ak sat on his haunches, which put his head just below Versa-eh's, shoulder.

"Don't worry, I won't forget about you." She opened a low cupboard and found a large bone. There was no meat on it, but he chomped on it gladly.

"We've found some villages that have other spices," Harta-ak said. "We trade a bag of salt for a quarter-bag of their spice."

"He is thinking we might be able to open a trading market like we found in Klaka-ah, where we armed you for your attack on Lasta-ah." She looked at Harta-ak with the same look of adoration he had seen on her face the day she met him. "He always has big ideas."

Harta-ak deflected the praise by changing the subject. "I'm nearly afraid to ask, but what is it you need from me? I admit, I'm not looking forward to leaving what we have built here."

"Where I came from, there was a story of a man named Damocles. He sat on a throne with a sharp sword hanging above him, suspended only by a single hair from a horse's tail."

Alex watched the two of them and saw that this powerful image struck home. Some ideas traversed the centuries.

"That is how I feel right now. As if the sword of Damocles hangs above our head, except we know exactly when the sword will fall—in four more summer solstices."

Versa-eh leaned forward, sober and focused. "We have talked about this very thing, but we have been unable to think of a plan to change our fate. What is yours?"

"I cannot stand to wait for them to come and kill or enslave us. I want to follow them back to their land and force them to agree to a truce."

Versa-eh smiled. "You want to travel to a land we do not know the location of, and with whatever tiny army we can put together, attack an entire people?"

"There were just four of them when they destroyed Lasta-ah," Harta-ak reminded her.

Alex raised his hand. "And admittedly, that was an easier thing to do than what I'm proposing. But here is what I need from you. I believe they are likely to leave one of their ships behind. I want to commandeer it and sail it back to where they came from."

Harta-ak blinked, then blinked again at the implication.

"How big is this ship that we are going to commandeer?"

"It would probably hold the barge you owned a hundred times over."

Harta-ak leaned back in his chair and whistled softly. "Who is going to captain a ship that size for you?"

"You, of course."

Chapter Six
Beyond the Call of Duty

Harta-ak's reaction to Alex's bold proclamation was not what he had anticipated.

He laughed. A quick exhalation of air, raised eyebrows and wide eyes.

"You're not serious."

"You are the closest thing to a sea captain within many days' ride of where we sit. Perhaps in all of Kragdon-ah. You have experience no one else has. Most importantly, I would trust you with my life."

Harta-ak leaned forward, raised the fingers on his left hand, and closed them one by one as he made point after point.

"I was a captain, but of a barge, where I could typically drop a pole and touch bottom. We rarely spent more than one night away from being docked. No matter what, I could always drop anchor and reconnoiter. None of those things are true in the voyage you are talking about. Yes, I once held the title of Captain, but you could take any citizen of Danta-ah and they would not be much less qualified than I am to command a ship like you speak of."

"I do not dispute any of what you just said. And yet, here I am. The most important element is trust. It's not just that I trust you to never betray me. I trust you to always make the best decision possible with the information you have. I know you are not truly qualified to oversee a ship like this. The challenge is that no one in Kragdon-ah is." Alex closed one eye as if he hated to say what he was about to. "I believe you are the best we have. But you are also the least-worst."

Harta-ak smiled ruefully at Alex's honesty.

Versa-eh was not smiling at all. Her brow was furrowed and her mouth pulled in a grim line. "But that is not the only thing you are asking of us, Manta-ak."

Alex opened his mouth to answer, but she continued on.

"You are asking us to do one of two things. Either we are separated for the first time since my husband rescued us from that stinking island. I wave him goodbye, knowing that the mission he is leaving on is one he will likely never return from. *Or*, I go with him and we give up everything we have built here and walk away from our chosen life, probably forever."

Her words struck Alex hard. He had made many sacrifices in his life, so it had become increasingly easy to ask others to do the same. He leaned back in his chair and looked around the cozy home, filled with love and happiness. To suit his own needs, he was asking people who had risked their lives again and again for him to give it all up.

He turned his eyes to the open-beam ceiling for a long moment. When he looked back at them, his eyes had softened.

I can captain this ship. I can drag Darand along with me and force him to show me everything he knows. Surely some of the Winten-ah landlubbers will have some natural ability to solve problems. Werda-ak is clever and figures things out quickly. I don't need to ask my friends to make yet another sacrifice for me.

Alex stood and moved around the table. He laid a hand on the shoulders of both Harta-ak and Versa-eh. He would have liked to envelop them both in a hug, but that was not done in Kragdon-ah.

Except by Lanta-eh, The Chosen One, the empath, the young girl he had grown to love deeply. The girl who had sacrificed herself for the tribe.

Being The Chosen One sucks. I don't know why I act like I am some-how the same so often.

Alex smiled at his two friends. "I am ashamed. There are times that I don't stop to think about the price I am asking people to pay. I take it back and thank you for helping me to see this. You are the greatest friends I have ever had."

Harta-ak started to speak, but Alex cut him off.

"I do have a favor to ask, though. If there are some citizens of Danta-ah who would like the adventure of a lifetime, I will need soldiers. I will train them on the voyage. But, you are right, they may never return to Danta-ah, so they need to be aware of that before they volunteer."

Alex hurried to the door, still not giving Versa-eh or Harta-ak time to speak. Over his shoulder, he said, "I am going to Rinta-ah to seek adventurers there, too. I will stop back here and see if anyone wants to come along."

Monda-ak sensed that Alex was leaving and bolted out the door in front of him. Alex stepped through, shut the door behind him, and strode to his horse. He jumped up and kicked the horse into motion. He was through the gate before he had a chance to see both Harta-ak and Versa-eh waving at him to stop.

When they were away from Danta-ah, Alex set Monda-ak free to hunt for his own meal. A bone is fine, but Monda-ak had need of much more.

Just before the sun went down, Alex heard the rush and roar of the Kranda-ah river ahead of him. He crested the ridge that looked down on the river—and the bridge that the Drakana had built.

There were two Drakana guards stationed at each end of the bridge.

Alex slowed the horse and gave a hand signal to Monda-ak to fall in behind. He raised his hand in greeting. The two guards, who stood on either side of the entrance with their guns pointing at the ground, raised a hand in return.

At a steady pace, Alex brought his horse up and onto the bridge deck. As he rode across, he glanced to his right, where the spar tree had once stood that had been the anchor for the rope bridge he had destroyed in crossing the Kranda-ah. The Drakana had toppled the tree, no doubt converting it to lumber to build the bridge he was crossing.

At the northern end of the bridge, the guards showed no more interest in bothering him than the first two had. Alex got the feeling they had received a duty none of them wanted. They had been left behind in a strange—and to them primitive—land, while their friends had returned to hearth and home.

Once on land again, Alex spurred his horse forward and saw the glow of a fire from the Rinta-ah guard shack up the hill. As in Danta-ah, the two sides kept an eye on each other, but nothing more.

"Gunta," Alex called ahead in the gathering darkness. "It is Manta-ak, come to visit Rinka-ak."

"Gunta, Manta-ak from Winten-ah. You are always welcome in Rinta-ah."

Alex approached Rinta-ah, which was built into a natural amphitheater, from below. The first thing he noticed was that the fence the Drakana had built was still in place. Now that they were in control of their city again, having the fence to discourage other attackers was a good thing.

Between the bridge across the river and this sturdy fence, the invaders had, in the end, done the tribe a favor. Of course, that favor came with the risk of their freedom or lives. There is always a trade-off.

Unlike his previous visit, when the fence had been impenetrable from one end to another, there was now a large gate. Tonight, it stood wide open and the torches and firepits of Rinta-ah seemed to welcome him.

The guards at the gate greeted Alex, who rode through and dismounted. Monda-ak fell in beside him. A young boy ran up and took the reins of the horse, leading it away toward a barn.

Looking up at the starfield popping out above, Alex said, "You can stable her for the night." The boy waved an acknowledgement, a bit too star-struck to answer. Since Alex had defeated the giant warrior Grunta-ak and saved the life of Rinka-ak, he was as much legend as he was man.

Rinka-ak, a tall, handsome man now in his mid-forties, walked leisurely toward Alex. "Just out to see old friends and enjoy our hard-won freedom?"

Alex touched his throat to indicate *no*. "The truth is, I cannot enjoy our freedom when I know it will come to an end before we are ready or able to extend it."

"Do you think we could challenge them to another Thundan? Buy ourselves another five years?"

Alex had not considered that possibility, so he let it run through his mind for a time.

"There are problems with that strategy."

"At this time, I would guess there are problems with any strategy," Rinka-ak observed.

Alex laughed a bit. That was a true statement.

Rinka-ak clapped Alex on the shoulder. "Come up to the hall. Dinner is just being served. Harta-ak has shared some of the new spices he found recently and our food tastes much better than it ever has."

Alex thought of demurring, saying that he'd had a bowl of cabbage stew in Danta-ah. But the welcoming lights and savory smells coming from the great hall convinced him not to object.

As the two of them walked into the hall and seated themselves at the head table, conversations lulled and all eyes turned to Alex.

He did not notice, preoccupied with his mission.

As soon as he was seated, Alex said, "The problem with the idea of just challenging them to a Thundan again is—what if they don't accept the challenge? Then we have invaders at the gate and we are back in the same horrible position we were in before."

Alex didn't mention his other objection—that he thought next time the Drakana would be much better prepared for any Thundan challenge. They had been relatively fortunate in their first challenges. The Drakana had relied on the elements of surprise, intimidation, and strength.

But Tinta-ak and Alex himself had defeated their giant and their beast Panga. He didn't think the invaders would leave such elements to chance again. He suspected that they would either refuse, or issue a challenge that favored them so heavily the challengers would have no chance to win.

Rinka-ak's eyes crinkled as he smiled at Alex. No matter the situation, he seemed to take everything in stride. Perhaps it came from facing almost certain death when he was just a young boy. It was obvious that, unlike Alex, he was capable of enjoying their remaining years of freedom.

"I suspect that you have a plan then, Manta-ak."

Alex outlined his plan—to capture one of the Drakana ships, to sail it back to their homeland and force them into a truce.

It was a ludicrous plan in many ways, but coming from Alex, Rinka-ak gave it full consideration.

"And what do you need of us?"

"I need your strength. I know it seems impossible that even with an army of five or six hundred soldiers, we can take on an entire nation, but I have a plan for that. My problem is finding that original army. The invaders have emptied out most of the fighters of Krag-don-ah and taken them into slavery."

Rinka-ak leaned back as a server brought trays of food and set them between him and Alex.

"Of course you have our strength. As much of it as you need."

"This will be dangerous. Many of those who leave will never return, if not all. I only want volunteers. People who can leave Rinta-ah with a clear conscience. If a fighter has obligations here—a parent, or spouse, or children, I don't want them to come."

"I understand," Rinka-ak answered. He stood and straightened his back. The coltish young boy who Alex had first met now stood nearly seven feet tall. His voice carried throughout the big hall.

"Manta-ak is leaving tomorrow on a dangerous mission. He needs our assistance. He tells me that those who go with him will likely never return."

A small boy at the back said, "I saw him defeat Panga all alone!"

Laughter rippled through the halls.

"If you are needed here, or if you simply want to stay in Rinta-ah, there is no shame in that. We will also need people here. But, if you have ever wondered what lies beyond the sunset, this is an opportunity to find out. He will leave at first light."

Rinka-ak sat back down and a buzz of conversation began immediately.

After dinner, Alex was shown to a private guest room that he suspected belonged to one of Rinka-ak's children. There was a soft bed and a rug for Monda-ak to lie on. Both of them were asleep in moments.

Alex awoke an hour before the morning light broke in the east. He did not know how many volunteers, if any, he would have to travel back to Winten-ah with him. Asking a tribe to loan him fighters temporarily was one thing. But this was essentially asking them to give their warriors up forever.

He opened the door and walked silently down the hall to the door outside. He took Monda-ak outside to answer nature's call, then went back inside. He intended to grab his pack and weapons and return to Winten-ah. He was surprised to find that Rinka-ak and what appeared to be his entire family were up and dressed.

Didn't know they were such early risers in Rinta-ah.

Rinka-ak stepped forward. "What will we need to bring with us?"

Alex was taken aback.

"I don't expect you to come. You have a village to run."

"I have been training my son to become chieftain for many years now. He has seen twenty summer solstices, which is more than I had seen when I became chief."

"And you have been a great chieftain," Alenta-eh, the wife of Rinka-ak said, draping a hand on his shoulder.

Alex did another double take. "Are you saying your whole family is coming?"

"Except for my son, who will stay behind with the tribe, yes."

Alex shook his head, trying to make sense of what he was hearing. "When did he become chieftain?"

"He will accept the role this afternoon, but it is all ceremonial. He does not need me here for that. We will leave with you now. There are dozens more warriors gathered at the gate, ready to go with you."

Alex was humbled at the faith they put in him.

"Some of them also want to bring their families, but they will all fight for us. I told them that if people were too old or too young, they would need to stay here."

Alex felt his throat tighten. He had been hoping to get perhaps ten warriors to accompany him.

"I cannot let you come with me," Alex said.

Rinka-ak started to object, but Alex held up his hand. "Of course I am grateful to have you and your family and all your warriors by my side. But you have a chance to pass the role of chieftain on to your son. That is something that you will never have the chance to experience again. Everyone who calls Rinka-ak home should see it. I will leave now, but you and everyone with you can come to Winten-ah in a few days. It will take us time to prepare everything anyway."

Rinka-ak put two fingers to his forehead in acknowledgement and smiled at Alex. "It will be my honor to see my son accept the mantle of chieftain. We will ride to Winten-ah soon."

Shaking his head in disbelief, Alex stepped outside the great hall and found his horse there, tied to a post. Alex swung up onto the saddle and rode toward the gate.

The gate had been closed for the night, but two guards moved it as Alex approached. He lifted a hand in greeting as he passed.

One of the guards said, "I am with you, Manta-ak." The other man simply held two fingers to his forehead, acknowledging the same truth.

Alex and Monda-ak bounded down the hill toward the bridge, which Alex had come to think of as the Drakana Bridge. Once again, there were guards on either end, but they simply stood as he rode past.

When Alex came to the cutoff toward Danta-ah, he hesitated. He dismounted and looked in the direction of the caldera. He knew people were there, going about their lives, making plans that had nothing to do with attacking a foreign nation with a pitifully small army. He knew he needed bodies to make that army, but at that moment, he felt he couldn't ask his friends who had already done so much for him, to be part of it.

He jumped up on his horse and pointed her toward Winten-ah. He clicked his tongue and said, "Come on, Monda-ak. Let's go home."

Chapter Seven
A Plan in Motion

When Alex and Monda-ak turned from the forest path to the clearing in front of the caves, it was obvious it was just another day in Winten-ah. Children ran and played, circling around Torana, who was taking turns throwing them high into the air and catching them.

Nanda-eh, Sanda, and the other archers were holding a competition at the far end of the clearing. Sanda gave him a quick wave, but immediately returned her focus toward her battle with Nanda-eh.

Alex climbed off the horse and straightened his back to work the kinks out of another long day's ride. A young boy broke free from those waiting in line for a Torana toss and ran to Alex.

"I will take him for you, Manta-ak," the boy said, smiling broadly and showing two missing teeth.

Alex ruffled the boy's hair then looked at Monda-ak. "We're home. Do what you want. I have to find Sekun-ak."

A decade or two earlier, Monda-ak would have run woofing into the circle of children, adding to their fun. Today, he trotted over to the shade offered by the tall krinta stalks, lay down, and closed his eyes.

"I wouldn't mind joining you," Alex said softly.

As it turned out, Alex did not need to go and find Sekun-ak. Sekun-ak found him just as he began to climb up the cliffside. He greeted him and suggested they go to the cave where the council meetings were held.

As they climbed, Sekun-ak said, "You had hoped to return with volunteers for your army, including Harta-ak. Is the fact you return alone a bad sign?"

"No," Alex began to explain, "I did ask Harta-ak, but I changed my mind. I just couldn't ask him to leave everything he has built there and risk never seeing it again. I do have good news though. When I spoke to Rinka-ak, he volunteered himself, and he is bringing dozens of warriors with him, including most of his family. He has named his son as the new chieftain, so he stayed behind to organize everything. I expect they will be here in a few days."

They entered the cave where a few chairs were scattered around a firepit that had no fire. Werda-ak the Younger and several of the other senior members of the tribe were waiting.

Alex's stomach churned. Everything he had planned could go wrong at this moment, depending on what Werda-ak had to say. Normally, Alex sat quietly listening as others took the floor and spoke at length. Today, he did not have the patience for that. As he was sitting down, he looked at Werda-ak and said, "Tell me what you saw."

Werda-ak had been sitting on one of the wooden, low-slung chairs, but stood, not unhappy to be the center of attention.

"It was very different from the last time we were there. It is a good thing we took a full group with us, because the ronit-ta were out in force. They attacked us three different times. I couldn't tell if it was the same group, or offshoots of the same group, or what. Nan-da-eh, Sanda-eh, and the other archers saved us."

Alex sat quietly, waiting for the one detail he craved, doing his best to be patient.

"When we reached the valley, we did as you said. We left the trail and climbed up through the dead trees to the small animal trail we followed last time. We went to the same bluff and looked down."

Alex found he was holding his breath and forced himself to moderate his breathing.

"Were the ships there?"

Werda-ak put his hand to his throat to indicate they were not.

Alex's heart sank. "None of them?"

"Where there were many ships last time, now there was only one."

"Yes!" Alex exclaimed, leaping to his feet. "Why didn't you say so?"

Werda-ak looked confused. "I just did."

"No, I mean—never mind. Was the one ship that was there like the others? Huge? Or was it smaller?"

"It looked exactly like the ships that we saw when you were with us."

Alex sat down, exultant that his plan was still alive.

Sekun-ak held up a hand. "When last we spoke, that is exactly what you thought Werda-ak would find." He tilted his head quizzically. "How did you know that?"

"I didn't *know* it. I just suspected it, and it is necessary for everything else to work. We would never have the time, materials, or knowledge to build one, so we would have no way to follow them."

"Yes, but what made you think that they would leave one ship behind and take the others?"

'It was just a guess. It's what I would have done if I was them. They left the smatterings of an army behind when they sailed away. I saw Drakana soldiers at both Danta-ah and the bridge across the Kranda-ah. If I saw them in those two locations, I'm sure they are scattered everywhere. Harta-ak said he thought they were just keeping an eye on us. Us, and everyone still free here in Kragdon-ah."

"So?"

"If you take all of the Drakana that are spread across Kragdon-ah, I think there are enough that they would be able to sail back home. If they begin to see something they don't like—if, for example, we arm ourselves, collect into one big army, or attempt to kill the remaining Drakana—they could take this ship and sail it home. For all I know, that is their plan. If Makinta is not planning on returning an army immediately, he may have ordered that these soldiers stay here and observe certain things for a year. Maybe two. Then they could return and give a full accounting. I can see a lot of possible reasons they left it behind."

"And somehow, this ship is integral to your plan?"

"Of course it is. We are going to attack it, capture it, and sail it back to Drakana. They will regret ever launching an attack on Kragdon-ah."

"Who will command this ship?"

"I will."

"In your previous life, did you ever do anything like this?"

"No," Alex said, unconsciously shaking his head, though it meant nothing to anyone present.

"But you are confident you can do this?"

Alex considered telling him the truth—that it scared him to death. That he was completely unsure he was capable of it. That there were times when he woke up in the deepest darkness of the night and thought he should just stay in Winten-ah, uncover the door, and take his daughters and Monda-ak home to Oregon. Those fever-thoughts at midnight always passed before the morning dawned.

Instead of sharing those fears, Alex smiled and said, "Of course."

Sekun-ak grinned at him as well—as though he knew the truth, but it didn't matter. There were limited choices for the Winten-ah to continue to exist as a free people.

Alex returned his attention back to Werda-ak. "Was there still an army of any size on the beach?"

"Nothing like what we saw before. There were two tents set up. We watched them for a long time before we returned home. I was able to count twenty soldiers camped there, but I can't be sure if that was everyone or if I counted some twice."

"And the ship? Could you see any activity on the ship?"

"There were at least as many of them on the ship. They were constantly busy, moving about."

"Soldiers?"

Werda-ak looked up, contemplating his answer. "I don't think so. They seemed to have more to do with the ship itself. That's what they worked on the whole time we watched them."

"Did you attempt to hunt for karak-ta eggs?"

Werda-ak put his hand to his throat, a downcast expression on his face. "No. The soldiers camped on the beach cut off our escape route from the karak-ta. We didn't want to reveal ourselves."

"You did well. Very well."

Werda-ak beamed, then sat down, realizing he had shared all the information he had.

"What is the next part of your plan?"

"We need to make as many weapons as we can. Lots of new arrows for the archers. They are going to be valuable in the attack. I will want as much food as we can carry. I do not know what stores, if any, they already have on board ship. I will lead a hunting party tomorrow. Can you do the same?"

"Of course," Sekun-ak said.

"Good. Have them salt as much meat as we can carry." Alex thought back to what he knew of long sailing voyages. "Ask them to find and prepare as much as they can in the way of storing fruit, vegetables, and berries. Dried is good, but I would like to start with as much fresh as we can." Alex contemplated trying to explain about scurvy, but instead he simply said, "We will need the goodness inside each of them."

The meeting broke up and everyone but Alex and Sekun-ak moved away, talking in small groups. Sekun-ak touched Alex's arm and said, "I have sent runners out to Garta-ah and Franta-ah. I think Tinta-ak would be very upset if we undertook an adventure and did not tell him about it."

"If they are coming, how long until you think they will arrive?"

"I sent the runners the morning you left. Any who are coming will be here within two days."

"Good. However many we have, we will leave on the morning of the third day."

"Before first light?" Sekun-ak asked. He was teasing his old friend. Alex always left on these journeys before first light.

Alex looked at the man who had once been his first enemy among the Winten-ah. The man who was now the brother he had never had.

Everyone thinks he is sour and humorless. It is just the weight of his role.

Alex allowed himself a small courtesy chuckle at Sekun-ak.

"Yes, we leave before first light."

Chapter Eight
Amassing a Motley Crew

The next two days passed quickly, a whirlwind of activity. Both Alex and Sekun-ak managed successful hunting trips each day, which overburdened the people who processed the meat. They recruited the children to cut the meat into strips and begin salting them. No fingers or noses were lost in the process.

On the evening of the second day, Alex and Sekun-ak met to strategize. First, they had to settle one important issue.

Sekun-ak very much wanted to come along.

For years, he had been training his daughter to take over as chieftain of the Winten-ah. The job chafed him and he longed for a time when he could be more free. She was killed in the first wave of the Drakana army, however. Now, there was no obvious person to give the leadership of the tribe.

It took time and a lot of persuasion, but Alex eventually convinced him that he had to stay in Winten-ah. The clincher was when Alex said, "If we win, but return to find that everything has gone wrong here at home, then we have still lost."

Sekun-ak could not argue with that, and with no natural successor in sight, he knew the only smart thing to do was to stay behind. Knowing that the journey Alex and so many of his other brothers, sisters, and friends were about to undertake would last years only made it worse. He was aware that when he watched them ride across the field and disappear into the forest, he might never see any of them again.

The mantle of responsibility chafed at him, but he had accepted it and could not find a way to rid himself of it. And so he agreed to stay.

As that day grew longer, Alex began to worry. No one from Danta-ah, Rinta-ah, Garta-ah, or Franta-ah had appeared. He was confident he could take the ship with only the warriors from Wintenah. But to have enough people to launch an offensive against the Drakana, he would need more bodies.

Amy tried to distract him by asking him to spar with her. She said being the smallest person in Kragdon-ah over the age of ten was sapping her confidence and she wanted to beat up on Alex to restore it.

That was a kind lie, of course. Amy had never lacked confidence in her life. Still, she and Alex stripped down to the basics and squared off in the open field. The sun was low over the hills, but it was still a warm late-spring afternoon.

Alex and Amy touched fingertips and circled each cautiously. They had sparred like this since Alex had returned to Oregon when she was four. Just when he thought he knew all her moves, she came up with something new.

A small crowd gathered around, as they always did when people wrestled or sparred, especially if the contestants were Alex and either of his daughters. Amy feinted a jab, then dropped down to do a leg sweep. It was not a killer move—more of a preliminary warm up. And yet, the crowd around them oohed.

That was an unusual reaction, which took Alex's attention away for a split second. Amy anticipated that Alex would back away from the sweep, but he was a step slow. Her foot connected with him just above the ankle and a half-moment later, Alex was on his back, staring up at the wispy white clouds in the sky.

Amy was on him in a flash, pressing her advantage, when they both heard the clamoring and yelling from the crowd.

Amy jumped up and extended a hand to her father. Walking toward them from the forest path were Rinka-ak, Alenta-eh, and two of their children. Directly behind them were Harta-ak, Versa-eh, and what appeared to be hundreds—not dozens—of volunteers.

Alex jogged to meet them and said, "I thought you were bringing a few dozen people!"

Rinka-ak smiled broadly, showing his even white teeth, and said, "I took advantage of the extra time to visit other tribes near us who avoided the sweep of the invaders. When I explained what you were doing, and why, this is the result." He turned slightly and waved his hand, encompassing all who accompanied him.

Alex looked at Harta-ak and Versa-eh. "I did not return because I feel as though I have asked too much of you already. You have built a life there."

Versa-eh knit her brows. "Do you not understand by now? We are all one family. When one of us is threatened, we all are. We could never leave you to deal with this on your own." She paused and glanced at Harta-ak. "I will always put my faith in those who have proved worthy of it over the years." She turned back to Alex and said, "And that includes you, Manta-ak."

"Come, come!" Alex said. He turned to Amy and in English said, "Run to Sekun-ak and tell him that we will have several hundred guests for dinner. We need to build a bonfire."

"On it," she answered, also in English, and sprinted for the caves.

"Do my eyes deceive me, or did your daughter put you on the ground as we approached?"

Alex grinned a little sheepishly. "The older I get, the faster she gets."

Rinka-ak lowered his voice confidentially. "It is the same with my sons. The world is the world."

Alex put two fingers to his forehead to acknowledge the truth of it.

At that moment, another roar sprang up, this time from people lined along the lower levels of the cliffside. They all looked and pointed toward the eastern side of Winten-ah. It was the lesser-traveled path out of the village—the same one Alex and the archers had used to escape the Drakana the year before.

Alex stood on his tiptoes, straining to see what they were looking at. He had to bob and weave around people, but finally got a clear view.

There was another long line of people streaming out of the foliage. In the lead were Tinta-ak and his wife Fantam-eh. They had a thick piece of wood resting on each of their shoulders. A gigantic boar swung from the wood.

When Tinta-ak saw Alex ahead, he waved his mighty fist above his head in greeting.

Alex was shocked for the second time in as many minutes at the size of the approaching crowd.

When they drew closer, Tinta-ak casually handed his end of the stick to the large man behind him, whose knees nearly buckled at the weight.

Tinta-ak ignored him and stepped forward to slam his hand down on Alex's shoulder, which *did* make Alex buckle for a moment. Again, Tinta-ak failed to notice.

"When are you going to learn, Manta-ak? You cannot leave on an adventure without me."

"I cannot imagine such a thing," Alex said. "I am so happy to see you."

"We met several of these beasts in the forests as we walked, and we thought they would make some good eating for us tonight."

"We are building a firepit right now," Alex confirmed.

Tinta-ak and Rinka-ak greeted each other as old friends.

Alex felt like he needed a moment to recover, so he slipped away through the crowd, though everyone who saw him shouted a greeting, including Brunda-ak, the chieftain from Garta-ah.

Alex finally worked his way through the crowd and up onto the second level of the cliffside.

Sekun-ak was there, waiting for him.

"I never dreamed..." Alex began.

"You need to stop underestimating what people will do for you." He pointed toward the crowd, which filled the huge field below. "They are here for you."

"I know," Alex said, a worried expression on his face. "And I hope their faith is not misplaced."

Sekun-ak left Alex to stare at the crowd below. As the chieftain of the home tribe, he had a long night ahead of him. He supervised the digging of the firepit, the lighting of the fire, and clearing enough space for each tribe to erect their tents for the night. They would leave those behind to hopefully reclaim on their return. Camping equipment was not necessary on a ship.

By the time darkness had fallen, a great bonfire pushed sparks and flames twenty feet into the air. Both groups had brought their fermented drinks and shared them liberally with the Winten-ah. For the sake of the mission that would leave early the next day, it was a good thing that there wasn't more than a single cup for everyone.

Just before midnight, the boars were pulled off the spit and carved up for a hungry and appreciative crowd.

While everyone laughed, ate, and drank, Alex, Sekun-ak, Amy, and the visiting chieftains strategized. Alex instructed Amy to do the near impossible and take a count of the visitors. Even with as many as had arrived, he wasn't worried about having too many to fit on the ship. Based on what Darand had told him about the capacity, he still believed they would have plenty of room. The challenge they might face would be feeding this many.

An army this size—perhaps the largest single gathering of tribes in Kragdon-ah in more than a century—would easily overwhelm the small force left behind on the beach. Alex stayed up late, picturing the terrain and considering what Werda-ak the Younger had told him he could expect.

By the darkest hour of the night, the revelers below had fallen asleep, either in the hastily erected tents, or under a blanket of stars.

That made Amy's job of counting much simpler. While the chiefs strategized about what was ahead, she slipped through the field, counting. She kept track on a piece of bark with a crude pencil. A far cry from the smart phone and tablet she had left behind in Oregon, but effective in the end.

Just as Alex and the chieftains were finally breaking to try and find an hour's worth of sleep, she returned. She shook her head in disbelief.

"I believe we will have slightly more than eight hundred people leave with us in the morning."

Alex let out a short, startled laugh. Even seeing the throng of people with his own eyes, it was more than he had anticipated.

Quietly, staring out into the remains of the fire in the field, he said, "We may still fall, but they will know we have been there."

Chapter Nine
The Beach

As much as Alex wanted to depart before first light, it did not happen.

As much as Alex wanted to think of this group as an army, they were not.

They were families who had left everything behind to join him. They were warriors, hunters, fishermen, cooks, weapon-makers, seamstresses, and adventurers. They were a large group of disparate people. They were not an army. Not yet, and not any time soon.

Alex began to push people to move thirty minutes before sunrise. They finally left for the coast two hours after. It would have to do.

The world is the world, he had to remind himself.

Alex arranged the march so that the best fighters would be at the front. If they ran into trouble head-on, he wanted to be as prepared as possible. He put another large group of competent warriors at the rear. He would not allow a rear flanking action to cripple them. He spread the rest of his fighters throughout the caravan. There were a few animals walking with them, including some milk-beasts that Alex hoped would provide calcium on the voyage, and a cart full of the Kragdon-ah equivalent of chickens. He would do his best to use them for their steady egg supply and not the other obvious use.

Alex stayed at the front, walking with Tinta-ak and Amy. Sanda was with the archers in the middle of the pack. If necessary, they could hop up on the carts carrying supplies and unleash hell either front or rear.

As they walked, Amy brought up several points that Alex had considered, but had not talked out with anyone.

"Have you ever thought that those red poles they gave us work both ways?"

"What do you mean?"

"We know that it means they will not attack us for four more years, but do you think they assume we won't attack them for the same reason? And that we are sacrificing whatever protection the tribes left behind might have by attacking them now?"

Alex let a small smile touch his lips. He loved his daughters more than the world, but he was most proud when they were using their natural skills to solve a problem. For Sanda, that was usually accomplished by putting an arrow through it. For Amy, it was turning a problem over and over in her mind until the rough edges were knocked off.

"Excellent thought. I did have that one myself. But we know that there are very few of the Drakana left in Kragdon-ah now."

"Unless they sent another ship out before these ships make the round trip."

"A possibility," Alex admitted, "but a slim chance. Why would they do that? I am confident they would wait for the intelligence back from this mission before they threw more resources into an unknown situation."

Amy nodded, allowing the point to pass.

"It's still a good thought, though," Alex continued. "It's entirely possible that these other guard units scattered around Kragdon-ah may come back to the beach to report in. This might be their headquarters, for all we know. If they come back and find them all slaughtered, they might decide to gather all their remaining force together and take it out on someone. That someone could easily be Winten-ah. We are the closest."

"And we have weakened them by bringing so many of their fighters."

"We *would* have weakened them even more, but when so many other volunteers showed up, Sekun-ak and I decided to leave more Winten-ah behind. They will be fine." Alex glanced at Amy and saw that she was not abashed to have run into a dead end with her objection, but was rolling the new information around in her mind.

Alex touched her shoulder. "There is always risk. If you eliminate all risk, you will also eliminate your chance to succeed."

Alex knew that the ronit-ta were back in their rightful place in the world, patrolling the plains that led to the beach. He believed that if they had been a smaller group, they would have met them somewhere along the line. With eight hundred armed people, dogs, and other animals that might sound the warning, the ronit-ta once again gave them a wide berth.

By mid-afternoon, Alex saw the outline of the valley that led to the beach ahead of them. He sent word back through the ranks that he wanted to stop and reconnoiter. With so many traveling so close together, it paid to alert everyone before applying the brakes. If not, it was inevitable that there would be pileups somewhere along the line.

Alex had gone over his plan dozens of times. He was in the odd position of having switched sides with the Drakana army. He now commanded the overwhelming force and preferred not to kill any of them he did not have to. Not that he intended to enslave them, but he harbored some hope that a few of them might be willing to join him. Not to fight their kin, but for a ride home. Alex at least had an offer he wanted to make them. An offer to a dead man was generally ineffective.

Alex drew the caravan to a halt. He conferred with Rinka-ak, Amy, Harta-ak and Versa-eh.

"Do you think they will have lookouts before we get to the encampment?" Versa-eh asked.

All eyes were on Alex.

"I certainly would. Having given up our superiority of numbers, I would want to know if we were being approached. The question is, how far out would they put them? If they are few in numbers, they are more likely to bring their lookouts closer to the camp instead of clear out here on this end of the valley."

"If we *knew* there were lookouts clear back here, what would we do?" Amy asked.

"If I knew they were here at the edge of the valley, I would send a small crew to dispatch them, hopefully before we were spotted. But, if we take the time to send a crew ahead, we will be sitting here for quite some time waiting for their return." Alex glanced at the sky, estimating how much daylight they had left. He did not want to fight the enemy in the dark if he could avoid it and he definitely did not want to camp out with eight hundred people on a hillside.

"If you eliminate all risk, you will also eliminate your chance to succeed," Amy said with a grin.

Alex gave her an acerbic look, then made a decision. "We'll move forward, but at half pace." He looked at Amy again. "Go back and find your sister. Tell her I need her up here. She's got the eyes of an eagle."

Amy headed back instantly and the caravan started to move forward. Before they got much closer, Alex heard the pounding of footsteps and didn't have to turn his head to know what he would see—Amy and Sanda, racing back toward him. It was a race Amy had lost a thousand times in a row, but she gave it everything she had anyway.

In English, Sanda said, "Agent Sanda Hawk reporting for duty, commander."

Alex sighed. "As we approach the hills, I want you to look for anything that might indicate an outpost or lookout. A flash of color that shouldn't be there, movement, anything."

"Do you want me to scout ahead?"

"No, I want you to do what I have asked you to do."

Amy held her hand up, a sign that something was tugging at the edge of her mind.

"Dad, this is all a waste."

"Why?" Alex immediately felt a sinking feeling in the pit of his stomach. When Amy said that, she was inevitably right about whatever she was going to say.

"When we ran just ahead of the caravan of prisoners last time we were here, we saw and heard them coming, so we ran up into the hills and looked back out over the plains. We could see the line for miles. If they have a lookout there, or anywhere along this ridgeline, they are going to spot us before we spot them."

Alex squinted his right eye and admitted to himself that she was, of course, right.

Did I really expect to sneak up on them with a group this size? I've got to get my crap together. These people are counting on me.

"You're right, you're right. I wasn't thinking. Let's just move forward as quickly as we can."

Alex picked up the pace and, as if in confirmation of what Amy was saying, they hadn't walked more than a minute when they heard the sound of a strident horn blast coming from up ahead. Fainter and farther away, they heard a repeat as the message was relayed.

Alex turned his head to the side and heard the third iteration of the message, so faint it almost felt like it was his imagination.

To Sanda, he said, "Go get your archers. I want them up here."

Sanda sprinted back the way she had come.

Alex leaned close to Amy. She often showed she was smarter than he was, but he still wanted to turn things into teachable moments. "Once they've spotted us, what do they do? Do they stay at their post, or return to their camp?"

"If we were a small band, they might hold their position. But they will be able to see we can overwhelm them. They will retreat."

"If they are smart, you are right."

Nanda-eh, Sanda, and the rest of the archer troupe arrived at the front and fell into step.

Ten minutes later, they entered the valley. Those fighters who had brought shields raised them to protect as much of the caravan as they could. It was no shield wall, but it would help against a random attack.

They passed the area where Alex was certain the lookout had been, but saw no sign of anyone.

The valley itself seemed completely vacant. Alex was sure there were eyes on them at least part of the time, but if so, they were well-hidden.

The farther into the valley they got, the more deliberate Alex's pace became. With the element of surprise gone, there was no real hurry. Finally, he saw the end of the valley where it opened up onto the stretch of sandy dunes that led to the beach.

Again, he turned to Amy and said, "I don't know if they'll have the guts to try and ambush us, but if I was going to set one up, it would be right there."

Over his shoulder, Alex said, "Slowing down, slowing down," and the word went back through the line.

Ahead, Alex saw a line of Drakana soldiers. At the front were four soldiers on their great warhorses. Both the soldiers and the horses wore heavy armor. Behind them stood a row of a dozen infantry, also armored and holding their rifles to their shoulders.

Alex knew that he had enough actual fighters at the front with him to overwhelm them, but he wanted to give them a chance to surrender. He split the archers into two groups, matched them with groups of warriors and sent them left and right, telling them to stay out of easy range.

Alex ordered two dozen of his shield warriors to the front to protect the column, then stepped in front, exposing himself. He was willing to gamble that the Drakana knew what a position they were in and would not want to risk their lives to take out one man.

Alex handed Amy his ax and sword and stepped forward with his hand raised in greeting. He walked forward with only Monda-ak at his side.

"Gunta, Drakana soldiers."

Alex noticed that the fact that he knew the name of their land hit home immediately. They had managed to keep that information secret during the entire invasion, but now it was out.

"Gunta," one of the soldiers on a warhorse answered and Alex homed in on him.

"I would like to come forward and speak with you. Are you willing?" Alex asked in the universal language.

The man didn't answer, but spurred his horse toward Alex at a walk.

They met in the middle of the open space. When he got close enough to see the man's face, Alex knew immediately he was scared to death. Whatever he had thought of being left behind in Kragdon-ah, Alex guessed he had never dreamed he would be facing an army this size.

Alex pointed to the ship floating in the harbor. "We are here to commandeer your ship."

"I cannot allow that to happen. I will be disgraced forever."

"I have choices for you. We will step aside and allow you to leave your post. Or you can surrender your weapons to us and stay here. Or you can die."

The man's eyes widened and his nostrils flared. Sitting atop his warhorse, he was six feet above Alex, but he knew he was in the inferior position.

He did not speak again, but whirled his horse and rode back to his men. Alex signaled both the groups that he had dispatched north and south to circle around slightly, forming a concave line around the small band of Drakana.

Alex waited patiently while the man on horseback rode around the infantry.

He is not the power. Whoever is in charge sent him out to see what information he could garner. Not what I would have done, but not a terrible plan.

Alex stood and waited while the minutes passed. The sun dipped toward the horizon, but Alex guessed they still had at least an hour of daylight left. No need to hurry them along just yet.

Eventually, the man Alex had spoken to returned, still on his warhorse. He did not approach Alex, but got back in line instead. A moment later, a man with long-dark hair tied up behind him walked around the line. He was dressed the same as the other soldiers, but did not wear armor and instead of a gun, he wore a sword attached to his belt.

The man approached Alex and said, "This will never hold."

"I do not need it to hold. I just need to know if you are willing to die in a wasted attempt to protect this piece of sand, or if you wish to surrender. That is what I offer you."

The man glared at Alex. It was obvious he had made his decision, but couldn't bring himself to announce whatever it was.

Finally, he reached down and fumbled with the scabbard that held his sword. When he got it loose, he solemnly offered it to Alex.

The beach was theirs.

Chapter Ten
Battle for the Boat

"**I**nstruct your men to lay down their weapons and dismount their horses."

The man who had given up his sword looked at Alex for a long moment, already regretting his choice. Eventually, he turned and muttered a few harsh words to the horsemen behind him, who dismounted at once. Then, more words barked at the infantry, who laid their guns on the ground.

Alex tossed the man's sword to Amy, then stepped closer to him. "*All* their weapons."

The man closed his eyes for two beats, then rapped out a longer staccato string of words that no one in Kragdon-ah recognized. Well, no one but perhaps Amy, who had a natural ability with language and had been secretly working with Darand to learn the language. She blinked as she tracked what he said.

At the early stages of learning a language, it is one thing to know certain words or even the construction of the language, but something else to try to keep up with a native speaker. Especially a pissed-off native speaker. Still, she was able to pick up the odd phrase and understand that the man was doing what her father had asked him to do.

One by one, the men untied swords, reached into hidden pockets, and produced a surprising amount of additional weaponry.

Alex pressed forward. "Now their armor."

The man who had surrendered opened his mouth to object, but was smart enough to see where that would end. One last time, he gave the order.

With the soldiers disarmed, Alex relaxed slightly. "Have your men put all their weapons and armor into a pile there," he said, indicating a spot on the sand. He turned and looked for Werda-ak.

"Run back to the nearest cart. Have them bring it to me, along with a team to unload its contents."

That obviously puzzled Werda-ak, but he did not want to question Alex in front of the enemy soldiers, so turned on his heel and ran.

Alex counted the men, who now looked less like soldiers and more like the prisoners they were, and found there were twenty-four of them. He turned to Rinka-ak. "Can you delegate a group of fifty to watch over them? Make sure they are armed and kill any who don't do what they are told or try to escape." He enunciated that last sentence slowly and carefully in the universal language, making sure that the man who had surrendered heard him.

Rinka-ak picked the men and stood them at guard around the captured soldiers. He went through the ranks picking out another fifty and telling them to switch out with the others every two hours.

When the prisoners were segregated from everyone, Alex heard a boom like rolling thunder. It was a familiar sound—one he had heard many times while the Drakana laid siege to Winten-ah.

The sound of a cannon being fired.

Alex dropped to one knee instinctively, but everyone around simply turned toward the noise.

Alex picked up the arc of the cannonball as it headed toward them but it was impossible to judge the trajectory. Impossible, that is, until the ball splashed into the surf twenty feet out.

"Everyone back up, back up."

Getting a caravan of people to start moving was a challenge. Getting a caravan of people that had come to a rest to start moving *backward* was worse. There was confusion as everyone milled around, unsure of what to do.

Alex spread his arms wide and asked Tinta-ak and Rinka-ak to do the same. Together, they pushed people back, but that just resulted in an unmovable clog.

There was another boom and Alex whirled his head around to track the shot. It was closer, but still splashed into the sea.

A third shot rang out and this cannonball landed in the sand.

Alex expected more to come, but there was only silence from then on. He guessed they had shot their maximum distance and without moving closer, couldn't do anything to them.

The sky was beginning to darken and Alex was glad that step one of the operation had gone so smoothly. He welcomed the dusk now, as he thought the next part of his plan would go better in darkness.

He grabbed Sanda and Amy and they walked toward the water. Casually, as they passed it, Alex nodded at a spot. "That's where I first came out of the door."

Sanda stared, but there was nothing but the rocky sand to mark the spot.

A few yards further along, they stood at the very edge of the waves. The ship still sat at anchor, but Alex could see activity on board. He had no doubt that those on board had noticed what was going on, even though no shots were fired. They were likely alerted by the lookouts the same as those on the beach.

"Can you see anything?" Alex asked Sanda.

"I see people moving about, but it's hard to tell what they are doing. I think I see one man looking back at us with a spyglass."

As one, the three of them lifted their hands and gave a friendly wave. Sarcasm ran freely through the Hawk family.

"What would you do if you were them?"

"Depends on what their orders are and why they were left behind. If it's simply to watch for an insurrection and report home, I'd say this qualifies, and they could be getting ready to sail. If they are supposed to gather information over time—say a year or two—then report back home, they will stay anchored."

Alex stared at the three masts. The sails were still gathered at the bottom of each.

"It doesn't appear that they are getting ready to flee," he observed. "I think that if I had seen an army this size approach the beach, I would have at least wanted to move out a little further. Maybe take a spin around the coast for a day or two, then sail by and see what the lay of the land was."

"Do you know what it takes to get a ship like that underway?" It was Harta-ak, who had come from behind them and stood staring at the vessel. "It is not an easy thing. Especially if you have a skeleton crew."

"This is why I am glad you came," Alex answered. "I wish I knew more about these matters."

Harta-ak raised his hands. "I am no expert either. That ship is bigger than any ten ships I have ever seen put together. There was nothing on the river that approached it." He stared at the ship, drinking it in from bow to stern. "But I am anxious to learn. What do we do now?"

"*We* don't do anything," Alex said with a grin. "You are too valuable. *I* am going to take a boarding party and attempt to take it over."

Harta-ak looked at the transport ship that was beached twenty yards away.

"Can you get enough fighters in there to do that?"

"I only know of one way to find out," Alex said. He turned and looked back at the beach. The cart had been brought up and their supplies had been offloaded. Alex strode to the pile and said, "Let's transport our goods inside their tents for now." While people went to work making that happen, he said, "Now, let's load all of their weapons and armor onto the cart."

Puzzled, Tinta-ak spoke up. "Why?"

"Because I do not want them to reclaim them and use them against us. If anyone feels they are under-armed, feel free to grab any of the swords, knives, or shields. In fact, pull a few sets of the armor out and put those in the tents as well. They might come in handy down the line." He looked around until he spotted someone he knew well and trusted. "Wenta-eh. I want you to take this cart and hook it to one of our horses. Then, take everything back to Sekun-ak. He will know how to dispose of their weapons. He's kind of an expert at that." He paused, considering what else needed to be done. "Who is our best with horses?"

There was a buzz of conversation that spread through the area as people discussed that and offered their opinions. Finally, the crowd separated and a somewhat-gawky teenage girl was pushed forward. A tall, thick man who Alex did not recognize stood with her.

"This is my daughter. She rides as if she was born on the back of a horse. All she ever thinks about are horses."

Tinta-ak said, "She is one of ours. I can vouch for her."

Alex turned to the man who had spoken. "Can you ride as well?"

The man reacted as though Alex had asked him if he still wet the bed. He snorted. "Of course."

Alex made a mental note that Tinta-ak's confidence seemed to run through his tribe. "I'd like you and your daughter to choose two other riders, at least one from Winten-ah."

Before he had a chance to continue, Werda-ak the Younger raised his hand and volunteered.

"Take these horses back to Sekun-ak as well. When you've delivered the cart and horses, come back here. I will need you back within two days. Do not leave until morning, though. No one should walk or ride across the plains in the night. They will likely not live to see daylight."

Alex turned away, his mind moving at a rapid clip.

What's next? What am I forgetting? How can I react when the plan goes awry?

Alex had already picked out his boarding party and now was just waiting for darkness to fall. There was only a sliver of a moon. He hoped that would help with a stealthy approach to the ship, though they would certainly be keeping a keen lookout for them.

He took his team aside and went over the plan one more time, then he judged it was dark enough that they could put things in motion.

Alex left Harta-ak and Rinka-ak in charge on the beach. He left Monda-ak with Amy, which took a bit of convincing. He knew there was no way to use him in this attack, though. He brought Tinta-ak along because he knew how intimidating he looked and thought that it would take more than one blow from any weapon to put him down. He would have loved to bring Torana for the same reason, but knew that as large as he was, he would have trouble scaling the ship. Fantam-eh would not hear of being left behind with Tinta-ak going, so she came along as well. Versa-eh insisted on going, though Harta-ak objected. She sweetly told him to shut up and that she would see him soon.

The rest of his team was made up of young, strong warriors who didn't mind risking their lives in the first real action of the campaign.

Alex split the archers into two groups, one led by Nanda-eh, the other by Sanda. They stood fifty yards apart, with the surf lapping at their feet.

Strong arms pulled the transport boat across the sand until it floated in the gentle surf. They timed their approach so that it coincided with the tide flowing out. Alex put himself in the bow of the boat since that was the place most likely to be hit as they approached. He and the four warriors behind him all carried their composite shields and would use them to protect the men behind when they got closer.

Even with the tide helping, it was not easy moving the boat. The four men who manned the oars strained against them, chanting together to keep in time.

The ship was mammoth, but it rose at both the bow and stern, leaving the lowest spot to the water in the middle. That was where the cannons were, and also where Alex intended to board.

He hoped they were an elusive, slow-moving image in the night sea, but the lookout on ship had sharp eyes and sounded the alarm, pointing right at them.

"Shields up," Alex commanded, and the five shields rose as one.

Moments later, a volley of gunshots sounded from the deck and Alex felt an impact against his shield. He ran a hand over his torso looking for a wound, but found none. At least from that distance, the composite shields held against their gunfire.

When they first arrived, Alex had seen cargo netting hanging down the side of the ship, but was not surprised to find they had raised it. The sailors on board were not stupid.

While the transport ship was still fifty yards away from the ship, Sanda's archers unleashed their longbows. The ship was at the outer edge of their range, and so there was no real chance for accuracy, but they let fly, hoping only to land arrows on the deck and scatter their defenses.

When Sanda's team's arrows were still arcing their way across the night sky, Nanda-eh's team let loose their own volley. The two groups took turns firing until Sanda saw that the transport was close to the large ship. Then she called out, "Stop!" and the barrage ceased.

When the boat got close enough to the ship—which looked even more impressive up close—Alex ordered them to pull alongside.

Tinta-ak whirled a rope with a three-pronged grappling hook over his head and threw it. It clanked against the side of the ship and fell back into the ocean. Tinta-ak tried again, with the same result.

That was when Versa-eh stepped forward and held her hand out. "It's not strength. It's technique. Watch." She twirled the rope smoothly around her head, spraying everyone around with salt water. When she released the hook, it sailed up and up and over the lower deck. She tugged on it and it caught.

Two young warriors had volunteered for the most dangerous job. They grabbed the rope and scrambled up. When they reached the top, they would be all alone and could be killed instantly. If so, they hurried to their death. Around one's shoulder was a rope ladder with hooks on the end. If they survived long enough, they would hang it over the edge and the others would climb up.

Alex wanted to close his eyes, but he could not. He watched the two lithe warriors brace their feet and pull themselves up the side of the ship. When they disappeared over the side, he expected to hear screams and sounds of a pitched battle, but it was silent. A moment later, the rope ladder dropped in front of him.

"Follow me, and remember what you are to do."

Alex's orders had been to fight where necessary, but to not kill unless they had to. He hoped to take at least a few of the sailors alive.

Alex reached the top and clambered over, aided by the strong hands of the warriors who had gone first. Every sense alert, Alex scanned around him. He expected gunfire or a screaming attack, but he saw no one. He stood lookout while the others scrambled up the ladder and onto the deck.

It was so dark, Alex had a difficult time seeing his own people right next to him.

To his left and right were sturdy steps that led up to the next decks. At that moment, a dozen men popped up and on an order from somewhere, fired as one.

Bullets ripped through the air. Two of Alex's people fell instantly. "Get them!" he shouted and led the charge toward the ladders. He had only taken a few steps when another dozen men popped up and fired down on them. Alex felt an impact on his calf, as though he had been hit hard with a sharp stick. He ignored it and led the charge up the ladder.

When he reached the top, he saw that the first dozen men had reloaded and had turned to face him. He did not hesitate, but gripping his two-bladed ax, he leaped directly at all of them. Tinta-ak was directly behind him and ten others clambered over the ladder and launched themselves at the Drakana sailors.

The guns went off, the smell of gunpowder hung heavy in the air and bullets flew.

The Drakana rifles were effective at a distance but useless for close combat. Their shots felled three of the Kragdon-ah warriors, but the rest jumped in with axes, swords, and hammers flailing.

The sailors scrabbled for their swords, or used their rifles as clubs, but stood no chance. These men were trained seamen, not trained fighters. The battle was over in seconds, with the sailors either dead or wounded on the deck, or holding up their hands in instant surrender.

Alex climbed to the highest spot available and scanned for more enemies, but saw none. The men in front of him were the only Drakana on board, or they were in hiding.

He jumped down, shouting, "Find rope and tie those who surrendered." To another man, he said, "Throw their guns overboard. Keep their swords."

Tinta-ak took the lead in organizing that. He was at least a foot taller than any of the Drakana and twice as broad. They knelt before him without being told.

Alex hurried to his wounded warriors. Two of them were lying dead on the deck. He recognized one as the man who had been first up the rope. Three others were sitting up, but with wounds that ranged from superficial—a gunshot graze of his scalp—to serious—a gaping wound in his side.

Fantem-eh rushed to Alex's side. "I am not a healer, but I can tend to our wounded for now. I'll start with you."

Alex was unsure what she meant. He looked down and saw a slick darkness that reflected the starlight from above. As soon as he saw his wound, he felt it as well.

There was a through-wound in the back of his calf. Another inch to the side and it would have hit his tibia. As it was, he had blood down both sides of his leg. In the heat of the moment, he hadn't felt it as more than an impact.

"Sit down," Fantem-eh commanded, pointing to a set of stairs that lead up toward the bow.

Battle injuries were not new for Alex, from shrapnel in Afghanistan to a crossbow arrow in the battle of Denta-ah.

Fantem-eh called out to Tinta-ak, who approached and bent over, trying to examine Alex's wound in the darkness.

"He'll live," Tinta-ak said. Fantem-eh spoke to him quickly in their own language and Tinta-ak hurried away.

Fantem-eh cleaned around the wound and within a few minutes, Tinta-ak returned holding a corked bottle. Fantem-eh pulled the cork out with her teeth, spit it out and took a swallow. She made a terrible face and said, "That is awful stuff. It is just what I need."

She poured copious amounts of the liquid into Alex's open wound.

The pain had throbbed in his leg, but that made it explode and a sharp cry escaped even through his clenched teeth.

"I told you he would live," Tinta-ak said and hurried away to check on their prisoners.

Fantem-eh bandaged the wound loosely so the healer could finish up when he arrived.

Alex stood, ignored the pain, and issued commands. He leaned over the side of the boat and shouted down to the four oarsmen. "Return to shore and bring as many fighters as you can carry, and a healer to care for our wounded."

He glanced around the open deck, which would be difficult to defend, as the Drakana had just discovered. He did his best, posting warriors as lookouts around the highest areas.

Only Alex's earlier orders stopped the Kragdon-ah warriors from quickly dispatching the wounded Drakana. They roughly searched those who had fought and were now wounded, then carried them to a corner of the deck where two warriors with heavy hammers stood over them.

The clean-up was not yet complete, but it was now nearly inevitable.

The ship belonged to Kragdon-ah.

Chapter Eleven
All Aboard

Once Fantam-eh had done everything she could for the injured Kragdon-ah warriors, Alex had her tend to the Drakana.

"You are saving them for me to kill?" she asked.

"No, I want to heal them if we can."

"I have never tried to heal an enemy unless they have pledged to become part of our tribe."

"This is a little different," Alex said. "I hope that when we heal them, they will pledge to help us." He chose his words carefully. He did not think there was much chance that the sailors would ever be part of one of their tribes. He did have hope that he could convince them to assist him in his plan, though.

Fantam-eh was obviously not convinced, but she did as Alex asked. Until a healer arrived, she was mostly limited to stopping the bleeding anyway.

With Fantam-eh on that task, Alex turned his mind back to military matters. This was not a ship in any normal sense of the word. It was more a city that sat on waves, and there would be hundreds of places the Drakana could potentially hide. To be able to make a voyage from Drakana to Kragdon-ah would require vast quantities of food and essentials, so the storeroom alone was likely to be mammoth. Then there would be staterooms, bunkhouse-style rooms, and dozens of others.

For the moment, Alex was happy to simply hold the decks and keep watch.

Meanwhile, the transport made it to shore, switched out oarsmen for more volunteers and returned to the ship. That first wave brought more fighters along with Harta-ak and Versa-eh.

Harta-ak touched lightly down on the deck and said, "It's been too long since I've felt water under my feet. This feels right."

He wanted to begin exploring the ship immediately, but having lost two of his warriors in the first skirmish, Alex was not in a mood to take chances.

It took almost thirty minutes for each round trip from shore to ship. Alex ordered the cargo netting lowered again, which made it easier for the people of Kragdon-ah to climb aboard.

By the time the first faint pink showed in the eastern sky, almost a quarter of the army had been transferred to the ship. With that many armed fighters on board, Alex felt confident enough that he broke them into teams of ten and sent them to search the rest of the ship.

Monda-ak took off at a rapid pace, sniffing every surface and investigating every room. If anyone was hiding, he would find them.

The first order of business was to find a light source. Even in the middle of the day, there would be dark and shadowy areas that would be difficult to search.

Alex finally thought to ask one of the round trips from the shore to bring a torch with them. Using that, and doing a little poking around, he found a number of oil lamps. He paused.

Would Sekun-ak think this is stama? Or is it just another form of a torch? Mentally, Alex flipped a coin and decided to use them.

He used the torch to light the wicks of the lamps and showed his fighters how to use them. They looked at the strange objects with suspicion at first, but when they saw how useful they were, they accepted them.

Antan-ak, the healer of the Rinta-ah tribe—who had once healed Alex after Panga flayed the flesh from his forearms—once again went to work on him. More than anything, Alex wanted to lead the search of the ship, but Antan-ak insisted he stretch out and raise his injured leg.

By that time, Amy and Sanda had made it to the boat, as well as Rinka-ak. There were now plenty of people who Alex trusted to carry out the search. He lay back, propped his leg up on a box and closed his eyes. He never would have thought it possible, but he fell asleep almost instantly.

When he awoke, it was full daylight and Versa-eh sat cross-legged on the deck next to him.

"I know you're going to ask," she said, "so let me tell you. We have searched the ship. We found many interesting things, but no more sailors. One of the Drakana speaks our universal language and he swears to us that they used everyone on board to try to repel our attack. I believe him."

Alex blinked, tried to reorient himself. He lifted his leg off the box, but it felt like it weighed a hundred pounds all by itself. The pain wasn't terrible, though. At least not until he moved, then he was reminded that he had been shot just a few hours earlier.

Alex pushed himself up onto his elbows anyway.

Versa-eh reached behind her and grabbed a stick. "Antan-ak said you would try to get up immediately and I was to give you this."

The stick was as thick as his wrist and looked like it had been cut from a tree very recently. It had a natural bend at the top and Alex saw that he could use it as a crutch. Versa-eh helped him to his feet and Alex made sure not to wince.

"How long was I out?"

Versa-eh looked at him uncertainly. There was no real method of keeping time in Kragdon-ah, as there was no need. They measured time in sunrises, the apex of the sun, and sunset.

"You slept as long as you needed to. You don't need to worry. We have been working."

Alex looked toward the beach and saw that there were still groups of people waiting to be ferried across to the ship. People were coming up from below decks with armloads of guns and throwing them into the ocean, likely never to be seen again. Harta-ak was standing under the mainsail, leaning over and talking to someone, but Alex couldn't make out who it was. Then Harta-ak moved slightly and he saw that it was Darand, speaking animatedly, gesturing this way and that at the sails and ropes.

Doing everything he can so we don't pitch him overboard, I guess.

Alex looked from Harta-ak and Darand to the captured Drakana, who sat in the same corner they had been in when he went to sleep. He noticed they were watching Darand closely.

Leaning awkwardly on his makeshift crutch, Alex limped over to them.

"Which of you can speak this language?"

A swarthy man smiled, showing several missing teeth. "I've been learning it."

"Good, but that might not be enough." Alex stood taller. "Harta-ak! Can you send Darand here to me?"

Harta-ak waved and a moment later, Darand hurried over.

Never thought he would be the one I would be using for a translator, but we work with what we have.

"Tell them who I am," Alex said.

Darand spoke in the Drakana language and went on for quite some time.

"I didn't need you to tell them my life story."

"I wanted to tell them they were dealing with someone important, so they would respect you."

"Fine," Alex said. "Tell them they have two choices. They can help us sail the ship, or we'll kill them where they sit."

Again, Darand went on for what seemed like a very long time, gesturing, and waving. He ended by drawing a thumb across his throat. Some things really *are* universal.

The captured sailors talked among themselves, before responding to Darand.

"They say that if they help you, they will be dead anyway, so you might as well kill them. I agree with them. I will kill them for you if you want."

"I appreciate your enthusiasm, but no. Tell them this. If they will help us sail this ship—and if they will train our men so they can do it themselves—when we get to Drakana, we will lock them up in the brig. We will turn them over to the first Drakana army we see and tell them they were captured as prisoners of war. They will be free to continue their lives. They could even be heroes who fought bravely against us, which they did."

Darand hesitated, then said, "Is that true for me, too?"

"Is that what you want?"

"I feel no loyalty to my country. They sentenced me to death and I only survived because of you. But I have a wife and child. I had given up hope of ever seeing them again."

"I will always take care of people who are loyal," Alex answered. "Now tell them what I said."

Alex waited, anticipating another long spiel from Darand, but this time, the message was conveyed in just a few sentences. The captured men put their heads together and spoke quietly. Finally, they answered Darand.

"They say they agree, but I do not know if I trust them. They still called me traitor, which seems wrong if they are making the same decision I did."

Alex considered, looking at the men before him. "Do you know any of these men?"

"Yes. I know him, him, and him," Darand said, pointing toward three men, but not the swarthy spokesman of the bunch.

"What do you know of them?"

Darand struggled for a moment, looking for words, then said, "They are men. They are not good or bad, they are just men."

"But are they sailors?"

"They are sailors, though they all have had different duties on board."

"Good. That's what I want." Alex looked around and his eyes landed on Rinka-ak. "On the next boat back to shore, I want all but these three men to go along. Treat them as we will treat the rest of the prisoners who surrendered."

Rinka-ak inspected the way the prisoners were tied. "One of the lessons my father passed on to me before he died was to never trust another man's knots."

"I am sorry I never met your father. I know we would have liked each other."

Rinka-ak put two fingers to his forehead and led the prisoners away.

The three men who remained looked confused, as though they were not sure whether they had just won or lost a peculiar lottery.

Alex turned back to Darand. "Thank you for being honest with me. I sent them away because I was afraid that with this many, they might feel like they could start trouble. With only three, I do not think they will be brave or foolish enough to do that."

Darand looked at the three men, who, at least at that moment, did not look brave at all.

"Tell them the offer stands for them, but they must mean it. They will have to work every day to train our men in how to run this ship."

Darand hesitated. "Then you should probably bring back the man who took a hammer blow to his left arm. He was our..." words seemed to fail him and he gestured, trying to make his point.

Alex believed he understood. He was their navigator. A critical component, indeed.

Alex called to Rinka-ak and said, "Hold up, friend. Bring the man with the injured arm back to me."

A moment later, the swap had been made, and an idea occurred to Alex. They had shown that they put value in their word when they had agreed to the terms of the Thundan.

"Tell them I want them to swear an oath, and I will do the same. If they help us learn how to sail this ship, we will do anything we can to protect them and deliver them safely back to their families. I swear it."

Darand took a long time to make that explanation, but eventually he turned back to Alex and said, "They swear it. Now I would trust them."

"Good," Alex said. "I will need you to be in three places at once. You will be our interpreter."

Darand placed two fingers to his forehead, showing he was not incapable of learning.

Alex raised his voice and said, "We pull up anchor and leave this harbor in three days."

Chapter Twelve
Preparing to Sail

Any number of interesting things happened over those three days.

One unanticipated side effect of life on a ship was seasickness. Even though the ship was at anchor, and though the chop of the waves was only a few inches, the ship still moved. Perpetually.

That small motion eventually disturbed something in the inner ear of many of the Kragdon-ah, causing severe vomiting, dehydration, and general malaise. Watching those who were afflicted by it, Alex couldn't help but remember his own sickness with a virus when he had first arrived in Kragdon-ah.

That brought another thought into his mind.

Why didn't Amy catch that same sickness? Sanda, he could understand. She was born in Kragdon-ah and would have had the natural immunity from her mother. But Amy was in the same position as Alex had been—entering this world in her twenties. Alex turned the question over in his mind for several minutes, but eventually gave up on solving it.

The world is the world. He had learned to take more and more comfort from the favorite phrase of the Winten-ah.

Alex himself did not get seasick. He had been sick to death the first time he spent an extended time on board a ship, but when he finally recovered, he never had it again. Something inside his body had adjusted to the motion. He hoped that would be the same for the rest of the Kragdon-ah. If they had to deal with this for the entire voyage, everyone would be well and truly miserable.

That was not, unfortunately, the case for Monda-ak. The huge dog got hugely sick for a time and deposited an incredible amount of dog vomit on the deck. He was miserable for twenty-four hours, then decided life was worth living again.

Another interesting turn was when Alex, Harta-ak and Versa-eh examined the storeroom more closely. He had anticipated it would be mostly empty after the long voyage, but was pleased to find it was still well-stocked.

Holding one of the oil lanterns to peer into the windowless room, Alex said, "They must have kept this ready to return home at a moment's notice."

He pried the lid off a barrel that stood as tall as his waist and was surprised to find that it was filled with rice—a perfect food to be stored for such a journey. There were other barrels filled with supplies—what appeared to be a form of flour, and two small barrels filled with honey.

That reminded Alex of his battle with the wasta-ta—the giant bees—and he wondered if perhaps their equivalent in Drakana were more easily tamed.

Another storage room had dry goods—canvas and needles as thick as a forefinger that Alex was sure could be used to repair sails.

The final storeroom was where weaponry had once been stored. The rifles had all gone overboard, cursed as stama, but there were more barrels here. A pyramid stack of cannonballs showed what those barrels contained—gunpowder. Alex would not let them dump it overboard. The cannons were definitely stama, which likely made the powder the same. Nonetheless, Alex couldn't bring himself to allow it to be destroyed. A single ship attempting to battle the army of an entire nation could not easily pass on such a weapon.

What if we are attacked at sea? Are there pirates in this world? Would they even dream of attacking a ship of this size? Boarding her like we did? What a prize it would be if they took her.

Alex closed the door to the storeroom with the gunpowder and cannonballs and ordered it barred. He also didn't want to take a chance that one of the Drakana would think to slip down and ignite the gunpowder, blowing a hole in the ship and undoubtedly killing them all.

On the second day, the convoy arrived back from Winten-ah. After he had sent them away, Alex realized that he had made a mistake by sending them all that way for so little gain. The guns they had sent to be destroyed by Sekun-ak could have just as easily been done away with as the others had—by dropping them in the ocean. Still, Alex knew that it would please Sekun-ak. He would relish both the destruction of the stama and the unspoken sign from Alex that he was not using them in his absence.

Initially, Alex had been unsure how to get the animals on board. For the first of many times, Darand proved invaluable. He showed Alex a sling system they had devised. Even larger animals like a horse or milk beast could be lifted from the transport boat onto the ship by wrapping the canvas sling around them and, through the strength of many men, pulling them on board.

By the end of the third day, everyone, and everything that Alex wanted on the ship was stored away. Harta-ak and his hand-picked crew worked with the captured Drakana tirelessly. From before first light until well-after dark, Harta-ak walked the ship, asking questions, watching tasks being performed, and doing them himself.

Alex watched him and was thankful Harta-ak and Versa-eh had decided to come along. He tried to picture himself performing the duties of captain and knew he would have done his best, but would have failed.

By sunset on the third day, most all of the people who had been suffering from seasickness felt it abate. Some took their first bite of food since they had left land behind.

For Alex, it felt like all was in readiness.

His final decision was what to do with the Drakana who he had captured but had no use for. The easy strategic decision would have been to simply kill them all.

To Alex, that would have felt like murder, nothing more. At least in theory, the Kragdon-ah had a truce with the Drakana. To attack them, to allow them to surrender, then to kill them would be unconscionable.

And yet, they were essentially at war, albeit an undeclared one to this point.

Alex met with his council, which included the chieftains and spouses of Rinta-ah, Garta-ah, Franta-ah and Danta-ah, along with Amy and Sanda.

They agreed they would leave the decision to Alex in the end, but each made their case. Most were in favor of simply killing them and leaving their bodies to predators, which would have likely been the karak-ta on the beach.

"We made the decision that we do not trust them to be part of our tribe," Rinka-ak said. "To me, that leaves a single viable option." He didn't have to say what he thought that option was.

That was the way in Kragdon-ah. No quarter asked or given. Each of them believed they would meet the same fate if the roles were reversed and so had no guilt about carrying it out.

Amy spoke on behalf of the prisoners, pointing out the ideas that Alex had already thought about, but couldn't come up with any strategic value to letting them live.

There were downsides to leaving them as they were. If they reconnected with other Drakana soldiers, they could arm themselves again and possibly attack one of their villages.

In the end, Alex simply could not bring himself to kill unarmed men, even enemies. He rode the transport ship back to shore to pick up the remaining Kragdon-ah who had been serving guard duty. He had left the crutch the healer had made for him on the ship. The idea of trying to walk across sand with a homemade crutch was ludicrous.

He ordered the guards to carry an armful of basic weapons—hammers and short swords—from the transport, and pile them at the water's edge.

Alex approached the man who had initially surrendered to him. He did not appear to be any worse for the wear of being held prisoner.

"We are leaving," Alex said simply. "You are free to go."

"Free to go?" the man spat back at Alex. "Why don't you just kill us?"

"That was the belief of most of my men," Alex agreed. "But I prefer to give you a chance to live." He pointed at the small pile of rudimentary weapons. "Those are yours now. Here is my advice for you." He tossed him a flint. "Build a fire. That will keep some predators away. I would get used to sleeping in trees. If you do, you might live."

Alex turned and limped back to the transport, very glad that he wouldn't have to walk on sand again for some time.

"What about food?" the man called, but Alex waded to the boat without looking back and they pushed away from shore.

None of the Drakana soldiers were ever seen or heard of again.

Chapter Thirteen
Anchors Aweigh

Alex Hawk had been around exceptionally complex technologies and weapons in the twenty-first century. He had also been around engineers, technicians, and pilots who understood that technology and how to use it.

Now, standing on the bow of what he considered to be equal to a fifteenth-century sailing vessel, he was, in more than one way, completely asea. Everything about a great sea-going vessel like this was more complex than anything else he had seen in Kragdon-ah, with the lone exception of the cruise missile he had found buried beside what had once been Denta-ah.

The challenge that he faced was that he had only four people who had some clue how everything worked. All four of those were part of the enemy force that Alex had captured and put to work, which was not always the most reliable labor force.

Still, he had no choice. One look at the rigging of the sails, or the navigation equipment, told him that his blithe confidence in his ability to figure things out as he went had been badly misplaced. Without the three captured sailors, Darand, and Harta-ak, he would have never managed to leave the little bay where they sat.

If he had managed, through some stroke of incredible luck, to figure out how to raise anchor and sails, he would have been every bit as likely to end up in what had once been Mexico or Alaska instead of Drakana, which he was sure lay somewhere far to the west.

He still wasn't sure where Drakana was located in twenty-first century terms. But based on the way Darand had described things to him, he was sure that if he found what had once been Hawaii, or Australia, or the Philippines, he would likely find Drakana there.

Their voyage of discovery started with pulling the anchor up. There was a mechanical winch with a number of long, strong wooden bars attached. Like an old-fashioned mill grinding flour, the bars were pushed forward and the anchor slowly wound forward.

Darand told him that this had once been among his duties and that it was horrible. He recommended that Alex pick out his strongest men to pull the anchor up.

Alex chose Torana and Tinta-ak. After those two, the other six didn't matter as much. As most things were, it was a challenge for Torana. His strength was incredible—likely equal to any two or three other men. But standing over nine feet tall, the bar was not built at a height that he could reach easily. The Drakana were all smaller than the average Kragdon-ah, and the Kragdon-ah were diminutive compared to Torana. Nonetheless, he bent his knees, hunched his shoulders, and put his incredible strength to the task, and they raised the anchor.

While anchored in the bay, the ship had moved slightly, rocked gently by the waves but as soon as they raised the anchor off the bottom, that movement became much more pronounced and the waves pushed the aft section of the ship toward the beach.

Harta-ak was the Captain of the vessel, but he was learning as well. He gave control of the ship to one of the three captured sailors. That man did not speak any language Harta-ak could understand. He barked his commands in the language of the Drakana. Amy, who had been studying their language from morning to night, translated those commands to the universal language.

Alex watched his daughter, who unconsciously took on a deeper, guttural voice that more closely matched the sailor she was translating for. When he pointed, stomped his feet, and swore in frustration, Amy did the same.

It was serious business, but watching Amy pantomime the man tickled Alex to a point that he had to turn away and look back toward the beach.

Harta-ak had given the order to raise anchor when dawn's first light had peeked over the eastern horizon. By the time the sun fully emerged, the sails were extended and the mighty ship had left the sheltering bay behind.

In the distance, karak-ta squawked their terrible song and circled endlessly over the rocks where they protected their nests. Alex watched them, unable to stop thinking of the first moments he had emerged from the door and met them face to face. As the shore faded, the distant birds fooled his eye so that they almost looked like the seagulls he had once mistaken them for.

There was a large deck at both the bow and stern of the ship—large enough that several hundred people could stand and look out where they were heading or where they had been.

The deck of the bow was empty—the vast expanse of open sea, nothing more than a rolling, endless horizon, was too much for those who had never before left Kragdon-ah.

The back deck was packed, with people watching the retreating shore of the only home they had ever known.

Alex climbed a few feet up on the stern mast, so he was higher than everyone watching Kragdon-ah slowly retreat. He let them have their moment, then, in a voice that carried over the wind and waves, said, "We will have a feast tonight! The cooks will need a few extra hands in the kitchen."

Alex knew the kitchen on a ship was called the galley, but he had discovered there were many new things that did not have a proper name in any of the Kragdon-ah languages.

There were more than enough volunteers to help out with the preparation of the feast. For the overflow, Alex and Harta-ak found other jobs that needed doing around the ship. The peoples of Kragdon-ah were workers. Alex recognized at once that he would need an endless series of tasks designed to keep everyone busy.

The best people for that job were Rinka-ak and Amy. They spent the rest of the day walking around the ship with one of the captured sailors. He was more than happy to point out all the grunt work that was necessary to keep a ship of this size shipshape. The more they did, the fewer jobs were left for him.

Alex found Harta-ak, who looked more harried than normal. "How goes it?" Alex asked.

"Here's the good news. We have only open seas before us for many days. There is not anything we can run into. But, come with me." They walked to the aft section of the ship. The waves were calm, but there was still substantially more chop than there had been when they were anchored. The ship had a continuous rolling motion that made it difficult for Alex to walk on his injured leg. The crutch was essentially useless on the moving deck.

As they walked, Alex said, "I've got to find someone to convert this crutch into a cane."

"Give it to me, then, and I'll have it done at once."

Alex wasn't sure of his ability to make it to the stern with no support, so he held onto the crutch for the moment.

Alex was able to climb the ladders that were everywhere on the ship, but only through using his arms almost exclusively and letting his injured leg dangle as he did. He was beginning to feel like one of those weightlifters at gyms back in the twenty-first century who continually skipped leg day.

Finally, they made it to the main deck. For the first time, Alex saw real gulls circling overhead. One circled, dropping closer and closer, then landed on a railing on the opposite end of the stern.

Like most things in Kragdon-ah, it was well oversized—perhaps two to three times as large as the birds Alex had seen growing up. Beyond the size of it, it appeared to be a gull in every other way. Still, Alex waited for the other shoe to drop. For the bird to suddenly fly at them and reveal a full set of sharp teeth and retractable claws in its webbed feet.

None of that happened. After the gull examined them for a few moments through its golden eyes, it seemed to let the wind blow it off its perch, drop to the water and soar higher and higher until it disappeared.

Harta-ak pointed behind them. "What do you see?"

There was no word for *wake* in Kragdon-ah, at least that Alex knew, so he said, "The trail we leave behind."

"Right. What does it look like?"

Alex wondered if this was a trick question. He stared at the wake, which looked like a dozen elongated Z-shapes strung together. Alex made a gesture with his hand.

Harta-ak put his arm out straight behind them, as though he was pointing back to the land of his birth. "That is what our trail should look like. Instead, it looks like our boat consumed too many karak-ta eggs last night and is still recovering."

Alex laughed, laid a hand on Harta-ak's shoulder and said, "As you say, there is nothing for us to run into out here. No sandbar where we will run aground. No other ships within many days journey, probably. We will improve."

Alex saw that the inefficient path was bothering Harta-ak.

"Maybe you should take a turn at the wheel."

Harta-ak had been so busy with a thousand details, the thought had never occurred to him. He smiled and his shoulders visibly relaxed.

"You stay here. I will send Torana to fetch you and take you wherever you want to go."

Harta-ak grabbed the crutch from Alex and with mischief in his eyes said, "Unless you want to catch me and take it back."

Alex did not try.

Instead, he sat and felt the bracing sea air against his face and closed his eyes against the bright sun. Monda-ak, who had finally gained his sea legs, rarely left his side.

There would be storms and darker days ahead. But for that moment, Alex Hawk was content.

Chapter Fourteen
The Eleventh Day

The Drakana, unlike all the tribes up and down the west coast of Kragdon-ah, had a written language. Of course, Alex couldn't read it and had to rely on the four Drakana on board to read it for him. Amy gave herself the task of learning the written language along with speaking it, but it was slow going.

The fact that they had a written language was helpful, though, because like virtually all ocean-crossing ships, they kept a logbook. That was of at least some help to Alex, though dated entries like "Landed at Prenta, Drakana," or "Left Trinitan, Drakana" were all meaningless to him.

But it did at least help him to understand approximately how long the journey was. It appeared that from the time they left what they considered to be the mainland of Drakana, it had taken them almost seven months to reach Kragdon-ah. But that was not all sailing time. They seemed to stop at various Drakana outposts every month or two to restock, which was smart. That likely helped them arrive in much better condition than if they had attempted to sail straight through.

Alex and company had started with a full larder, and they had their animals that would help replenish it to a certain extent—the milk beasts for milk, cream, and butter, and chickens for eggs. He had placed Werda-ak in charge of the fishermen who had lines in the water from the lower decks all during daylight hours. Deep sea fishing was very different from river and lake fishing, but at least he had some idea of the basic concepts. They soon learned that fishing from the ship was feast or famine. They either pulled in fish as quickly as they could get their line in, or they went for days on end catching nothing.

Even with those attempts at resupplying on the go, Alex knew they would not be able to make the one-hundred-and-fifty sailing days to arrive at Drakana proper.

That was all right. As was so often the case, Alex had a plan that would solve that problem.

He also realized that his one-hundred-and-fifty-day estimate was almost certainly optimistic. That was how many sea-days it had taken the ship to reach Kragdon-ah with an experienced crew. Their wake was undoubtedly as straight as an arrow. Harta-ak was handicapped by a large crew more than willing—they scampered up and down the netting and masts—but clueless. The three captured sailors were already spread as thin as the shadow of a single hair.

As impatient as Alex was, he resolved to not show that to anyone—especially Harta-ak. The Captain already had enough of a load on his shoulders. He didn't need Alex adding pressure.

Through Amy's translation, Torana offered to carry Alex wherever he needed to go until his leg healed. Alex hated being reliant on anyone or anything, but he had to admit that trying to walk on a deck that tossed and moved unpredictably on a leg that had been shot clean through a few days earlier was a bad idea.

And so, the incongruous pair of Alex and Torana became a normal sight around the ship. If Alex stood at the stern watching their wake—which had now become a hobby for him—Torana was there, too, standing with infinite patience. Alex could only imagine what went through his mind most times.

He had been raised to serve only one purpose—to kill with his bare hands. Now he had been adopted by a group of people he had been trained to think of as the enemy, and they had shown him only kindness. His hands—the size of a large ham—now only picked up Alex and played with children.

His favorite of those children was Sista-eh, who had now seen five summer solstices. When Torana had first arrived, she had judged the other children were too rough on him and took charge. She was that kind of girl. Alex could envision her becoming chieftain of the Winten-ah in a few decades. She and Torana were almost inseparable. Even when he was carrying Alex somewhere, Sista-eh was very likely perched on his left shoulder.

Even for a nine-and-a-half-foot-tall giant, there is no perfect way to carry a six-foot-tall man. It came down to two choices—a fireman's carry, with Alex slung over Torana's shoulder looking at his posterior—or cradled like a small child.

Alex would have preferred the fireman's carry. The view wasn't necessarily lovely, but it felt a bit more adult. Torana, however, did not give Alex a choice. He would simply scoop him up in his arms and off they would go, with Alex "driving" by pointing where he wanted to go. If the hundreds of Kragdon-ah who saw Alex carried like a baby found it funny, they at least waited until he was out of sight to let their smiles show.

As promised, Harta-ak had the useless crutch turned into a cane, with a large knob on top to make it easy to hold. In one of the storerooms, someone had found a crate of what Alex assumed was the same material Nissina's suit had been made out of. It was malleable, but gave a great grip against even wet, slippery surfaces. It was wrapped around the bottom of the cane and Alex became as mobile as he could. Even so, Torana and Sista-eh lingered.

The Drakana navigator did his best to show Harta-ak how to plot a route and take readings from the position of the sun and the stars. That man had spent a lifetime learning the intricacies of his craft, however, and it was impossible for Harta-ak to absorb more than a tiny percentage of what the man knew.

They had been out to sea for ten days and had enjoyed perfect weather. Steady winds, sunshine, and only a few wispy white clouds had marked their days.

That ended on the eleventh day.

As best as Alex could determine, they were on a west-southwest course when an impressive bank of dark clouds appeared on the horizon. Before Alex had even noticed the impending change in the weather, the three Drakana sailors began running around the decks issuing orders.

That was normally useless because of the language differences, but this time, their meaning was clear. Everything that wasn't already lashed down needed to be, or it had to be moved below.

Many hands can make quick work, but many bodies on the ladders and tight enclosures of the passageways had the opposite effect. Torana carried Alex to the bow and he stood watching the clouds. Judging the speed of an oncoming storm is almost impossible, and Alex proved hopeless at it. He estimated how far it was to the horizon where the storm was first showing, then guessed at their own speed and how fast the storm might be approaching.

After all that guesswork, he guessed that they had forty-five minutes until the storm was on them.

He was horribly wrong.

Five minutes later, the wind picked up dramatically and the first warm, heavy drops of rain splattered against the deck.

Torana did not wait for Alex to tell him where he needed to go. He picked him up and placed him on his hip like a harried mother with her child in a supermarket. Torana typically used the ladders to go from upper to lower decks, but now he bypassed that nicety, as he had experienced sudden-onset squalls before.

Harta-ak, the three sailors, and a large group of volunteers were up in the rigging, hurrying to get the sails down before the heaviest of the winds hit.

The wheel was at a high point for visibility and was exposed to the elements. The winds whipped across the decks as dozens of men tried to tie the sails off. Harta-ak called for a long rope and lashed himself to the wheel so he wouldn't be tossed overboard.

The navigator could not stand to leave him alone there and so lashed himself to Harta-ak. The two of them would eventually be the best witnesses to the storm, although they were so shaken by it they both chose not to speak of it.

Everyone else hurried below decks, closing doors tight behind them to keep as much water out as they could.

Monda-ak scampered after them, making himself as small as a three-hundred-pound dog ever could be. He lay down, placed his head between his paws and stared at Alex, looking for reassurance.

Above, the winds howled and shrieked, tossing the massive ship up one wave and plunging down into the trough of the next.

Alex did his best to calm everyone around him.

"This feels bad, but remember, this ship is built to withstand storms exactly like this. I'm sure it endured storms this bad and worse on the voyage to Kragdon-ah."

Across the room, Darand raised his voice and said, "Oh no, Manta-ak. I have never seen a storm come up so sudden and strong."

Alex tilted his head to the side as if to say, 'Really?' but chose not to argue with him.

As quickly as the storm had arrived, Alex knew it was fast-moving. He hoped that it would pass over them quickly.

That hope was not fulfilled.

It had been mid-afternoon when the first dark clouds were spotted. When the storm hit them full-on, the sky darkened immediately so that it felt like dusk. And then it raged, tossing the ship hither and fro like a child's toy for enough hours that the darkness became complete.

Below decks, with the doors closed, it was very dark, but Alex would not allow any of the oil lamps to be lit. In the grip of the squall, which had now become a full-fledged ocean storm, they would only be a fire hazard.

And so they huddled together in the dark, waiting for the obscene rocking—where it felt like they were going over half a dozen times—to cease.

And then, as quickly as it had come on them, it stopped.

After the wailing winds, creaking timbers and thunderous impacts of loose boxes slamming about, the quiet was almost deafening.

Alex threw the door open and limped a few steps before Torana, who had been hunched quietly behind him, bracing him during the entire storm, caught him and plucked him up.

They stepped into a certain kind of chaos that only results from having survived a hurricane in a bottle.

Monda-ak jumped through the door, scampering around like a puppy let loose after hours in a kennel.

Above, the stars shone brightly, offering a promise of better things to come.

The deck was strewn with detritus—broken crates and boxes, shattered glass, tattered bits of canvas that had somehow caught purchase somewhere.

Alex pointed up to the wheel, where Harta-ak and the navigator were still untangling themselves from the ropes. They would be forever bonded by what they had survived together.

Versa-eh rushed ahead of Alex and helped to untangle them.

When they were both loose, Harta-ak turned to the smaller man and laid his hand on his shoulder in the universal Kragdon-ah pledge of friendship. The smaller man saluted him in return.

"That's it, right? It's over?" someone asked from below deck.

Alex turned toward the unseen voice and said, "Unless you'd like to sail back and go through it again."

No one answered.

Harta-ak took charge and said that cleanup could commence as soon as it was light. Until then, everyone should get some rest. They would need it in the morning.

Chapter Fifteen
Dead Calm

The next morning dawned calm. Not just calm as in a beautiful day, but calm as in the ocean being so still they felt they were on a lake instead of what had once been called the Pacific Ocean.

Ever since they left Kragdon-ah, there had always been some small bit of wind that the mighty sails could corral and use to move them along.

On this morning, they might as well have been a ship in a bottle, protected from all elements.

Torana carried Alex above deck and set him gently down.

"This is normal, right? A calm like this after a storm?"

"I don't know. I have never seen a storm like that before," Harta-ak answered.

Amy presented the question to the navigator in her broken Drakana language.

He corrected her words a few times, but eventually got the gist. He answered her slowly.

She turned to Alex and said, "He says a quiet like this can come at any time. It might come after a storm, but not only. They have a word for it: *tragon mig*. That just means *death of the wind*, as far as I can tell."

"Can you ask him how long it will be like this?"

Another round of back and forth later, she turned to her father. "He said that is like asking *how long is a piece of rope?* The answer depends on the rope in question."

Alex let himself smile a bit. "He's right. That was a dumb question. He's our navigator, not a weatherman. One more question, though. Ask him if he thinks the storm blew us off course."

After several long exchanges, Amy said, "He is sure we are off course now, but he won't know where we are until the stars come out tonight."

Alex looked around at the chaos that was everywhere. He called his lieutenants to him. "Each of you grab twenty-five people and take a different section. Don't throw anything away, but section off anything that is broken. We may need to use it to repair something else."

He looked up at the masts and was grateful to see that they were still pointing skyward. If one of them had splintered and fallen, he didn't know what that would mean to them, but he knew it wouldn't be good.

He turned to Harta-ak and the navigator. "Will you do a survey of our key systems—the rigging and sails, and give me a report?"

"We'll start on it now," Harta-ak said, and he and the navigator set off together.

"Friends forever now, I think," Alex commented to Amy. "Do you know his name?" He pointed at the navigator.

"No."

"Find out, will you? I'm tired of just calling him the navigator. He's done enough for us that I can at least learn his name."

Amy chased down the two of them, had a quick conversation and returned to Alex. "His name is Pictin."

"Their names are so weird, but I'm sure Manta-ak, Amy, and Harta-ak sound the same to him."

Alex felt useless as he stood on the upper deck and watched everyone around him working to repair the damage of the storm.

He wanted desperately to pitch in and help, but the healers who had worked on his leg all had the same admonition—move as little as possible. Bending, squatting, picking up and moving debris did not fit with that, so Alex fought against his instincts and simply watched others work.

He couldn't be sure how long it would be until they made land-fall again. Before the storm, he had thought it might be thirty days, but now it was impossible to know. Wherever they did find land, Alex anticipated a battle. Harta-ak was the captain on the ship, but once they hit land again, he knew everyone would look to him. He needed to be back to full-strength, or at least, close to it.

As he watched others work, a flare of movement caught his eye. He swiveled his head and saw a long, sleek flash of gray that disap-peared instantly. He didn't have to wait long for another and another just like it to appear. They had been found by a pod of dolphins.

Or at least they had the form of dolphins. They had a long snout and curved in and out of the water in a fashion reminiscent of the dire wolves in the tall grass of the plains. These aquatic mammals were even more outsized than the ronit-ta.

Alex gave one short, sharp whistle and everyone looked at him. He pointed to the port side of the ship and those who could, moved there and stared. Amy and Sanda hurried up to him, laughing like lit-tle girls. Monda-ak saw where everyone was looking and jumped up, putting his front paws on a railing. When he saw the dolphins swim-ming and playing, he barked at them. One rose up on its rear fin as if to tease him into jumping.

Alex laid a hand on his head and said, "Stay, big boy. If they get you in the water, I don't think you'll like it very much." Monda-ak didn't jump, but he strained to see more clearly.

"If that's how big the dolphins are here, imagine what a sperm whale will look like," Alex said.

Amy and Sanda looked at him with wide eyes and said as one, "I'll pass!"

As huge as the ship was, Alex was afraid that a full-grown whale might be able to seriously damage it if it wanted.

For a moment, he had a weird fantasy of somehow harnessing the power of these giant dolphins to pull them out of the doldrums they suddenly found themselves in. An image of half a dozen of the huge, powerful swimmers pulling the boat along flashed across his brain. He laughed a little to himself at the impossible idea.

The dolphins swam silently, often clearing the water to jump over one another. One of the two Drakana sailors, whose name Alex still did not know, approached him. He gesticulated wildly and spoke rapidly. Amy asked him to slow down, then turned to Alex. "He says there is what we would call a harpoon in one of the store rooms. He wants permission to get it and kill one of them. He says their meat is a delicacy."

Amy waited, wide-eyed.

Alex looked down at the dolphins shining in the sun. He saw intelligence in their eyes and they appeared to be smiling. He would have never thought of killing one, but was it any different than when he killed and field-dressed an elk?

Both the man and Amy looked at him expectantly, but expecting completely opposite answers from him.

"Tell him that these are sacred animals to us, so we can't kill them."

"Do you think he will believe that? He knows we have never been to sea before."

"It doesn't matter whether he believes it or not. Just tell him."

Amy turned to the man and spoke slowly. Before she was finished, the man spat on the deck, whirled on his heel, and walked away.

After a few minutes, the dolphin-like creatures tired of teasing Monda-ak and couldn't find anything else to amuse themselves with. Like the storm, they disappeared as quickly as they had arrived.

Everyone returned to work in the eerie quiet. Alex contemplated teaching at least some of the Kragdon-ah a sea shanty. He knew all the words to many verses of *What Do You Do with a Drunken Sailor*, including one or two that had a sprinkling of profanity. Again, an image leaped unbidden into his mind. A Disneyfied version of his crew, sweeping, scrubbing, and singing the shanty.

"I think I'm losing it," Alex said, but the only person near him was Torana. If the giant had an opinion on Alex's sanity, he kept it to himself.

A full day's work returned the ship to a good order. They had been lucky. Things had been tossed and broken, and some things had been swept overboard, but everyone had survived and nothing critical was damaged beyond repair.

It was better while the cleanup went on. Everyone focused on that, instead of leaning over the edge of the ship looking at the listless water. Harta-ak did what he could to keep everyone busy, but there was only so much busy work on hand. As the strange calm stretched into a second, third, and fourth day, the crew grew restless.

Alex and Harta-ak consulted with Pictin. They asked him if he had ever seen a calm like this go on so long.

He admitted he had not, but was confident that it would soon pass.

Alex taught the crew how to play mumbly peg, or at least he taught them to play the way he had learned as a boy in Oregon. Two players stood six feet apart. A unit of measure was agreed upon, usually a stick that was six inches long or so. The first player threw a knife at the foot of the second. If the knife stuck and was within the agreed upon unit of measure, that player had to move their foot to where the knife was. Then it was their turn. They continued to throw the knife back and forth, legs splayed farther and farther apart, until one of the combatants fell over.

Unsurprising to Alex, Sanda emerged as the undefeated champion. She had her father's competitive streak, had a great eye, and was wicked with a knife. Amy was almost equally skilled, having grown up playing the game, but facing opponents with a foot and a half of height on her, they outstretched her every time.

Soon enough, there were small games breaking out all over the decks, with onlookers rooting for their friends and small bets being placed.

That went on until a warrior from Rinta-ah threw a little too enthusiastically and put his knife clean through the foot of a warrior from Danta-ah. The tribes got along well, but inflicting a wound like that tested the limits of friendship.

That was the end of mumbly peg on the ship, as Alex banned it and gave the injured warrior a full week off from all duties to recover.

The various tribes broke out their own methods for dealing with their stalled predicament.

The Winten-ah had their holy woman stand on the bow of the ship and chant to the forefathers, asking them to breathe life into their sails. If the forefathers heard, they remained unresponsive.

Tinta-ak and Fantem-eh were next up. They did a dance their tribe had danced for dozens of generations. It was like nothing Alex had ever seen before, though it did end with Tinta-ak picking Fantem-eh up over his head as though she was Jennifer Grey at the end of *Dirty Dancing*. Since Fantem-eh was three hundred solidly muscled pounds, that made for an impressive sight, but the winds themselves remained unimpressed.

Rinka-ak and his wife brought special burning rolls of herbs onto the deck with them. They moved to all four corners of the ship, silently waving the smoking rolls at all points in between.

The first two attempts had no effect whatsoever.

They ended their third tour of the boat where it began, standing in the bow. They dramatically held their burning herbs aloft, silently saying a prayer to their gods.

This time the efforts of the Rinta-ah brought a profound reaction, though not the one they sought.

The huge ship, which hadn't moved in days, listed horribly to the right. Even those who had grown accustomed to the vagaries of uncertain footing were caught off guard. In three seconds, the only beings still standing were Monda-ak and the other animals that had the benefit of extra legs.

Alex, still favoring his right leg, was sent tumbling across the deck. He instinctively tucked and rolled, going with the momentum. The first person to regain their feet was Torana, who rushed to Alex and picked him up, then set about moving around the tilting ship.

Harta-ak and Pictin ran to the bow just as an impossibly long tentacle reached up over the side and wrapped around the deck.

A moment later, two more humongous tentacles wrapped around the railing, then snaked out, touching everything in their path. A moment later a creature pulled itself on deck.

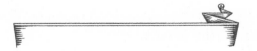

Chapter Sixteen
The Giant Squid

Even Alex Hawk, a battle-hardened warrior who might have said he had seen everything, froze. What had suddenly lifted itself onto the bow of the ship was simply impossible, or so the human brain seemed to say.

ALEX HAD READ ABOUT giant squid in the twenty-first century, but they were mysterious creatures even then. Seeing such a creature in the oceans of Kragdon-ah was more than just mysterious, it was completely terrifying. Alex had once read a report of a giant squid that had reached one-hundred-feet in length. That would have been a baby next to this monster.

The squid moved its tentacles about, attaching and releasing thousands upon thousands of suckers. Each sucker was bigger than a platter and made a sucking sound when it caught and released. It made for a disconcerting concerto of sound that further froze the hearts of the bravest warriors.

Rinka-ak and his wife, Alenta-eh, who were the nearest to the behemoth, jumped to get away, but not quickly enough. The vibrations of their footsteps seemed to attract the attention of one of the long tentacles, which reached toward both of them curiously. It easily wrapped around the two of them and held them curled in its embrace. A moment later, the tentacle lifted high into the air and flung both of them into the water.

A moment later, a tentacle grabbed Darand, who in many ways had started this whole plan by telling Alex about the Drakana, and dragged him across the deck, slamming him into obstacles as he went. A moment later, the creature flung Darand high into the sky. He didn't come crashing down into the water initially, though. Instead, he landed awkwardly on the railing of the bow, then slipped silently over the side.

Alex attempted to take command. He knew that at least a few of his people were good swimmers, including Amy and Werda-ak the Younger, who stood nearby, completely unsure of what to do.

"Jump overboard. Make sure they are safe and try to help them up the netting."

What to do with the monstrosity that boasted tentacles that were at least a hundred feet long was another matter altogether.

Tinta-ak rushed at one of the tentacles, screaming a war cry and lifting his huge battle ax above his head. He slammed it down perhaps twenty feet back from the tip. It was obvious he expected the ax to cleave clean through the tentacle, leaving the creature wounded. Instead, his ax simply bounced off and left only the tiniest of marks.

The blow did serve to attract the creature's unblinking eye, however. It withdrew the tentacle he had attacked and enfolded Tinta-ak in another. As it had done a moment before, it lifted the tentacle into the eye and tossed Tinta-ak over its head as though he weighed nothing. Tinta-ak's scream of frustration turned to fright as he plunged toward the sea, then was cut off abruptly.

Alex leaned over the side and yelled to Amy and Werda-ak the Younger. "Stay there. Help those who cannot swim get back to the boat."

A number of the warriors who had been on deck ran below. Alex could not guess whether it was to hide or to arm themselves. The first group to reemerge with weapons in hand was Nanda-eh, Sanda, and the rest of the archers. They scattered so as not to present a focused target for retaliation.

They did not wait for an order to fire from Nanda-eh. As soon as one of them got into position, they put arrow to string, pulled and fired. There was never any question of hitting the target. Whether their arrows could do any damage was quickly resolved. The arrows either bounced harmlessly off or sank into the squid's flesh to no apparent effect.

Other warriors reappeared with their weapons of choice and charged bravely at the gigantic beast. Every weapon they tried was useless. Swords, axes, thrown knives, and pikes all had no impact on it.

The squid continued to treat the ship like a buffet crawling with edible tidbits. It didn't try to eat anyone there and then, but simply tossed dozens of people overboard, as if saving them for snacking on later.

Sanda, who had grown up hearing of her mother's exploits with a bow, climbed a mast high enough that she actually managed to look down at the squid. She braced herself on a rope, drew and aimed. She had seen that other archers' shots were useless, but she had a plan. She remembered how her mother had saved the army by piercing go-dat-ta's eye with a single shot. The eye of the giant bear was miniscule compared to the squid, which had huge eyes meant to drink in every bit of available light in the murky deep.

She aimed and let fly. The squid seemed to sense the arrow coming and moved its head just enough that that the arrow bounced harmlessly away. Sanda cursed and fired again with the same result. Two more shots also fell uselessly away.

The squid had managed to identify where the threat was coming from, though. It reached one of its impossibly long tentacles up and up and wrapped it around Sanda. It pulled her away from the mast effortlessly, then held her high up over the deck.

Alex saw his daughter squirming helplessly in the grip of the squid and he cried out. To his eye, it looked like Sanda had irritated the creature so much that it was considering smashing her into the deck. Instead, after a moment's ride that she would undoubtedly remember for the rest of her life, the squid flung her out into the ocean.

Alex allowed himself to breathe again, but could not imagine how to combat this enemy. It was so large as to be invulnerable to any attack they could mount. For a moment he thought longingly of the guns they had tossed overboard, but decided that those would be equally useless. He contemplated just ordering everyone below until the beast from the deep tired of living on their deck, but he couldn't even do that until he arranged to rescue the dozens of people who had been thrown in the water.

At that moment, a heavy door flung open. It led to a little-used corridor where the dry goods were stored. Versa-eh stood in the doorway empty handed, but with a look of intense purpose on her face.

Alex wanted to call out to her to ask what she was doing, but the words died in his throat.

Versa-eh reached behind her and pulled a heavy toggle harpoon out—no doubt the same harpoon the man had wanted to retrieve to kill the dolphin. It was so long and heavy that, as strong as she was, she dragged it behind her instead of actually lifting it. She managed to get it through the door and it clanged onto the deck. The head of the harpoon had two points, both deadly looking. The bar was made of some heavy metal and the wood that surrounded one end was ancient and scarred.

Alex's heart raced. It was a huge weapon for a more-than-huge opponent. The problem was, how to use it effectively. He glanced at the cannon pointing out to sea. The idea of running to a storeroom, finding the powder, loading it, and firing it at the creature was ludicrous, even if the cannon barrel would accept and fire it.

Alex watched Versa-eh struggle and despaired that anyone would be able to lift it and get enough thrust to do any damage.

While Alex had this conversation with himself, more warriors poured out of every passageway and threw themselves uselessly at the giant squid who seemed to be entertaining itself throwing them overboard.

Before Alex could come up with a plan, his constant bodyguard, Torana, abandoned him to his fate.

Monda-ak, on the other hand ran toward the tentacles, barking and snapping. The squid didn't seem to fear the giant dog—or anything else—but it did manage to keep its tentacles out away from his teeth.

The giant was not fast under normal conditions, but he jumped down from the upper deck and landed with a crash below. He lumbered toward Versa-eh. Two other warriors had also noticed her and rushed to help. They had picked the heavy harpoon off the deck, but it was obvious that there was no way they could effectively combine their manpower to throw it.

When the shadow of Torana fell across them, they gladly released the weapon to him. The giant held the heavy harpoon in one hand, finding the balance of the weapon. When he found it, he adjusted his grip. Versa-eh touched him and pointed to her face.

Torana did not acknowledge her, but turned to face the squid. He took five, then ten running steps. He was perilously close to the body of the squid and Alex had no doubt he would be plucked up like everyone else.

Before that could happen, Torana bunched the muscles in his strong right arm and threw. His form was not perfect, but he did manage to get a zip of momentum behind the harpoon. The weight of the weapon did the rest.

It flew toward the squid and hit it in its huge eye. Unlike the arrows and other weapons thrown at it, the harpoon did what it was designed to do. The deadly barbs sank into the beast's eye all the way up to the hilt.

Squids are deadly silent hunters and when the tables were turned and it became the hunted, this mammoth squid remained silent. That is not to say there wasn't a reaction to Torana's throw. The long tentacles, which had been snaking everywhere over the surface of the boat retracted instantly. The main body of the squid, which had perched on the bow, hurled backwards over the railing and into the water. It twisted in the air and hit the water like a bullet, making only the smallest splash.

It did not dive and disappear immediately. First, it swam perhaps twenty feet below the surface. When it was directly under a group of swimmers, it reached up with its tentacles and plucked two, three, four, then five of them, getting two swimmers with a single tentacle at the last possible moment.

Only then did it dive, dragging the unfortunate Kragdon-ah in its grasp to their inevitable death.

For a moment, silence reigned on deck, then Alex shouted, "Anyone who can swim, go overboard. Help those who cannot stay afloat."

He knew he should stay where he was and oversee the rescue operation from there, but he could not stand idly by any longer. He climbed onto the railing and dove into the water. He surfaced, shocked by how cold it was, then looked for the nearest person struggling. It was a young warrior that Alex did not know. He was much bigger than Alex and he recognized that the danger was not past. Alex could easily drown if a non-swimmer drug him down in their panic.

Alex watched the man's head slip below the waves. As he swam toward him, he waited for the head to pop back up, but it did not. Alex grabbed a lungful of air and dove down. The man was sinking, but slowly. Alex dove sharply, grabbed the man by the arm, then kicked hard for the surface. That was the danger moment. If the man began thrashing and grasping onto Alex, they could both easily drown.

The man remained calm, looking at Alex with placid brown eyes. It was possible that he had already accepted his own death. Alex grabbed him under one arm, stretched himself out, and kicked toward the boat.

The bandage had come off his injured leg and though the cold water might numb the wound eventually, at the moment it hurt like someone was exploring it with a hot poker.

He made it to the netting, helped the man up onto it, then swam back from the ship a few feet. "Lower the transport boat. Throw anything that might float into the water!"

The boat should have undoubtedly been the first thing in the water, but in the chaos of a crisis, it was impossible to remember everything.

Above, people scrambled to do exactly that. Alex pushed away and looked for more people who needed help.

Slowly, those who could swim were the only ones left in the water. All others had either been helped to safety or had drowned.

Tinta-ak, who had been one of the first into the water, was among the last to leave. As he was so often, he was amused at the prospect of a close brush with death. He swam to Alex and said, "What a story we will have to tell."

"By the time you tell this story back in Franta-ah, you will have ridden a shark to rescue people."

Tinta-ak's eyes lit up at the thought and he laughed. He looked more closely at Alex and said, "We are safe now, Manta-ak. You do not look well. Let's return to the ship."

Tinta-ak was correct. Alex did not look well. All the swimming had softened the scab that was forming on both sides of his leg. The swimming and exertion had washed it completely away and he was now bleeding into the water. Alex had been joking about sharks, but when he looked down and saw the blood seeping from his leg, he remembered the incredible distance a shark could detect that smell.

Tinta-ak lifted Alex onto the rope netting as Alex had lifted others. Sanda, who had swum up behind them, climbed agilely up the rope and helped lift her father up onto the deck.

Antan-ak, the healer from Rinta-ah, made Alex lie down on the spot and examined the wound. He frowned and said, "Manta-ak, you have set yourself back to the beginning of the wound."

In his exhaustion, Alex nodded, then remembered where he was and put two fingers to his forehead. A setback in his healing was a small price to pay for saving the lives of his brothers and sisters.

Amy and Sanda both hovered over him, concern etched across their faces.

While the healer worked on him, Alex began to give them orders to carry out.

To Amy, he said, "Get a head count from each chieftain. I want to know how many we lost, and their names."

To Sanda, "Organize the best swimmers and form a line to retrieve anything of value we threw overboard." He thought for a moment, then said, "Have someone keep a lookout. If any dangerous creatures approach, get out. There's nothing we threw overboard that is worth any of your lives."

Alex looked around for anyone else he could give orders to, but saw only Harta-ak and Versa-eh. Everyone else was already at their tasks.

He smiled at Versa-eh and said, "How many times are you going to save us?"

"I didn't do anything. It was your giant who saved us."

"You know better. As usual, it was your idea that saved us. Torana was the muscle, but you were the brain."

Alex tried to sit up, but Harta-ak put a gentle hand on his chest and pushed him back down.

"We are on the ship. I am still the captain. I am ordering you to your cabin, where Antan-ak can take care of you."

Alex thought of objecting, but the bone-weariness convinced him otherwise.

He gave up and lay back on the deck.

A storm to end all storms, then an attack by a giant squid. What's next?

'What's next?" is a question that no adventurer should ever ask.

It will always be answered.

Chapter Seventeen
Mists Out of Time

The attack of the giant squid cost the various tribes eight people. Alex ordered a watch on all sides of the ship for twenty-four hours in case the bodies of those who had drowned came to the surface, as dead bodies do.

If there had been the usual wind and waves, it was possible, even likely, that the current would have carried the bodies miles away.

In the eerie calm they found themselves, though, that did not happen. Three bodies were spotted and retrieved.

Each tribe took care of their own dead as they always did, although the burial was necessarily at sea, as there was no way to keep the bodies from deteriorating until they reached landfall.

Unlike those who were taken to the deep by the giant squid, the families of those who simply drowned at least got to say a proper goodbye. Those who were taken by the cephalopod were never sighted again, but everyone was sure what had happened to them. Their hope was that they had drowned first, before anything else took place.

Some on the ship believed that the dead calm had summoned the squid, or perhaps vice-versa. In any case, after the attack of the giant creature, most people expected the wind to return.

It did not.

The ship floated where it was, barely moving from hour to hour or day to day.

One theory was put forward that perhaps they had all died, weren't aware of it, and this was their afterlife. That idea soon passed as being too horrible to contemplate.

There was a crow's nest high up in the rigging, more than a hundred feet above the deck. The people of Kragdon-ah were all natural climbers and there was a steady stream of volunteers to climb up and take a watch there.

Mid-afternoon of the third day after the squid attack, the lookout shouted down, "I see something."

Boredom had overtaken almost everyone. The exceptions were Harta-ak, who still felt like he was on a crash-course to learn ocean sailing, and Amy, who was doing the same with the Drakana language. Everyone else was anxious for some type of excitement.

The lookout didn't specify which direction he saw something, so people rushed to port and starboard, forward and aft. They put their hands over their eyes to block the sun and scanned the horizon, but could not see anything.

Torana lifted Alex up so he could see. Since his dive into the sea, as Antan-ak had warned, the healing of his leg had essentially gone back to square one. Alex peered in all directions, but could not see anything.

He craned his neck toward the lookout and shouted, "What is it you see? A ship? Something else coming to kill us?"

The lookout did not answer, but simply pointed to the port side of the ship. These were landlubbers, and they had not yet grasped all the directional terms.

Thanks to Torana, Alex was taller than anyone else, but he still could not see anything but the same stretch of calm water he had been looking at day after day.

Again, Alex called up. "What is it?"

The lookout hesitated and Alex briefly considered trying to climb up himself just so he could see. Just the thought of climbing the ropes gave his wounded leg a twinge, so he waited patiently.

"I just see white."

"White? Like a sail?" Alex couldn't decide if another ship approaching them would be good or bad.

"No. Just...white. White clouds."

Alex stared again and this time, thought he could just make out a white fringe along the horizon. As he watched, the thin line became more defined.

"Fog," he said to himself.

He looked up into the clear blue sky and warm sun.

"That doesn't make any sense."

Harta-ak appeared beside him.

"These are not the conditions for fog."

"Right. So what is that coming at us, then? Smoke?"

Alex looked up at the rigging and ropes. They all hung as limply as they had for the previous week.

"And how is it moving toward us if there is no wind?" Alex asked.

"What can we do?" Harta-ak wondered.

"I don't think there is anything to be done. Sit here like an animal in a trap and wait for whatever it is to reach us."

By then, everyone who wasn't assigned to a specific duty lined the port side of the ship from bow to stern. An onrushing fog bank wasn't great entertainment, but at least it was *different*.

As the whiteness drew closer, it created an optical illusion. It felt like the ship was moving, and the white cloudiness was standing still. Alex continually had to look down at the water beside the ship to clear his head and work out what was what.

The closer the whiteness drew, the less it looked like a fog bank. Fog was a bit misty at the edges, and there were always areas where it was thicker and thinner.

Whatever this was, it was different. This was more like a thick white cloud had been plucked from the sky and set on the ocean, then blown toward them.

Alex again craned his neck and shouted up to the lookout. "Can you feel any wind up there?"

"No, Manta-ak," the man said, and it was obvious he had made the same connection—how was this fog moving with no obvious wind?

"I don't like this," Alex said quietly to Harta-ak, but he couldn't think of a single thing to do. If there had been wind, they could have run at full sail and attempted to outrun it. Deep in his heart, Alex believed that wouldn't have made any difference either.

As the bank of white grew closer and closer, Alex could see that it was moving faster than he had originally thought. With no perspective it was almost impossible to judge.

When Alex guessed it was within a hundred yards of the ship he leaned over the side of the railing, trying to see anything at all within the white.

There was nothing.

From there, things happened quickly.

Just before the whiteness hit them, the temperature dropped.

There was no dramatic pause.

With a sound reminiscent of a cork being pulled from a bottle, the whiteness enveloped the ship.

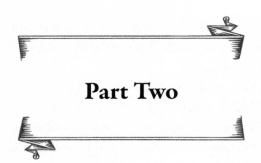

Part Two

Chapter Eighteen
A Mystery

Alex Hawk looked around him, a deeply puzzled expression on his face. Monda-ak stood beside him, panting as if nothing in the world was wrong.

Alex felt as though he was waking from a dream as long as Rip Van Winkle's. There were cobwebs in every corner of his mind and even the cold bracing sea air did not blow them away.

He looked to his left. Amy and Sanda stood together. They also appeared to not quite be all there.

To his right, Harta-ak, Versa-eh, and Tinta-ak all wore the same expression.

It was such a passingly odd feeling, Alex reached out and touched his daughters, just to make sure they were really there.

"I'm here, Dad," they both said in English. They almost never spoke in English when Kragdon-ah were present.

Alex glanced around and saw that instead of the normal scurrying activity, *everyone* was standing still as though hypnotized by someone who had neglected to snap them fully awake.

That was when things got *weird*.

As the ship shifted in the waves, Alex took a step forward to balance himself.

He had grown accustomed to every step costing him something in pain and suffering, especially since he had torn the wound open in the ocean trying to rescue people.

And that was what was weird. That step did not hurt at all. It felt like all the millions of steps Alex had experienced before his calf was shot clean through by a Drakana bullet.

Alex steadied himself and again noticed a distinct lack of pain in his leg. He knelt and looked at the wound.

Except, it wasn't a wound at all.

It was a *scar*.

The skin where the entry and exit wound had been, was now a raised white color that stood out from the tanned skin around it. Thin white lines emanated out from the scar.

Alex touched the scar with wonder. There was no pain at all.

Amy and Sanda bent down to see what he was looking at. When they saw the scar where the open wound should be, they both gasped.

"How is that possible?" Sanda asked.

"It isn't, is it?" Alex answered.

Amy shook her head, still trying to clear it, and looked at her father for the first time. "Dad, what happened to you?"

Alex instinctively patted himself to make sure he was still there. "What do you mean?"

Alex and Sanda exchanged a meaningful glance.

"First," Amy said, "You're skin and bones. Look." She loosened the ties on his shirt and pulled it up. "I could play the xylophone on your ribs. And your beard. It's almost to your waist."

"I shaved just a few days ago," Alex said with wonder, running his fingers through his long, graying beard. He looked around. "You girls are skinny, too. You too," he said to Harta-ak and Versa-eh. "It looks like we've been on half rations for months. But how can that be? I can remember the good breakfast I had this morning."

"Can you?" Amy asked. "What was it?"

Alex opened his mouth to answer, then slowly shut it. He had been sure he could remember breakfast, but there was nothing but a black hole in his memory.

"What *can* you remember?" Amy pressed.

"I..." Alex started, then stopped again. He took a step backward, looked up and to his left, and scratched his chin. He was the very picture of a man trying unsuccessfully to chase down an errant memory. Finally, he said, "What about you? What do you remember? Or you, or you?" he said, including everyone around him in the question.

"I remember being on the ship," Amy offered, but it was weak.

"Sure, sure," Alex said. "I have a vague memory of being on the ship, too, but what specifically do you remember?"

"I remember..." she hesitated, then in a spurt said, "I remember learning the language of the Drakana," triumphantly. Then her hand flew to her forehead in shock. "Wait! I don't remember just learning it. I can speak it! I can think in it! I know Drakana now!"

"My bullet wound, you learning a new language, something very mysterious is up."

"The squid," Versa-eh said, as though it was as much a question as it was a statement.

Everyone stopped, and it was as if the same memory was poured into all their minds at once.

"Of course!" several of them exclaimed.

"How could we ever forget that?" Alex asked. He nodded his head as if in answer to some driving internal rhythm. "And then the calm. Right?"

The others looked blankly at him, then smiles spread across their faces as the memory once again completed itself in their minds.

"That's right," Harta-ak said. "We were in the middle of a dead calm that we thought would never end!"

"And then the lookout saw a fog bank or something approaching us," Alex said excitedly, sure that they were about to crack the mystery wide open.

"Right!" Harta-ak agreed. "We saw the fog coming and..." he winced and rubbed his hand across his face. "And..."

"And..." Alex picked up, sure that the next memory was coming.

It never appeared.

"I can't remember anything after seeing the fog bank."

"Me either," Amy said.

Sanda, she of the sharpest eyes, was the first to notice the next anomaly.

She pointed a shaking finger at the bow of the ship. "But maybe they can explain what happened to us."

All heads swiveled in the direction she pointed.

Two men stood smiling down at them.

Alex had never seen either of them before.

Chapter Nineteen
The Mystery Deepens

Alex's first instinct was to yell out "Grab them!" They were strangers who had not been on the ship when they sailed into the fog. There was no way to know what their intentions were.

There was something about them—the way they stood, a certain familiarity and comfort that forestalled that action.

The two men were very different—both from each other and from everyone else on board the ship.

The first man carried himself well. He was short by Kragdon-ah standards, but he still stood close to six feet tall. He had a beard as well, but it was a more well-trimmed mustache and goatee. He was dressed in what Alex thought of as perhaps seventeenth- or eighteenth-century garb—heavy swashbuckling boots, a broad belt, a white shirt tucked into his pants and a tan vest.

The second man was shorter still, a remarkable sight in a world where the average person approached seven feet tall. He was bald and smiling, with laugh lines etched deeply in his face. His hands were folded placidly in front of him. Most unusual of all, he wore the orange robes of the monks Alex had encountered on his journey around Kragdon-ah.

Like Alex and everyone else on the boat, they seemed on the verge of being emaciated. Even Monda-ak, who always managed to find food in unlikely places, was thinner than he had ever been.

Around him, people still seemed to be waking up, waiting for full consciousness and their memories to return to them.

Alex jumped up a ladder and hurried to the bow. It was impossible for him not to be pleased at how well his leg was healed. He had been afraid that he would have to lead his troops into battle on only one leg.

Alex approached the two men. Their body language did not change, though the taller of the two men drew a deep breath and let it out slowly, as though he knew there was a long ordeal ahead of him. The monk's smile—sweet and innocent—never faltered.

"Who are you?" Alex demanded. He had an entire litany of questions lined up, but started with the most basic.

"Hello, Alex who is also known as Manta-ak," the taller man answered. "I am Charles Hawthorne. This gentleman beside me with the charming smile is known only as Quintan. He does not speak."

Alex blinked. The man had answered him in English. With a proper English accent.

How is any of this possible? A memory sprang to Alex's mind of his friend Dan Hadaller chiding him: *You stepped through a door that flung you through time. But it is* this *you choose to find remarkable?*

"I'm going to need some explanations from you."

"Which I'm afraid I am not going to be able to give you," Hawthorne said with obvious regret. "I would like to, sincerely. It would be wonderful to explain everything and put your mind at ease, but I simply cannot."

Amy had caught up to Alex and stared dumbfounded at the man. "Dad, he's speaking English. How is this possible? Where did they come from?"

"He says he will not answer our questions, but I am sure he will change his mind soon enough." Alex turned back to Hawthorne. "Let's start with where you're from."

"You above all people should know how difficult that question is to answer. Where are you from? Is Alex Hawk from a mythical, faraway land known as Oregon? Was Manta-ak born on the day you stumbled through the shimmering door and battled the karak-ta on the beach?"

Alex narrowed his eyes at Hawthorne. "You seem to know a great deal about me. It seems that we are on unequal footing."

"We are on unequal footing in that regard *now*. In my recent memory, you knew all the answers to the questions you are asking me and much, much more."

Alex looked skyward. He was almost glad that the orange-robed monk didn't speak. He remembered how frustrated he was in trying to get answers out of Tokin-ak. If this Hawthorne was this frustrating, he couldn't imagine how a monk given to speaking in platitudes and unhelpful honesty would be.

Heavy footsteps approached behind Alex.

It was Tinta-ak. "Manta-ak! Fantem-eh is missing."

A missing person took precedence over grilling the unexplained visitors. Alex didn't bother to ask if he had searched the whole boat. That was a ridiculous idea—the ship would take hours to search completely and they had only been awake for a few minutes.

Alex immediately took charge and organized a crew to begin the search, breaking them up into groups to cover each different section. While Alex went through that process, Hawthorne stood silent, a concerned expression on his face, but not wanting to interrupt.

Just when the searchers were ready to begin, another voice cried out that someone was missing. Then another, and another.

Alex sent the groups out with orders to report back to him as soon as anyone or anything unusual was found.

The search parties scattered and Alex turned back to his two unusual visitors. He was surprised to see that Hawthorne was holding a scroll.

"I am sorry to share this with you, but you yourself asked me to do this to save everyone pain." He handed the scroll to Alex, who unrolled it.

He unrolled the parchment and saw that it was just a list of names, including Fantem-eh, Wenta-eh, the warrior who had burst through the wall in Alex's basement, and a dozen others. At the top of the list was a single word.

Dead.

Alex's heart sank. He might have questioned the list and its veracity, but he could not.

It was in his own handwriting.

Chapter Twenty
Searching for a Memory

There was a whirlwind of activity on board the ship. Alex did not let the list—even though it was in his own handwriting—stop the search. If it had been Amy, Sanda, or Monda-ak who had gone missing, he would have torn every board loose before he gave up looking for them. He wouldn't deny the same satisfaction to the worried searchers.

Still, in his heart, Alex knew. Somehow, they had been enveloped in a fog bank and had emerged some unknown time later. It was hard for him to accept, but Alex knew that the missing time had to be measured in years, likely, not months. Terrible wounds like he had suffered don't heal up and scar over so decisively in just a few months.

Worse than the unknown passage of time, was the apparent loss of life. In a battle, there are stakes. People fight and die. When it is over, the loved ones of the dead can grieve over them but know they fell protecting something they believed in. With a sudden and un-explained disappearance like this, there was no healing grief. Only unanswered questions.

"I have more questions for you," Alex said to Hawthorne.

"Of course. I will answer any that I can, but I fear that won't be many."

"Can you tell me why we are all so underfed? I notice that in-cludes the two of you, as well."

"Just the obvious. There is no food on board. We have all been hungry for months now. We rationed the best we could, but this is the end result."

Alex turned to Amy and Sanda. "Go check the supplies and check back with me." He looked about for anyone who wasn't actively searching for the missing. His first thought was that he wanted Werda-ak the Younger, but of course he was off searching for his mother Wenta-eh.

Alex selected a handful of Winten-ah and told them to find the fishing poles and hooks and anything that could be used for bait, then get their lines in the water. Fish—fatty, rich fish—would be the perfect antidote to the malnutrition they were all suffering.

To Hawthorne, Alex said, "Why didn't we fish if we were hungry?"

"There is so much I cannot tell you, but I will say that we did. There were no fish on the other side of the fog. We were in a doldrums for months where we were the only life that existed. I believe you will have much better luck now that we are here."

Alex glared at Hawthorne, who was driving him to distraction. On the one hand, he wanted to threaten to throw him overboard if he didn't tell him what he needed to know. On the other, it was obvious that there was a relationship here that Alex simply couldn't remember. The fact that Hawthorne knew so much about him—and the death scroll—was testament to that.

Alex chose five more warriors who were just standing around on the deck below them. People seemed to be coming out of the haze they were in at different times. "Go grab weapons from the armory, then come back here and guard these two."

The five warriors—three men and two women—took off at a run. They seemed pleased to have something to do other than try to remember the unrememberable.

"I'm going to search you for weapons," Alex said.

"Of course," Hawthorne said. "You told me to place my weapons in the hold when we saw the wall of fog approaching. We knew that my appearance on board would seem sudden and mysterious. Both of my pistols are in a lockbox in the weapons area. The key to it is here," he said, dangling a silver key from a chain he wore around his neck.

Alex ignored what he said and searched both the men, but came up with nothing.

A moment later, the guards had returned, carrying swords, spears, and hammers.

"Guard them. If either one makes a move, toss them overboard."

Hawthorne smiled at Alex—an expression that conveyed something too familiar for the situation. "Do you mind if we sit? Like you, we are weak with hunger."

Alex pointed to the railing. "Sit here with your back against the rail."

"Aye aye, Manta-ak," Hawthorne said and he and Quintan eased to the ground with a sigh. "Good luck with your fishing. We could all use that."

When he had opened his eyes, Alex had no idea what time it was. He also had no idea what day it was or where on earth he might be. Now that he was coming to grips with the idea that they might have been floating unchecked for untold months, he needed to find out the answers to both those questions.

He looked up at the darkening sky and saw the clear sky already dotted with the earliest appearance of stars.

Amy and Sanda returned, wearing the same grim expression.

"Unless we want to eat an old pair of boots I found, there is no food at all in the stores."

Alex nodded. He had expected that.

"Amy, find Pictin and bring him here."

From his left Alex heard an excited whoop. Hope sprang into his heart that someone who had been missing had been found. If one was found, they all could be.

It was not a missing person, but it was something else that had obviously been missing—food.

One of the fishermen pulled a huge fish up. It was big enough that Alex was surprised the line hadn't snapped landing it. Immediately, another cry of victory from the other side and another fish was brought on board.

To Sanda, he said, "Get the cooks to fire up the stove. Get the fish processors standing by with knives sharpened. I want these fish cut up into fillets and frying immediately. Save the guts for bait. Go!"

By the time he had given the order, two more fish had landed, flopping wetly on the deck.

If nothing else, their period of starvation seemed to be coming to an end.

Pictin approached, a haunted look in his eyes. It was obvious he was not adapting well to the new situation.

To Amy, Alex said, "Ask him if he can tell how long we were in the fog. More importantly, ask him where we are." Alex paused, blinked, and said, "Wait. Holy hell, I can ask him myself. I may not be as fluent as you, but somehow I can speak Drakana. I must have learned it when we were in the fog."

Then it was Pictin's turn to blink and look surprised.

"That's not all. I can speak your language," he said in the universal language of Kragdon-ah.

Curiouser and curiouser.

"That will make things easier," Alex observed, though he was thoroughly nonplussed at this most recent attack on what seemed reasonable and right. "Here's what I need to know. A lot of time passed from the moment we went into the fog until when we came back." He hitched up his pants leg to show the scar. "But I don't know *how much* time. I need you to tell me two things if you can—where we are, and how much time we have lost."

Alex was concerned that while they were in the fog, a thousand years might have passed. If so, Drakana likely would have proceeded with its plans, Kragdon-ah would be a conquered part of their dynasty, and everyone they knew would be dead.

"Can you tell all that by looking at the stars?"

"Of course." Pictin looked up at the deepening gloom. "I will get my log book." He turned and headed toward the cabin he shared with the two other Drakana. Alex had made the decision to allow them free run of the ship. With so few, he wasn't worried about an insurrection.

Activity increased around Alex. The fishermen had pulled fish up until their arms ached. Whatever had caused the fish to abandon them in the fog had perhaps caused them to emerge to this great windfall.

He caught a group of people who were wheeling the fish back to be cleaned and cooked. "Tell the cooks to only prepare enough to give everyone a single serving. We can have more in the morning. I don't want people making themselves sick by gorging on it."

The leader of the crew acknowledged Alex's order and wheeled the cart, heavy with still-dying fish that each looked like they weighed thirty pounds, toward the kitchen.

Searchers were beginning to return to the main deck. They looked lost and demoralized. Alex gathered them together and stood on a box so they could all see and hear him.

"My friends, I fear we have lost those who we value, our brothers, sisters, wives, and friends. Something has happened, and I wish I could tell you what it is, but I cannot."

As he spoke more and more people gathered around to listen. He had thought he was speaking just to those who had lost someone close to them, but realized everyone needed to hear what he had to say.

"None of us know what happened while we were inside the fog. We do not yet know how long we were there, or how far we have traveled." Alex glanced first at Hawthorne, then at Pictin. "We are working to answer those questions, but I fear some things may never be known."

He fished in his pocket and pulled out the scroll Hawthorne had given him.

"I can't explain it, but I somehow left myself a list of those who died while we were in the fog. I wish I had taken more time to explain things, but all I can say is that I must have had my reasons. Now," he said, holding the scroll up, "I will never tell you to stop searching for your loved ones. I know I would keep searching. But I believe this list is likely true, and our brothers and sisters are dead."

He turned to Sanda. "Bring me a lantern." She unhooked one and held it up. Alex uncurled the scroll and began to read the names. He thought he might have heard gasps of pain or shock as each group heard the name of someone close to them, but he did not. Each time he glanced up from the scroll, all he saw was impassive faces.

With one exception. When he read the name Fantem-eh, Tinta-ak's chin fell to his chest. For long moments, he did not look up, but his shoulders began to shake.

Fantem-eh's name was the last one on the list. Sanda took the lantern and hung it back up, then went to Tinta-ak and laid her head against his broad chest.

"I wish I knew more about what happened to those we lost, but I do not. You have my word that if I learn anything new, I will share it with you at once."

Alex drew a deep breath and let it out.

"I know we are all hungry. The sea has blessed us with a bounty tonight. We will have a feast of fish, but please do not overeat. Our stomachs have shrunk and we could make ourselves sick."

Alex searched his brain for something motivational or positive to say, but the words would not come. Soon, the crowds dispersed. It was possible they still did not fully accept that the people they loved were dead, but Alex's words had brought them farther along that path to acceptance.

Soon, the cooks called people to eat in shifts. That was not a hard sell, although there was never any pushing, shoving, or urge to cut ahead in line. The people of Kragdon-ah were unfailingly polite, filled with what had once been called small-town values in a long-lost world.

Alex stood on the starboard side of the ship, staring out into the falling darkness. Amy and Sanda came and stood beside him, but did not speak.

When he turned and saw them, he was surprised they were there. He had been lost in deep thoughts. As soon as he did, he kicked back into his role of leader.

"Will you make sure that a serving of the fish is taken to our two new guests?"

They smiled comfortingly at him and disappeared below. They were soon replaced by Pictin.

"I have done as you asked." He spoke again in the universal language, apparently almost as comfortable in it as he was in his own language.

Alex turned, hungry for any information that might help solve the mystery.

Pictin's face, lit by the flickering light of a nearby lantern, seemed pale to Alex's eye.

"I took the measurements and ran my figures twice just to be sure," he said by way of prelude.

Alex felt impatient and wanted to say, 'Get to the point!' But he didn't. Instead, he calmed himself and said, "Excellent. Thank you. What did you find?"

"According to the stars, we did not spend any time at all in the fog. The last entry in my log shows that exactly twenty-four hours have lapsed since I took my last reading."

This was another impossibility, of course. Alex's healed leg, the fact that everyone on board had nearly starved to death belied the possibility that no time had passed.

"That is why you began by telling me you checked your figures twice."

"Yes," Pictin confirmed. He took a confidential step toward Alex and lifted his shirt. In addition to being able to see his ribs, there was a long scar that ran from his left collarbone to his sternum. It was not as fully healed as Alex's wound, but it was obvious it was not fresh. "I did not have this wound before we sailed into the fog. None of it makes sense."

"That is something I can completely agree with. What about our location? Are we in the same spot as well?"

"No, not at all. We are very near to the spot where we were first planning to stop." He lifted his face against the breeze, which had returned since they had come out of the fog.

"Depending on the winds, we will arrive there in just a few days."

Chapter Twenty-One
Hawthorne

Alex's mind immediately shifted into a new gear. He had been running round and round in mental circles, trying to figure out what had happened to them. Now, knowing that the first step in his campaign to strike back at Drakana was imminent, he began to forget about the mystery and focus on more immediate concerns.

He stepped to the bow, where Hawthorne and Quintan still sat. The five men assigned to guard them did not seem to be on high alert. Instead, they were so lost in conversation with the prisoners that they did not hear Alex approach. He stood directly behind them and cleared his throat. They jumped, guilty.

They did not apologize, but took two steps back and hung their heads, abashed at being caught derelict in their duties.

Alex knelt beside them. "You were speaking to them in our language," Alex observed.

Hawthorne nodded.

"What other languages do you speak?"

Hawthorne grinned. "This world or ours?"

"Nothing is easy with you, is it?"

"I suppose not. From our world, I speak English, Spanish, and Portuguese well. A little Dutch and French. From our present surroundings, I speak Drakana and your universal language. I was just speaking to your guards about the differences between their primary tongue and this common language you all speak. It's quite fascinating how it's all developed, really."

"Is that what you are, then? A linguist?"

"No. I am a pilot."

Hawthorne's use of the word put Alex in mind of a man sitting in the cockpit of an airplane. Which, based on the apparent time frame of the man's clothing, seemed incongruous.

Alex narrowed his eyes at him, trying to decipher what he meant.

"As in a ship's pilot. I suppose you might call me a navigator, though for a long time, I have also been a captain. Before that, I think I did much the same job as your man there," he said, nodding to Pictin, who appeared to be triple-checking his figures.

"Pictin is definitely not my man," Alex observed.

"So you told me. I got the feeling there was a time when you were enemies. As our time together went on, the two of you seemed to mend that." Hawthorne put a finger to his lips. "I must be careful. I don't want to tell you too much."

"You seem a decent sort," Alex said. That was the best he was prepared to say about the Englishman at the moment. "Why are you being so purposefully obtuse?"

"Oh, I thought I told you. You insisted on it. You swore me to secrecy. You said it was absolutely necessary and that I shouldn't tell you much of anything, even on penalty of death. You have only yourself to blame."

Alex considered that. It did sound like him, but he couldn't begin to understand why he had chosen to hamstring himself this way.

"I've had only myself to blame for most of my life's problems," Alex observed.

Hawthorne mimed a tip of his cap to Alex, who turned his gaze to Quintan.

"Is there anything I should know about him?"

"You've met the monks before. You told me the story of your journey around Kragdon-ah. You spent a good portion of that journey riding with one of them, did you not?"

"I did," Alex said, and couldn't help smiling a bit at the memory.

"Then there is not much more I can add. They are a mystery to me as well. Here's something you may not know, though. They are not strictly a Kragdon-ah phenomenon. They are everywhere. Sometimes I think they are the true power in the world, though they would never admit it."

Quintan had been staring out into the darkness as though he did not understand a word they had been saying. At that last comment, he turned his face toward them. As always, his face was inscrutable, but there was the faintest touch of a smile on his lips. Alex and Hawthorne were speaking English, which caused Alex to consider how much this silent monk might really know.

Almost to himself, Alex said, "What am I to do with the two of you?"

Hawthorne hooked a thumb at Quintan. "He's just hitching a ride to get to where he needs to go. As for me? If I were you, I would use me." He glanced at Pictin. "I know you've got your own pilot there, but you never know when another experienced sailor might come in handy. I will want to work for my room and board. I never expect anything for free. Just tell me what you need. My pistols and swords are at your service as well."

It was Alex's turn to grin. "About that. These people think of weapons like that as being bad juju. They call it stama. If they find your pistols, they will more than likely toss them overboard."

Hawthorne winced at the thought of it. "I would appreciate it, then, if you would see that they don't find them. They are dear to me."

"I will do what I can." Alex hesitated, unsure of the proper path. As he so often did, he went with his instincts. He stood and extended a hand to Hawthorne—an old-fashioned handshake, not the Kragdon-ah greeting. "I am probably crazy to trust you—a man out of time who simply appeared on board my ship, but my gut tells me you mean us no harm."

"A man out of time, hmm? That could be applied to you as well. I will do everything I can to once again earn your trust."

Alex considered that *once again*, then put it aside. Perhaps when these adventures were over, Hawthorne could tell him everything.

"There is something we never found time to talk about. You are one ship going against an entire nation. How can you possibly hope to prevail?"

Alex took a few minutes and went over the highlights of the previous year with him. He emphasized how overwhelming the force had been that had landed on Kragdon-ah, and how the tribes that were on board the ship had barely escaped being enslaved.

"So," Hawthorne said slowly, "you had two choices. Live out the four years of peace, with the knowledge that you would soon be enslaved, or attack them."

"Precisely. And so, here we are."

"Which brings me back to the same question. How can you hope to prevail against such an overwhelming force?"

"I hope to use their strength against them."

"How so?" Hawthorne said, intrigued now.

"Their strength is that they are everywhere. A man named Darand, who we have brought along with us—"

"—Oh yes, I know Darand, of course."

"—of course. Darand traded information about his country for his own life. He told me how the Drakana Empire stretches everywhere. I was trained in military strategy. Being everywhere is fine, but it is impossible to defend everywhere. You can build up an impressive defense in key areas, but others are likely lightly guarded. That will be our entry."

Hawthorne held his chin in one hand and tapped a finger against his cheek. Alex could see that he was working his way through the problem.

"For the rest, you will have to see," Alex finished. "But for now, we will provide the two of you a cabin."

"Unless something has changed recently, we already have one. With your permission, I will be off to it. I think tomorrow will be a busy day."

Chapter Twenty-Two
Landfall

Alex spent the next two days doing the best he could to return strength to his warriors. He wished he had some leftover stores of fruits and vegetables, but he knew that would have to wait a bit. For now, they feasted on the bounty the sea provided, and that was enough.

From the day they had set out from Kragdon-ah, Alex had been pointing to one spot on the map. After consulting with Darand to identify it as a spot to start his campaign, he had worked tirelessly with Harta-ak and Pictin to steer toward it.

Alex was not capable enough with geography to be able to identify what this island was called in his own time. It would be a challenge for most people from the twenty-first century to be able to identify more than a few islands if they were presented with a map of the Pacific, but that doesn't mean they weren't there. In fact, there were dozens of larger islands and thousands of smaller ones.

Alex had made this chosen island his target because Darand had been there himself and was able to give him some intelligence about it. The island itself was small—perhaps twenty-five miles across in one direction and forty in the other. The key for Alex was that there was more than one settlement of some size on it. The largest city had a population of a thousand people, according to Darand, but a smaller settlement on the other side of the island only had a few hundred.

This second settlement was primarily agricultural and would be less-heavily defended.

The large city had a nice port because the city had become something of a hub for shipping the fruit they grew to the rest of Drakana. However, there was also a port in the smaller city so shipments could be loaded in two locations at once during heavy harvests.

Alex had spent the previous two days going over plans with his brain trust, which included Harta-ak and Versa-eh, Rinka-ak, Sanda and Amy, and Tinta-ak, who insisted on being involved to take his mind off his grief. In the end, Alex added Hawthorne as well. He had weighed that decision carefully, but could not see a nefarious reason for his appearance on board. His navigational and sailing knowledge was definitely a plus.

The Drakana on board had been instrumental in giving him information, but he would never include them in an attack plan against their own nation.

The island came into sight shortly after first light. They had circled around it, giving it a wide berth, so their approach from the northwest should go undetected.

Although they had some intelligence from Darand about the layout of the island, and he had drawn them a crude map showing the ports and cities, they were still approaching with less-than-ideal intelligence.

Part of Alex's attack plan included not alerting the bigger, better-armed city until it was too late if at all possible. He had drilled Darand about the communication methods his people used. He had been concerned that they had some sort of instant communication, like a telegraph. Darand had sworn that, at least when he had last seen the Drakana Empire, they still relied on messengers.

Their ship was too large to approach the island closely without risk of coming aground, but with the expertise of Pictin and Hawthorne working as a team, they found a spot that was only a few miles away from the smaller village that was shallow enough to drop anchor, but deep enough to keep them afloat.

They dropped the anchor, then lowered the transport boat into the choppy sea. A dozen strong men and women, included four of Nanda-eh's archers, climbed down rope ladders and rowed toward a tiny, deserted cove with a small beach.

Alex and most everyone gathered on the starboard side of the ship and watched their progress. When they got close to the beach, two men jumped overboard to haul them up onto the sand. They had estimated the depth of the water incorrectly, though. Instead of touching bottom, their heads disappeared beneath the waves. A moment later, they popped up and grabbed hold of the small boat. The oarsmen continued to pull on their oars, and a few seconds later, the two men were walking along, pulling the boat with them. Everyone but the people manning the oars jumped out and helped pull the boat well up onto the beach.

Alex found himself holding his breath. This was the very first step of his planned campaign against the Drakana. If disaster struck here, it would bode poorly for the rest of his plan.

His worry was for nothing, though. The men and women both flashed hand signs that all was well, then they disappeared into the lush vegetation that surrounded the cove. The oarsmen returned the boat to the ship and climbed the ladder aboard before raising the transport boat back into its place.

Those warriors did not have a true map of the island. But they had the innate sense of direction that all Kragdon-ah seemed to possess. Even this far from home, if you asked them where they were born, their arm would instantly and unerringly point the correct direction. They *did* have Pictin's crude map and that showed them the general direction they wanted to go. The rest was up to them.

Alex wanted to give them time to get themselves into position, so he stayed at anchor for a few hours. It was a nervous time, as it always is just before a battle is fought. They had eaten their protein, sharpened their weapons, and gone over the plan—such as it was.

Someone suggested a game of mumbly peg, but Alex quickly put a stop to that. He wanted his warriors to have all their toes when the battle was joined.

Eventually, Alex gauged that he had given them enough of a head start and Torana and a few others turned the wheel and raised the anchor.

Alex had ordered the Drakana flag—a solid black background with vertical red stripes—to fly above the tallest mast since they had left Kragdon-ah. He had hoped that if they ran into another Drakana ship, it would buy them more time and cause some confusion. Now, he was glad for it, because although they were certainly not expected, he hoped they would be able to slip into the port with little fanfare.

That part of Alex's plan worked like a charm. They sailed out to sea, then circled and turned toward the port as though they were coming from far away, not just around the corner.

Alex ordered all his warriors below decks. He didn't know what their immediate reception might be like, but he thought it would be a lot friendlier with only a skeleton crew showing.

He didn't want to force the four captured Drakana to be part of an elaborate masquerade because he thought that would renege on the deal he had made with them to try to get them to safety. Instead, he dressed them all as slave laborers in torn rags and put them up in the sails to carry out orders as they drifted into port.

He also took the Drakana clothing he had found and dressed those who he thought could best pass for Drakana in the proper outfits.

Harta-ak, typical of the natives of Kragdon-ah, was nearly seven feet tall, so he hid below, along with other giants like Tinta-ak and the true giant, Torana. Hawthorne, Alex, and a few others could do a better job of disguising themselves, and they had the advantage of being able to speak the language.

Hawthorne gave the order and they trimmed the sails and slipped gently into port. He expertly maneuvered the ship alongside the dock and Alex and others disguised as Drakana threw ropes to men on the docks. If those men suspected anything, they did not show it. It seemed it was just a slightly unexpected occurrence, nothing more.

The second Alex judged they were tied up securely, he turned and shouted, "Now!"

Warriors poured through every door that led below decks. Many of the first through were Nanda-eh's archers. They had their short bows today, as they knew they needed accuracy, not distance. They climbed quickly up to assigned spots in the rigging, put arrows to string, and drew and held at the men on the dock below.

Other warriors silently ran to the upper decks and leaped to the docks in a swarm, carrying swords, clubs, hammers, and axes.

The men on the docks were not fighters. If there was a weapon anywhere in the area, it was not evident. They all backed away with their hands in the air.

One man turned and sprinted toward the small village that sat behind the docks.

"Sanda, put him down," Alex ordered.

In a split second, Sanda sighted and released. The arrow whipped through the air and struck the man low in the back. She had another arrow nocked before that one struck home, but Alex raised his hand.

No one else made a move.

Alex hopped up onto the dock and in a voice designed to carry, he said, "We have come to accept your surrender. We do not want to hurt you," in Drakana.

The men on the dock turned and stared at the man writhing in pain with an arrow in his buttocks.

"If you just don't make any sudden movements, we will not hurt you. If you raise a weapon against us, we will kill you."

There were perhaps fifty people milling around between the town and the dock and hundreds of Alex's warriors. No one seemed intent on putting up a fight.

That was when first Tinta-ak, then Torana stepped onto the deck.

The men on the docks gaped and stared at the doorway where they had emerged as though it was possible that something even more wondrous was about to appear.

From high in the rigging, Nanda-eh called, "I can see three men who left a building and are running away."

"Can you get them?" Alex answered.

"No, they are too far."

"We will let them go, then."

Alex turned back to the men who stood stock still on the dock. "Who is the leader of this village?"

Half a dozen hands pointed at a wizened old woman who stood in the center of a group of men. Her hair was a ratty gray and she leaned on a tall cane in front of her.

To Alex's eye, she looked to be over a hundred years old.

As he walked to her, there was a hubbub that came from the direction the runners had gone. In a moment, the source became clear. The warriors they had dropped off at the cove hours before were returning the runners to the village. They had managed to find the primary road between the village and the city. Once they met that challenge, subduing the runners was simple.

The warriors and Alex both grinned at the success of the plan and their own cleverness.

Immediately, their glass house was crushed by a large rock.

Alex had rounded up all the villagers he could see and the warriors surrounded them in a dirt area in front of a long wooden structure.

He had not yet searched all the small boats that were tied up to the docks.

One of those boats had a single sail and a small cabin. A few feet above the waterline there were what looked to be three small ports. Silently, a wooden covering was removed from the portholes from inside the ship and three long oars appeared. A skinny, frightened boy, who appeared to be no more than ten or eleven years old popped up, threw off the single rope, then hustled back into the cabin.

The oars dipped into the water and the ship moved away from the dock.

"Stop them!" Alex yelled, berating himself for not searching the boats.

Half a dozen of Alex's warriors ran down the dock to try to catch the ship. It was obvious they could not catch it, but when they came to the end of the dock, they dove into the water and swam after the small craft. One of them actually managed to touch one of the oars, but could not hold on.

As soon as the boat was a few yards from the dock, the young boy popped up again and raised the sail. It caught the breeze and ended any chance of the warriors catching it.

"Shall we give chase, Manta-ak?" a sailor on board their ship shouted down.

Alex did not answer, but Harta-ak did. "No, we will never catch them. On the open sea, with a good wind, we are faster. But they will be wherever they are going by the time we get out of port. They are gone."

"Which means our time frame just tightened up considerably."

Alex had asked Darand what the military capabilities were like on this island, but beyond a few generic statements that Drakana was always prepared for an invasion, he didn't know much.

Alex turned to Harta-ak and said, "We'll continue with our plan and adjust as we need to. Get all the warriors off the ship and prepare to launch."

Ten minutes later, the warriors were all formed up into their squads on the dirt patch. To Alex's eye, they still looked like a ragtag bunch—they didn't have a uniform, and their weapons were diverse and primitive. But with fourteen squads of fifty men, their sheer numbers alone gave them a certain weight.

Harta-ak prepared to take the remaining men, including the Drakana sailors, on board the ship.

"When it is safe for you to return, we will light a signal fire here on the beach and keep it burning. Give us two days, then check for the fire, but don't come too close. We can't risk losing the ship."

Harta-ak gave a crisp salute—a habit he had already picked up from Hawthorne—and led his small crew back on board the ship. The ropes that tied them to the dock were thrown off, sails were raised, and they slowly moved away from the port.

It had been Alex's plan to have the ship leave. When he took the battle to the forces on the other side of the island, he didn't want to have to leave a segment of his army behind to guard the boat. Not to mention he didn't think they were prepared to have a battle while they were stuck in port. In the end, he thought it was better just to send the ship out to open seas where it would be safe from attack.

Even though it had been his idea, Alex still felt a twinge of regret as he watched the ship head for the horizon.

He finally turned back to the old woman. Until the small ship escaped, Alex had intended to negotiate for their surrender on the spot. That seemed like a losing strategy now that they knew the cavalry would inevitably be on the way.

He looked at the long building behind the old woman and asked, "What is that building?" in the Drakana language.

"It is where we process what we grow and prepare it for shipment."

Alex turned to Amy. "Grab one of the squad leaders and take their men. Search the building for anything that could be used as a weapon. Bring that out and dump it here. Double time."

Amy gestured at the squad leader nearest her and they hurried up the gentle ramp and through the wide double doors that were obviously intended for horse-drawn carts to pass through.

"When we've cleared the building, I'm going to put all your people inside. We will not mistreat you. We will feed you."

"There is no need to feed us," the old woman said. "There is a kitchen. It is where we have our lunches."

"Good enough," Alex said and turned to meet with Rinka-ak, Tinta-ak, Versa-eh, and the rest of his advisors. He called the leader of the small band he had dropped off earlier to get a situation report on what the land looked like ahead. He already missed the steady advice of Harta-ak and Hawthorne, but it couldn't be helped. They were needed on the ship.

Amy led the squad back outside. There had been no weapons inside, but they carried armfuls of a short, curved knife that was obviously used to prepare whatever fruit they processed here.

Alex caught a glimpse of a cart that was full of the fruit, which looked like an oversized pineapple. He made a mental note to fill their storerooms on the ship once they had won.

His warriors herded the workers into the long building and he decided to only leave a dozen men behind to guard all of them. He watched the men and women as they were led into the storeroom. For people who were suddenly attacked as they were going about their daily business, they seemed to take it in stride.

I may have to reevaluate what the Drakana people are like. Maybe there is no average Drakana person and they still maintain the personality they had before they were conquered.

Alex and his lieutenants had drilled the squads in how to march while they were on board the ship, but space had been limited and this would be their first real contact with the enemy. Alex was not at all sure how they would hold up. Would they fight as a single unit or break down at the first sound of gunfire?

Alex put himself at the head of the column and began their march toward the city on the other side of the island. He estimated it was twenty miles away, but knew that if the army approached them, they could meet them much sooner.

Chapter Twenty-Three
The First Skirmish

The march toward the city was taxing. On the ocean, the weather was warm, but there was typically a breeze and the coolness of the water to balance things out. Now they were marching at a steady pace through a jungle that was not only hot, but humid. A sudden rain shower drenched them but didn't bring relief from the heat, as it was even more humid when they marched in their wet clothes.

Alex's army did not have enough shields to go around, but he did have enough for the unit that marched in front of the column. The composite shields were as light as they could have been constructed while still having stopping power, but carrying them in the ready position for mile after mile was wearing.

After a march of a few miles, Alex halted the line. The warriors in front did not complain, but it was obvious by the rivers of sweat and strain on their faces that leading the march and holding the shields ready was taking its toll.

At the same time, the road they were on offered too many spots for a possible ambush to let them proceed with no protection.

Alex solved the dilemma by sending the front squad to the back and moving all others up one spot. He resolved to not push each squad so hard and to switch them out more often. He wanted them to be fresh when the battle finally arrived, whether that was later to-day or sometime the following day.

Alex always marched with the front unit. The road was wide, well-maintained, and easy to walk on. But it was still a road through thick foliage and plenty of rolling hills, which offered potential for ambushes.

The hardest part of preparing for this campaign was that they did not know the true strength of the resistance they might face. Alex had some grasp on their weapons, as he was sure they would be armed like the invaders who had come to Kragdon-ah. What he didn't know was whether he would be facing an army that numbered one hundred, five hundred, or thousands of soldiers. If it was the latter, he would need to beat a retreat to the ship and come up with a different place to begin.

Alex kept his head on a swivel and made sure his marchers were as silent as possible. Their only sound was the rise and fall of hundreds and hundreds of feet. He kept Monda-ak near and whispered to him, "Tell me if you smell anything new."

The road took a bend first to the right, then to the left to move around a rock outcropping. Alex looked up at it and had a single thought: *this would be an excellent spot to fire down on us.*

He hadn't even finished the thought before he heard a cry above, then a volley of shots.

Alex instinctively jumped toward the cover of the heavy plants on the side of the road. He glanced behind him and saw that his army was doing the same, with the exception of four of his men who were sprawled out on the compact dirt with blood oozing from gunshot wounds.

He did not wait to see if the gunmen were still waiting to fire at anyone who came to their rescue. He and Penta-ak, the squad leader who was at the front of the column, ran back into the line of fire and each picked up or half-dragged two of the injured men into cover.

The other two who had been shot had managed to crawl to the relative safety of the foliage.

Alex called "Healer!" down the line, then sent an order for everyone to stay behind the bushes until further notice.

Alex checked himself to make sure he hadn't caught a bullet or ricochet without realizing it in the heat of the moment, but found he was uninjured. He flashed a hand signal to Monda-ak to follow him quietly and stepped into the brush.

There were few actual trees, but the dominant plant species was a bush that sprouted tall, thick shoots about six feet into the air, where they bloomed into thick, broad leaves. It made Alex's ascent up the hill relatively easy.

The hill was not tall and it only took him a few minutes to reach where he estimated the ambushers had been. He circled around them and popped up over a ledge to discover that the ambush area was deserted. There was no sign that they had even been there, aside from the flattened grass where he guessed they had lain on their stomachs and waited for their approach.

Alex and Monda-ak hurried back down the hill.

"They're gone. They can pick an ambush spot, take a few shots, then hurry on to the next and do it again all the way to the city. We can't afford to play this game."

Tinta-ak had come forward and said, "The next time they fire at us, let's just charge them. They will kill some of us, but we will kill *all* of them."

"No. I have a different idea. Tinta-ak, I want you to take my place at the front of the army. March them at a steady pace along the trail. If you reach another ambush, just take everyone into the nearest cover and wait for me. I'm going to try to make sure you don't get ambushed at all."

"What do we do with our wounded?"

"Leave one of our healers and ten warriors here to guard them and keep them safe. Move them off the trail. We'll be back for them as soon as we can."

Tinta-ak moved to carry out the orders.

Alex picked out ten warriors, Sanda, and three of her archers. "Follow me."

He led his small contingent back up the hill to where the Drakana had lain in wait for them. He put his arm around Monda-ak. "Find their scent. We are going to follow them. Don't go too fast, though. Got it?"

Monda-ak put his nose to the ground and went around in circles a few times, identifying the scent he wanted. When he had it, he stood tall and looked at Alex.

"Slowly," Alex told Monda-ak. "We want to sneak up on them."

Monda-ak turned and moved slowly ahead of them. Soon, Alex realized that they were on some sort of small game trail like he had often followed through the forests of Kragdon-ah. The fact that there was a visible trail and the scent was fresh made it easy to track the Drakana.

After half a mile, Alex, Monda-ak, and his small band climbed a small rise. Before they reached the top of it, Alex clicked his tongue once and Monda-ak froze, waiting. Slowly, Alex crept alone over the top of the small hill and saw a band of a dozen soldiers lying on their stomachs on a small bluff that looked over the trail. They each had several of the broad leaves positioned over their head. Alex glanced to his right and saw that once again the road below emerged from a turn. The front squad would be vulnerable before they knew they were under attack.

Alex slid silently back down the small hill and gave orders to his group. He placed his archers at the top of the hill, then lined the rest of his warriors up in a single file behind him.

He gripped his twin-bladed ax in his right hand and his short sword in his left. Without a word, he launched himself over the hill and sprinted toward the dozen armed men below. Monda-ak soon caught and passed Alex and was the first to reach the soldiers.

The men below all carried rifles, which were perfect for an ambush but a poor weapon when attacked from behind. Alex's warriors stayed in single file as they followed, which created a good line of visibility for the four archers. They had arrows already nocked and their first volley hit home—four strikes—before Monda-ak reached the first man.

Monda-ak leaped onto a man in the middle, crushing him below his weight and closing his jaws over the man's head with a crunch.

Alex was second to arrive and though the man he chose had a leather helmet on, Alex's ax was so sharp and swung with such strength, it cleaved right through helmet, skull, and into the man's spine. Alex put a foot into the man's chest and pulled to free his weapon, but by the time he had it loose, the archers and his other warriors had attacked. All twelve of the Drakana were dead or dying at their feet.

Those who were not dead presented a small conundrum. He didn't want to leave more of his people behind to care for these men, but he hated the tradition of the Kragdon-ah to kill instead of capture. Then he remembered that this army had invaded his land, enslaved those who only wanted to live in peace.

There would be a time and strategy for mercy, but here, in the first skirmish of his war against Drakana, was not it. He gave a signal and the warriors quickly finished off the enemy.

Alex's first instinct was to gather the weapons and begin training a new unit of rifle-equipped Kragdon-ah warriors. But he had promised Sekun-ak that he would not lose the war for the soul of Kragdon-ah just to win a battle.

There was no place to easily dispose of the Drakana rifles—their *stama*, so they simply left them behind.

Alex and Monda-ak led the warriors down the hill and were waiting for the army when it came around the bend.

The legend of Manta-ak grew once again.

Chapter Twenty-Four
The Battle of Lakunadan

Alex and his army were cautious from that point on. Each time they came to a bend in the trail, they sent a small, shielded group ahead to check for further ambushes. There were none. Alex and his small band had taken out the only ambush crew that had been sent to harass them. He soon concluded that the primary purpose was not to kill or maim them in great number, but simply to slow them down.

After a few more miles, they came to a spot where the trail emerged from the jungle into open, verdant farmland. The sun hung low in the sky, already turning the clouds purple and red against the horizon. Alex did not know how far they were from the city, but he felt they were not close yet.

Cities are like the beating heart of an area. As roads leave the heart, they are wide and prosperous, with businesses and houses clinging to them on all sides. The farther from the heart those roads travel, the thinner they become until they finally end as a single lane path like the one they had been walking on all day.

The land around them had opened up into a flat vista, but there was still only open fields and the occasional hut or lean-to for buildings.

With the sun setting and the city still distant, Alex made the decision to make camp where they were while there was still enough light to see. He elected to not have a big fire at their camp, but had a team gather wood for a bonfire anyway. The army made a simple camp to the eastern side of the road, but Alex ordered the fire built a hundred yards away, on the western side. If attackers came, they would likely be attracted to that area first and find only an open field.

Everyone else simply hunkered down where they were and ate some of the meager food they had confiscated from the small village. Not enough to satisfy every appetite, but enough to keep hunger pangs away.

Alex set up a perimeter of sentries fifty strides out from the group and spaced them only twenty strides apart. He scheduled them on approximately a three-hour rotation.

Most of the warriors settled into excited conversation. Today was the first day that they had touched a land that was not part of Kragdon-ah. At least, it was the first day aside from the unknown possibilities of the missing months in the fog.

In the deepest part of the night, there was a sound and the alarm was raised. A hundred warriors were on their feet and at the scene of the cry in moments. No person was sighted, but using a torch and Monda-ak's nose, they did find the hoofprints of what looked like a deer or antelope that led back into the jungle. If it had stumbled into their camp in the daylight, they would have had more food for their stores, but it escaped unharmed.

Before the first light showed in the east, Alex had his army up and marching down the road. They made good time with fresh legs and before long, they began to see scattered houses here and there. Alex approached the first with trepidation, but when he broke down the door, it was empty. He checked the next four houses with the same result and finally figured out that all outlying people had been brought back to the city.

Alex created a small team of people to check each house and find whatever useful supplies were inside. They found several carts designed to be pulled by a horse. They had not unloaded any of their horses from the ship, but they had plenty of manpower. They loaded the carts with whatever foodstuff they could find—which included loaves of bread, jars of honey, and a strange purple paste that was apparently considered edible by the natives.

Alex and Amy talked as they moved toward the city.

"Based on what we have seen so far, what conclusions can we draw?" Alex asked her.

Amy was not fast to answer, but then she never was. She preferred to speak correctly instead of quickly.

"The easy way we were able to take the village shows that they were not expecting to be attacked. Their defenses there were non-existent. However, the fact that they had a group ready to attack us on the trail tells me that the city's defenses will be much greater. I would guess that as the squad of men passed through here, they told everyone to flee to the city, and fast. That would explain why they left food behind for us to find."

"As usual, I can't fault your logic. What do you think we will find at the city?"

"Darand told us that they had excellent defenses in their port. I think they would probably have something set up to be ready for an attack like we are launching from the other side of the island."

"What would that look like, do you think?"

After a pause of several dozen steps, she said, "A wall, perhaps? That would fit with the idea that they gathered their people together. Stay inside their walls. Of course, it's also possible that they didn't want to waste the time and resources on building a wall. If that's the case, they probably have other booby traps set up for us. Maybe spiked barriers, ambush spots, dugouts or trenches where they can pop up and fire on us."

"You paint a rosy picture, daughter of mine." Alex winked at her, obviously proud of her ability to think things through. While Amy had been talking, he had been scanning the horizon. "I think one of your predictions has already come to pass," he said, pointing ahead.

Perhaps a quarter-mile ahead, there was a stone structure that stretched as far as they could see, east to west. It was not impossibly tall—perhaps eight to ten feet. It was a solid unbroken line with four guard towers in the area they could see. There was only a single gate, which would funnel them down to a pinch point—advantageous to the defenders, difficult for the attackers.

Alex assumed that they had already been spotted by those in the guard houses, but that wasn't unexpected. This would be more of a battle of preparation than a sneak attack in the night.

Alex stopped the column of marchers and had them break into the separate squads. He wanted to make it easy for the Drakana to count their numbers, hoping that it would seem overwhelming—just as their attackers had overwhelmed Kragdon-ah villages and forced them to ground.

"One thing I just thought of," Amy said.

Alex's mind was elsewhere, already concocting strategies to storm a walled city protected by guns. He turned to look at Amy.

"We don't know how far it is to the next Drakana settlement, but isn't it likely that they've already dispatched a ship with a message that we are here?"

"It is, but we just didn't have the firepower to stop that. It means that our advantage of surprise ends here. It will be harder from now on."

"The first thing we will need to do is establish where their weapons become effective. I will need some volunteers for this."

As expected, every single hand around him shot into the air. Alex chose fifteen warriors who, by his eyeball, were approximately the same height. "Gather a shield for each of you. Do you remember how I showed you to do the shield wall on board the ship? We are going to do something like that. It won't be a true shield wall, because I don't want you to engage with the enemy like that yet."

The warriors formed into something that almost looked like an organized shield wall. Alex found Nanda-eh and said, "Take your whole squad of archers with their longbows and march behind the shield wall. When they stop, fire two volleys of arrows over the wall. There's no need to aim for anything in particular, just put the arrows over the wall. They won't be ready for that and we are certain to find a few of them."

Alex wedged himself inside the group of shield warriors. From the center of them, he quietly said, "Slow march."

The small contingent of warriors—a group of shield-bearers followed by a squad of hunkered-down archers—must have looked strange to the guards in the towers. Those guards showed their discipline and did not fire on the group until they grew closer.

When they did fire their guns, it was as a single unit—Alex noticed and filed that information away, as it meant a certain level of training.

The shield-bearers did not slow their march, though Alex could feel them tense as they waited for the onslaught of bullets. It never came. Alex called for his unit to halt, then took the tip of the spear he had brought with him and dragged it back and forth at his feet, marking the spot.

They marched forward at a snail's pace, waiting for the next volley. When it came, the bullets hit the shields, but did not penetrate. Alex made another mark in the road.

Another ten paces and another volley rent the air. This time, the bullets impacted the shields and one of the frontline warriors cursed.

"Are you shot?" Alex asked urgently.

Still holding his shield, the man said, "Just in my forearm."

Alex made a third and final mark in the road, then said, "Nanda-eh, two volleys over the wall now."

Behind them, the archers stood straight and tall and got a clear view of the wall and guard posts for the first time. They already had their arrows nocked, and with no need to aim, released and dropped back down behind the shields.

"One more," Alex said, and the archers responded.

One of the unaimed arrows flew like it had eyes and pierced the throat of one of the guards in the tower, who tumbled over backwards. Other screams came from the other side of the wall.

The Drakana may have drawn first blood, but Alex knew they had made their presence known.

"Back now, slowly," Alex commanded, and the small group slowly retreated to out of range of the guns.

Back with the bulk of his army, Alex spoke to Tinta-ak, Rinka-ak, and his other lieutenants. "Move your squads and have them form up just behind the first line I drew in the road. Keep a row of warriors with shields up at the front in case they get lucky with a shot. Rotate people through the front row so they stay alert."

The road into the city was broad here and there was room for three squads across if they spread onto the cleared area on the side. The other squads fell into formation behind them.

Alex was contemplating the very best way to breach the stone wall when the gate in the middle began to creak open. The gate was obviously heavily reinforced because it opened very slowly. Alex began counting in his head and realized that it had taken at least ninety seconds for it to swing fully open.

He stood in front of his squads and said, "Be ready to attack that opening at my command."

A moment later, a man dressed in fine leather armor astride a beautiful warhorse walked his steed out through the opening. Behind him, two more men rode on almost-identical horses. Each of them carried a flagpole with a solid-red flag moving slightly in the breeze.

"Hold steady," Alex said quietly. "But stay ready. Attack if I give the order."

Alex looked the man in front over carefully. If he was armed, it didn't show. The same was true of the men behind him. Still, Alex was smart enough to stay where he was—out of the range of the gunmen on the wall.

When the man in the lead was ten strides away, he halted his warhorse with the slightest tug on the reins.

"I am Bantam. What do you want with our city?"

"We are here to accept your full surrender and capitulation to us. I require you to lay down your weapons, open your gates, and instruct all citizens to do as we say."

The words seemed to strike Bantam like a blow. He moved back several inches in his saddle, then recovered himself.

"If that is what you want, you have three choices. You can turn around and march back to your ship and sail away peacefully and never return. Or, you can persist in attacking a well-armed city in the Drakana Empire, which means this meadow will run red with your blood and the screams of your ridiculous force will echo for a generation."

"Very poetic," Alex said. "But you said we had three choices. That is only two."

"Ah, yes," Bantam said delicately. "You can have sexual relations with the ghosts of your ancestors."

Alex couldn't help himself. He let out a small burst of laughter. He heard Amy behind him, who still spoke Drakana better than he did, also laugh. Most of the warriors around Alex had not understood a word that had been said, but when they saw Alex laugh, they did as well.

Soon, Bantam was faced with hundreds of warriors laughing in his face. It was almost certainly not the reaction he had sought.

Without another word, he clicked his tongue, turned the horse, and headed at a trot toward the gate.

Alex did not hesitate. At the top of his lungs, he screamed, "Charge them!" then trilled his own war cry and sprinted toward the gate. Monda-ak ran ahead of him, tongue wagging, eating up ground even faster than the warhorses ahead of him. He caught up to Bantam's horse just before the gate, leaped, and took Bantam himself clean out of his saddle. The man landed with a burst of air, then took a deep breath to scream. It was a sad little scream, and it was the last sound he ever made, as Monda-ak closed his mighty jaws over his head and crushed the man's skull.

The two riders in front heard the commotion. Instead of wheeling to defend Bantam, they kicked their heels and their warhorses sprinted toward the gate. As they did, they screamed, "Close the gate! Close the gate!"

The process of opening the gate had been slow and closing it was not any faster. Before it was even a quarter shut, Alex and Monda-ak hit the opening, followed by a screaming horde of Kragdon-ah warriors.

Chapter Twenty-Five
The Battle of Lakunadan Redux

A lex heard one bullet whiz by his head and another hit the road between him and Monda-ak, then ricocheted away.

He had no idea what size the force was that he would be attacking, but he was sure that they would never have an opportunity to just pour in through the open gate again.

He burst through the gate with his army at his back and saw that the two men on the warhorses had turned to face him. One yelled, "Throw me a weapon!" to someone in the guard house. Before he had a chance to receive it, Alex charged him. He swung his ax in a smooth arc and it hit the man just above the knee, severing it. The man screamed and fell off one side of the horse. The bottom half of his leg fell off the other side.

Alex did not stop to kill him, but saw a line of gunmen opening fire on those who poured through the gate. As he watched, one man aimed carefully and fired, taking down a charging Kragdon-ah warrior.

Alex zeroed in on that man and sprinted toward him, closing the distance in seconds. The man saw him coming, calmly reloaded, and was a split second away from raising the gun to fire when Alex bowled him over, running him through with his short sword.

Monda-ak was like a demon, growling, leaping, tearing at anyone who got close to him.

The chaos of the battlefield took over from there. It was soon obvious that Bantam's boast of a heavily defended city was incorrect. Alex estimated that there were perhaps one hundred actual soldiers behind the wall. Everyone else was a civilian and had found discretion to be the better part of valor by retreating inside whatever building was available.

It was obvious that the battle would go the way of the Kragdonah. It was just a question of how heavy their casualties would be from the Drakana guns.

Alex saw the third man who had been on horseback. He whirled his horse left, then right, taking in the carnage around him. He saw the same thing Alex did—his forces were destined to die at the hands of these invaders.

He stood high in his saddle and shouted, "Cease! Stop firing! Lay down your guns."

A battle in full motion is not like a switch that can be turned off. For a few moments after his command, there was still the sound of gunshots and the ring of metal against metal. Nanda-eh and her archers had taken the high ground from those on the wall and had clambered to the top.

When the man on horseback called for a cease-fire, she gave the same command to her archers, who looked down on the entire village square below them.

"Lay down your arms," the man shouted again, and this time it was easier to hear him. His soldiers were hesitant, as they faced a mob of wild-eyed, half-naked warriors. Still, it was obvious to all by then that even with their guns, they would all be cut down sooner rather than later.

"Where is your commander?" the man on horseback shouted.

"Here," Alex said, stepping toward him. "I still want what I did when we were outside the wall. I will accept your unconditional surrender. Nothing less."

Alex's words were harsh, but he stood on a cobblestone street wet with the blood of the Drakana and his own men. It was not a time for equivocation. The battle had been determined. The only thing remaining to know was the final death toll.

"I surrender," the man said quietly.

"Get down from your horse, approach me and tell me that."

The man glared balefully at Alex. Given the opportunity, he would have gladly told every one of his men to turn their guns on him. He was not being given that opportunity.

He gracefully dismounted from his huge horse and Alex was surprised to see that the man was shorter than him. He had looked huge sitting astride the warhorse.

"On behalf of Drakana and the village of Lakunadan, I surrender."

There was no raucous cheer from the Kragdon-ah. Dozens of them were wounded. Five lay unmoving in the street.

"What do you wish of us?" the commander asked.

"You have three choices," Alex said. "You can agree to disavow your allegiance to Drakana and swear to fight with us as our friend and ally. Or you can choose an honorable death and we will grant you that favor with as little fanfare as possible."

That was, of course, only two choices, but the Drakana commander was smart enough not to ask for the third option. He was already certain what it would be.

There were roughly fifty Drakana soldiers still standing. Perhaps half that many were dead or dying on the cobblestone street. Every eye fixed on the commander, waiting for his decision.

"Until this generation, the people of Lakunadan were a sovereign nation, responsible only to themselves. What will happen to them?"

"That is no longer any of your concern. What happens between us and the people of Lakunadan is going to happen, no matter what your decision is."

Alex got the feeling the man was perhaps stalling for time, looking for a better option that did not exist.

"I could make the choice for all, and the men would follow what I say. I choose not to do that. I will allow them to each choose for themselves."

Alex opened his mouth to answer him, but the commander dropped a small, razor sharp knife from the long sleeve of his shirt. With a movement so swift that no one beside Monda-ak even had a chance to move, he slammed it deep into his own chest, piercing his heart.

He slumped to the pavement, eyes glazed before he had completed the fall.

Alex's head swiveled from one group of the Drakana soldiers to the next. None of them seemed surprised by the sudden action, but none of them showed a sign of following his lead.

Alex stepped over the former commander's body and into a small clearing in the middle of the square. To his lieutenants, he said, "Gather their weapons and pile them here. Put our prisoners in there for the moment." He pointed to a small, dead-end alley between two buildings. There was a brick wall that stood perhaps twelve feet tall at the far end. "They will be safe there."

"Who is in charge of this city now that this man is dead?"

Another ancient woman, who could have been the twin of the woman he had seen at the village, stepped forward. "I am Timpata. I was the leader of this city when he was still alive, and I still am now, if you allow me to continue. That man was the leader of the Drakana army. Nothing more."

Alex heard pride in her voice, but it was the kind of satisfaction that can go with a long life well-lived.

"We will discuss your role soon. For now, I need whatever healers you have here in the city to care for the wounded Drakana. We have our own healers, but they are not fully equipped. I will need you to help them with any supplies they need."

"I will put our medicine people at your disposal. Now," she said with great dignity, "I am going to take a nap. It is too hot and there has been too much excitement." She was not asking permission, and it was not a question. She turned and tottered off with a small retinue behind her.

Alex searched for his least-injured squad. Unsurprisingly, it was one he had placed at the back. He called the squad leader to him and said, "Return to the village. Light a signal fire. When Harta-ak returns there, load up our stores with as much of that fruit as we can eat before it spoils. Then sail around the island and dock the ship here. There will be no resistance by then."

Alex started to turn away, then remembered a detail that had almost escaped him. "Who speaks for the town while your leader is napping?"

A young woman of perhaps twenty-five stepped toward him. "I am Trema. She is my grandmother. I cannot speak for her, but perhaps I can help you."

"I need a horse and cart. Not a horse like this," Alex said, gesturing at the warhorse standing alone, still saddled. "A work horse that can pull the cart."

Trema did not speak but walked calmly to a building on the other side of the square. She reemerged a few moments later and called to Alex. "I will have it brought to you."

Alex turned his attention back to his lieutenant. "When the horse and cart get here, take it with you. When you find our wounded on the trail, load them on the cart and return them to the ship."

The man put two fingers to his forehead, said, "Yes, Manta-ak," and hurried off to gather his men.

Alex walked to the stone wall, found a ladder that led to one of the guard houses and climbed up. Nanda-eh and Sanda were standing guard, arrows nocked and watching the Drakana soldiers suspiciously.

"I do not trust them," she said.

"I do not need you to trust them yet, but I may eventually. Remember this. When they invaded our land and had the upper hand on us in every way, they still held to the word they gave us when we defeated their champions at Thundan. That doesn't mean every Drakana is trustworthy, but it is a good start."

Sanda nudged Nanda-eh in a way that suggested an intimacy Alex had not been aware of. Quietly, Sanda whispered, "I told you. We cannot always trust them, but we can always trust my father."

Nanda-eh leaned her head toward Sanda and they briefly touched foreheads in acknowledgement.

Alex left them and climbed on top of the stone wall. From that height, he could see the outline of the city as it spread out before him. The first battle had been easier than he had thought. He knew Amy was correct, though, and that the Drakana here had undoubtedly sent word on to other islands and settlements that there were invaders attacking.

The Battle of Lakunadan was over.

The war against the Drakana had barely begun.

Chapter Twenty-Six
Looking Forward

With the battle finished, the negotiations began.

Alex looked at those discussions as two separate things. The first was negotiating with the remaining Drakana army. The second was dealing with the people of Lakunadan.

The negotiation with the Drakana troops was simple. Alex set up a table in the middle of the square and brought the soldiers to him one at a time. He gave each soldier the same choice he had given the commander: surrender and become part of his own army, or choose an honorable and quick death.

Alex's preference would have been to give them more options, such as a possible banishment, but it just wasn't practical. If they chose not to join him, he would be leaving a potential army behind that might eventually catch up. He didn't want to fight the same soldier twice, and he didn't want to have to fight on two fronts. So, he gave them the hard choice.

Alex explained to each man what that would mean—that they would be enlisted into his army to fight against their own people. He made it clear that they would be Kragdon-ah from that moment forward, and that their life in Drakana was over.

Or they could choose death.

It was a risky strategy that Alex had discussed long into the night with his best advisors.

"What do you do," Rinka-ak had asked, "if you arm them, make them part of us, and at a crucial moment, they betray us?"

Alex agreed that would be catastrophic, and he could not guarantee that wouldn't happen. He always came back to how the Drakana responded in Kragdon-ah when losing a Thundan had thwarted them. They had a completely superior military position and could have easily reneged on the deal they made, but they had not. That gave Alex faith that once a Drakana agreed to become a Kragdon-ah, they would remain so.

The first five men Alex questioned agreed easily. They were stripped of their Drakana uniforms and dressed in the style of a Lakunadan villager.

The sixth man presented Alex with a question.

"I have a family. If I know I will never see my wife, son, and daughter again, I will choose to die now. However, if it ever becomes possible for them to join me in my new home and you will allow it, I will pledge my life to you."

Alex considered that for a long moment before answering. He told the man to wait and walked to where Amy was watching the proceedings.

In English, he asked her, "What are the pros and cons of answering him each way?"

"The pros are easy. Look at him as he sits there. Even with his fate on the line, he looks confident and relaxed. He did not just agree as the others did. That tells me he is an unusual man, and could be valuable to us. The cons could be more hidden. If you promise him, you are promising everyone. If we somehow manage to survive the conflicts ahead and return home, will we have room to take all those families with us?"

"Good. Of course, there is another answer. If they fight bravely for us and we conquer Drakana, we could give those soldiers a ship of their own and let them find a place where they could build their own life. There are a lot of options for us."

Alex returned to the table, sat down, and looked the man in the eye.

"I cannot promise to go and look for your family. However, if there is ever an opportunity to reunite you with your family, I will allow them to come with us."

The man stood and snapped off a sharp salute. "Then you have my pledge."

Amy's words rang in Alex's mind. He trusted her instinct and thought she was right about this man—he was extraordinary.

"What is your name?"

"Grantan," the man said.

"Good. Grantan, I am Manta-ak. I want you to do something for me. Go to the remaining Drakana and tell them what we have agreed to. I will extend the same offer to all of them. Your first duty as a Kragdon-ah is to find out whether or not the rest of the men wish to live and fight for us, or die an honorable death. I am going to create a squad of those men and I am putting you in charge."

The man did not beam. His chest did not swell. He simply acknowledged what Alex had said and left to go to work. Alex could not help himself. He already liked Grantan and prayed that he had made the right decision here.

The truth was, unless they converted the natives and Drakana to their cause at most stops along the way, they would have no chance when they got to Drakana proper. It made for a good balance of power. Alex needed them, and they needed Alex if they wished to live.

Unsurprisingly, the remaining men all chose to declare fealty to Alex and Kragdon-ah.

Alex had his first squad of Drakana soldiers. Soon, he would have to decide what to do with them.

Going into the battle, Alex had thought of this island as one entity—Drakana. Once he had time to look around and ask a few questions, he could see that was not the case.

Lakunadan was very much like Kragdon-ah. Until thirteen years earlier, they had lived as a sovereign people, a matriarchy. They had grown the fruit that Alex thought of as oversized pineapples, but only enough for themselves. They lived a relaxed, easy-going lifestyle that included swimming and fishing in the plentiful sea, evening song festivals around the fire, and long naps in the heat of the afternoon.

They rarely had arguments, and when they did—one farmer thinking another was encroaching on his land, for instance—it was settled by the woman who was the oldest person in the village. When she passed on, whoever was next oldest became the new chieftain.

When Alex first sat down with Timpata, the current chief of the village, she had pointed out the wisdom of their approach. "Those of us who are the oldest have seen the most. We have a perspective the young and strong do not. Eternity stretches before us, which helps us make decisions that will benefit the tribe for hundreds of solstices, not just the now. When a grandmother dies, the whole village mourns the loss of knowledge."

Lakunadan had been easy pickings for the Drakana. When they had arrived, there had not been a true port built on either side of the island. The bay beside the city provided a perfect spot for the Drakana to anchor and invade.

The Drakana were not the first people to visit Lakunadan. People from other islands both near and far had traveled in what Alex believed were the equivalent of large outrigger canoes. There were adventurers who went from island to island, but most of the population of Lakunadan was content to stay home and enjoy the peace of perpetual good weather and easily available food. It was a good life and most Lakunadan were happy to live it never having gone more than two miles from the spot where they were born.

When the Drakana landed, the Lakunadan people were not hostile. They treated them as just another visitor.

That ended when the commander of the Drakana ceremonially beheaded the chieftain on first meeting her.

The Lakunadan revolted, of course, and fought back however they could. It was impossible for a people who had known nothing but peace to be prepared for a warlike enemy who appeared on their beach.

The Lakunadan revolt was soon put down, with as little loss of life as the Drakana could manage. They could have easily wiped out the native population, of course, but as in Kragdon-ah, they looked at those natives as potential property.

The Lakunadan had no choice but to acquiesce to the wishes of the Drakana and so reluctantly became the latest piece of the Drakana nation.

On the surface, they cooperated completely with the Drakana. They allowed them to take what they wanted from the island and let them turn their life of leisure into long days of breaking more ground and growing more fruit. They let the Drakana builders—who may have very well been the best in the world at this moment—build docks to create a port on both sides of the island. The Drakana also oversaw the slave labor that built the road that connected the village to the city and the stone wall that Alex had breached so easily.

The people of the former Lakunadan—now known simply as Drakana, as all conquered nations were—never showed any visible signs of resistance. The Drakana left a military presence big enough to ensure that any uprising would be quickly quelled. Those imported Drakana soldiers were happy with their new assignments. They were a continual show of strength on the island, but soon adapted themselves to the lives the natives had lived for thousands of years, swimming, relaxing, and napping in the heat of the day.

The Lakunadan showed a submissive face to the world, but in their homes and gathering places, they never lost sight of their ultimate goal—to be their own mistresses again.

When Alex learned that, it changed how he dealt with Timpata. Since before he had left Kragdon-ah, he had planned on negotiating a certain percentage of each country's best and brightest to be contributed to his hopefully growing army.

As in adding the captured Drakana, he had figured that was the only way that he was going to be able to have a sizable enough force to be able to make an actual dent when he got to Drakana proper.

After he listened to Timpata recount the history of Lakunadan, though, he knew could not ask any more of them. To Alex's mind, they were just the same as the people of Kragdon-ah—minding their own business when they were attacked and subjugated by an aggressive enemy.

Alex entered the small hut that passed for a home for Timpata. She offered him a drink that was a favorite of the Lakunadan. They drank it hot in the morning, then let it cool and drank it at room temperature through the rest of the day. It was early in the day, so it was still warm. Alex did not like any hot beverage and had tried—and greatly disliked—this particular drink the day before.

Still, this conversation was as much ritual as it was business, so he accepted the cup and took a sip.

"Thank you," Alex said.

Timpata touched her own cup to her lips, then put it on the table. "Now that you have conquered the Drakana, what is it you want from us?"

"When we arrived here, we did not know what to expect. We thought you were just a happy part of the Drakana nation."

"When you sailed to our island, we cheered, even though it was silently," the old woman spoke in the language of the Drakana—their only common language. "When you sailed around to the other side of our land and put men on the beach, we saw you, but we did not say anything to the Drakana. We knew it was possible that you would be even worse than our conquerors, but nothing could be too much worse than losing our entire way of life as we have. My mother always told me that those who oppose the people who oppose me are likely to be my ally. When I saw you come through the gate, running straight toward those guns, acting without fear, I knew you were the answer to our prayers."

Timpata signaled to her granddaughter Trema, who leaned down close. The old chieftain whispered in her ear, then sent her away.

Timpata continued. "We will attempt to arm ourselves and be in a better position to defend our island if they come back, but I know that even then, we will never be able to withstand an invasion from them. Still, we will tear down the docks they built to land their trading and war ships. If nothing else, we will make it hard for them to conquer us again." She paused, as though she might have lost her train of thought, then snapped back. "You will want their ships, yes?"

"Yes," Alex said.

"Good. I do not want them here. Will you have enough people to sail them?"

"The men who were once Drakana have agreed to become part of our tribe now. With them, we will have enough."

"Do you want our strongest too?"

"Once, I thought that would be my plan. Now that I have seen your beautiful island and people, I cannot take any of them away from here. That would not be fair to you or to them."

"Then I will not force anyone to go. Those who need to stay here and take care of families will stay. But some have already told me they want to go with you. They know they may never return home, but they believe that by fighting with you, they will do what they can to stop the Drakana from returning. Will they be welcome?"

"Of course."

"If I had seen ten fewer solstices, I would go myself," Timpata said. A sudden fire flared in her eyes that spoke of faraway sunsets and adventures. It quickly died out.

"I would be honored to have had you," Alex said.

After receiving no response, he looked closer at the old woman. She was asleep.

Alex crept out of her small house, though he had the feeling that if he had tap danced a flamenco on the way out, it would not have woken her.

When he stepped outside her hut, Trema had returned, bringing another old woman with her. "This is Hanta. She has something she wishes to tell you."

Alex turned and gave Hanta his undivided attention. Like Timpata, she was ancient. Gravity was doing its work and she seemed to be collapsing in on herself.

"We are not a warlike people," Hanta said, with no other preface, as though she had rehearsed this speech. "That is why we were so easily put down. But not all of us are so gentle. There is word of a place where all those who lived in lands conquered by the Drakana but were able to escape now live. Among all those refugees, they have raised a mighty army that will someday take on our conquerors."

The old woman made what Alex would have called an 'OK' sign with her thumb and forefingers and spat after saying that last.

She had Alex's attention. He saw Amy across the square and motioned for her to hurry to him. She ran across the square, her long dark hair flying out behind her.

"I want you to listen to what this woman says," Alex said. "Go on, Hanta."

The old woman looked at Amy with sharp eyes and must have thought she passed muster because she continued on.

"The location of this island where the refugees train and fight and build weapons is unknown."

Alex's shoulders sagged a bit. To Amy, in English, he said, "Just another myth to keep hope alive most likely."

The old woman did not speak English, but she recognized Alex's dismissive tone. For a moment, Alex thought she was going to turn her back on him and leave. There seemed to be a battle inside her, but finally she said, "We have a special child here. In our tribe, she is called Sofina, which means *our chosen one*."

That phrase—chosen one—staggered Alex and he was immediately lost in his own thoughts. Lanta-eh, who was the Winten-ah Chosen One had been dead for decades. Like Alex's other great loss, his love Senta-eh, he carried her memory with him everywhere. But that memory was locked in a steel box deep inside him that he rarely opened.

Hearing that phrase had an instant effect on him as his memories of Lanta-eh flooded through him. He had first known her as a child, and she had never had a chance to be much more than that. For a moment, Alex found himself standing on the hillside known as Prata-ah, staring at the statue that the visitor Emily had made right before his eyes. In that moment, she was there. She smiled and reached for him. She was the only Winten-ah who ever hugged Alex. She did so again, but it was a ghostly hug and her image dissipated around him.

When he opened his eyes again, he was back in Lakunadan and all three women were staring at him.

"Sofina," Alex said. "The chosen one."

Hanta looked from Alex to Amy, then back. "Yes, Sofina. As I said, I am sending her with you. She knows how to find the place where the army gathers."

Chapter Twenty-Seven
In Search of a Mystery

Harta-ak returned to the main port two days later. He dropped the gangplank and Alex waved at him from the dock.

"I feel a little guilty leaving all the hard work to you," Harta-ak said.

Alex waved him off. "We had a hammer to kill a single fly here. It was better to have you safe at sea. If we lose this ship, we lose everything."

That was when something caught Alex's eye. At the front of the ship, just under the bow, there was white cursive lettering that read, *The Senta-eh.*

In English.

Alex's jaw dropped open. He couldn't imagine who would have done that. He pointed to it and said, "Did you do that?"

Harta-ak looked at what Alex pointed at and squinted. It was obvious he had not noticed it either. It would not be visible from on board the ship.

"I don't know what that is," Harta-ak answered.

"It's in English, the language from where I come from. It says, *The Senta-eh.*"

"I guess that is the name of our ship then. I could not have picked out a better one."

"I agree, but who did this, and when?" Alex saw Sanda and Amy at the end of the dock, searching through some boxes. He waved them down and pointed to the words. "Did you two do this?"

Their eyebrows raised in surprise. As one, they both said, "No, Dad."

"It must be another mystery from the fog," Amy said.

That made sense to Alex, but he couldn't help staring at it. He had never thought of naming the ship. But somehow, seeing her name there—even in a language she would not have recognized—was comforting. Alex let his gaze rest on the name and communed with her spirit for a moment before returning to the business at hand. It felt to Alex like his past was running like the wind to catch up to him.

Timpata ordered stores of every kind loaded onto the ship until the storerooms overflowed. She gave them not just the fruits and vegetables, which would go bad soon, but also ground wheat, honey, and other stores that would get them through long weeks at sea.

There were no Drakana ships that approached the size of what Alex had instantly begun to think of as *The Senta-eh*, but they did have two smaller ships that would serve a good purpose. Each of them had room for a hundred men, but Alex had less than fifty of the former Drakana soldiers, so he split them among the two ships.

The good news was that there were a number of actual sailors among those he captured and did not kill. Between Pictin, the men he trained on the voyage to Lakunadan, Hawthorne, and the new recruits, Alex felt like he almost had a legitimate crew.

He had more of the original Kragdon-ah warriors on board *The Senta-eh* than he needed, so he assigned some of them to the smaller boats. He didn't want the former Drakana soldiers to feel alone and isolated. It was important that they were assimilated into their new tribe.

He met Sofina, and as he had so often been with Lanta-eh, he was impressed with her presence and knowledge. When Hanta had said she was her great-granddaughter, he had been sure she would be just a child. Instead, she proved just how old Hanta was, as she appeared to be about twenty—not that much younger than Sanda and Amy.

In fact, Sanda, Amy, Nanda-eh and her archers all welcomed Sofina with smiles and promises of stories to tell.

Ten days after they had taken their first surreptitious trip around Lakunadan, *The Senta-eh* and its two companion ships shoved off from the dock toward open waters. Alex stood with Amy and Sanda on the aft deck of the ship.

As the city shrank into the distance, Alex pointed out two things.

First, he pointed back at the docks. Lakunadan workers were already going at it hammer and tongs, dismantling it. If the Drakana did ever come back, they would be starting over.

Second, he pointed at the wake behind them. It may not have been as arrow straight as Harta-ak, Pictin, or Hawthorne would have liked, but it was nothing close to the zig-zag zipper pattern that Harta-ak had shown him at the beginning of the voyage.

They were making progress.

As soon as Lakunadan faded over the horizon, Alex met his advisors in what had once been the captain's quarters. He wished he had a map he could dramatically unroll on the large table in the middle of the room, point to a spot and say, "There's our destination."

However, there was no map. Even though everyone on Lakunadan had heard of this mysterious island of rebels and insurgents, no one had any concrete idea where it was.

When Alex explained where they were heading, Harta-ak asked the logical question. "How do we find this place if no one knows where it is?"

Alex looked around the table. Rinka-ak, Sanda, Tinta-ak, Versa-eh, and Amy were nodding their heads in agreement.

Alex drew a deep breath and said one word. "Sofina."

"The woman we picked up in Lakunadan?" Tinta-ak asked. "She's been there, then?"

Alex hesitated. "No, actually she hasn't."

A small uproar erupted around the table. Alex didn't try to quell it, but let it run its course. "Everything you're saying and even what you're not saying because you don't want to call me crazy is valid. I won't downplay your concerns. But let me tell you why I think it's worth our efforts to find this place."

Alex pushed his chair back and stood, gathering his thoughts.

"We are trying to accomplish the impossible—setting out with less than a thousand people to conquer an entire people. When the Drakana came to conquer us, they brought twenty-thousand soldiers and they were attacking a people who weren't expecting to be attacked."

"We've always known what the odds are," Rinka-ak said. "Some fights are worth fighting anyway."

Alex smiled at him, loving him for the boy he had once been and the man he had grown into.

"My original plan was to find the vulnerable outer edge of the Drakana Empire, conquer it, and use those people to reinforce our strength. Then, to go to the next spot with that larger army and hopefully defeat them and add them to our size."

"And we are succeeding," Versa-eh said. "Why abandon a plan that is working?"

"My plan to free the tribes of Kragdon-ah by challenging the Drakana to Thundan was working, too. Tinta-ak defeated their giant. I defeated their creature from hell."

Alex did not really need to finish that story. They all knew what had happened next.

"And when we lost the third challenge, all was lost until my great friends came and rescued me. Except this story is different. If we lose—if someone sinks this ship, or we lose a battle badly—there is no one to come and rescue us. We will have failed. And we won't have failed only ourselves. We will have failed every person in Kragdon-ah who we are fighting for."

"Why didn't you tell us this before?" Sanda asked.

Alex looked at the ceiling, then said, "Because it was the best plan we had. Because I always believe I will find a way to make these crazy plans work. And that's what I'm trying to do now—make this crazy plan work."

Harta-ak spoke up. "You are our leader, and we will always trust you. But I think we should put a time limit on looking for this magical place that may or may not exist. How long do you think it should take us to find it?"

"Sofina has no idea about distance or time. Perhaps a moon cycle?"

"Then I propose this—if we spend two moon cycles looking for this place and do not find it, we will return to our original plan. We will fight and do the best we can. Agreed?"

Alex looked from face to face. Some agreed, some thought that perhaps Harta-ak was being too generous in his timeframe. Still, it was Manta-ak.

They agreed to give Alex two cycles of the moon to find this magical land of ready-made resistance fighters.

"One last question, though," Harta-ak said. "If this young woman has never been there—if there are no visible landmarks—how is she going to help us find this place?"

In answer, Alex asked all the Kragdon-ah warriors to stand and face him. "Show me where the place of your birth is."

As one, every arm shot up and pointed over Alex's right shoulder.

"There you go. To the best of my knowledge, Sofina was not born in this place, but she tells me she can point to the direction it lies."

"How is that possible?" Amy asked.

"How is it possible that they all just did that?" Alex answered. "I don't know. Like you, I am trunti. We don't have that built in compass."

"I do," Sanda said. "I never realized it before. But when you asked, my hand involuntarily pointed in the same direction."

"A gift from your mother. You are not trunti," Alex said with a slightly sad smile. He looked around at his friends. "I do not understand any of it. One thing I have learned is that there are times that I just need to have faith. This is one of those times."

Chapter Twenty-Eight
Race Against the Moon Cycle

It made for an odd sight. At the top deck, when Harta-ak, Pictin, or Hawthorne were at the wheel, a young woman stood beside them. Once an hour or so, whoever was in charge of navigation at that moment would turn and ask her a question. She would unerringly indicate a compass point. Often, it was in a straight line ahead. But several times each day, she would point slightly to port or starboard and the pilot would make a slight adjustment.

That young woman—Sofina—didn't mind her long hours spent beside the wheel. She had never left the shores of Lakunadan before. Having the opportunity to stand atop the ship and feel the strong, salty breeze brought her only happiness.

And she had questions. One sunny afternoon, she noticed that her hair was blowing left to right, in a completely different direction than they were traveling. She stayed silent and thought about that for a long time, but could not solve the puzzle of how the wind blew in one direction and they moved in another.

Finally, she gave up. She tapped Hawthorne, who happened to be piloting the ship, on the shoulder and asked, "How does the wind blow across us, but we move forward?"

Hawthorne flashed his rakish grin. He enjoyed the company of all, it seemed, but was especially content in Sofina's presence.

"It seems like a mystery, doesn't it? I'll give you the same answer my grandfather gave me when I asked that same question as a boy. 'Little Duck,' he said, for that was my nickname, 'Little Duck, always remember this. It is not the wind, but the sail that determines the direction.' That was my first lesson, and now it is yours."

Sofina did not answer, but instead felt the wind against the side of her face and looked up at the great sails billowing above. A man stood on the deck under the mainsail, shouting orders and those above scrambled to carry them out. The shouting man was one of the Drakana sailors. The men and women above were from Winten-ah, and Rinta-ah. They had begun to work together as a team.

When everyone had agreed to give Alex two moon cycles to find this land he was looking for, he had hoped to find it within the week.

As it turned out, the moon waxed, waned, and began to wax again with no sight of land at all. Sofina pushed them unerringly west-southwest. The ship ran night and day, night and day, gobbling up the nautical miles as fast as the wind would carry them.

Alex filled the endless days by rotating the crews among the three ships and training different groups in different disciplines. Alex used a strategy he had developed before he fought his first battle against Denta-ah. He personally trained one group. Then he picked the best and most-receptive warriors and gave them additional, intensive training. They then became trainers.

He found that the former Drakana soldiers had been well-trained and had good discipline, but were too reliant on the superiority of their guns. They had become accustomed to people who had never seen such a weapon fleeing in fear at the idea that it could spit death from a distance. As Alex had shown them in Lakunadan, if an army was willing to run right into the teeth of those guns, they quickly became useless.

So Alex concentrated on teaching them other weapons that would be valuable in those situations. The Drakana guns were superior to distance weapons like spears or atlatls, so Alex didn't bother with them. He did show them the superiority of something as simple as a cudgel in hand-to-hand fighting.

As he had suspected, Grantan, the former Drakana he had made a lieutenant, caught on quickly and embraced the techniques. Other former Drakana did not accept them as easily.

One afternoon, Alex was standing on an upper deck watching Grantan train his charges. When Grantan brought the cudgel out, ripples of discontent spread through the ranks.

"We were part of the greatest fighting force the world has ever known," one man said. "Now we are fighting with clubs like someone who lives in caves?"

Alex hung back to see how Grantan would handle this objection.

"Yes, exactly. The men who wielded this weapon *did* live in caves. They also beat us in a fair fight with inferior weapons. What does that say?"

"I think it says that they caught us by surprise, and you are right that we need to learn to be a better fighter once our guns are made useless. But I'll take a sharp blade over a chunk of wood any day."

Alex vaulted over the railing and landed behind Grantan. "I'll take that bet."

The man who had spoken raised his hand, deflecting the idea. "I will not fight you, Manta-ak. If I were to hurt you, Grantan would punish me severely."

Alex held his hand out to Grantan, who tossed him the cudgel. Alex moved it a bit, getting the weight and feel of it. "I'll tell you what. Pick an ally. You two can pick whatever bladed weapons you want and I will only use the cudgel. Fight as hard as you can. If you manage to draw even a drop of my blood, I will give you each your own units to train and your own private quarters."

Grantan stepped back and made a slight bow toward Alex. Dugand, the man who had complained, looked at the man to his right. That man suddenly became interested in what was happening up in the sails.

"Come on, Parden. Don't be a coward. Two of us against him. I would like to have my own squad to train, wouldn't you?"

Parden seemed uninterested, but finally said, "I'll take that sword," pointing to a rack of weapons. He plucked the sword out and ran his finger along it. It was razor-sharp with a sharpened end.

Dugand selected two short knives from the rack and began twirling and tossing them in the air, catching them by the handle. It was obvious he was familiar with bladed weapons.

Alex looked up at the gathering crowd and spotted Tinta-ak, who was grinning in anticipation. "Hold onto Monda-ak. I don't want him jumping into the middle of this."

Tinta-ak put two fingers to his forehead in acknowledgement.

Alex turned his attention back to his two opponents. He held his cudgel loosely in his hand, weight balanced, ready for an attack.

"I guess we can—" Dugand interrupted himself by throwing one of the knives on a flat arc at Alex's midsection.

Alex had suspected an attack like that, but he was still nearly pierced. He managed to get the cudgel up to deflect the knife, which clattered to the deck.

"You move pretty fast for an older man," Dugand said, but it was not a compliment.

Alex did not react.

Dugand skittered around Alex and retrieved the knife. Parden hoped to catch Alex off-guard and swung his sword at his right side in a flat vicious arc. The effort he put behind the swing showed that he was not concerned about possibly decapitating Alex.

The blow was strong enough that if Alex had simply blocked the sword with the cudgel, it might have gone right through it or knocked it from his grasp. Instead, Alex surprised Parden by stepping toward him and, holding the cudgel in both hands, he struck up at his hands.

Parden howled. The sword dropped to the deck and Parden stepped back, flinging his injured hand around to get the sting out of it.

Alex didn't hesitate, but continued the attack. Still holding the cudgel in both hands, he let his grip slip down a bit and jabbed it into the center of Parden's face. Parden tried to duck out of the way, but wasn't fast enough. The cudgel smashed into his nose and he sprawled backward, tripping and going right over the deck. A short scream was punctuated with a splash as he hit the water.

Alex paid him no mind. He was sure Dugand would choose the moment to attack. He whirled around and saw that Dugand was indeed closing on him. He whipped the knives around in tight, concentric circles, making it difficult for Alex to find an opening. Alex turned sideways to Dugand and leaned slightly back from the whizzing blades.

Dugand feinted left, then attacked with the blade in his right hand.

Alex ignored the initial feint, then ducked under the true attack. At the same moment, he swung the cudgel viciously at Dugand's left thigh. It connected with a meaty smack and Dugand went down like a corpse cut from a limb.

Alex did not press his attack, but backed off, bouncing lightly on his feet.

Dugand muttered something under his breath, but it was in a language Alex did not understand.

"Do you yield?"

"Of course not. I still have two knives and you have that stupid piece of wood."

"True enough. But I have two legs and you have only one."

The man waved Alex away and managed to pull himself onto his right leg. Alex waited patiently.

Dugand took a single step forward. His damaged left leg would not support his weight and he pitched forward on the deck, slamming his face into the wood. In doing so, he dropped both knives.

Alex slapped at them with his cudgel, sending them whirling across the deck. He looked up and winked at Tinta-ak, who was now laughing uproariously.

"You'll be all right in a few days," Alex said to Dugan. "Then we will begin again with cudgel lessons." He looked up to see who was at the wheel and saw it was Hawthorne.

"Ahoy, Pilot," Alex said in English. "We'll need to circle back. We've got one in the water."

"It will be easier if I flag down one of the other vessels and have them pick him up. They're a lot more nimble than we are."

Alex waved his approval at him. Hawthorne had a sailor send a message to the smallest of the two ships to pull alongside. He shouted orders over his head to cut the sail and slow the ship while they waited for the smaller vessel to retrieve the man bobbing in their wake.

Five minutes later, *The Senta-eh* had slowed to a crawl and the smaller vessel had turned back to rescue Parden.

While they waited for the smaller ship to catch back up, Hawthorne scanned the horizon. With a start, he saw something that should not be there. It was not land. It looked like it might be a tall sail.

He shouted at a man to climb to the crow's nest and report back.

The young man scrambled up and from his superior height, called out, "Ship on the horizon!"

Alex hurried to Hawthorne's side. "No way to know who it is, is there?"

"Not at this distance. But I can't think of any circumstance in which seeing another ship can be good."

"Can we outrun them?"

Harta-ak, who had been asleep below decks, had hurried up in time to hear the call from the crow's nest. He peered out toward the horizon and muttered a long-forgotten Lasta-ah curse word.

Hawthorne, meanwhile, took a number of things into account before answering. He looked at the direction of the wind, the direction the ship was approaching, and the fact that *The Senta-eh* had just cut the sails and slowed to a crawl.

He looked at Alex and said, "We can keep ahead of them for a time, but even if we abandon our course, they will catch us eventually."

"Do it," Alex said. "Keep us together as much as possible, but find as much speed as you can."

"Will do," Hawthorne said, then looked at Harta-ak. "Captain, do you want to take over?"

"It's your shift, it's your ship, Pilot."

Hawthorne barked orders and turned the ship sharply to the north, trying to find the best use of the wind.

A sailing ship chase is an odd thing. Distances can be closed and a hunter can run the hunted down eventually, but it is a chase in slow motion.

The three pilots—Hawthorne, Pictin, and Harta-ak—ran with the wind, but the other ship slowly, inexorably closed on them.

By the time darkness fell that night, anyone standing on the bridge could make out the details of their pursuer. In the fading darkness, everyone passed the lone spyglass they had around so they could see in greater detail.

It was obvious that the ship was somewhat smaller than *The Senta-eh*, but it was definitely faster. More worrisome to Alex and Harta-ak was that the same flag flew as the false flag they sailed under.

"What are the chances they are not Drakana either?" Alex asked.

"It's possibly a pirate vessel," Hawthorne agreed. "But it is not likely. I believe it is more likely they have been looking for us."

"Why?" Tinta-ak asked.

"Because we know a vessel left Lakunadan carrying word of our arrival with bad intentions," Hawthorne explained. "If the Drakana had any warships in the area, I think they would have crisscrossed the ocean looking for us."

"Is that what that is, then? A warship?" Alex asked.

Hawthorne handed him the spyglass. "Focus on the side of the ship when it turns toward us. What do you see?"

"Cannons," Alex answered. "One, two, three, four. Four cannons."

"We have a few cannons too, as you know, but given your Kragdon-ah tendency to not use guns, I'm not sure how much good that will do us," Hawthorne said.

"Even if we do decide to use them, we only have a few men on board who have ever fired a cannon. I think if it comes to a sea battle, we're in trouble."

Harta-ak ended the speculation with the great Kragdon-ah truism.

"The world is the world," he said. "Let's see what the morning brings."

No one slept well that night, knowing an enemy was closing in.

As the sky lightened in the pre-dawn hours, everyone lined up and had a look at their pursuers close up.

The spyglass was no longer necessary.

"I can see which ones shaved this morning," Alex observed. He didn't mention that they all wore Drakana uniforms and carried guns.

"They're turning away," Hart-ak said, watching the path of the Drakana ship carefully.

"That should make me feel better, but it doesn't," Alex said.

"They're going after our other ships."

"Who is captaining those ships?" Alex asked.

"Fredon and Handan," Harta-ak answered.

"Drakana soldiers," Hawthorne said. "We could be outnumbered three to one here, and they all know how to use their firepower."

"*Former* Drakana soldiers," Alex said hopefully. "Now they are soldiers and sailors of Kragdon-ah."

From over their heads, the lookout in the crow's nest shouted. "Land! Land ahead!"

"There!" Alex said, pointing at a thin line of green that appeared on the horizon at that moment. "Head for that! If we're going to be in a sea battle, I'd rather be close to land."

The Senta-eh adjusted her course to aim directly at the land slowly showing on the horizon.

The Drakana ship aimed toward one of the two ships they had claimed in Lakunadan. The enemy ship was faster than *The Senta-eh*, but the smaller Kragdon-ah vessel was nearly its match.

Alex went to the railing and watched both the chase and the approaching land.

"They're leading them away from us!" Alex said.

"That's one way of looking at it," Hawthorne observed. "Or they could be just running away."

For a few more minutes, both the two smaller Kragdon-ah ships and their pursuers grew smaller, while the land mass ahead grew larger.

Then the captain of the Drakana ship made a decision. He turned his ship back toward *The Senta-eh*. He had either come to the conclusion he couldn't catch them, or believed he had scared them away.

The Drakana ship took an angle toward the land mass, looking like it would intercept *The Senta-eh*.

"What do you say, Manta-ak?" Harta-ak asked. "Turn back toward open sea or continue our course for land."

"Running for open water will only delay the inevitable. Hold our course," Alex said.

Harta-ak, Pictin, and Hawthorne worked together, plotting the best angle, setting the sails for maximum speed.

None of it mattered. Within thirty minutes, the Drakana ship had closed and was once again within firing range.

"They're not signaling, asking us to slow or stop. I think they just mean to take us," Hawthorne said. "I've been here before."

The Drakana vessel pulled alongside *The Senta-eh*. Men stood stationed behind each of the four cannons. Behind them, another man gave a command that carried across the distance between them.

Four men lit four fuses.

Alex and everyone else on *The Senta-eh* waited helplessly.

Chapter Twenty-Nine
Cannonballs Fly

Four cannons boomed, the recoil pushing them back onto the deck. Four cannonballs flew through the air.

Four cannonballs crashed into *The Senta-eh.*

They hit with an impact that shuddered the ship. One shot had sailed high and hit the mainsail mast, splintering it fifty feet above the deck. It tilted dangerously and sails covered several decks.

Alex rushed to the side to see how badly the other shots had damaged them, but from that vantage point could not see. He didn't have time to worry about it anyway. After firing their initial volley, the Drakana ship had pulled alongside and seemed intent on boarding them.

"To arms!" Hawthorne yelled as chaos erupted on *The Senta-eh.*

The Drakana ship heaved alongside *The Senta-eh* and men stood by with large hooks attached to thick ropes.

"They're boarding us!" Harta-ak shouted.

"They will live to regret that, if they live at all," Alex said. "Torana, where are you?"

An instant later, Torana was by his side as though he had only been waiting to be summoned. "Amy!"

"Here," she said from behind him.

"When they have attached themselves to us, I want Torana to take our thickest rope and tie the two ships together. Can you tell him that?"

"Dad, you're speaking Drakana. He can understand. You just told him yourself."

She and Torana walked toward the pile of the thickest ship's rope, which was as big as a normal man's bicep. Torana lifted the pile effortlessly, slung it over his shoulder and walked to the port side.

The grappling hooks attached and the two boats were pulled together. Drakana soldiers climbed into a tall position on their masts and fired indiscriminately at whoever was on *The Senta-eh*.

"Amy, tell Torana now!"

She and the giant went to work.

Alex found Tinta-ak. "Before they can board us, I want to board them. Take as many men as you can and jump on their ship. Kill them or throw them overboard, I don't care."

Tinta-ak yelled, "To me!" and men ran to him. Tinta-ak led the charge of the men—made up of men from many different Kragdon-ah tribes, former Drakana soldiers, and a few Lakunadan warriors—right into the teeth of the guns.

Tinta-ak was the first casualty. He was hit twice by gunfire and crumpled to the deck of *The Senta-eh*. Undeterred, the men leaped over and around him and jumped onto the Drakana ship.

Alex rushed to Tinta-ak and attempted to pull him out of the battle that raged around him. He was too heavy. "Amy! Torana!"

The giant had just winched the two ships together with the heavy rope.

"Help me move him to safety!" Alex reached under one of Tinta-ak's bloody shoulders, but Torana gently pushed him away. The giant knelt and scooped Tinta-ak—the second largest member of the Kragdon-ah army—in his arms like a child. Once, the two men had met as enemies. Now, Torana followed Amy below decks with the limp body of Tinta-ak.

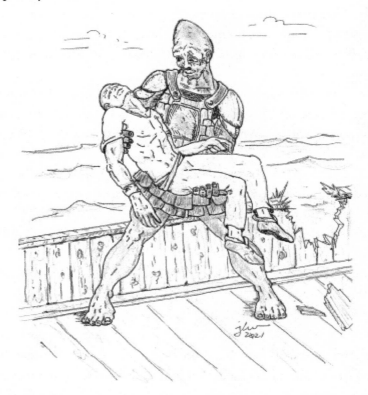

ALEX LONGED TO JOIN the battle that was taking place where the two decks were lashed together, but he couldn't just go past those who had been wounded by the initial volley of gunfire. He moved from person to person, doing instantaneous triage—moving those who were badly wounded behind a wall or into a passageway, then helping those who could still walk below decks.

When he came back onto the main deck, movement in the ropes that dangled from the masts caught his eye. He looked up to see that Nanda-eh, Sanda, and the other archers had climbed up to get a better vantage point. Once they were high, they found a way to brace themselves and nocked their arrows.

The battle was a mass of confusion below them, so they didn't fire quickly. Instead, they picked their target, aimed carefully, and let fly. After two rounds of arrows flying toward the Drakana vessel, Alex realized there were no more gunshots. There was still the sound of scuffles and the ringing of blades on blades, but the echoing gunfire had ceased.

Alex ran to the spot where the two ships had been lashed together to get a view of the battle, but as he reached that spot, *The Senta-eh* groaned, timbers smashed against each other and the ship tilted wildly to the port side.

The Drakana ship was half as big as *The Senta-eh* and was now lashed to it tightly. When *The Senta-eh* tilted so strongly, it took that ship with it for the ride.

Alex had a hard time just holding his balance on the shifting deck.

He saw Harta-ak and Hawthorne above and shouted, "What do we do?"

They leaped over the railing and ran to Alex just as he lost his footing. It was only Harta-ak's quick reflexes that allowed him to grab Alex and pull him back on board. Hawthorne, meanwhile, wrapped one arm around a deck railing and the other around Harta-ak.

"I've been on ships that have sunk before," Hawthorne said. "One of their cannons fired a mortal blow and I believe we are going down."

Alex wanted to shout, 'No!' but he knew that denying the inevitable only wasted valuable time.

"Let's throw everything that will float overboard, then. We've got injured and people who cannot swim. We need things for them to hold onto. Let's get everyone up from below decks, too, or they will be trapped there."

The three men scattered, telling men to throw barrels, doors ripped off their hinges, empty boxes, and anything else that might float overboard. Alex found Amy and Sanda and told them they were likely sinking. "Get in the water now and help people who cannot swim stay afloat as much as you can."

The Senta-eh took another lurch to the port side, partially capsizing the Drakana ship as she did.

"Hurry! Go!"

Amy and Sanda did not hesitate. With their weapons bouncing on their backs—the bow and arrows for Sanda, the katana for Amy—they ran uphill to the railing on the starboard side. They climbed up and cut neat dives down into the water and immediately began searching for people who were struggling.

People poured out of the doors and passageways. Many were dripping wet already, which showed how damaged the ship was.

Alex stood on the main deck directing traffic, telling everyone to get overboard. "If you can swim, find those who can't and help them. Find debris and help them to it!"

Torana emerged from below decks, once again carrying Tinta-ak. Alex's heart sank. Under the best of circumstances, Tinta-ak was not a great swimmer and Torana was no better. Being shipwrecked miles from the nearest land was not the best of circumstances and Alex was afraid he would lose them both.

Torana laid Tinta-ak gently on the deck and cast his eyes around, looking for something. A huge chunk of a mast had splintered off when the cannonball hit it. Torana tried to lift it, but for a moment he only strained, and Alex thought it was too big even for him. Torana screwed up his face in concentration, got his huge hands under the wood and lifted again. The size of it staggered him, but he took three fast steps to the side, peered over, then tossed the wood into the water.

He picked Tinta-ak up once again, stepped over the railing, and disappeared over the side.

Alex rushed to where Torana had disappeared and saw that the huge piece of the mast was bobbing in the water. Torana had one arm wrapped around it and the other around Tinta-ak.

Alex abandoned them to their fates and hurried through the ship, looking for stragglers below decks and helping them up and over the side.

The Senta-eh heaved to the port once again and with sickening certainty, Alex knew the end was near.

He looked every direction and saw only Pictin, Hawthorne, and Harta-ak.

"Come on," Alex said. "We're not going down with the ship! Overboard with all of us."

A moment later, the three pilots had jumped overboard and Alex found that he and Monda-ak were momentarily alone on the tilting, tossing deck. He looked around at the chaos that had been an organized ship only a few hours earlier. Now all order was gone.

As was Alex's grand plan to invade Drakana.

Still, he had lives he was responsible for, including the four-legged one standing beside him, looking at him with the same trusting expression as always.

Alex laid a hand on Monda-ak's neck and said, "Come on, time for the next adventure."

They leaped from the deck into the cold water.

Chapter Thirty
Adrift

If this had been a movie, *The Senta-eh* would have dramatically gone down at the same moment that Alex and Monda-ak leaped into the water.

Instead, the ship simply floated where it was for another long minute, then the pressure it exerted on the Drakana ship finally caused Torana's knots and the grappling hooks to release. The Drakana ship bobbed away, though Alex thought it was likely there was no one left alive on board.

As soon as *The Senta-eh* broke free of the Drakana ship, it foundered. It flopped all the way over to the port side and one of its remaining masts slammed into the Drakana ship, damaging it further.

Alex found a piece of floating timber and helped Monda-ak get his front paws on it so he could float without expending all his energy. Then he began to swim from person to person, looking for those who were slipping beneath the waves. He knew it was inevitable that he wouldn't be able to save everyone, but he moved as quickly as he could.

His first thought was to get people stable in the water and then claim the Drakana ship as their own. It likely wouldn't be comfortable to have so many of them on board, but it was infinitely better than bobbing like corks in the ocean.

Then he saw the first plumes of black and gray smoke coming from the Drakana ship. Moments later, an explosion rocked the ship and Alex knew that if anyone *had* been alive on board, they no longer were. Less than a minute later, a second and third explosion boomed as the flames found the stores of gunpowder and other weaponry and the whole ship above the waterline began to burn.

Alex knew that the death of the ship was also the likely death knell for many of his army. He lifted his head and found the dark outline of the land mass they had been hurtling toward when they were caught by the Drakana. It was difficult to estimate distances while bobbing in the water, but when they had been attacked, he thought they were only a mile or two away.

There was nothing to do but swim for it.

Alex found a barrel bobbing in front of him that was currently unoccupied. He grabbed it and did his best to pull himself up out of the water. He pitched his voice to carry as far as it would.

"Anyone who can swim, head for land. I think you can make it. If you can't swim, call for help or hold on to something that is floating. We will find a way to get you there."

Harta-ak and Versa-eh swam smoothly up beside Alex. "We will stay here and help you with those who are injured or cannot swim."

"Me too," Sanda and Amy said together.

Alex turned to his daughters. "Go with the swimmers. When you get to the land, gather some wood. We'll need to build a fire to keep warm through the night."

Soon, a flock of humans were swimming for the shore as if they were migrating. Amy and Sanda did their best to keep the group together and encouraged anyone who fell behind. It was soon obvious that they would not be able to swim straight to land. Amy swam in front of the pack and showed everyone how to do the dead man's float, which allowed them to rest for a bit before they swam again. She soon had the group coordinated—swim, float, swim, float.

Meanwhile, Alex tried to get a count of how many were still with him, holding on to whatever floated. "If you've got something good that will keep you afloat, hold on and kick toward the shore. It will be slow going, but you will make it before the sun sets."

Alex didn't want to state the obvious: *we really don't want all of us floating in the ocean in the middle of the night.* He remembered how dangerous the waters of the Okrent River had been the last time he had been shipwrecked. He didn't think that the ocean would be any safer.

Alex estimated that he had perhaps a quarter of his army around him. Two hundred or so human lives he was responsible for who were too wounded to swim or simply didn't know how.

Behind him, Versa-eh's voice cried out. "Manta-ak! Look!"

Alex turned and saw a beautiful sight—one of the two boats they had commandeered in Lakunadan was sailing toward them. Alex waved his arms to attract their attention then realized how ridiculous that was—they were sailing toward the burning Drakana ship—a far superior attractant.

The ship didn't appear to be too far away, but now that a possible rescue was at hand, its progress seemed slow. Alex swam from one small group to another, encouraging everyone to hold on.

Eventually, the boat approached, cutting speed before it reached them so it essentially drifted into the debris and survivors.

Fredon, the Drakana who had been piloting the smallest vessel when they were attacked, leaned overboard. "We'll pick you up!"

"We need to be smart about it," Alex said. "We need to put the most-injured on board with you. You're not going to have room for us all. Have you got any netting you can throw over the side to help people climb up?"

Fredon disappeared for a moment, then he and two other men draped a strong net over the side. Alex climbed halfway up and called to Harta-ak. "Come up here with me. Versa-eh, can you guide people over and we will lift them onto the boat?"

Those who could maneuver moved toward the boat, including Torana. The giant could not swim, but he clung to the mast he had thrown overboard for he and Tinta-ak.

In Drakana, Alex told Torana what to do.

Torana put Tinta-ak over one shoulder and reached for the net with the other.

Alex hadn't been sure if he and Harta-ak together could lift someone as large as Tinta-ak up the net, but Torana scrambled right up with him flung over his shoulder. Once on board, he leaned back over and looked at Alex. He made a shooing gesture with his hand.

Even amidst this complete disaster, Alex couldn't help chuckling a little bit. He dropped down into the water with a splash and Torana swung his leg over the railing and positioned himself halfway down the netting.

One by one, Alex brought the most-wounded people to the small ship. Harta-ak reached down and lifted them high enough for Torana to grab them. The giant then lifted them over his head to the men waiting for them above. It was a prodigious display of strength, but nothing Torana did surprised Alex any more.

Soon, Alex had all the wounded he could find on board the ship.

Fredon leaned over and shouted at him. "We're almost full. We can fit maybe two or three more, including the giant."

Alex thought about that. He knew Torana would be helpful in unloading the wounded at the beach. He cast around and picked out two others who were not badly wounded, but were flagging from trying to stay afloat.

"Room for one more giant dog?" Alex queried.

A pause, then Fredon answered, "We'll make room for Monda-ak."

Alex helped Monda-ak start up the netting, until Torana reached down, grabbed him by the scruff of his neck and lifted him onto the deck. One more in a series of things Alex had never expected to see when he woke up that day.

"Take these to shore, then come back for the rest of us," Alex called.

Fredon disappeared from view and a minute later the sails raised and the ship moved toward shore.

Alex watched it disappear and wished it Godspeed. He didn't know how long he would be able to keep everyone afloat in his small armada of hangers-on.

The shipwrecked members of *The Senta-eh* were now split into four groups. The swimmers were making progress in reaching shore. The group who had something to hold onto and could kick and move were moving, but much more slowly. The wounded on board Fredon's ship had it easiest, but were in the worst shape.

And then there were Alex and his charges. When Fredon's boat disappeared, Alex counted the heads around him. He came up with twenty-nine, including himself, Harta-ak, and Versa-eh.

He swam from person to person, offering encouragement and helping them adjust their grip on whatever piece of flotsam they clung to.

As he waited for Fredon to return with the boat, he did another count. Twenty-seven.

Alex swam in a hurried circle, looking for any head that had slipped under the waves. He could not find anyone.

He counted again. Twenty-six.

"If you are too tired to hold on any more, call me and I will help you! Don't just let go!"

After what felt like hours—and the sun was low in the sky—he saw Fredon returning.

Alex counted again and found only twenty-three people. At that moment, he felt a tingling in his feet, knowing how exposed he was.

When the ship pulled up alongside, Alex was thrilled to see that Torana had returned to complete the rescue mission. He had done his best to keep everyone in one location, which made it easier to get them all up onto the boat.

Torana, Harta-ak, and Versa-eh formed a line and lifted the exhausted Drakana and Kragdon-ah people up and onto the boat. Alex heard a huge woof and saw Monda-ak's head appear over the side. He had no doubt insisted on returning for Alex, and who was going to tell him no?

As the last person was lifted up, Alex reached for a hold of his own on the netting.

If not a final answer, he got a substantial clue how people had gone missing over the past few hours. A slick gray tentacle grasped his ankle and pulled on it. Not a gentle tug, but a *come sleep in the deep with me* pull.

Alex shook his leg to loosen the grip, but that had no effect.

He looked up and said, "Something's got me. Pulling me back in." Harta-ak leaned over the side and grasped Alex's outstretched hand, pulling up strongly. That lifted Alex mostly out of the water, but did nothing to loosen the grasp of the tentacle.

"It won't let go," Alex said, calm, but beginning to feel some sense of inevitability in the grip.

The tentacle wrapped around his foot pulled him down and Harta-ak's grip loosened, no matter how he strained to hold on.

Torana climbed over the side and down the netting. He dangled his own legs in the water and lifted Alex up. The tentacle moved with Alex, but would not let him go.

Torana looked up at the boat and held a massive hand out for help. He made a wordless sound of frustration—the first sound Alex had ever heard come from him.

It was Harta-ak who knew what he wanted. "Throw him a sword!"

Fredon leaned overboard and dangled a sword to Torana. At least, it looked like a sword when Fredon held it. In Torana's hands, it looked like a long knife.

No matter. The giant wrapped his hand all the way around the handle and hacked down at the water below Alex's leg again and again.

Alex closed his eyes and attempted to remain very still, but was not confident he would still have a foot when Torana was done.

Finally, Alex felt the pressure ease on his leg. Harta-ak was suddenly free to lift him up onto the deck.

As soon as his feet hit the deck, Alex turned back over the side to help Harta-ak and Torana up out of the water. He got Harta-ak up, but by the time he reached out to Torana, two more tentacles had emerged from the water. One wrapped around his leg and another around his waist.

Alex looked desperately around for another weapon to join the battle, but could not find anything.

Torana once again swung the sword in mighty arcs, hacking at the gray tentacles around him. In a moment, he cut clean through them and was free. He scrambled up onto the deck with surprising agility. Being nearly eaten by a giant squid will light a fire under you.

For the first time since they had spotted the Drakana ship alongside them, Alex felt like he could breathe.

"Let's get to shore. I've got to see what we're up against now."

Chapter Thirty-One
Stranded

T he land they had seen had been just an obscure dark blob on the horizon at the time.

It soon became something more—their possible salvation.

As Fredon steered the ship toward land, Alex was pleased to see that they were not passing any of the swimmers. Even those who were just pushing debris to the island had either made it or had met a watery end at the end of a tentacle.

Alex was most concerned about those who were injured and how they would care for them, but that was a problem he would deal with when they reached the beach. That freed him up to study the land mass ahead.

Approaching from this angle, it was impossible to tell what type of land it was. It could have been a small island, a part of a chain of islands that led to a large land mass, or a peninsula of some sort.

The first thing Alex noted was the steep, sharp cliffs that ran along almost all of the outer edge of the land. Those cliffs sprang up at such a sharp angle that he doubted even the Winten-ah, long renowned as great climbers, would be able to easily get to the top.

The beach—which was a very nice name for what was, in reality, a little sandy spit—was formed where three of these cliffs dropped down to the ocean. The only way to get to the beach was from the sea, which should protect them from predators. It also would make finding food very difficult unless they could pull it from the ocean.

He recalled the horrible little island he had been stranded on decades before, and the poor food pickings that were there.

"We didn't survive that and getting sunk today just to starve to death here," Alex said.

"What's that?" Harta-ak said, and Alex realized he had spoken in English.

"Nothing," Alex said, then returned to the problem at hand.

"Is there a smaller transport boat on this ship?" Alex asked, and realized he should have made himself more familiar with what they had seized in Lakunadan.

"No boat," Fredon answered. "We are too small."

"How many cabins do you have? How many can you sleep?"

"Ten cabins. Two bunks in each cabin, and the captain's quarters. There is a larger bed in there that could hold three or four if they know each other well."

"We're going to convert this ship into our floating hospital," Alex decided. "This will give us the best chance to heal our wounded and give them rest. Everyone else will sleep on the beach. Do you have a flint?"

Fredon reached into his pocket and tossed a flint to Alex.

"What about supplies?"

"We were well stocked when we left Lakunadan, but that was a long time ago. Our storeroom is not empty, but," he looked pointedly at the beach, "we might have enough to feed everyone one or two meals, then that will be it."

"Fishing equipment?"

"Yes," Fredon said. "If the fish are catchable here."

Alex sighed.

So many problems, so few tools to solve them.

"One thing," Fredon said. "It is a good idea to use this ship to house the injured. But we will need to keep at least a few sailors on board. You won't want to have a ship of just healers and patients."

Alex put two fingers to his forehead in acknowledgement, then remembered that the Drakana did not use that gesture.

The ship came within fifty yards of the shore when Fredon said, "We'll drop anchor here. If we get much closer, I'm afraid we'll run aground."

Harta-ak and Alex helped Fredon lower the anchor, which was much smaller than the one on *The Senta-eh*.

Alex called to Monda-ak and the two of them jumped into the water. Alex was surprised to find that the water was only chest deep for him. If Monda-ak raised his snout a bit, he could stand on the rocky bottom and still breathe.

With Harta-ak, Versa-eh and the others right behind him, Alex and Monda-ak hurried to the shore. The beach seemed even smaller once he was standing on it.

Still, it was dry, and Amy and Sanda had done as he had asked. There was a big pile of wood in the sand. Alex threw Sanda the flint and said, "Let's get a big fire going. We're all wet and exhausted and I don't know how cold it's going to be overnight."

He tended to Tinta-ak first, as he had been the worst injured. At least, the worst of those still breathing.

Tinta-ak was conscious now, but he didn't seem at all focused. Instead, he shivered and tossed his huge bald head back and forth as if in the grasp of a nightmare.

Antan-ak, the Rinta-ah healer, had done his best to tend to Tinta-ak's wounds. He was not used to dealing with the destruction a bullet wound can bring, but he had removed the lead from the wounds and done the best he could under terrible conditions.

When Alex took him aside, Antan-ak said honestly, "I do not know if he will live. We will know more by morning. If he is still alive then, it will be a good sign."

"I could say the same for any of us," Alex observed, but then asked, "Will it hurt him if I move him? I think we can make him more comfortable out on the ship."

'It would be better if he didn't go into the water again. I will have to rebandage his wounds if he does."

Alex looked closer at the bandages and saw that they weren't really bandages at all. They were strips of cloth Antan-ak had torn off his own clothes.

"If you have to rebandage his wounds, you might be naked," Alex said.

"So be it," the old man said.

"I think I've got a better idea. Amy?"

Amy hurried to her father's side.

"Can you ask Torana to carry Tinta-ak out to the boat without getting him wet?"

Amy looked at her father like he was losing it. "Tell him yourself."

"Right, right," Alex said. He turned to Torana and relayed the message again, this time in Drakana.

Torana did not reply, but scooped Tinta-ak up and carried him gently into the waves. Where the water had come up to Alex's chest beside the boat, it barely reached above Torana's waist.

One by one, Torana became the ambulance that safely carried the wounded to the ship. His last trip, he also carried Antan-ak, much to the old healer's delight.

With the wounded momentarily taken care of and a fire crackling in the firepit, Alex let himself relax a little. When he did, he realized he was so exhausted he could barely stand. When his adrenaline was on full tilt, he could still pretend he was the Alex Hawk of old. Without it, he felt beyond mortal.

Amy noticed her father wavering and led him to the fire. "Here. Lay your head down for just a few minutes. I will set the guard rotations."

Alex opened his mouth to say something, but Amy put a finger to his lips. "I will post guards along the cliffs in case something comes down, and at the water's edge in case something comes up from the deep. Leave it to me. Rest."

Alex smiled and truly let go, knowing Amy had the situation in hand. He closed his eyes and fell into a deep sleep immediately.

While he slept, Amy, Sanda, Harta-ak, Versa-eh, and Rinka-ak organized scavenger groups to grab the residue of *The Senta-eh* and haul it up onto the beach. They salvaged everything—boxes, timbers, pots—anything that might be useful.

As soon as darkness fell, rain began to fall. At first, it was a gentle rain.

Amy ordered more wood on the fire and as the rain increased, it hissed and sizzled as it met the flames.

That polite rain was just the introduction.

The drops turned huge, heavy, and pounding.

The bonfire continued to sizzle, but as the skies opened more, it was obvious it could not continue to burn.

The rain was hard enough that it woke Alex from even his deep slumber. He sat up, blinked the water from his eyes and looked momentarily lost. In his dream, he had been camping out, but it had been in Oregon, and Amy and Sanda were just little girls.

The full-grown version of his daughters knelt beside him and Sanda shouted over the pounding rain. "The fire has gone out. There's no shelter."

"Then the best we can do," Alex said, "is collect the rain water. We'll need fresh water if we can't reach any. Take anything that will hold water and put it face up."

"What else can we do?" Amy said.

Alex shrugged. "Nothing. Our wounded are protected on the ship. For the rest of us, we will just have to survive the night."

Chapter Thirty-Two
Extremes

I t was a long, miserable night.

Alex would have sworn it was impossible for it to rain any harder than it was when he woke up.

He was wrong.

The rain hammered down on them so hard that each of the castaways looked for anything they could put over their heads. Not to stay dry—there was no chance of that—but to stop the relentless pounding of raindrops on their skulls.

There was no shelter of any kind on the small beach. With no fire, hundreds of people huddled together in their shared misery.

Alex began to think it was possible they had been flung through another door—one which led to an endless night that stretched for years.

As quickly as it began, the rain slackened, then disappeared entirely. The clouds, which had blocked out the starfield, moved away and bright spots of light appeared.

The sky lightened in the east and as soon as the sun peered over the horizon, temperatures soared.

They were in the tropics, but Alex had still been worried about hypothermia overnight.

There was a brief period of time when all welcomed the rising temperatures. People stripped off their wet clothes and laid them out on the sand to dry.

The semi-eternity of the horrible night soon faded and people began to joke about it. They were a resilient bunch.

As the sun rose in the sky, the temperature climbed to quickly become unbearably hot. Steam rose everywhere on the beach as the sun quick-dried their clothes, the debris, and the unburned wood in the firepit.

Amy found Alex and said, "Does it seem awfully hot to you? Like, hotter than anything we ever felt when we were on the ocean?"

"It's not your imagination. At least during the day, we can go in the water to escape the heat."

"As long as those aren't waiting for us," Amy said, pointing to Alex's left leg. The skin on the leg was still red and puffy where the squid's tentacle had wrapped around it.

"Good point. If it's this hot early in the morning, imagine what it's going to be like by mid-afternoon."

"I don't think anyone got any sleep last night," Amy said. "Maybe we can all take a siesta this afternoon to get through it."

"Just make sure your guards are alert and rotating out," Alex answered. "I'm going out to the boat to check on our wounded."

Alex and Monda-ak splashed out into the water, but Alex turned to the dog and said, "You should wait for me here. I won't be long. I don't want to have to lift you up onto the boat again."

Monda-ak had a wide array of expressions, which ranged from "I'm hungry," to "I'm a little sleepy," to "I'm going to eat that man's head." At this moment, he found his best, "I'm hurt, but that's fine" expression and with as much dignity as he could muster, turned back to the beach.

Amy's mention of the squid that had grabbed him the day before made Alex a little more cautious as he made his way to the boat.

"I should have learned more about squids when I had the chance," he muttered to himself. "But I suppose that's true of a lot of things."

He boarded the ship and found Antan-ak tending to the least-wounded, who had been exposed to the same rain as those on the beach. Those who were worse off were below deck in the cabins.

Alex looked at Antan-ak and could tell that he'd had the same amount of sleep as everyone else, which is to say none. There were bags under his eyes and his eyelids drooped heavily.

Alex put his hand on his shoulder and said, "You need to get some rest, too. You won't be able to help anyone if you drop from exhaustion."

"We lost two more in the night. I did what I could." He pointed to a small piece of canvas on the deck, which looked suspiciously like two bodies.

"Tinta-ak?" Alex asked, dreading the answer.

Behind him, a deep voice rumbled, "You will not get rid of me so easily."

Alex whirled around and there was Tinta-ak. He did not look well, but he was actually standing mostly upright.

"I knew you were too tough to let a few bullets take you down!" Alex nearly shouted. He wanted to run and hug his friend, but held back.

"He has the recuperation of an alecs-ta," Antan-ak said, referring to the donkey-like creature the Kragdon-ah used as pack animals.

Tinta-ak took that as a compliment. "Give me another day and I will be ready to take on those cursed fools who attacked us."

"No need for that," Alex said. "They're all dead."

"Lucky for them," Tinta-ak said and Alex could see a little of the big man's own vitality already starting to return.

"I will send Torana out to retrieve the bodies of those who died in the night and we will find a place to bury them on the island." Alex turned and looked for Fredon. "Did you get hit with a hard rain in the night?"

"Long and hard," Fredon agreed. "I thought those of you on the beach might need something, or I would have tried to outrun it."

"I'd say that would be good," Alex said thoughtfully. "No reason for you to get battered like we did. If we get another storm like that, go ahead and try. For now, I have a different job for you."

"What do you need?"

"I'd like to know what kind of land we've washed up onto. Why don't you take the ship and sail around. See what the lay of the land is."

"I will need a few more sailors if we want to make good time."

"I'll send a few out with Torana when he comes to retrieve the bodies."

"I'm going to come with you," Tinta-ak said. "I'm no longer wounded."

"The blood seeping through your bandages tells a different story," Alex said. "Stay here on the boat for another day. There is nothing to do on the beach anyway."

Alex jumped overboard and swam toward shore until the water was too shallow to swim in.

People by the hundreds were lying in the shallows—the best way to escape the sweltering heat, but still stay relatively safe from whatever ocean predators were around.

Alex looked up at the cliffs in the heat of the day and decided again that they were too steep, with uncertain handholds, to be climbable. He found Amy and had her dispatch Torana to the boat to retrieve the bodies of those who died overnight. He found four people and told them to start digging the graves as close to the cliffs as they could, but to switch out with others. The blazing sun was too hot for any one person to do too much.

Just like that, Alex ran out of things to do. He had been moving, keeping busy, since *The Senta-eh* had sunk. With nothing to occupy his mind, the true desperation of their situation sank in.

Alex moved off to be as by himself as he could be on the crowded beach. He put his back against a cliff and let things sink in.

We are lost. Shipwrecked in a remote area where no one will know to look for us. We have no food and will only be able to stay here for a few weeks before we start succumbing to the terrible heat, the even worse rain, and the lack of food.

He plucked a long blade of grass out of the soil and unconsciously put it in his mouth, just as he had done as a child lying on his back in the fields of Central Oregon.

And my idea to take the fight to the Drakana? That's over. I've lost too many warriors and my plan to fight my way up the chain to Drakana is a non-starter.

He let his mind drift back to Winten-ah, which looked like paradise to his mind at that moment. He could picture Sekun-ak and the remaining members of the tribe going about their business—hunting, planting, telling stories around the fire at night. He was suddenly very homesick for his unlikely home.

What have I done? Taken these people away from their homes with a promise of a victory we will never be able to see. They will die on foreign soil without ever seeing home again and it is because of me.

Amy and Sanda came and sat down on either side of Alex. They didn't speak, but they both laid their head on his shoulder.

That simple connection with his daughters stilled his racing thoughts and he drifted off in the baking heat.

Hours later, he was awakened by a shout of "Fredon has returned!"

Alex stood up, stiff and sore from falling asleep in an uncomfortable position and limped out toward the water. The first thing he noticed was that three people were standing in water up to their waist, fishing. The second was that there was a long stick jammed into the sand in the water. He looked more closely and saw that there were fish on a piece of rope attached to it.

He heard a banging sound to his left and saw that a team of men had found rocks and were beating at an area of the cliff where it naturally receded. Their intent was immediately clear—if there were no cliffs to shelter themselves on the beach, they would begin to make them.

Another team had dug the graves at the back of the beach and four people were filling the dirt in. Apparently, Alex had slept through the burial ceremony.

Alex had taken his moment to wallow in doubt, guilt, and self-pity. While he was doing that, the group of people he had brought together had pitched in and started living. He couldn't help smiling a little.

He waded out to the ship and Fredon was waiting for him. Alex didn't even climb into the boat before Fredon started his report.

"It's just an island, Manta-ak. Not a very big island at that. I think you found the only place where you could have come ashore on the whole thing. Everywhere else, the cliffs drop down straight into the water. It is an inhospitable place."

A bit of Alex's good mood dissipated.

"When everyone who is going to has healed, I'd like you to take the ship out and look for any other islands within a day or two from here. We can't come close to fitting everyone on this ship, but if we find someplace better, we can make trips back and forth until we move everyone."

Alex chose not to add, 'We'll never be able to survive here long-term,' but in his heart he knew it was true.

Chapter Thirty-Three
Misery

The second night and day on the island followed the weather pattern of the first. With darkness, rain swept in and turned to something else—a wet assault on their senses.

Men and women worked constantly chipping away at the base of the cliffs, trying to carve out a shelter from the pounding rain. Constant chipping away was not a short-term solution, especially with so many bodies that needed protection from the weather.

The baking sun—so much worse on the island than it was on the ship—returned the next morning. On either end of the cycles, there was a brief, glorious hour when the weather was like paradise. The other twenty-two hours of the day were miserable. The rainwater they collected each night was enough to keep people from dying of thirst, but by the sweltering heat of the afternoon, everyone longed for a cool drink.

On the third day, Nanda-eh tried to climb the cliffs. A popular theory on the beach was that there was a plateau on top of the cliffs, filled with fruits, edible plants, game, and running water.

Alex was not one to tell anyone that something was impossible, so he watched her climb.

The lower part of the cliff did not present a difficult challenge. There were hand and foot holds aplenty, and Nanda-eh made great progress.

The middle section was much tougher. The plentiful places to grasp and stand on slowed to a trickle. What holds there were funneled her into one single path. That path led to a spot where the cliff above actually bulged out above her head.

Sweat poured off her in rivulets as she searched for any path that might get around that bulge. There was none.

Her arms began to shake, her fingers quivered in their last grip.

She let go with a frustrated "Gah!" and tumbled backward toward the earth. Her feet brushed against the cliffside and she pushed away from it as she fell, so she wouldn't land on the rocks below.

Instead, she fell on sand. Certainly better than falling onto boulders, but still not ideal.

She kept her momentum going and rolled, absorbing some of the impact, but it was obvious she wouldn't pop back up from a fall like that.

She didn't have to. Sanda and her other archers rushed to her side. They surrounded her and made her stay down while they assessed her injuries and air found its way back into her lungs.

The final injury toll was a painful broken rib, a separated shoulder, and a sprained wrist. It could have been worse, but she wouldn't be pulling her bowstring back for a time.

After watching Nanda-eh's spectacular fall, no one else attempted to scale the cliffs.

Alex knew that the small beach that had been their salvation was not sufficient for a long-term plan, so he continued to send Fredon out in search of something better.

Initially, the ship sailed eight hours west of Shipwreck Isle, as Amy had dubbed it. Then he circled around it, slowly closing in on his starting spot.

After a week of that, the ship had not identified so much as a pile of rocks sticking up out of the water.

The conditions on Shipwreck Isle wore on the hundreds of people who were stranded there. They fished from sunup to when the nightly rains arrived and they caught enough of the odd, yellow-silver flat fish to keep everyone alive. They noticed that those fish were slowly moving away from the island and it grew harder and harder to catch enough to give even a small portion to everyone.

Some brave soul swam out far enough that they reached around the cliffs. As Fredon had said, there was no place else they could find that would hold more than one or two people.

However, they did find some green seaweed that got caught in a small, rocky cove. The brave swimmer returned to the beach with it wrapped around them like a suit.

Alex and everyone else took turns examining the thick, green strands, trying to decide if it was safe to eat. Tinta-ak made the decision for them. He grabbed a bulb and took a mighty chomp out of it.

Everyone stood back to gauge his reaction.

He made a terrible face, but kept chewing. Finally, after a monumental struggle, he forced himself to swallow. He took a moment to recover, then smiled brightly and said, "It's delicious!"

Everyone laughed, but no one believed it was delicious or even palatable.

Tinta-ak was like a celebrity for the next few hours, as everyone watched him to see if he doubled over with sudden diarrhea or fell to all fours with nausea.

After twenty-four hours, Alex was willing to admit that the seaweed might provide them with some of the nutrients they were missing in their fish-only diet. A team of the best swimmers went to the small cove each morning and brought back enough of the green ropes and bulbs to give some to everyone in the tribe.

Alex and his wise friends made the very best they could out of the situation, but they knew they could only stay in that spot for so long before they began to die off. Each morning, the tribe looked a little more ragged after having survived another round of beyond-torrential rains.

Quietly, Alex, Amy, Sanda, Rinka-ak, Hawthorne, Versa-eh and Harta-ak began to plan for the worst. If people started to die from the horrible situation they were in, they would have no choice but to pile as many people as possible in the boat and head out, sailing until they found a better spot, whether that spot was days, weeks, or months away.

That plan would be devastating, as everyone knew that once the ship left Shipwreck Isle, there was a legitimate chance they might never see it again. That being the case, Alex insisted he would stay on the island and keep things going in the hope of the ship's return. They figured that they could fit one hundred people on board, so that meant the bulk of people who had sailed on *The Senta-eh* would be left behind, likely to perish.

Once the plan was talked about, dissected, and looked at from every angle, Alex tabled it. Splitting up his army was the last thing he wanted to do—he just wanted to be prepared in case he had to do it.

One night Alex and Monda-ak sat on the beach, bracing themselves for the inevitable night-storm. For the moment, they sat in the brief respite between too much heat and too much rain. For those few minutes each evening, it really did look like they were on a tropical paradise.

Alex leaned back against Monda-ak, who was the most comfortable pillow on Shipwreck Isle. He stared up at the moon and realized it was back to the same phase it had been when he had agreed to give up his search for the rebellion in two months. That time had passed, but the search itself had been exchanged for a simple fight for survival.

The next morning, an hour after the rain had ceased and just as the incredible heat of the day was beginning to crank up, Sanda stood on her toes and stared at the horizon. She turned to Nanda-eh, who was never far from her, and said, "Do I see something on the horizon? Or have I just been staring at it for so long that my mind is fooling me?"

Nanda-eh, who was another six inches taller than Sanda, but whose eyes were not as good, said, "I don't think I see anything."

Sanda ran to the cliff and climbed up until she was twenty feet off the ground. She craned her neck so that she could look over her shoulder.

"Ship! I see a ship!"

That got everyone's attention and hundreds of people abandoned whatever they were doing and hurried to the water's edge.

Sanda held on to her spot on the side of the cliff and looked over her shoulder again, trying to verify that the ship was heading toward them. What she saw was so surprising that it made her lose her grip and tumble to the sand.

Chapter Thirty-Four
Rescue

Sanda's tumble to the sand below was from a much lower height than Nanda-eh's had been and she just rolled forward, then jumped to her feet.

She caught her father's eye and said, "It's not a ship. It's *ships*! A lot of ships!"

That started a buzz of conversation that ran through the gathered throng of castaways.

"Are we rescued?" "Is it the Drakana come back to finish us off?" "How many ships?"

Alex did not join in on the speculation. His lifelong motto was *hope for the best, prepare for the worst.*

Most of their weapons had been lost in the shipwreck, but a few had made it ashore with a sword, or knife. None of Nanda-eh's archers had landed with both their bow *and* their arrows. However, a few of them had their bows and a few had landed with arrows.

"Don't gather in one spot. Disperse as much as we can. We don't want to make it easy for them in case of a cannon shot." As soon as he said it, Alex looked around the small, exposed beach and realized there was nowhere to hide. "Anyone who has a weapon, move to the waterline. Everyone else, move back."

That was a logical command, but the truth was, Alex was just burning off nervous energy while he waited to see what their fate would be. If someone really wanted to do away with them, it would be as simple as anchoring in the small harbor and pelting them with cannonballs and gunshots. They would have no answer for that.

If Fredon had been there, Alex would have sent him to the other side of the island, or out to open sea to protect the vessel. That ship was out on its endless mission to find more hospitable surroundings, though, and wasn't due back for several days.

Still, Alex had his ragtag army as ready as they could be.

It didn't take long before it was obvious that there were at least six ships, and that they were heading directly toward them.

Alex and everyone stood transfixed, watching the slowly approaching sails.

After almost an hour, someone with sharp eyes shouted, "That's Handan's ship!"

Alex couldn't understand how someone could look at a small smear of white and brown on the horizon and make out that it was a specific ship. He began to realize that his eyes were not as good as they had once been.

Alex huddled with Amy and Hawthorne. "If it truly is Handan's ship, what is that likely to mean?" He looked from Amy to Hawthorne and back.

Finally it was Hawthorne who spoke up.

"We never knew what Handan's intentions were when he left us as the Drakana ship was attacking us. It's possible that they started out running from the larger ship, then decided to strike out on their own."

"Possible," Alex agreed, "but unlikely. It would be a very different response than we saw from Fredon, and Handan's ship had a large number of Kragdon-ah on board. I don't think they'd let him mutiny and run."

"Since there are other ships with him," Amy observed, "I think it's most likely he went to get help."

"I'd love for that to be true, but how does it make sense? Where would he find help?"

"I think he found the Resistance against the Drakana."

Alex and Hawthorne considered that. "How would he find them? We have Sofina here," Alex pointed out.

"What else makes sense?" Amy asked. "We've got multiple ships coming toward us, led by Handan's ship." She hesitated, then continued, "I guess it's possible that Handan was captured and forced to reveal our whereabouts, and now they're coming to finish the job." She switched from the universal language to English. "But think of Occam's Razor, Dad. All things being equal, the simplest answer is usually the right one."

Alex laughed. He had first used that argument against Amy when she was ten years old. He raised his hand in defeat. "The good news is, we'll know very shortly."

Less than an hour later, Handan's ship sailed into the natural harbor. Handan himself stood on the bow of the ship and leaped into the water as soon as they got close enough. He was beaming.

"I didn't know what to do!" he shouted at Alex as soon as he picked him out on the beach. "I didn't know if I should turn around and help, or if I should go looking for these guys." He indicated *these guys* by waving his arm vaguely at the five ships behind him. None of the ships that accompanied him were as big as *The Senta-eh*, but several were larger than either Handan or Fredon's ship.

Alex made a quick calculation and figured if the ships weren't full, then everyone on the beach could fit easily onboard the ships.

For the first time since he had set foot on the beach, Alex felt his insides unclench a little. He didn't know what was ahead yet, but at that moment the future seemed suddenly brighter.

It turned out that the bigger ships, which anchored farther out from shore, were mostly empty. They looked like warships, with four to six cannons protruding from each side, but for this trip, they were transport ships.

A man leaned over the side of Handan's ship and in Drakana said, "Who is this Manta-ak?"

Alex smiled tentatively and raised a hand in greeting. "I am Manta-ak."

The man leaped over the side of the ship and landed in the water gracefully, with barely a ripple. This was impressive, based on the size of the man. He was not tall, at least not like the Kragdon-ah, although he still stood a few inches taller than Alex. His chest was broad and tan, with many ink-black tattoos. He had the neck of a bull and long, curly hair that hung well down his back. His most striking feature was his smile. When he smiled, his face—also partially covered in black tattoos—changed from fearsome to welcoming.

"I am Akima." He waved a huge, heavily-muscled arm toward the ships behind him. "These are my friends. We heard you needed a little help and that you want to fight the Drakana. That has been our goal for more than one hundred solstices."

Alex had given up on his dream of attacking the Drakana when the mast of *The Senta-eh* had been shattered by a cannonball shot and eventually sunk. He had turned his mind to more immediate tasks—keeping his charges alive, and perhaps finding a way to return them to Kragdon-ah.

Now, seeing these ships and this impressive man in front of him, hope bloomed.

Alex stepped toward Akima and extended his right hand, intending to put it on his shoulder in the Kragdon-ah greeting. Akima was having none of that. He batted Alex's hand away and embraced him so strongly that Alex felt his back pop up and down his spine.

Up close, Alex got a better look at Akima's face. He had originally thought him to be a young man. Now he saw that there were fine lines around his eyes and mouth and a certain wisdom that flashed in his eyes.

Akima looked around the beach and then wiped sweat off his brow. "Are you ready to get off this island that has been forgotten by the gods? I think it was put here for one purpose only—to give you a place to wait for us."

"I am ready," Alex said, then paused. "But we have a ship out searching for a new home for us. I will need to wait here until they return. If it is possible, maybe we can load people onto the ships and be ready to leave when it returns?"

"That is an excellent plan," Akima agreed. "But first, you must be hungry and thirsty. We have brought everything we need for a feast. We will eat and drink tonight, then get ready to leave tomorrow, if your ship has returned."

Akima's head turned suddenly and a flash of recognition crossed his face. "Sofina?"

The young girl ran to him and hugged him.

"Wait, how do you know Sofina?"

"She was born on our island. We take many of our children and send them to other nations the Drakana have conquered. That way, we can stay hidden, but if someone really wants to find us, they can use them as a navigation system." He turned back to Sofina. "Your Auntie will be very glad to see you."

The young girl grinned, hugged Akima again, and walked away.

Alex reminded himself again that he was not the only person who made long-term plans. For the moment, he looked forward to only spending one more night on Shipwreck Isle under its nightly pounding rains.

"I wish we had more to offer in the way of hospitality," Alex said as he pointed to the beach, devoid of everything except hungry people. "I'm afraid all we have to offer is our appetites."

That was enough. Akima had brought everything else. They dropped one transport ship after another into the water from the bigger ships and rowed to shore. Each was heavily loaded with everything needed for a feast. Boxes of fruits and vegetables. Huge containers of some sort of meat, and barrel after barrel of ale.

The men from the ship went immediately to work, building a fire, preparing the fruits and vegetables, and making sauces and gravies that made everyone nearly mad with hunger.

As the sun went down, Alex announced that they were in the magical hour between too-hot and too-wet, and the feast commenced.

Alex wondered if Akima was the leader of the Resistance. He was certainly the leader of the expedition, but there was no way to know if his leadership extended over the entire operation, except to ask.

Alex, Akima, Amy, Sanda, Rinka-ak, Hawthorne, and Tinta-ak sat in a circle. Harta-ak and Versa-eh sat knee-to-knee, talking quietly. Monda-ak sat directly behind Alex. His stomach was already full, as the cooks had delighted in feeding scraps to him. The humans all had a flat piece of wood heaped with food.

It was all delicious, including the meat, which turned out to be octopus, prepared in a rich, red sauce.

After a diet of nothing but fish and seaweed over the previous month, Alex was sure that so much rich food would cause a lot of gastrointestinal distress over the next few hours. He had no interest in saying anything and ruining the jubilant mood. Still, Alex, Amy, and Sanda did not overindulge, instead simply sampling each delicacy.

Alcohol was not prevalent in Winten-ah, so the warriors he had brought with him drank the ale like it was water. It was not long before most of the castaways were passed out in various corners of the beach.

The rain came, but softened by the warm glow of the ale and the fine food in their bellies, most everyone got the best sleep they'd had in weeks.

Alex was anxious to spend time talking and strategizing with Akima, but the rain made any kind of conversation impossible. At one point, Akima offered to take Alex onboard one of the ships so he could get better rest, but Alex demurred. He couldn't imagine leaving his troops on the beach, absorbing the pounding rain while he was snug in a bed somewhere.

And so they all passed their final night on Shipwreck Isle together on the sand and, as always, were grateful when the sun rose, the rain stopped, and the temperature climbed.

It was Sanda who once again saw the sail of Fredon's ship first. They watched it for long minutes, but soon realized that it had stopped.

"He's uncertain what this is, and I don't blame him," Alex said. Turning to Handan, he said, "Let's go meet him—tell him all is well."

Alex and a few others—Amy, Sanda, and Monda-ak included—climbed onboard the small ship and set sail. It didn't take long until they pulled alongside Fredon's ship.

"I didn't find a thing, and I guess it doesn't matter," was the first thing Fredon shouted when he saw Alex and Handan on board. "Are we rescued then?"

"We are rescued!"

Chapter Thirty-Five
The Hidden City

They had left Shipwreck Isle five days earlier and the ships had sailed within sight of each other ever since.

Akima, who had elected to travel with Alex on the smaller ship, said that they were not taking the most-direct route, because that was too dangerous. It would have taken them through waters where Drakana vessels were known to patrol, looking specifically for them.

Akima was able to shine some light on the attack that had sunk *The Senta-eh*. One thing Alex had never been able to figure out was why the Drakana ship had been so anxious to board them. The Drakana ship had more firepower and could have easily sunk them from a distance.

Alex posed the question to Akima.

"Why would they try to board us when we were such a big ship? They couldn't have known that we had eight hundred warriors on board and that we would swamp them immediately, but they couldn't have known we *didn't* either."

Akima smiled, as he did so often. "You had the bad luck to be mistaken for us."

"They saw their own Drakana ship and thought it might be you?"

"We have taken many of their ships. We haven't engaged in a direct land battle with them yet, but we've been harassing them at sea, and they us, for many years. They no doubt saw your big ship accompanied by two smaller ships and thought you were us. That would fit our pattern."

"But still, why would they attempt to board such a large ship when they were blind?"

"Because we have been fighting so long, we think we know each other's patterns. Sometimes that can lead us to make bad decisions."

"I'm not sure I follow."

"We often sail big ships with just a small crew. We don't ever want to get into hand-to-hand combat with them. We prefer to hunt them on the open sea, fire a few shots at them and run. We don't need a large crew for that—just enough to get the most speed out of the sails. When they came across you, they thought you were just another of our ships out to harass them with a tiny crew. They wanted to board you, kill you, and claim the ship."

"Except they had already knocked our mast down and struck a fatal blow at our waterline."

"I would guess that was a mistake." Akima was somber for a moment, then his face lit up. "But it was the last mistake any of them ever made!" He laughed a deep, throaty laugh that echoed around the ship.

And now, Alex Hawk stood on the bow of Handan's ship. A fresh ocean breeze ruffled his long hair and although the sun was shining, it was pleasant, not oppressive.

The island that held the city that Akima called Rontan was dead ahead. As they approached the island, Alex could see the wisdom of their choice of location. As at Shipwreck Isle, steep, imposing cliffs rose from the water's edge and the ocean lapped at jagged rocks as far as the eye could see.

If Alex had sailed by it, he would have rejected it as just another worthless pile of rocks.

Rontan had been formed many years earlier by a few outcasts from one of the nations that Drakana had conquered. Over the years, it had grown until it was a legitimate nation of its own, made up entirely of those who were seeking refuge from Drakana.

It had been just an island of misfits until a man Akima called Nakama had arrived. Most of the refugees arrived starving, disheveled, and with nothing but the clothes on their back.

Nakama arrived with a small fleet of ships, a cache of weapons, and a desire to overthrow Drakana. He was welcomed with open arms and it quickly became obvious Nakama was the leader Rontan needed.

Akima and all the rest of the people who lived in Rontan had thought that Nakama would lead them in a glorious quest to strike back at Drakana and reclaim the lands they had all lost.

Nakama proved to be cautious, however. He wanted to wait until he felt the odds tilted in their favor before they attacked. Instead of a huge frontal attack, he satisfied himself with quick guerilla actions, intended to unnerve and sting the Drakana.

Nakama had pursued this strategy for so long, he had grown old. He was still beloved among the outcasts of Rontan, but these past few years, there had been whispers behind closed doors.

Why do we not attack? We are stronger than we have ever been. While we wait, Drakana grows stronger yet. Soon, we will have waited too long and they will be too huge to attack.

Nakama was still beloved for the relative prosperity he had brought to Rontan, but his cautious approach was being called into question more and more.

Handan cut their speed and floated gently as they approached the island. A number of the larger ships continued to sail directly toward the cliffs as if they were intent on smashing themselves against it.

Those bigger ships turned slowly to the south, then banked back to the right. One by one, just when it seemed they would run aground or into the rocks, they disappeared.

"There is an inlet that runs deep into the island, but the only way to see it is to approach it from the correct angle. If you're not close enough, or if you have the wrong angle, all you will see is cliffs. It is our natural camouflage and what has let us grow to the size we are without interference."

Handan turned the wheel over to a boy who had obviously been commanding boats since he was in diapers. The boy didn't need to shave yet, but he handled the ship—and barked out orders to those in the rigging—like a veteran.

Handan jumped down to where Alex and Akima were. "I'm not ready to take a ship to Rontan yet. It's tricky."

"How did you find them, then, if you didn't go into the city? And how did you find them at all, since Sofina was our built-in navigation system?"

"I didn't find them—they found me. Sofina was our compass, yes, but she had been pointing the same south-southwest direction since we left Lakunadan. When we got separated from you, I thought the best thing I could do was to get help. I knew this boat was too small to do you much good in a battle. So we kept sailing in this direction. At first, I expected the ship that attacked us to come after us."

"Hard for them to do that when it ended up burning to the waterline," Alex observed.

"That explained that, then, all right. We kept to that same line and eventually came to what you see in front of us. I figured that might be it, but I couldn't find any way in. Didn't matter, though. They must have a good watch set up. I wasn't here for more than a few minutes before three other boats came to check me out. I told them who we were, what we were trying to do, and one of their pilots led me into the city. It's not just finding the opening in the rock, but once you're in, you've got to know the right route, or you'll end up aground or crashed against the rocks."

"A natural defense system," Alex said. "Good for them."

"Good for us," Handan said. "If you still want to take the fight to Drakana, it's good to have a hidden place to launch those plans from."

Alex looked at Handan closely to see if there was a sign he was being disingenuous. He didn't see any. Until a month or two earlier, Handan had been a captain of the Drakana navy. Now he seemed to have converted completely to the idea that the Drakana were the enemy.

"Have you always been Drakana?" Alex asked him suddenly.

Handan smiled. "That's not always a simple question, is it? I was born into a land that was called Drakana, yes. I never had any choice about what I would be. I grew up on sailing ships, so I was destined to be in the Drakana fleet. But our city hadn't always been Drakana. Even twenty-five solstices ago, we were an independent nation. The Drakana conquered our land, but they did not conquer our spirit. Like the people who live in Rontan, we always believed a day would arrive when we would once again be free."

Which made it that much easier to declare your allegiance to a new nation when the opportunity became available, Alex mused. *You can conquer a city, put it at the tip of a sword, but that doesn't conquer the hearts of the people who live there.*

The young boy at the wheel stood with a relaxed posture as he guided the ship into the opening between the cliffs. For a moment, they sailed directly into a fogbank and Alex had an immediate sense of déjà vu. He tensed slightly, but as the ship approached the fog, it dissipated, as real fog does. They sailed right through it without any sound effects.

Chapter Thirty-Six
Rontan

As the ship wound its way through the inlet, Alex began to feel like he was in a primitive version of *The African Queen*. At times, the water was wide and their young pilot kept them in the middle, full speed ahead. At others, he ordered the sails down or turned so that they didn't catch any wind at all. They drifted as the water twisted and turned, but the boy always had them where they needed to be.

In Alex's mind, he expected to sail beyond the cliffs to find a city. That wasn't the case. They meandered inland for more than an hour.

There were times that the jungle vegetation threatened to close in on them. Long vines hung heavily from trees that reached out over the water. Occasionally Alex thought he saw those vines move, which gave him a start, as he had thought no snake could possibly be that big.

Eventually, the waterway widened into a most amazing sight.

The ocean fed into an inland bay that was more than a mile across. A city of sorts had been built up around that bay.

There was so much to see that Alex couldn't take it all in at once.

Some of the buildings around the port were taller than anything he had ever seen built in this world. His eyes fell on one particular structure that wasn't just broad—it also stood four stories tall. It was the Kragdon-ah version of a skyscraper, he supposed.

Beyond the size of the city, what floated in the harbor was even more impressive.

Ships.

Lots of ships. So many that Alex couldn't count them all initially.

It wasn't just the sheer volume either. There was an incredible variety. There were two ships that were as large as *The Senta-eh* had been. Alex could see at least another five or six that were only somewhat smaller. Then there were dozens more vessels that obviously served different purposes, including smaller ships equipped with cannons, and low barge-like ships that would be able to carry a lot of cargo or people.

After being back in Kragdon-ah for several years, Alex had once again become accustomed to thinking of a *city* as having a few hundred people in it. In fact, when *The Senta-eh* was still afloat, it was the largest concentration of humanity he had seen, aside from the miles-long caravan.

Rontan, however, was once again an exception. There were people everywhere. Every ship, every barge, every dock was filled with people hustling and bustling, going about their daily lives.

Their young pilot guided them to a dock and Handan tossed a rope to a man standing by who attached it to a pier.

"Come," Akima said to Alex. "Nakama will want to meet with you."

"I'd like my council to come as well."

"Of course! Bring as many as you want."

For just a moment, Alex's sixth sense tingled.

That's exactly what he would say if he was leading us into a trap. Sure, bring everyone into the palace, so we can behead you all at once.

Alex shook his head.

That makes no sense. Why rescue us when they could have simply left us there to starve? Sometimes a hand up is just a hand up, nothing more.

Stepping off the dock and onto cobblestoned streets was a surreal experience for Alex, but at least he, Amy, and Sanda had experience with civilizations. Alex hadn't nailed down Hawthorne's exact history, but he seemed right at home in this environment. Harta-ak and Versa-eh had at least spent time in the larger towns that dotted the giant river that now split the former Midwest of the United States from the former East Coast. Even their eyes were wide, though, as they took it all in.

Alex could only imagine what was going through the minds of Tinta-ak, and Rinka-ak, whose idea of civilization was a world lit only by fire.

There were no internal combustion engines—civilization here hadn't progressed that far, but it was crowded with people, animals, carts, and buildings that encroached against the narrow streets and other buildings.

To Alex, it looked like what a New England whaling village might have looked like in the eighteenth century.

As people passed them, they stared—especially at Tinta-ak, who was the largest person they had perhaps ever seen, as Torana had stayed behind on one of the ships. No one looked unfriendly or questioned why they were there, however. It was as though if you were present in their town, you were automatically one of them.

Akima and his small coterie wound through the crowded streets until they reached the four-story building Alex had spotted from the ship. Like all the other buildings in the city, it was not beautiful. Beautification did not seem to be a priority in this city. There were no statues, or gardens, or murals anywhere. Every single building—and every person, for that matter—seemed designed for a specific purpose with no other thought in mind.

It made for an efficient, if somewhat plain, environment.

That same homely feeling extended inside the large building. Wood plank floors and unadorned walls were the order of the day.

Akima led them up a staircase to the second, then third, floor, where he pushed open a door into a large, open room. It reminded Alex of the uppermost cave in Winten-ah, a place where a large meeting could take place.

Instead of a firepit, though, there was just a long wooden table with chairs scattered around it and a large window at one end of the room. There were two people already there, an old man with a shock of long, white hair and an equally impressive white beard, and a younger man who hovered behind him.

Akima, who had been one of the most informal people Alex had ever met, suddenly struck a more rigid pose. His back erect, he said, "These are the leaders of the expedition we rescued today." He turned to Alex. "Manta-ak, this is Nakama." He didn't bother to introduce the second man.

Alex was unsure of how to greet Nakama. Every group and culture he met in this world seemed to have its own version of a greeting.

Nakama solved the problem by standing and approaching Alex with his hand extended just as a twenty-first century man might have. Instinctively, Alex reached out and took the old man's hand. Nakama pumped Alex's hand three times, then moved on through the rest of the group, doing the same with everyone else.

Amy, Sanda, and Hawthorne knew what to do, but the others seemed a bit puzzled by the handshake.

"I have already heard interesting stories about you, Manta-ak, and your group of adventurers," Nakama said in Drakana.

"I'm afraid to ask," Alex said in the same language.

Nakama smiled and Alex relaxed a little. There was no malice in the man's expression, no hint of duplicity.

"When your sailor Handan came here and asked us for help in rescuing you from the tiny island you were on, we questioned him carefully. We have survived here for many years by being careful. He

told us how the Drakana had come to your own land and attempted to conquer you as they have done with so many others. And that
you had decided to fight back and attack them, instead of cowering,
waiting to be enslaved or killed."

Alex looked closely at Nakama. There was something about him
that put Alex in mind of Tokin-ak, the old monk who had played
such a large part in his rescue of Lanta-eh. Although slightly bent
from age, his eyes were still lit by a fire within. Alex made a mental
note not to underestimate him or what he said.

"We are in need of a man who doesn't always do what is expected. It will take surprising decisions and not playing it safe if we are to
ever launch a successful attack against our mutual enemy."

"*Our mutual enemy,*" Alex mused. "You have me at an unfair advantage. You know my history, but I don't know much of anything
about you and yours."

"My story is a simple one," the old man said, a twinkle in his eyes.
"You see, I was to become Makinta, god of the Drakana."

Chapter Thirty-Seven
When Makinta is not Makinta

Most of the faces around the table remained blank. Only Alex, Amy, and Sanda had a reaction, as they had already talked among themselves of such a possibility.

"I think your story is way more interesting than mine," Alex observed.

Nakama bowed his head slightly, acknowledging that.

Hawthorne raised a hand, as if for permission to speak. "Sorry, but I'm completely lost here. How were you to become Makinta? Isn't there already a Makinta?"

"There have been a number of Makintas," Nakama said, not quite agreeing.

"I think I know what you're going to say," Alex said, "but I think you should walk us through from the beginning."

Nakama bowed his head slightly again, then began his story.

"I was the oldest son born to the man who was known as Makinta. As such, I was privy to much information and training that others who were not so high-born never received." He paused, seemed to reconsider where he was in the story. "I better start a little farther back."

Tinta-ak and the rest of the Kragdon-ah looked relieved, as they were lost.

"Here is a brief history of Drakana," Nakama began. He gave a brief recap of the same history that Darand had given in the caves of Winten-ah. He told of how the tribe that eventually became the Drakana had once been as small and poor as any other, until a man who called himself Makinta appeared one day. The man was dressed strangely, and brought magic items with him that no one in the village had ever seen. He spoke a strange language and the people of the village believed him to be a god.

"Makinta did not disabuse them of that idea, in fact, he encouraged it," Nakama went on. "Soon enough, using the magic items he brought with him, he built that village up from a small, inconsequential place to something that should be feared. The power and influence of that village, which Makinta renamed Drakana, grew until it controlled everything in the land where it had started."

Most of that information wasn't new to the recently rescued group, but it provided a good framework for understanding what Nakama said next.

"Makinta said he was a god, and that he would live forever. Instead, he grew old and feeble like everyone else did. No one dared to question his power, because to do so was to choose death for yourself and your family. Still, there were whispers. That was when Makinta said he was going to transfer his soul into the body of another. He chose to become his oldest son, or so he said. When Makinta passed away, it became a day of celebration and feasting, because he was once again young and strong."

Rinka-ak nodded. In his tribe, leadership was essentially passed the same way, without the pretense of the transfer of souls.

"Makinta transferred his soul many times, choosing his oldest son each time he grew old. My own father was chosen to be Makinta for that same reason, and as his oldest son, I was given the same honor."

Nakama's eyes grew misty as he stared out the window. Sunshine poured in, but it was obvious that the old man's thoughts were many years and miles away.

"Like many fathers and sons, we did not always agree on everything. I thought that would change when I became him."

Nakama sighed and there was a heavy silence in the room. No one wanted to interrupt him.

"Instead, he told me a story of generations of lies. Makinta—the original, real Makinta—had been dead for hundreds of years. But he had passed the knowledge he had brought with him down to his son and told him enough about the strange world he came from that his son could pretend to be him. That happened from father to son for generations, with each son living out the lie and 'becoming' Makinta."

"But you did not?" Alex guessed.

"I did not," Nekuna agreed. "I did not..." he trailed off, once again lost in his thoughts for a moment before snapping back. "My father was a very smart man. Even though I tried to hide it, he could see that I was not happy about deceiving our people. My father decided that I was not worthy to be Makinta. That created a problem, though. How could he leave me alive? What if I told anyone what I knew? It would be embarrassing, or might have caused an uprising."

"But you are here, so he did not kill you," Alex said with a slight smile.

"I was awakened by my servant in the middle of the night. He told me that if I did not leave at that moment—still wearing my night clothes—I would be murdered. This man had looked after me since I was the smallest boy. I trusted him more than anyone. He and I slipped out of the palace in the dark of night. My servant had a small ship waiting for us, piloted by a man and his family who also wanted to get out of Drakana and away from my father. We sailed into the night with no real plan other than escape."

"How did you end up here?" Alex asked.

"Luck, I suppose. We did not know Rontan existed, and in truth, it did not exist as you see it today. When I arrived as a young man who had seen less than twenty solstices, there were only a few people here living a poor existence, hiding from my father. I brought something they did not know, however. I brought knowledge—about the way things worked, about our shipping routes, about everything. That was why he wanted me dead."

Nakama sat back as though he had reached the end of his story.

"My younger brother is now Makinta, but he is also an old man. He will have long-since begun training his son, my nephew, to become the next Makinta."

"Thank you for telling us," Alex said. "I have to ask—why did you never attack? Did you not think you were strong enough? Did you just want to live here in peace?"

"I wish I could say that was the case," Nakama said. "But as I have grown older, I have a new perspective, both on myself and the world around me."

Alex guessed that the old man might be tiring. His hands, even resting on the table in front of him, shook with slight tremors and his chin drooped as if his head had grown too heavy to hold up.

"I think I was born to be an administrator. I am good at organizing things. I am proud of what I have done in building this town. But our mission from the day I arrived was to fight my brother, free the people he has enslaved, and reveal the truth. I never believed we were ready, even though we may have been. It is my greatest failure."

Alex could see the pain in the old man's face and heard it in his voice.

Alex pushed his chair back and walked to the window. There was no glass in it, but heavy shutters hung on either side, ready to shut out the rain should it come. The street below was crammed with people hurrying from one place to another, waving and greeting friends as they moved.

Alex waved his hand at the street below. "There's no way you can think of yourself as a failure. Look at what you've helped build here!"

Akima stood and went to Nakama's side. The big man put a gentle hand over Nakama's palsied hands, calming them.

"We need a warrior, Manta-ak. Someone who can lead us against our enemy."

Alex didn't say anything. Instead, Tinta-ak stood and said, "We have the greatest warrior I have ever seen with us. He beat me in hand-to-hand combat, then showed me how to beat others. He led us into battle against a fortress and we burned it to the ground."

Harta-ak stood next and said, "I watched him destroy a city with only three people and a dog."

"Yes," Alex said, "but that dog was Monda-ak, so that has to count for extra."

Monda-ak's huge tail beat against the wood floor at the mention of his name.

"He fought a godat-ta nearly as large as this building singlehanded and killed him."

"Again," Alex said. "Monda-ak. I have never gone into battle alone. He is always with me."

Akima looked fondly down at Nakama. "We do not require any convincing. We will put our resources at your command, if you will lead us, Manta-ak."

Nakama gathered the last of his strength and stood, shuffling toward Alex.

"I am sorry to ask this of you. It is a horrible responsibility."

Sanda and Amy glanced at each other and smiled. They knew how their father did with horrible responsibilities.

They were what he lived for.

Chapter Thirty-Eight
War on the Horizon

Alex Hawk walked along the docks, going over ships and inventory. Again.

Amy was beside him, a clipboard—or at least what passed for a clipboard in this part of the world—tucked under her arm.

They had been in Rontan for a full month.

Somehow the city had swelled enough to take in and feed the hundreds of refugees that Alex brought with him. They had not only fed and clothed them, they had also armed them. Most importantly, several thousand citizens had agreed to follow him into a head-on confrontation with the Drakana.

The city was energized and everywhere Alex went, he was greeted with "Any day now, right?" or the slightly grumpier, "It's about time!"

There had been some among the Rontan citizenry who wanted to charge into that conflict the day after Alex agreed to lead the army. That fed into Alex's desire as well, but he had the better sense to take the time needed to prepare.

Alex had seen how the Drakana fought—their strengths, their weaknesses, and he found that the Rontan army was the same in many ways. That was not surprising, since it was the only type of warfare any of them had ever seen.

Alex knew that the Drakana tended to rely on their superior weaponry—specifically their cannons, rifles, pistols, and warhorses—too much. That was sufficient when they faced an opposing force whose greatest weapon was a few longbow archers.

One question Alex had faced was whether the Kragdon-ah forces would be accepting of fighting alongside allies who used stama at all. A war had been fought in Danta-ah for essentially that reason. He gathered Tinta-ak, Harta-ak and Versa-eh, and Rinka-ak to him and discussed it.

"I will never ask our forces to use anything that resembles stama. But these people we are joining with have only known how to fight using these weapons. If we take them away now, they will be mostly useless. What do we say?"

Harta-ak spoke first. "I come from a part of Kragdon-ah where we have a very relaxed idea of what stama is. I will have no problem with it."

Alex looked to Tinta-ak and Rinka-ak. "I trust you to speak for your tribes."

The two men, one muscled and brutish looking, the other tall and refined, looked at each other. Finally, it was Rinka-ak who spoke. "It is the existence, not just of ourselves, but of those we love who we left behind that is at stake. We will never use stama."

"We do not *need* stama," Tinta-ak added.

"But we will happily fight alongside our allies who use what they have in battle."

"We are agreed, then," Alex said.

Amy leaned forward and said quietly to Alex, "What would Sekun-ak say about that?"

Alex closed his eyes for a long moment. Equally quietly, he said, "He would not like it. In truth, he would probably forbid it."

"But Sekun-ak is not here," Amy said, finishing his thought.

"Yes, Sekun-ak is not here."

He turned his attention back to the others. "So, as I was saying, their reliance on weaponry was fine when matched against an overwhelmed force. But if they ever met an armed force that was equally well-armed and more than willing to engage in close-in fighting, they would be at a disadvantage."

Alex spent the month training the Rontan army in how to face an enemy that was literally in their face. It was difficult to get an exact count of how many soldiers were in the Rontan army, but Amy had pegged the number at around five thousand. That was too many for Alex to train, obviously, but he did it as he always did.

He started by taking his best fighters, including Tinta-ak, Grantan, Sanda, and his other lieutenants who he had trained on board during the voyage, and making them platoon leaders. Those leaders walked through the basics with their own charges, then picked the most natural fighters and enrolled them in intensive training for a few days.

After that, those volunteers trained squads during the day and then received more intense training from Alex and his key people at night.

They had worked sunup to sundown for a month.

Alex had also worked with the weapon makers to ensure that every person that sailed with him would be suitably equipped for whatever job they needed.

Nanda-eh and her archers had mostly lost their bows when *The Senta-eh* had gone down, but it turned out there was an old man—perhaps older than Nakama himself—who was a skilled bow maker. His skills had not been required in the previous decades, as the Rontan army had relied on gunpowder and rifles, but Nanda-eh and Sanda met him with open arms.

It was impossible for Alex to envision exactly what the conflicts ahead would look like, so he tried to prepare for every eventuality. That included having the weapon makers create enough shields that

Alex could recreate his shield wall with several squads if the need arose.

After a month of frenzied activity, Alex was finally satisfied with the store of weapons at his disposal.

Alex had noted that no one came forward to challenge him as Tinta-ak once had. His reputation now preceded him and no one wanted to try their hand at taking him down a notch. That was fine with Alex. He felt his old wounds a little more every year and those years were beginning to pile up on him.

Alex and his council had decided that a month would be sufficient for the training. With that time gone, Alex would have liked to have another month. But, after Nakama's slow-but-steady approach, Alex knew he needed to inspire action.

Now that they were going to leave the next morning, Alex was filled with nervous energy, just as he always was before a big campaign.

"What am I forgetting?"

"To not be nervous?" Amy answered. "We've planned everything within an inch of its life. I don't think you've forgotten anything."

Switching to English, Alex said, "Do you remember Mike Tyson?"

That surprised Amy. They almost never spoke about things back in the time she was born. Neither she nor Sanda ever seemed nostalgic for what they had left behind. She squinted one eye shut and said, "I think so. Boxer?"

Alex laughed. "Just shows how fleeting fame is. When I was a kid, he was one of the most famous people on the planet."

"I would say that when you were a kid, dinosaurs walked the Earth, but that's more like right now than then."

Alex pretended not to hear that. "Yes, he was a boxer. He said, 'Everyone has a plan until they get punched in the mouth.'"

"He sounds like a kind and gentle man. So, isn't it best if we punch them in the mouth first?"

"That's my girl," Alex said, hugging her close. "I wish there was a way I could protect you. I couldn't stand it if anything happened to you or your sister."

"We feel the same way about you, you know. What's the chance we can keep you away from the thick of things?"

Alex saw the truth of that. "None," he admitted.

"Then let's not dwell on it."

Alex and all the warriors he had brought with him from Kragdon-ah, along with strays he had picked up along the way, like Hawthorne, Quintan, and Grantan, would be on one ship. Harta-ak would once again be the captain, and Hawthorne and Pictin would take the other turns at the wheel.

Alex had been mourning the loss of the ship he had hijacked back in Kragdon-ah. Not because of any particular fondness for the ship itself—though it served its purpose nicely. His sadness was because of the connection to Senta-eh.

Sanda had done what she could to take care of that. She had rigged a platform from the deck above and sat there one long afternoon, painting a new name on the side of the bow.

When she was done, she stood, stretched, and said to herself, "I dub thee the Senta-eh II. May you live on longer than your predecessor."

The new ship was dramatically different than *The Senta-eh*. It had a similar capacity, but was more of what Alex would have thought of as a typical European design. That fact alone made Hawthorne happy, as it was exactly what he was used to sailing.

The only thing that mattered to Alex was that it was big, fast, and would be the ship that led the fleet into Drakana, just as the Drakana had once sailed into Kragdon-ah.

They also had a guest of honor on board.

Alex had assumed that Nakama would stay behind when they sailed, but the old man insisted on coming along. Alex put him into the captain's cabin along with Akima and a personal aide named Treptan, who was almost as old as Nakama himself.

The sun dipped below the horizon in the west and Alex turned to Amy. "Let's go on board. I want to leave early."

"I didn't think we'd have a noon departure," Amy said with a wink.

Chapter Thirty-Nine
The Wind at Their Backs

Harta-ak was the captain and Pictin and Hawthorne acted as his co-pilots, but that didn't take effect until they hit open water. As they maneuvered through the winding inlet that led from Rontan to the ocean, the same young boy who had piloted them in now piloted them out.

When they hit the open water, he grinned at Harta-ak and bowed slightly, as if to say, *I did the hard part. I think you can take it from here.*

With sails full and the wind at their backs, Alex relaxed a little. Nakama had told him that it would take weeks to arrive at Drakana proper, especially with the route they were taking.

The Rontan had been in a running sea battle with the Drakana for so long that they both knew each other's normal routes. That meant that Akima and the other Rontan pilots had planned out a route that would avoid the normal passageways. They didn't want to tip Drakana off to their imminent arrival until it was too late for them to prepare.

The weeks passed easily. Alex used the time to continue training everyone, just as his lieutenants did on each ship in the fleet. The weather was fair and no giant sea monsters attacked them as they sped toward Drakana.

Nakama spent most of his time in his cabin, resting. On the evening of the twentieth day of the voyage, he emerged with Akima and Treptan supporting him on either side. The old man was relatively stable on dry land, but the tossing of the ship made him unsteady. His arrival on the bridge caused everyone to stand a little straighter.

Nakama considered himself a failure because he had not had the nerve to pull off an attack against Drakana. It was obvious from the way the Rontan people looked at him that he was alone in that opinion. Everyone who knew him seemed to love him.

To Alex, the old man was one of the most interesting people he had ever met. He had been born into privilege and, if he had desired it, could have been an emperor/god head of everything he saw. It was only down to an intrinsic sense of honor and fair play that he had been put—at a very young age—into such a horrible position. Flee or die.

Alex thought back to where he was when he was a late teenager, and what decision he would have made at that time. He couldn't be sure he would have had the emotional wherewithal to leave everything he had ever known at a moment's notice and never look back.

To be fair, that was the same age in which he had enlisted, so that wasn't that far off.

"Just come for some fresh air?" Alex asked Nakama.

"The old man pointed a finger ahead and to their right. "We are almost there. We will arrive early tomorrow if this fair wind that has been pushing us along holds."

Alex's stomach tightened, just a little. He had grown anxious to get the attack over with, but knowing it was imminent sent him into a spin of considerations and new plans.

Nakama looked at him with wise eyes. "You have made all the preparations. You are ready."

Alex was immediately taken back to a memory of standing outside the gates of Lasta-ah. He had traveled across the entirety of what had once been the United States on horseback and on foot. He had made that journey for one purpose—to rescue Lanta-eh. And there, standing outside those gates, even with the plan in place and ready to execute, he had come to doubt himself. Senta-eh had said something very similar to him then, and her words echoed across his memory.

I hope you are with me, wife. I hope you will be the wind at my back and the strength in my arm.

Nakama's eyes fell on Quintan. The orange-robed monk stood away from everyone, silent as ever. It didn't matter how crowded a situation was, Quintan was an island to himself. Alex was surprised to see a look of disgust on Nakama's face. Alex had always assumed that the monks were neutral figures. Perhaps simple observers, nothing more.

Alex leaned in close to Nakama and whispered, "Does something about Quintan bother you?"

"Not Quintan himself," Nakama answered equally quietly. "It is the same with him and all his brothers. You should never mistake them as a friend or ally. They are neither."

Alex glanced at Quintan, who had turned away and was looking serenely out to sea. He thought of Tokin-ak, who had indeed seemed like a friend. Unconsciously, his hand touched the half-circle that he always wore around his neck—a gift from many years earlier.

"I will keep that in mind. Thank you, Nakama."

The bitterness left the old man's face and he said, "I am tired now." His eyes swept the horizon and he took as deep a breath as his lungs would allow. "We will see Drakana proper before the sun sets tomorrow."

Nakama, Akima, and Treptan disappeared below decks.

"And they will see us," Alex said to himself.

Quintan turned and looked at Alex, a guileless smile touching the corners of his lips.

Tinta-ak, Hawthorne, and Harta-ak approached Alex.

"I've cut off the ale for the night," Hawthorne said. "Best not to have any detrimental effects on the morning of a battle." His words were jovial, but there was a tightness in his voice and Alex realized that everyone was on edge.

Everyone, but Tinta-ak, that is. The big man seemed so keyed up that Alex thought he could perhaps dive overboard and swim to Drakana. Since he had lost his wife in the still-unexplained fog, he had been disconsolate. Only the promise of the thrill of battle had rescued his mood.

"Nakama says we will arrive in Drakana tomorrow afternoon," Alex said to Harta-ak.

"Good," Harta-ak answered. "We will fall back into the middle of the grouping, tomorrow, then. Let the ships who have better people on the big guns take the lead and soften them up."

Alex had decided long before not to try and teach the Kragdon-ah how to use stama. He would leave them as they are. The Rontan did not suffer from the same dislike of technology, however, so they would lead the initial battle.

Alex expected to encounter resistance from the Drakana ships when they were still distant from the port where they were going to attack. In truth, he was slightly surprised that even using this little-used route, they hadn't been attacked already.

Ever since they had been plucked from Shipwreck Isle, everything had proceeded smoothly.

It made Alex nervous.

As it should have.

Chapter Forty
Drakana

Alex suspected they were getting close to Drakana when he began to see more and more birds circling overhead.

His suspicions were confirmed when Nakama once again appeared and asked to be escorted to the bow.

"I have not seen Drakana since I was spirited away in the middle of the night," he said. "I am anxious to see it again."

The Senta-eh II had fallen back in the midst of the flotilla.

A man in the crow's nest of the ship in front of them shouted, "Land!" and his voice carried back to them. A moment later, Sanda, who was in the crow's nest of their ship, shouted out the same.

Alex looked around and saw that hundreds of his warriors had gathered at the bow and lined along both sides of the ship.

"If you don't have a job to do on deck, get below and prepare for battle. That is your job, not gawking at what cannot yet be seen. We do not want to reveal our true strength until we have to."

Alex's lieutenants took charge and gathered their squads, ushering them below decks to prepare for whatever may come.

The flotilla had circled around Drakana and approached it from the west. With the setting sun behind them, Alex hoped that it would buy them a few more moments before they were spotted.

That sunset lit the sails of the ships, turning them from white to blood red.

Above their heads, Sanda spotted something else.

"The city is burning!"

"What?" Alex exclaimed, and climbed up a rope ladder until he was twenty feet off the deck. He cupped his hand over his eyes and squinted.

Sanda was correct. There was a reddish glow from the city and once he focused his eyes, he could see columns of smoke rising up from a dozen different spots around the city.

Alex slid back down the rope ladder and tried to get a grip on what this could mean.

"Why would the city be on fire?" Alex asked everyone, but his eyes were on Nakama.

The old man closed his eyes, deep in thought for a moment, then said, "I have no idea. They must be under attack."

"From whom? We are all here!"

A small smile touched the lips of Nakama, as though he had figured out the answer to a difficult puzzle.

"The Northmen."

Akima took in Nakama's words and said, "Of course. They are finally here."

"I don't understand," Alex said. "Who are the Northmen?"

A gust of wind rippled the sails loudly and whatever Nakama intended to answer, his voice was carried away.

Akima leaned in closer to Alex. In a voice that carried on the wind, he said, "The only enemy who has ever stood up to the Drakana. Makinta spread over the entire world, but he made a mistake the day he invaded the Northmen. They did not have the weapons or training that Makinta's forces did, but it did not matter. They are ferocious fighters that do not seem to care if they live or die. Makinta marched his ships and guns into their country like he did everywhere and they ran straight at him. The Drakana guns blazed, the Northmen fell, and it did not matter. Another wave of them leaped over the bodies of the fallen and attacked. Again and again, until they were on top of the riflemen. As soon as it came down to hand-to-hand fighting, there was no fight, really."

The wind died suddenly and Nakama saw an opportunity to finish the story. "The Northmen are the most feared and legendary fighters in the world. My father told me of a man who was pinned to the ground by a spear stuck all the way through him and into the ground. He pulled the spear out of his own chest and used it to kill the man who had speared him. Attacking the Northmen was the worst mistake the Drakana ever made."

Alex leaned forward to catch every word.

"A few of our soldiers made it back to our boats and were able to sail home, but knew they would never again challenge the Northmen on the field of battle. It was impossible, even with our guns against their swords. My father's greatest fear was that someday the Northmen would bring the fight to us. If this city is on fire, I believe that is what happened. I cannot think of any other enemy who could have done this."

Alex looked up into the sky, trying to think as quickly as he could. He had spent months preparing for a particular kind of battle, against a specific opponent. Was it possible that they would not need to fight that battle at all? Could they simply believe that the war was over and turn around and sail back to Kragdon-ah?

As soon as Alex asked himself that question, he knew the answer. As long as there was a single Kragdon-ah man, woman, or child held captive in slavery in Drakana, he could not leave them.

"What do we do now?" Alex mused. He was mostly talking to himself, but if anyone wanted to pop up with a suggestion, he was more than willing to listen. He looked from Amy to Tinta-ak, to Hawthorne, then back to Nakama. No one answered.

"You cannot fight the Northmen," Nakama noted. "No one can. You might have used some of the same strategies they use to defeat the Drakana, but you will never beat them that way. They will kill anyone who stands in their way."

"Do we need to fight them? They are the enemy of the Drakana. We are the enemy of the Drakana. Could we work together?"

Nakama looked down at the deck. When his gaze returned to Alex, he said, "The Northmen are an insular people. They barely tolerate anyone who was not born in the same village. They hate outsiders of all stripes. I do not think they would work with you or anyone."

"What did we mean to accomplish by coming here?" Amy asked. "To ensure that the Drakana would not come back to Kragdon-ah. If the Northmen have wiped them out, that mission might have been met, even though not by us."

"We had two missions," Alex reminded her. "To keep the Drakana from returning and to retrieve the people of Kragdon-ah from slavery."

Amy closed her eyes. "Of course," she said. But then, she swept her arm toward the city on fire, its red glow now easily seen. "But how?"

"We sail into the city and find them."

Chapter Forty-One
A City on Fire

A nd so it was that Alex Hawk, born in Central Oregon in the late twentieth century, stood in the bow of a sailing ship and sailed into a city that, only a few hours before, had been the capital city of the most powerful nation in this world a hundred millennia after he had been born.

A city that was now on fire.

Alex had Amy on one side, Sanda on the other. He hugged them both close to him. He had done everything he could to make sure they weren't exposed to the dangers that were inherent in this world. They had come anyway. He had worried himself sick the first few days, weeks, and months they were in Kragdon-ah.

Then, he'd had an epiphany of sorts. He pictured his own parents, and what they would have thought if they'd been forced to watch him when he was on active duty. What if they had seen him as he prepared for a mission that would almost certainly turn deadly at some point? Would they have been worried about him? Of course they would. Would they have stopped him? No. They trusted him to make his own decisions. They respected the fact that it was his life and he was capable of making his own choices.

And so it had to be with Amy and Sanda. Of course Alex worried about them. He hated every moment that they were in harm's way.

But he needed to allow them to make their own choices and find their own path in life.

As they drew closer, Alex could see what a city Drakana had been. In Rontan, he had been impressed to see a four-story building. In Drakana, that building would have been lost among the towering structures around it. The architecture was difficult for Alex to wrap his mind around. There were turrets and steeply sweeping rooflines that spoke of an effort at beauty, not just functionality.

To Alex's eye, it all looked like it might be razed to the ground by the next morning.

They sailed into the harbor, where Alex had expected to meet stiff resistance. Instead, there was no one present. There was no one to greet them as each of the ships pulled into what had been a huge and bustling seaport.

No one, that is, except for one orange-robed monk, who stood with the same placid expression that they all seemed to have. Alex looked at Quintan.

"Is he here for you?"

Quintan remained as silent as ever, but did raise a hand in greeting to the man who stood on the dock.

"Why do you think these Northmen have not torched the dock yet?" Alex asked Nakama.

"Look around. There should be a hundred ships tied up here. Instead, the harbor is almost empty. I believe the Drakana ships saw how the battle was going and headed out to sea. I'm sure the Northmen will get here eventually and destroy this. For now, I do not think it was a priority target."

Each ship pulled into an empty slip or slot alongside a dock and sailors scrambled overboard to tie them down. Gangplanks were lowered to the dock and men and women touched solid ground for the first time since they had sailed from Rontan.

Alex remembered guiltily that he had sent his men below to prepare for the fight. He sent his lieutenants to bring them up and form them up on the docks. He had emptied out about half the nearly eight-hundred warriors when Sanda shouted, "People approaching. I see torches."

"How many?" Alex asked.

"Ten, maybe a few more" Sanda said. "They are coming at a run, so it's hard to tell."

"Armed?"

"Oh yes," Sanda said as she strung her bow and nocked an arrow. Nanda-eh and the other archers climbed up into the sails and did the same.

Alex put a row of his most-trusted warriors at the front of the dock and they formed into a competent shield wall. Alex himself stood in front of the shields with Monda-ak by his side.

The cobblestone road that ran from the city proper down to the docks was twisty and steep.

The men didn't march in any formation, but the bobbing torches showed that they were not dawdling. When they finally came into view, Alex could see that they all had long, matted, wild hair, and beards that covered most of their faces. It was a warm day, and outside of their knee-high boots, shields, and weapons, they were not wearing armor, or even much in the way of clothing.

Each of the approaching warriors had a large wooden shield that had various designs painted on them, and a sword or spear strapped across their back. They all held long, sputtering torches in their right hands.

They didn't slow as they approached the soldiers Alex had formed up in front of *The Senta-eh II*. When they were still twenty strides away from both the ship and Alex's men, they each threw their torch—either at the sails or onto the deck of the ship itself. Only then did they step back, draw their weapons, and seem to notice that they were facing hundreds of enemy soldiers.

The leader of the group watched as his men's torches landed and began to burn. He reached his own arm back and released the torch in an end over end arc that hit a sail right at the feet of one of Nanda-eh's archers, who fell awkwardly to the deck.

Nanda-eh did not hesitate, but said, "Fire!" Her dozen archers had a second arrow in the air before the first hit home. Four arrows hit the man who had thrown the torch into the sails.

To Alex's eye, any of the arrows looked like they could be a fatal blow—three struck him in the chest and a fourth pierced him just below his throat. The man staggered back then launched himself at Alex and the shield wall.

Alex's mouth dropped open slightly as he watched the obviously mortally wounded man rush toward him. The man never had a chance to reach Alex or anyone. Torana, who Alex had left on deck, jumped down onto the dock and ran toward the man. Before Torana could get there, Monda-ak leaped up and knocked the injured man first to his knees, then flat on his back. The last thing that Northman ever saw was a vengeful pair of canine eyes and a gaping mouth full of sharp teeth. Torana wrestled the man away from Monda-ak, lifted him over his head and hurled him like a rag doll against the side of the ship.

The battle was engaged.

The hundreds of men Alex had on the dock were at something of a disadvantage, because there wasn't room to bring more than a few dozen at a time into play. Still, between the archers in the rigging firing relentlessly and the fact that the attacking Northmen were outnumbered almost one hundred to one, they eventually fell.

By then, the dock was slick with blood. Alex looked around him and saw that twenty of his own men were dead or badly injured.

Alex turned to those on board. "Put that fire out!"

He shook his head. *We shouldn't have lost anyone to a force this small. I can't imagine if we meet them on an equal battlefield.*

The Northmen had fought until they died, so there was nothing to do with them except kick their bodies over the side of the dock and into the water.

Alex arranged for his own dead and dying to be brought back onto the ship to be cared for.

"Dad!" Sanda shouted from above. "More torches coming."

Alex called out to his lieutenants to move their squads forward. There was an empty square at the end of the dock where they could form up into units that would allow them to use their numerical advantage.

Alex called up to Nanda-eh. "Stay there. As soon as those men get close enough, fire on them."

Arrows might not stop them, but it will slow them down, by God.

The next wave of Northmen didn't bother to attack the boat but threw themselves straight at the assembled warriors, swinging mighty axes, throwing heavy spears, and swinging spiked balls at the end of a chain.

The first squad tried to form a shield wall, but the ferocity of the attack shattered the shields and drove them back until the first line tripped and fell backward. That encouraged the Northmen, who ran and dove into the scrum, swinging their melee weapons and screaming indecipherable words.

Alex's squads did their best to meet ferocity with ferocity, but the sheer animal push of the Northmen resulted in more of his warriors falling than he ever would have imagined.

Like the wave that came before them, these Northmen were so outnumbered that they never had a chance, but they fought as though they were sure they would rise to fight again tomorrow.

Torana proved to be a marvel. Alex had become so used to seeing him play gently with the children that he had forgotten what a body that big could do when used in anger. Time and again, Torana ig-nored the jabs and stabs of their weapons and simply picked them up and slammed them over his knee, breaking their backs. Monda-ak worked in tandem with him, putting each of the men out of their agony.

Darkness had fallen and the only light came from the burning buildings of the fallen city.

Alex knew they were trapped if they remained in the closed-off area of the harbor so he ordered his lieutenants to march the men up the road to the town proper.

As they marched, they ran into more small roving bands of the Northmen. Time and again, Alex watched as groups as small as three men ran at a squad of a hundred men. It looked like suicide to Alex but it did have an unsettling effect on his warriors.

How do you fight an army that truly does not care if it lives or dies?

Chapter Forty-Two
Drakana Redux

Alex had wanted to land at Drakana with a large army to take on the huge resistance he expected to find there but now found the overwhelming number of men to be a challenge. They were in a strange city with an unknown enemy and he had a difficult time grounding himself and forming a plan.

Initially, Alex expected to run into the main body of the Northmen army. They marched through the city, but there didn't seem to be any main force—just bands roaming the streets drunkenly in search of spoils.

Alex divided up his squads and sent them in different directions down the main streets, trying to root out the groups of Northmen. That fighting—small, intense skirmishes—lasted through much of the night. By the first light of morning, the city felt like a ghost town.

Alex gathered his council together in a building that had been spared the worst of the destruction of the city. Fires were still burning in many places, but everything that could burn in this location had done so. This building had been spared. He had left Nakama safely on board *The Senta-eh II* the night before, but sent Torana to fetch him. Ten minutes later the giant returned cradling the old man in his arms.

The full council consisted of Alex, Amy, Sanda, Nanda-eh, Rin-ka-ak, Harta-ak, Versa-eh, Tinta-ak, Grantan, Hawthorne, Akima, and Nakama. Quintan and the other orange-robed monk were also there, though they rarely spoke.

The building Alex had chosen as their temporary headquarters was built of stone, and so had not been burned. It had been thoroughly ransacked, but most of the furniture was just overturned, not completely destroyed. They met in a large downstairs room where a long table had survived. They turned the table back up onto its four legs, then found the least-damaged chairs and set them up as well.

Alex automatically moved Nakama to the head of one end of the table and he chose to stand at the opposite end.

Alex spoke first. "We come from different places and we have different goals for what we are trying to accomplish," Alex began. "But I don't think any of us expected this." He looked from face to face and there was no disagreement.

"Those of us who came from Kragdon-ah wanted to smash Drakana and make it impossible for them to return and conquer us. Those of you who came from Rontan wanted something similar. I think the Northmen did that for us already, and after seeing how they fight even in small groups, it is easy to understand how it happened."

Alex took a deep breath and looked at Nakama.

"We have another mission. We need to find our people who were kidnapped and enslaved. Once we have found them, we can return to Kragdon-ah. I have no quarrel with the Northmen, but they seem to have a quarrel with anyone who stands in front of them. I don't think they see any difference between the Drakana and us. We are simply another enemy. I am open to ideas as to how we can find our people."

"The problem is, we have no idea what happened to those who were brought here," Amy said. "They could have made them fight the Northmen and they could all be dead already. Or, they could have sent them to another part of Drakana, and they could all be safe and waiting for us to come and rescue them. How do we know?"

A movement caught the corner of Alex's eye. Quintan and the other monk had turned their heads toward each other and exchanged a meaningful glance.

Alex held a hand up. He looked at the monk with Quintan. "None of us know where our people went, because we weren't here when they arrived from Kragdon-ah. But you were here, weren't you?"

The monks were well-known for two things—minding their own business and answering questions posed to them in the most unhelpful way possible. They always told the truth, but often did it in a way that led the person who asked astray.

In this case, the second monk simply bowed his head toward Alex.

"Do you know where they all are?"

"I do not."

It was the first time Alex had heard the man speak. Alex thought back on his many conversations with Tokin-ak and how often he had managed to become confused or make bad decisions, even though Tokin-ak only spoke the truth.

"Do you know where they *might* be?"

"I know where *some* of them are," the monk said.

Alex sighed. *Typical.*

"Those whose location you know. Where are they?"

"The Summer Palace," the monk said, and it seemed a straightforward and simple answer.

Only Nakama had a reaction to that answer. The old man sucked in his breath, sucked his teeth, and said, "Of course, of course. That is what my brother would do."

Alex looked at Nakama and asked the obvious question. "What's the Summer Palace?"

"Drakana lies in the lowlands and the summers can be quite unpleasant. Heat, humidity, and biting bugs can ruin anyone's mood.

Five generations ago, the Makinta at the time ordered a summer palace built high in the mountains. In the wintertime, it is impossible to reach, as the road there is treacherous. Every Makinta since then has spent the worst months in the Summer Palace. It is cool there, even on the hottest days, and there is a pleasant breeze that keeps the insects from feasting on you."

"How far is this place?"

"It is within a day's walk if conditions are right," Nakama answered.

"What are the right conditions?"

"With a horde of Northmen on your heels, wanting to kill you."

"That is a motivation, yes," Alex said. "Why would your brother leave his city and retreat there?"

"If my brother left this city, he knew Drakana had fallen. He is hoping to find a place that is defensible, with tall, strong walls he can hide behind and hope that the Northmen get tired of their quest for vengeance and settle for destroying everything else."

"Is it? Defensible, I mean." Now that Alex knew that his fellow Kragdon-ah were likely there, that had become an important question to him.

"Oh, yes," Nakama answered. "There is only a single road that leads to the Summer Palace. It is not more than twenty feet across at any point. It switches this way and that and there are sharp cliffs that fall off to either side of the road. When you finally reach the palace, you will find a very tall wall that is as thick as a man laid from toe to head. My brother no doubt retreated behind those walls and doubly reinforced the walls behind him."

Alex drummed his fingers on the table, lost in thoughts and strategies. After a moment, he shook his head. "Why would he take slaves with him? If they are trapped behind thick walls, resources will undoubtedly become scarce quickly. Will he want to feed those extra mouths?"

"No doubt he will not, and they will be put to death as soon as it pleases him. He would have taken them with him because he undoubtedly took everything of value from the city and he needed them to carry the heaviest valuables."

"Then we need to go to this Summer Palace and rescue them," Alex offered.

Nakama looked truly pained, but said, "I'm afraid that will be impossible."

Alex had heard people use that word many times, just before he accomplished something.

"Why?"

Patiently, the old man said, "How many of the Northmen did you find here in the city?"

"Not many. Maybe two hundred at the most."

"When you look around what was once a great city, with a massive defensive force I would have said was the best in the world, do you think two hundred fighters could have defeated it?"

"No, these were just the stragglers left behind to mop up and look for valuables."

"I believe you are correct," Nakama said. "I also believe that the main force of the Northmen chased my brother up the mountain. If they caught them before they got behind the walls, then they are all dead. If they did not catch them, then they are safe, but the entire Northmen army stands on that one narrow road between us and them. Either way, it will be impossible to rescue them until the Northmen leave."

Impatiently, Alex said, "These Northmen have just traveled how far to attack and level Drakana? Once they have them cornered, why would they just give up and go home?"

"I agree. They wouldn't. That is why I believe you will find the Northmen stretched out on the road leading to the palace, and there they will stay until they find a way in or my brother tries to negotiate out of desperation."

"They don't look like people that are much for negotiating."

Nakama smiled with a tinge of bitterness. "They only have one negotiating tactic, and that is to kill you."

"I will not accept that there is no way to rescue the people we sailed across the ocean to get."

"It's not quite as impossible as all that," Hawthorne said.

Alex's head snapped around. "How so?"

"There is another way into this Summer Palace."

"Why didn't you say so? Let's go," Alex said, standing.

"Oh, I don't know how to get there." He pointed a finger at Quintan and the other monk. "They do."

Chapter Forty-Three
The Monks

Alex strode to the two orange-robed monks. Unlike the average person from Kragdon-ah, these monks were not exceptionally tall. In fact, standing in front of them, Alex looked them both in the eye. He didn't speak for a few moments, but just held their gaze.

"Do you know of a second way to get into the Summer Palace?"

The second monk, whose name Alex still did not know, stared placidly back at him. It occurred to Alex that if the man simply clammed up, there was nothing he could do to persuade him. What was he going to do—get physical with a monk?

"We do," the man answered finally.

Alex relaxed visibly. "I need you to take me there."

"I will not."

It was a simple declarative statement. There was no drama, no heat, and no room for negotiating. *I will not.*

"Why?"

The monk smiled, which infuriated Alex a little. "That is always an excellent question, Manta-ak. Why?"

Alex waited, but beyond that single statement, the man seemed not to be inclined to speak.

Alex tilted his head back and took a deep breath. He looked for something that the monks might want or need that he could offer in exchange for passage into the Summer Palace. He came up blank.

The monks seemed to want for nothing. If they had a grand plan for the world, it was not obvious. They always struck Alex as passive observers more than anything.

He riffled through his mind, looking for anything.

He remembered that the monks had been in communication with Lanta-eh as she attempted to communicate with the visitors who came from far away.

Why did they help us then? Why will they not help us now?

"Is there anything I can give you, anything I can help you with so that you will help us?"

The man shrugged, and it was such a human gesture, and one that Alex saw so rarely in Kragdon-ah, that it touched him.

After another moment's long silence, the monk said, "There is nothing we need. We do not keep possessions. We are simple observers of the world, nothing more."

Frustrated, Alex spun on his heels and walked away. As he did, his shirt opened and the half-circle necklace that Tokin-ak had given him so many years before became visible. The monks didn't say anything, but Amy noticed that the necklace obviously caught their attention.

Alex himself was distracted with his own thoughts and didn't notice anything. He walked back to the head of the table and sat down, momentarily lost in thought. Eventually, he snapped his head up and seemed to realize where he was. He looked around the table, then settled on Nakama.

"What is your plan from here?"

"I would very much like to speak to my brother again before I die," the old man said. "I don't know if I'll get that chance."

Alex hadn't asked Tinta-ak what his plan was, but he made it known anyway. He stood up, pounded his fist against the table and said, "We came here to fight an army and save our people. If that army is gone, I think we should fight the people who defeated them."

Alex did not dismiss that idea out of hand.

Could we defeat the Northmen?

He envisioned what Nakama had told him about the Summer Palace. The miles of long, twisting road with steep drop-offs on either side. Then he pictured fighters like they had met in the streets of Drakana. Men who flew into berserker-like rages at the mere sight of an enemy. He considered what it would be like to fight them in a place where there would be no way to use any numerical superiority.

Alex saw death. He saw one bloody skirmish after another that ended with his army—his friends and the people he loved most—thrown broken down those unforgiving cliffs.

"I understand why you want that. I will fight them if I have to. But if there is a better way, I want to take the time to look for it."

If anyone other than Alex had said that to Tinta-ak, it would not have gone well. The two men had known each other for so many years, and had fought so many battles together, they knew each other's hearts. Neither had ever had cause to doubt the other.

Instead of arguing, Tinta-ak sat back down.

Alex knew the matter was settled for the moment, but not forever.

Amy leaned close to him and said, "Dad, can I talk to you outside for a minute?"

Alex shrugged, still frustrated that he hadn't been able to solve this problem.

Amy led Alex outside the room and quietly said, "Your necklace."

Alex touched it, as he had done thousands of times over the preceding decades. It had not left his body since Tokin-ak had given it to him as a gift the last time he had seen him.

"What about it?"

"There's something about it. When you were talking to the monks, I watched their eyes when they saw it. Especially the one that speaks. It definitely attracted his attention. I just thought that since it was a gift from a monk, it might influence them somehow."

"Like a monk version of being able to cut in line?" Alex said with a smile, his sense of humor slowly returning.

"Something like that," Amy said. She turned to walk back into the meeting room. "But if you've got better ideas, that's no problem."

Kids. She knows I am out of ideas.

Alex walked back to where the monks stood against the wall.

He opened his shirt front and grasped the half-circle stone. He held it out toward them.

"Do you recognize this?"

"Yes," the monk said simply. "It is half of a pomoro stone."

"I didn't know it had a name."

The monk tore his eyes away from it. "It looks ordinary," he said, "but there are only ten pomoro stones in the world."

"Huh," Alex said, and dropped the necklace back inside his shirt. "Ten? Must be pretty valuable, then."

"No," the monk said quietly. "Value indicates it has a price that could be paid. The pomoro stones have no value because they are beyond price."

And I've been carrying it around my neck all these years.

"Are they all split in half?"

"No," the monk answered. "Only one has ever been split."

"Huh," Alex said again, nodding his head. He slipped the leather of the necklace back into his shirt. "How can you tell this isn't just some piece of rock I picked up somewhere?"

The monk did not answer his question directly. Instead, he said, "We can tell. If I pointed at her"—he indicated Amy—" and said, 'That is your daughter,' would you be able to tell her apart from any other woman I pointed to?"

"Of course I would."

"And so it is for pomoro stones."

For the first time that day, Alex felt like he had something to ne-gotiate with. Alex had realized years before that if there was bargain-ing to do, he should not be the one to do it. It seemed inevitable that he would miss some obvious detail and make a poor bargain. Because that was true, he hesitated to ever enter into any negotiation.

Amy knew this about her father. She stepped beside him, laid a hand on his shoulder, and said, "We'll give you the pomoro stone in exchange for you leading us through the secret passage to the Sum-mer Palace."

"Will we?" Alex said. He touched the small half-circle that hung around his neck. He had never considered giving it up under any cir-cumstance. It wasn't the sudden value that the monks ascribed to the stone that made Alex hesitant to part with it. It had been with him so long, it would be like trading away a part of him.

Amy stood on tiptoes and quietly whispered in Alex's ear. "Have you ever thought that maybe Tokin-ak gave you this stone for this very moment? Is that possible?"

Alex's expression softened as he thought of his old friend. "Knowing him, it's not just possible, it is likely."

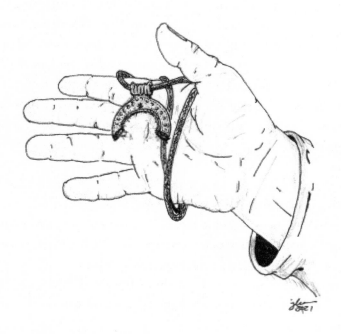

ALEX SLIPPED THE NECKLACE off and held it in front of him. If the monks wanted it badly, they did not show it. Their faces remained impassive. "Well? Alex demanded. "If I give you this, will you show me the way into the Summer Palace?"

"It is dangerous," the monk said. "You may very well die trying."

"I've heard that before," Alex said, "but here I am, still breathing."

"It is a secret we have kept for many years. If we take you there, you must go alone."

"That's fine," Alex said. "But Monda-ak goes with me everywhere."

Monda-ak had been asleep on the floor, but lifted his head at the sound of his name.

The monk said, "Then we do not have a bargain. It would be impossible to take him along."

Alex glanced at Monda-ak, then at Amy and Sanda. They both nodded at him. Of course they would keep the dog company, though he would be ferociously out of sorts while he was separated from Alex.

"All right. Just me then."

The monk held his hand out and Alex regretfully let the stone touch the man's palm and the leather draped over his fingers. The monk slipped the necklace over his own head and said, "We will leave at sunset."

Chapter Forty-Four
The Tunnel

As the sun dipped low on the horizon, Alex, Quintan, and the other monk, who Alex learned was named Bratan, said goodbye to everyone and walked on a small path that led away from town.

The army and council did not feel comfortable living in the burned-out city, so they buried the dead and returned to their ships. They would keep guards posted around the clock and would shove off if they saw the Northmen returning.

Alex did not expect the Northmen to return to the city, however. They had already looted it for everything of value that remained after Makinta fled. He was sure they would be laying siege to the Summer Palace.

Alex said a difficult goodbye to Monda-ak, who seemed inclined to not forgive him for being left behind.

Alex, Quintan, and Bratan set out at a brisk pace. The monks were excellent walkers.

Alex was the only one who was armed, thought the monks did have their orange robes, which seemed to be better than armor, at least against the human predators of this world.

"Are the Northmen peaceful toward you?" Alex asked.

Bratan considered that for a long time as he walked. Finally, with a smile, he said, "I don't know if the Northmen are *peaceful* toward anyone, or anything. However, they do not bother us. We have our monasteries in their land, just as we do everywhere."

"Just curious," Alex asked, "but why are we leaving so late in the day?"

"All monks know of this passage to the Summer Palace. However, even Makinta does not know of it. That is why I did not want to take you. It is one of our most secret secrets."

"And we'll be less likely to be spotted after dark. Of course. What if someone is following us?"

"No one is following us," Bratan said. "If they were, I would know."

They walked in silence for a few miles. They set out along the ocean, but their path turned inland and they walked upstream of a small river.

Alex felt like one of his own appendages was missing. He never went anywhere without Monda-ak and realized that while that breed of animal was famous for being inextricably bonded with their human, that was a two-way street.

It was a cloudy night, so no stars or moon shone down on them. Still, the monks walked confidently, never stumbling, as though they were in bright sunshine. Alex marveled at that for a moment until he remembered how Tokin-ak, though completely blind, saw more than any sighted person he knew.

After a long walk, Bratan broke the silence by quietly saying, "This way." He stepped off the path they had been following onto a small trail. Alex was happy to have guides who had the apparent ability to see in the dark, but at the same time, he longed for a good flashlight so he could see too.

A sudden form, somehow darker than the darkness that surrounded them, loomed up before them. Alex slowed and squinted, and realized it was a cliff. He closed his eyes and envisioned the path they had followed since they left the city. He had a hunch they had walked around a mountain until they were perhaps at the backside of where the Summer Palace was located. He craned his neck and looked up, but of course he could see nothing at all.

Quintan reached out with his walking stick and tapped on a massive boulder that sat at the bottom of the cliff. For a moment, Alex had a weird vision that the whole mountain would dissolve into a giant staircase that would lead them up to the palace.

His life would have been easier and much less dangerous had that been true.

Instead, Bratan turned to Alex and said, "Will you move the boulder?"

Alex flashed back on a similar request Tokin-ak had once made of him when they approached the monastery in Kragdon-ah. That boulder had been massive, just like this one, but moved aside at the slightest touch. At least, it moved aside at the slightest touch from the right person.

This time, Alex was ready. He didn't strain, or grunt, or really put his shoulder into the task. Instead, he placed a palm on the side of the boulder, which he would have guessed weighed four or five tons. He gave a slight push and the boulder moved as if it was weightless.

Behind the rock, there was a small cavern. Alex would not have thought it possible, but when he stepped into it, everything grew darker still. He heard the sound of Bratan moving the boulder behind them and knew they were trapped in the small room.

He could not see his own hand an inch in front of his face, but he relied on his other senses. He could hear the sound of water dripping into a pool of water with a regular *plink, plink, plink.* He could smell a dank, mossy smell. The air was cool against his face and he felt a slight breeze coming from off to his right.

Bratan lightly touched Alex's elbow and led him gently over some uneven ground. The sound of the water dropping into a pool grew louder.

"We will stay here and wait," Bratan said.

The way his voice echoed, Alex knew they had moved into a much larger chamber.

Alex blinked rapidly, but there was no difference in his vision whether his eyes were open or closed. There simply is no adjusting to the pitch darkness of a cave.

A sudden pinpoint of light appeared in the distance over their heads, followed by the sound of a rush of water. Alex heard water rushing toward them and felt a sudden urge to flee, as though he was about to be washed away.

Bratan sensed this and laid a calming hand on Alex's shoulder. "We are fine."

The last of those words was lost as a huge quantity of water dropped into the pool in front of them. The pinpoint of light disappeared, as though it had perhaps been a figment of his imagination.

Small drops of cool water sprayed up in an arc from the pool and settled on Alex's face. He closed his eyes and wiped his face.

"That will happen at regular intervals. Water will run down the shaft and wash anyone or anything away that is clinging to the walls."

"Why do I get the feeling you're about to tell me the shaft is the secret way into the palace?"

"It is indeed. I did tell you that it was dangerous and that you might very well die."

"Glad to see you didn't oversell the experience," Alex mumbled. "What do we need to do so that we don't get washed away and crushed at the bottom of the shaft?"

"Not we. You."

"Hold on, you're not coming with me?"

"Our bargain was that I would show you the way into the palace. I have done that, and I will tell you how to climb the shaft. If you survive, there is another of our brotherhood that will be waiting for you. You must reach the top before it becomes light, though, or you will have to hide until it becomes dark again. We cannot let the secret of this shaft become known by anyone."

"Got it," Alex said with a tinge of bitterness. "No problem."

"Here is what you need to do. There are small recesses built into the shaft. You need to learn the rhythm of the falling water, then climb from recess to recess in between the water falling. If you stand in the recess, you will not be washed away. There are nine of them."

"Is there a ladder?"

"Ladder?" Bratan said. "Yes, of a sort. It is possible to climb it and not be washed down."

"Have you done it?"

"No," Bratan said simply.

"Show me where to start."

Bratan led Alex to the wall next to the pool. The rush of water had once again been reduced to a steady drip-drip-drip. The monk took Alex's right hand and placed it on a small protuberance that could be used as a hand or foothold. Then he placed Alex's left hand on an identical bulge.

Bratan did not speak again, but Alex heard the two monks' footsteps as they walked away. A moment later, he heard the rock slide open, then shut.

Alex knew he was alone. In total darkness. With a task that, no matter what angle he looked at it from, seemed impossible.

Chapter Forty-Five
The Climb

Alex wished he had started counting when the water had fallen. Bratan had said the water fell at regular intervals. Alex could not understand the mechanism that would cause that to happen, but he accepted it. However, not knowing what the interval was made the information slightly useless.

Alex felt the need to climb as soon as the water fell again, though. He could try to time the water and make it to the first safe spot at the same time. He tried to estimate where he was standing in relation to the falling water. He couldn't judge whether he was out of the impact range where he stood or not.

Only one way to find out.

As it turned out, he was not out of the range.

Alex had craned his neck, knowing that the previous time the water had rushed down, it had been preceded by a point of light well above his head.

Once again, he saw the light—though there was no obvious form to it—at the same time the sound of the water came to his ears. He braced himself tight against the wall, holding onto the two hand-holds.

It seemed like it took a long time for the water to reach Alex. When it did, it dropped onto his head and shoulders with tremendous force. Even with his feet solidly on the ground, it staggered him slightly.

It drenched him and, even if he *had* been able to see, it would have blinded him.

Alex took a deep breath and began to cough as the last remnants of the falling water went in his mouth and down his throat. The coughing spasm went on for a few seconds and he realized he had not begun counting.

Shit. One, two, three, four...

He pulled himself up using the handholds, then felt with his feet and found a similar purchase for them. He grasped blindly over his head and found another handhold and then another. He pulled himself up again and braced his feet against the previous outcroppings.

It didn't take long for his shoulders to begin to ache and his fingers to grow numb from the cold water and grasping the tiny knobs of rock so tightly.

Ninety-eight, ninety-nine, one-hundred...

He tried to estimate how far he had climbed, but doing that little bit of math while continuing to count was more than he could handle.

He felt like he had climbed a great height, but knew he could very well still be toward the bottom of the shaft. His had a vision of a steep cliff that climbed up hundreds and hundreds of feet, essentially taunting him with *and you're climbing up inside that.*

Two-hundred-thirteen, two-hundred-fourteen, two-hundred-fifteen...

It seemed like it had already been too long since the water had fallen, and he knew it must be time for it to come. He searched desperately above him for the promised indent in the rock.

His fingers stretched and grasped, but all he found was more handholds, allowing him to continue to propel himself up, up, up.

Three-hundred-forty, three-hundred-forty-one, three-hundred-forty-two...

Alex's fingers finally found something that was not just another small outcropping to grab onto. It was a ledge.

Alex threw his head back and looked up. The pinpoint of light appeared.

The water was coming.

It felt like all the strength had drained from his arms. He knew that if the water found him still clinging to the rock, he would be smashed into the rocks below. The desperation of that thought caused him to leap up off the final toehold he had. He managed to get most of his chest on the platform as he heard the water directly above him.

He tried to curl up into a ball on the recessed ledge, but did not move his legs out of the way quickly enough.

The water slammed into his lower legs and he felt himself being pulled inexorably off the ledge. He flailed his arms, looking for anything to hold onto. Finally, his right hand found a crease in the rock and he jammed his fingers in. That gave him enough leverage to arrest his slide and he pulled himself back onto the ledge and away from the waterfall.

The muscles in his legs and arms were burning and he had a difficult time catching his breath, which came in ragged bursts.

That's one? Bratan said there were nine of these. There is no way I can do this eight more times.

The small voice in the very back of Alex's mind whispered to him quietly.

What choice do you have?

Alex knew that in order to make it from station to station before the water fell again, he would need to time his climb perfectly. He also knew that based on how his strength was flagging already, the climb itself would likely kill him if he jumped back out into the shaft immediately.

Instead, he gave himself a respite. He felt around in the total darkness and calculated the size of his small ledge. It was perhaps three feet deep—just enough to pull himself out of the way of the rushing water.

Alex sat with his back against the cold wall. His clothes and hair were wet and even though it had been a warm day, he was shivering.

Tucked back into the small shelf, he did not see the pinpoint of light when it once again appeared. He did hear the water rushing toward him, and felt incredulous.

It just fell. The interval must be changing.

He shook his head to clear his mind and waited for the last of the water to fall. He reached above the shelf and found another set of small rocks to grasp onto.

He sighed, mumbled, "Right, what choice do I have?" and pulled himself up.

As it turned out, the distances between shelves were all different. The climb from the floor of the shaft to that first protective indent in the rock was by far the longest.

Alex didn't know if that was by the design of whoever built this torture chamber, or if it was dictated by the natural layout of the shaft.

In any case, Alex made the trip between the first indented ledge and the second with almost a full minute to spare.

His muscles still screamed at him, and he took at least one rest period between each climb, but he slowly made his way up the slick wall in the darkness.

When he arrived at the seventh ledge, he had begun to think that he might survive the climb. That seventh leg had been a bit longer, and Alex had barely beaten the water, but he was there.

He pulled his exhausted body up onto the ledge, wishing for the hundredth time in the span of a few hours that he was twenty years younger.

He kneeled for a long moment on the hard ledge, then stood up to try to stretch some of the ache out of his lower back, which was beginning to spasm.

When he stood, he felt his head brush against something soft and furry.

His blood ran cold and it took every ounce of mental strength not to simply leap back out into the abyss of the shaft and plunge to his death.

Whatever he touched gave off an annoyed squeak of a sound that instantly told Alex it was a bat. Or perhaps bats, plural.

For just a moment, Alex lost his mind. He began to scream and pinwheel his arms while shaking his head from side to side like a madman.

Over his head, a small family of bats took flight with a flutter of leathery wings.

Alex ran his hands over his face, his neck, his bare arms, trying to determine if any of them were on him, or if they had bitten or scratched him.

Physically, he was unharmed. In other ways, he was disturbed and nearing the end of his rope.

He groped blindly around him. If there were more creepy-crawly things sharing the platform with him, he wanted to know it right then.

There was nothing there, and Alex allowed himself to relax and breathe. He stamped his feet, wriggled his hands, and tried to get his blood to circulate and bring some strength back to his limbs.

He contemplated just curling up and taking a two-hour nap, but his driving sense of responsibility would not allow him to fully rest.

Bratan had said that if he did not reach the top by first light, whoever was there to help him would be gone until darkness fell again. Alex couldn't tell how much time had passed since he had started his climb. It felt both like an eternity that might have stretched on for weeks and also mere moments since he had started.

Alex waited until the water whooshed by him again and forced himself out into the vertical corridor, climbing, climbing, forever climbing.

The eighth rest spot did not present any more unusual challenges. No centipedes that were three feet long, or eyeless, skittering cockroaches that wanted to share their platform with him.

He leaned his head out slightly and looked up. Each climb, each new platform, brought him closer to whatever the source of the water was. Just as he looked up, he felt a sense of movement not far above his head. The light was no longer just a pinpoint. He could see the source of the light was a burning torch that showed for a moment, then winked out. As it did, the water poured and poured and ran down the shaft.

Alex chose not to rest. He was too close to his goal for that. As soon as the last gallons of water passed him, he began the climb. The final leg was the shortest. He only transferred from one handhold to another four times when he felt a long, flat platform above him and to his right.

He used the last of his strength to pull himself up and actually had time to catch his breath before the ceiling above him began to move. It lowered toward him, but stopped a foot above his head. The water splashed out and the ceiling returned to its original position.

Behind him, a voice said, "I was about to leave. Hurry and come with me."

Chapter Forty-Six
The Summer Palace

Alex did not question the unseen person behind the voice. He was too exhausted for questions or arguments. He simply reached his hand out in front of him and walked in the direction of the voice.

A strong hand gripped his elbow and pulled him to the right and up a short set of stones set into the rock.

"Stay here," the voice said. Then Alex heard a sound that was very much like the rolling, scraping sound the huge boulder at the foot of the cliff had made when it slid away.

It was still dark outside, although normal darkness, with a minimum of ambient light from the skies, which suddenly seemed very bright to Alex.

Alex turned in a circle, trying to get his bearings. Behind him, he heard the sound of running water. When he turned toward it, he saw a circle of torches suspended over what appeared to be a swimming pool. A small stream flowed into the pool, filling it. The light from the flames glittered and danced on the water.

Then, Alex saw what had caused the phenomenon of the water filling the shaft. When the pool filled to a certain point, it became unstable and slowly tipped over, dropping the full weight of its water into the shaft. Seen from below, the torches above the pool would appear as a pinpoint of light.

Alex smiled to himself and shook his head.

Ingenious. Who would ever want to look down into the dark shaft below? And with the sliding boulders at the top and bottom, it will remain a secret passageway forever.

"I am Thelon," the man beside him said.

Alex looked and saw that he was dressed in the same orange robes as all the monks. This man had a hideous scar that ran from the left side of his jaw up across his sightless left eye and into his scalp.

"Manta-ak," Alex said.

The man did not acknowledge that. Alex remembered that all the monks seemed to practice some sort of telepathy. That was how Thelon had known he was coming.

"Can I see Makinta?"

Thelon turned a slightly surprised eye on Alex. "Makinta presents himself as a god."

"Interesting choice of words," Alex noted. "*Presents himself...*"

"Which is to say that one does not crawl out of a well dripping wet and disheveled and walk right into Makinta's bedroom for a conference."

"Does he know I am here?"

"He does not. We thought that you would likely fail and die in the climb. If that had happened, we would have received the pomoro stone at no risk to ourselves. That was a risk worth taking."

"How many people have climbed up that way?"

"Oh, no one," he said, and seemed quite proud. Since the monks typically displayed no emotion at all, it stood out on his face. "Makinta himself ordered the pool that drains itself to be built over the natural shaft. We saw an opportunity for future gain and installed the handholds and safety spots. But no one has ever actually used it before."

Alex reminded himself once again that he needed to check out these bargains he made before committing to them.

Ignoring the fact that the monks thought he would be killed in the climb, Alex said, "What do I need to do to see him?"

"Leave it to me," Thelon said. "I will be with him while he lunches. I often have his ear and I will see what I can do. For now, I will take you to our humble monastery here in the palace."

They walked along a path of finely ground white gravel. To his left, Alex could see the tall, thick wall that served as the only protection from the Northmen. If they were attempting to scale it or break through it, there was no sign or sound of it.

Inside the wall, everything was placid. There were winding paths, gardens, and what looked like meditation spots.

"Where are the slaves kept?"

"It may not seem it from here, but the Summer Palace is quite extensive. Where we stand was once a natural valley. As you can see, it was protected on three sides by impassable cliffs. All that was left to do was build the wall across the front. Doing so gave a huge, easily protected piece of land to develop. We are standing in the Summer Palace proper. It is designed to meet the taste of Makinta."

Thelon pointed to a broader path that led away toward one of the looming cliffs.

"If you follow that path, it will lead you to another section of what is, in reality, a small city. That is where the servants and slaves work. There are gardens there, as well, but where these gardens are planted for their beauty, those are designed to provide nutrition."

"I'd like to go there. I want to see if some of our people are truly there."

"It would not be wise for you to walk around the palace alone. As long as you are with me, you will not be questioned. Come with me to the monastery and rest. You must be tired after a long night."

Alex had run on adrenaline for the previous hours, but now the legitimate chance of dying was past. At Thelon's suggestion that he must be tired, Alex realized he was perhaps as exhausted as he had ever been. It would be wise for him to rest before facing Makinta.

"Agreed," Alex said, and Thelon gestured to a path to his right. "It's not far. We earn our keep here in the palace by maintaining the gardens and the well. Makinta decreed that we should live nearby them."

Alex had learned long ago that when someone referred to their home as *humble*, it was typically a humble-brag, like calling a huge mansion on the water *our humble little summer place.*

In this case, Thelon was not bragging. The monastery building was non-descript, with the only stand-out architectural detail being a sharply pitched roof that rose higher than the building itself.

Inside, the space was not divided into spaces, but was one open room, though obviously divided into different uses. The majority of the space was taken up by two rows of sleeping pallets. One corner of the room had a wood stove that was vented to the outside. Besides that, there was a long, low table. There was no other furniture.

Two other monks approached Alex as soon as he and Thelon stepped inside. Politely but firmly, they indicated that Alex should sit and remove his moccasins. One monk washed Alex's feet and the other did the same for Thelon.

It was an odd feeling for Alex to have clean feet while the rest of him was so smelly and grungy from his climb.

"Before you rest, you should bathe."

Bathing was not a popular concept among the tribes of Kragdon-ah. In fact, Alex had never seen anything like a bathtub anywhere since he had first stepped through the door.

The monks led Alex through the room and slid a door to a small patio outside. There was a tub large enough for five or six people to sit in. Alex couldn't tell what metal had been used to make it, but it was warm to his touch because there were the coals of a fire that had burned down beneath it.

He stripped down—having mostly lost his innate modesty since coming to Kragdon-ah—and stepped into the warm, fragrant water.

It was, he decided, among the best moments of his life. His tired, aching arms and legs accepted the heat and at least partially forgave him for what he had put them through.

Alex let himself slip beneath the water before popping back up with a smile.

Thelon stood beside him with a washcloth and small bar of soap. Alex accepted it, held it to his nose and inhaled. It smelled of lavender, which he had seen growing in the gardens outside.

If you've got to make a last stand, I'd say this is the place to do it.

Alex washed himself, slightly ashamed of how dirty he had made the water.

They're going to have to drain the whole thing and start over again after I get out.

After fifteen minutes, Alex reluctantly climbed out of the tub and dried himself with the towel Thelon had left behind for him. He reached for his clothes, but saw that they were gone.

Thelon reappeared with a robe.

"We are washing your clothes," he said simply. "You should sleep now."

Alex did not need to be told twice. After the hellish climb and hours facing death, followed by the cleansing hot water, he was dead on his feet. His legs were leaden and he could barely keep his eyes open.

Thelon led him to a pallet and he collapsed across it, asleep within seconds.

Chapter Forty-Seven
Makinta

Alex didn't so much as move for the next four hours.

When Thelon stood over him and said, "Manta-ak," he still didn't move. The monk knelt beside him and laid a hand on his shoulder.

Alex came out of his deep sleep with a jump. He was unused to being woken up.

Thelon gave Alex a moment to reconnoiter where he was. His eyes were slightly unfocused, but only for a moment. Then, "Makinta?"

"It is time," Thelon said.

Alex sat up and realized he had fallen asleep in the robe. He looked about and saw that his filthy clothes had been washed, dried somehow, and were folded at the foot of the pallet.

Two minutes later, he and Thelon were walking toward the *palace* part of the Summer Palace.

It wasn't a massive building, as palaces went, but it was three-stories tall, with more of the steeply slanting ornamental rooflines that the monk's monastery had. The walls were a gleaming white, while the roof was a deep red.

Outside, Alex paused and listened. He could hear some noise coming from the tall wall. When he looked in that direction, he saw that a line of Drakana soldiers stood twenty feet back from the wall, rifles at the ready. If any stray Northman made his way over, he would meet a hail of bullets. Tough fighter or not, anyone who is shot ten or twelve times is likely to die.

There were tall double doors that led into an entryway that soared up to the tallest point of the ceiling. The net effect was to make Alex feel very small. He guessed that was the whole plan.

There were more armed soldiers lined all along the polished wood floor and walls of the entry.

Alex had no idea where his meeting with Makinta would take place. An opulent garden? A business-like conference room?

It was neither. Makinta sat on a no-doubt-about-it epic throne at the end of a long gold and red carpet runner. Alex made a note of the fact that Makinta liked the trappings of power.

Makinta was, not unexpectedly, an old man. Alex was sure that by this point, he was already well into training his son to be the next Makinta.

A stray thought occurred to Alex. *Has any son ever jumped the gun and helped dear old dad on to his final reward a little early? Likely so, but it's not going to be something they discuss in polite company.*

As he drew closer, Alex couldn't help but notice the remarkable resemblance between Makinta and Nakama. They were brothers, so that wasn't unlikely, but it was so uncanny that Alex thought Nakama might have fooled people into believing he was Makinta if they didn't look too closely.

Thelon stopped ten feet in front of the throne and Alex took his cue from that. That close to the man, Alex could begin to see the differences between Nakama and Makinta. Where Nakama's eyes were kind, Makinta had the bird-like focus of a hawk about to swoop down on a field mouse. Where Nakama was often smiling or laughing, Makinta had pursed lips and a drawn expression.

Alex was glad he was aligned with the brother and not the god-head. He had to remind himself that he needed to strike a deal with the man in front of him to make things work, though.

Thelon cleared his throat, looked passively at the floor a few feet in front of him and said, "This is Manta-ak from Winten-ah in Krag-don-ah."

Just hearing the name of his adopted home was enough to make Alex homesick, but he put that out of his mind and focused.

Makinta did not speak, but turned to an advisor who stood be-side him. The man hustled away and Makinta turned his attention back to Alex.

"Thelon asked me for the favor of my time. What do you want?"

Straight to the point. All right, that's how we'll play it.

"I am here to help you defeat the Northmen," Alex said in Drakana.

Makinta's attention had already been drifting away, but that brought him back around. He smiled, and Alex instantly decided he liked the dour version of Makinta better than this attempt at pleas-antry. A smile did not sit well on his face.

Makinta leaned forward and at least feigned interest. "Do you have a weapon I am not aware of? An army of super-fighters trained to take on that horde from the north?" He focused on Thelon and said, "How did this man get here? I don't remember approving him. Is he one of the slaves?"

Thelon stared at the floor in front of him and became as mute as Quintan.

Alex took a step toward Makinta and the guards on either side of the throne casually leveled their rifles at him.

"If you don't find a solution soon, Drakana may cease to exist. In the best case, the country you have ruled over for centuries will be se-verely damaged."

It rankled Alex, but he had made the decision to play along with the idea that this person in front of him was the same Makinta that had lived for hundreds of years.

Makinta's face clouded over. It was plain that no one spoke unpleasant truths to him. He wondered how he had been convinced to retreat to the Summer Palace. *Your Grace, the palace in the mountains is so pleasant this time of year. Let's go there and take everything of value with us.*

"I offer you a solution. It is not without risks, and there will be a price paid by all of us, but it is the only way I can see both of us accomplishing what we want."

And that price will be paid by the many that lay down their lives, while you sit on your throne and ask for battle reports. But it can't be helped.

"I'm listening," Makinta said grudgingly.

"I *do* have an army. They are not super-soldiers, but they are well trained and they are currently sitting in what was your capital city until very recently."

That statement impacted Makinta. He leaned toward one of his advisors, whispered something, but received no answer.

"My fighters are willing to face the Northmen on the field of combat. I would say that people like that are in short supply for you."

Makinta's eyes hooded like a cobra's.

"We have superior numbers, but I don't believe that is enough to defeat the Northmen. I have seen them fight. They are unmatched. However, at this minute, their army is camped outside your walls here and stretched out for miles down the road that leads to this palace. We essentially have them in a pincer, though they don't know it yet. I believe that if we both attack them aggressively, we can meet in the middle as allies, with the Northmen vanquished."

Makinta blinked and Alex's image of facing a cobra only increased.

"You have an army. In my city."

Alex did not answer. The worst Makinta could do in his present position was kill him. Beyond that, the formerly most powerful man in the world was powerless.

Suddenly, Makinta's eyes flew wide with recognition. He leaned toward his advisor again and whispered a question urgently. The man cupped his hand over the emperor's ear and gave him a short answer.

"Manta-ak. That name has been niggling at my brain. Now I have placed you. You challenged my commanders to Thundan." Again, he leaned over and whispered urgently to his aide de camp. "Or at least you are presenting yourself as him. Are you the man who killed Panga in hand-to-hand combat?"

Alex held both arms up. Webs of scars ran up both of them from the wrists to past his elbows. "I killed Panga, but he left his mark on me."

Makinta held up a hand. "Well enough. Wait here for a moment." The aide beside him reached down and helped the old man to his feet. He disappeared through a door situated behind the throne.

That gave Alex a moment to look around the throne room. Rich tapestries with intricate designs hung down the walls. Now that it was empty, he could see the throne more clearly. It was made of polished wood and obviously hand carved. A dragon's tail began on the right arm and that carving concluded with the roaring head of the dragon at the top. The left side was the same, but it was a lion instead of a dragon.

Outside the throne room, the floors had been wood, but this room was white with natural gray designs running through it—marble, to Alex's eye.

Even though Makinta was gone, the guards beside the throne and placed along the wall did not relax. Alex realized there were two dozen weapons pointed at him. That did not concern him much. Weapons had been pointed in his direction much of his adult life.

Minutes ticked by, then the door behind the throne opened again. Makinta stepped through, followed by his aide and a third man.

Alex gawked with recognition. It was Mandran, the commander of the army he had first encountered. The man Alex sat beside when Torana had thrown Tinta-ak into him, shattering his leg. That was confirmed as Mandran fully appeared. All this time later, he still walked with the aid of a cane.

Makinta sat on the throne with a sigh of relief, then said, "I brought this man to identify you, Manta-ak, but I see it is not necessary. I can tell from both your expressions that you know each other."

Alex looked more closely at Mandran. The intervening years had not treated him especially kindly. His face sagged, there were dark circles under his eyes, and he was dressed, not as an army commander, but in the garb of a common soldier.

Makinta did not bother to even speak to Mandran. Instead he waved him away dismissively.

Mandran looked at Alex, but there was no heat, no hatred in his gaze. Whatever feelings he had once had for him, he had long since come to grips with them. Head bowed, and with as much dignity as he could muster, he limped through the door.

Makinta also stared at Alex, obviously somewhat more interested in him now that he had a better understanding of who he was.

"Manta-ak from Prindan Zand, I am curious. The ways of those people are quite backward. How did you manage to get from there to here?"

Alex considered what to tell him. As usual, he decided the truth was the best option.

"You left a ship behind in Kragdon-ah," Alex said, purposefully not using the insulting name for Kragdon-ah that Makinta had. "We attacked the men guarding it, dispatched them, then stole the ship and sailed it here."

He decided to leave out the part about that ship being sunk by Makinta's men and his subsequent rescue by Nakama. He thought it was best to keep Makinta's brother's arrival in Drakana a secret.

Makinta leaned forward and rested his chin in his hand.

"I'm having a hard time thinking of a reason why I shouldn't execute you for piracy right now."

In response, the soldiers beside him raised their rifles to their shoulders, ready to carry out the execution order.

"I'll give you a reason. Because if you kill me, you will slowly starve to death trapped in your palace. This is a beautiful place, but it is not self-sustaining here. You will kill the slaves first, but that won't help. Who will raise what food you are producing then? Soon some of your soldiers will be forced to kill the others, just so the food can be stretched farther. In the end, it won't matter. You'll be eating nothing more than scraps off your beautiful plates on your hand-carved table."

Alex didn't actually know that Makinta had a hand-carved dining room table. It was just a guess based on everything he had seen up to that point.

"And what happens to you then? Try to escape over the wall in the dark? The Northmen will still be there, waiting for you." Alex's eyes bored into Makinta's. "There is no good end for you without me. I am your hope for salvation."

Makinta narrowed his eyes, hating Alex, but recognizing the truth of his words.

"What is it you want from me?" It was obvious the words—and the fact he was forced to enter into a negotiation with Alex—were painful to him.

Alex had spent long hours in consultation with Hawthorne, Akima, Nakama, Amy, Sanda, and Grantan about what the answer to this question should be.

Alex held up his hand and ticked off his demands on his fingers. "You must aid us in the fight. At our signal, you must open your gate and allow the Northmen in to fight you. I can strategize with your commanders to set traps for them. While you fight them here, we will also attack them from behind. They will be forced to fight on two fronts."

Alex could see that Makinta was already having his doubts.

"Once we beat the Northmen, and the last of them are killed, you will free all the people who were kidnapped and brought here from Kragdon-ah. You will give us enough ships to transport them home. Once we are there, we will have no need of the ships again, so your people who are there can sail them home to you if you wish. Finally, you must agree to never attack the people of Kragdon-ah again."

"Feh," Makinta said, explosively. "I will never agree to such terms."

"Then you should kill me now and begin the wait for the same fate yourself at the hands of the Northmen. I will point this out, though. How much good will those enslaved people do you when you can't feed them? How much good do those ships do you when you are run through by a Northman's sword? How will you conceive of another attack on Kragdon-ah when you are dead?"

These were likely the harshest words anyone had ever dared to speak to this Makinta or any of the preceding Makintas.

He did not take it well. He turned to his aide and said, "Take him into custody. Put him in chains. Let him rot."

Chapter Forty-Eight
In Chains

Alex did not resist as the soldiers approached him and grabbed him roughly by each arm. They hustled him out of the palace, along the white-graveled path that led to a small, open square. There was a tall, thick post sunk deep into the ground there. Short iron shackles hung limply down the sides.

Out of his peripheral vision, Alex scoped the two guards out. Alex estimated that he could have taken them out rather easily. They were not expecting him to push back. They were armed, but it was with rifles, which were not good for close combat, and with pistols, but those were pushed into their belts.

In the end, Alex couldn't see where taking the guards out would lead, so he let them take him to the rough pole.

The guards pushed Alex's face into the post, wrapped his arms around it, then stuck his hands in the shackles and clasped them shut.

Without a word, they turned on their heels and walked away.

It wasn't a comfortable position, but if Alex shifted his weight this way or that, he could find an adequate way to stand for a few minutes at a time. The shackles were attached to a chain that ran through a bolt at the top of the post. They were nearly eight feet off the ground, which meant that Alex could not sit or even squat, but was forced to stand on the balls of his feet.

It was mid-afternoon and the sun was high overhead. It beat relentlessly down on Alex, whose mind worked constantly, trying to think of a way out of his predicament.

If he could free himself from the chains, he could make his way to the hidden door and climb back down the shaft. But even if he could, what then? He would have risked the horrible climb for nothing, and they would be in the same position.

Nakama would be in some sort of control of the city, but that hold would be tenuous at best and they would likely be overrun once the Northmen dispatched Makinta and returned.

Alex would still not have rescued the people he had come to save.

Everything he had done to get to Drakana would be for naught.

He fidgeted with the shackles and chains, trying to get an estimate of how strong they were. They did not show any easy method of escape.

Alex lifted his head and looked around the area. Very few people passed near him closely enough that he could even shout at them. Perhaps having people chained in the public square was common enough that it didn't even attract attention.

He began watching each person as they passed, looking to see if he recognized anyone. Finally, after several hours had passed, he saw someone.

A dark-skinned man that was almost a foot taller than anyone else Alex had seen in the Summer Palace passed by. In the universal language of Kragdon-ah, Alex called, "Gunta, friend, gunta. Can you help me?"

Alex couldn't be sure the man was from Kragdon-ah, of course, he could simply be a tall man with dark skin from Drakana.

Whatever the case, the man did not respond, aside from quickening his step. In moments, he was in the long shadows cast by the palace, then disappeared.

After five hours being chained to the post, Alex hurt everywhere. He had managed to keep his face out of the direct sunlight most of the time, but he was still overheated and terribly thirsty.

Eventually, the sun went down and the temperatures dropped. Alex wondered how cold it got at the top of the mountain at this time of year. He wondered if anyone would appear to give him water or food. Eventually, he decided that would not be the case and, as Makinta had said, he was being left to rot.

A new plan came into Alex's mind. He would find a way to escape—that part of the plan was still unclear. Once he did, instead of fleeing back down the shaft, he would sneak into the castle, take out Makinta's guards, and kill the god himself.

He wasn't sure how that would help him strategically, but it was a fantasy to help him get through the long, increasingly cold night.

Once complete darkness fell, Alex tried something new.

He wrapped his arms and legs around the pole and shimmied up to the top. He thought perhaps the bolt that held the chains at the top could be worked free. It was a lot of work to climb up, as the chains constantly interfered, but eventually he made it.

Only to discover that, as with so much of what the Drakana built, the bolt was affixed properly and could not be budged.

He slid back down to the bottom. His arms and legs hadn't fully recovered from his ordeal in the shaft the night before and now his muscles were once again being tested to their limit.

Alex Hawk was not a man much given over to despair, but he felt it wash over him.

He thought of Amy, Sanda, and Monda-ak, and how they would wonder about what happened to him if he never returned. He thought of the cliffside and his brother Sekun-ak. He thought of all the people on his council who had trusted him to solve this problem. He knew he was letting all of them down, and regretted not taking out the guards who had chained him.

The sun rose, but things did not look any brighter to Alex. The heat returned almost immediately and brought increased thirst.

Hours more passed, and as hard as Alex thought, nothing came to mind to extricate himself from this dire situation.

Most of the day had passed when two guards approached the post. Without a word, they unshackled him. Freed from the constraints, Alex's legs nearly collapsed under him. His shoulders were on fire and every muscle throbbed.

The soldiers turned Alex back toward the palace and pushed him ahead. He stumbled and came close to falling, but managed to stay semi-upright. He rolled his shoulders, shook his hands, and did his best to push some circulation back through his limbs.

There was no thought in his mind of attacking the guards. In the condition he was in, he knew there was no way he could have effectively fought them.

The guards had still not spoken, but guided him on the same path they had taken him the day before. When they approached the palace, the doors swung open and he was escorted inside.

The soldiers who lined up on both sides of the entryway ignored him as he passed. Just as he had been the day before, he was escorted into the throne room. Makinta once again sat on his throne.

Alex did his best to straighten his posture and walk as though he was not in pain.

When he approached within fifteen feet of Makinta, the guards grabbed his elbows and stopped him.

For long moments, the two men looked at each other. Alex had no interest in speaking first. He couldn't imagine what he would say.

Finally, after the dead silence played on in the room for an uncomfortable time, Makinta said, "I have decided to give you another chance to speak to me. Your demands yesterday were ridiculous. I will not be told what to do by someone like you."

Alex still did not speak.

"Have you reconsidered what you require from me?"

"I have not. I will not. I cannot," Alex said softly.

Makinta closed his eyes as though he was pained.

"Take him away. Chain him."

Alex went through the same routine as he had the day before. Arms chained over his head, face against the pole.

"He will do this to you until you die, you know," one guard said.

"So be it," Alex said.

The second night and day seemed even longer than the previous cycle had been.

Alex had not slept at all the previous night, but this time he somehow fell into a troubled slumber, full of pain and dancing shadows.

At midday the following day, the same charade played out. Alex was released from his shackles. This time he *did* collapse when loosened. It took everything he had to manage to stand. He believed some sort of permanent damage had been done to his shoulders and upper back. He was not sure he would ever walk upright again.

Alex had once read of one of the men who had been accused of witchcraft in Salem, Massachusetts. He had not been hanged, but instead had been pressed to death. That was accomplished by putting the man in an indent in the ground, then laying heavy rocks on him. Each time the inquisitors gave the man a chance to confess he said only two words: "More weight."

Finally, the inevitable happened and the man expired, unable to breathe because of the weight on his chest.

It had begun to feel like he might be playing out the same cycle, with Makinta playing the role of the inquisitor and Alex as the crushed man.

After a few steps, Alex was able to walk in more or less a straight line into the throne room.

This time, Makinta did not wait, but simply said, "Well? Have you changed your mind?"

Through parched lips, Alex said, "I have not. I will not. I cannot."

Alex was drug back and chained.

He was semi-delirious now, muttering "I cannot," over and over again.

Darkness fell. Alex swayed slightly at the end of the chains, no longer able to support himself.

He had not had water in two days and knew he would not likely survive another cycle like this.

His strategic mind, which was always his greatest weapon, was now useless, lost in an endless jumble of images, desires, and nightmares.

It was the darkest hour when two men slipped out of the shadows to him. One—a foot taller than Alex—lifted him up and relieved the pressure on his arms. The other—also tall and lanky—cradled Alex's head back and used a bag to squirt water past his parched lips and tongue.

Alex coughed and woke fully for the first time in hours.

The man who held him off the ground whispered, "Gunta, Manta-ak."

The water helped revive Alex. He had to work his throat several times to be able to accept the water. He focused on not coughing because he didn't want to attract any attention.

"Thank you," Alex said hoarsely. "You've got to leave me."

"We are sorry we couldn't come to your aid sooner. We didn't want to tip off our overseer, then we would not be able to do you any good."

"It's fine, don't worry about it," Alex said, still a little disconnected. When he stopped to think, he couldn't be sure what language he had spoken in.

The tall man with the dark skin looked around, then said, "Here, take a little more water. Not too much, or it will make your stomach clench."

Alex gratefully accepted the life-giving water.

The man who carried the bag let it drop, then rubbed his hands together to generate warmth. He then rubbed them over Alex's shoulder and upper back.

"We can get you down, if you would like."

Alex wanted that more than anything he could imagine.

"No. Thank you for the water. I am better now. Please go back to our people and tell them we are here to rescue them."

"We have already told them. As soon as I recognized you, I knew that somehow, you had followed us and that you were here to take us home."

The way he said that last word—*home*—it gave the impression he had said *heaven* or *nirvana* or some such.

Hearing that revitalized Alex as much as the water. It gave him renewed purpose.

"We must leave now, before we are discovered," the man who had been holding Alex off the ground said, gently lowering him. "If you are still here tomorrow, we will come back. Gunta, Manta-ak."

They slipped away into the shadows.

The next day, Alex was still physically destroyed by his two days on the pole, but he felt slightly better to have had his thirst quenched in the night. He didn't let on about that, though, and this time fell completely down when he was released. He acted as though he could not walk and allowed the soldiers to carry him into the throne room. They dropped him at the feet of Makinta.

"This is getting us nowhere," Makinta said, his frustration evident.

Alex was on all fours and let his head hang down.

"You will die before you agree to reasonable terms, won't you?"

Alex managed to pull his legs underneath him and sat back on his heels. The effort of that cost him most of his remaining strength.

He tried to push his tongue out between his chapped lips, but it would not go. Finally, he managed to croak out, "I will die first."

"Feh," Makinta said. "I will never understand unreasonable people." He glared at Alex, who was unmoved. He felt so near to death he was beyond caring.

Makinta raised one bejeweled hand, ready to send Alex back to the pole, this time likely never to return.

Just before he made his pronouncement, the man who stood beside him moved his head forward and whispered in Makinta's ear.

A flash of irritation spread across Makinta's face, but he whispered something back and the man left. Makinta continued to stare at Alex, his lip curled in distaste.

Moments later, Mandran came limping in. He and Makinta huddled together, speaking quietly for a long time. It was obvious who held the power between the two of them. It was the godhead, not the disgraced soldier. And yet, Mandran did not back down.

Finally, Makinta took a long breath and held it. He dismissed Mandran with a wave, then turned back to Alex.

Alex was not aware Makinta was looking at him. He had a difficult time lifting his head up.

Makinta's next words shocked him.

"Fine. I agree to your terms."

The sudden agreement electrified Alex and gave him a strength he didn't think he would ever possess again.

"You will attack from here while we attack from below?"

"Yes."

"You will let the people of Kragdon-ah go free?"

"Yes," Makinta said, with increasing petulance.

Alex didn't care. This was one bargain he wasn't going to lose. He couldn't afford to.

"You will give us ships to return home." It wasn't a question any more, but a statement.

Makinta sighed. "Yes."

"And you agree and bind all future incarnations of yourself to never attack Kragdon-ah again."

Makinta was silent, as though mentally counting to ten. "I agree, for me and all my future incarnations."

"Then we have a deal," Alex said, and collapsed onto the fine marble floor, unconscious.

Chapter Forty-Nine
Recovery

As soon as Alex and Makinta reached an agreement, everything changed. Alex went from an opponent to be broken down to an ally to be cared for.

Makinta stood and left the throne room, but not before giving instructions to his ever-present aide. That man made arrangements for Alex to be picked up and carried to a private room with a plush, comfortable bed.

Alex lapsed in and out of consciousness for twenty-four hours, but he finally settled into a healing deep sleep. He slept through the rest of that day and through the night.

He was awakened by sunshine slanting in through a high window in his room. He had not recovered from his ordeal, but he was ahead of where he was when he had collapsed in the throne room.

As soon as his feet hit the floor, an older woman with steel-gray hair and laugh lines around her eyes hurried in. She presented Alex with a warm damp cloth and indicated he should wash his face.

Before he was done with that, she had poured a large cup of some sort of hot beverage and pushed it into his hands. Alex had experienced mixed results with hot drinks in Kragdon-ah, so he hesitated. The woman was not going to take no for an answer. She pushed the cup toward Alex's lips.

He sipped hesitantly, then drank greedily. It was warm but not hot and had a sweet, delicious flavor that warmed him as it went down.

The woman smiled in an *I told you so* sort of way and poured him another cup, which he also drank eagerly.

She carried the small tray out of the room and was immediately replaced by a younger woman with another tray.

"Your stomach is empty, so we do not want to put too much into it at once. Start with this," she said, lifting a lid on the tray and revealing a small selection of warm rolls.

Alex would have bet that he wasn't hungry, even though he hadn't eaten in days. The smell that wafted off the rolls—sweet, with an aroma of herbs he did not recognize—changed his mind instantly.

Maybe living in the Summer Palace wouldn't be all that bad after all.

The second woman smiled at Alex and removed the tray.

The same moment she left the room, another woman appeared with clean clothes for him. What he had previously worn had been stained and damaged by his days chained to the pole.

The new clothes were finer than anything he had worn since he arrived in Kragdon-ah. The shirt was soft and loose, with what looked like ivory buttons down the front. The pants were made of soft cotton with a built-in belt.

The third woman left and Alex found himself alone in the room. He stood to put on his new clothes and discovered he was not as recovered as he had thought he was when he was still flat on his back. His knees buckled slightly before they decided to hold him. A knot of muscles screamed at him from his upper back and his shoulders felt like they had been ripped off and stuck back at a wrong angle.

He gently tried to roll his neck and decided that was a bad idea. *Slow and steady.*

He eventually managed to get dressed and when he came out of his room the third woman was waiting for him.

"This way," she said, indicating a long hallway. There were doors off both sides of the hallway, but they went to the room all the way at the end.

Inside, ten men in uniform sat around the table. Alex was surprised to see that Mandran was one of them. Alex had assumed that he had been busted so far down in rank that he would not be attending meetings like this.

It was Mandran who stood and introduced Alex to the room. "This is Manta-ak of Kragdon-ah." He did not bother to introduce all the men around the table, but he did gesture to the man at the head of the table. "Manta-ak, this is Kimda. He is in charge of the Drakana army."

Alex nodded at the man, still unsure of what the proper Drakana greeting would be.

"Sit," Kimda said, indicating the chair at the other end of the table.

Alex decided to just be quiet and listen. He could only imagine how this looked to them. They were in charge of an army that had been defeated badly, even though they possessed superior technology. And now, Makinta was forcing this outsider on them.

I don't expect anyone here is happy to see me.

Kimda surprised him. He leaned forward and clasped his hands on the table in front of him. "Mandran says you were a more than worthy opponent in his dealings with you."

Alex's eyes flitted to Mandran, whose face was impassive and stared straight ahead.

"There is something you should know. Makinta was set to send you back to the pole. Mandran risked his own life by interceding on your behalf."

That truly shocked Alex.

He turned to face Mandran. "Why would you do that?"

"We are losing. I saw how you managed your forces when we had the upper hand. You not only survived, you thrived. When all normal avenues have been exhausted, we need to look for a solution that is not normal. That is you."

"I had no idea. Thank you for that faith in me. I will do everything I can to deserve it."

"We are in a difficult position here," Kimda said. "We are trapped behind our own walls. Makinta has made a pact with you that we will fight the barbarians from the north on this end while you fight them from the other. Based on our dealings with them, I wonder what input you might have so that we are not simply sending our men to the slaughter."

That says something about you as a leader of men. You got your tail kicked, but instead of pouting about it, you're reaching out for help.

Alex knew he would have to take Kimda seriously.

"How many fighting men do we have within the walls?"

"I still believe we may have the remainder of the Northmen's force slightly outnumbered. Our problem is, we once had them heavily outnumbered and they have evened those odds." Kimda looked to the man to his right and said, "How many total men are still under our command?"

"Slightly over three thousand troops."

Alex nodded to himself. "And how are they equipped?"

"Fully equipped," Kimda said. "One of our weapons storerooms is here behind the wall."

"We fought the Northmen in the streets of your city," Alex said. "Even though we had thousands of warriors and they had only left behind small, wandering bands, they killed many more of our people than they should have. They are fierce fighters who will try to kill you even as they draw their own last breath."

"That is our experience as well," Kimda confirmed. "It is unpleasant to think about, but I believe each of their fighters killed four or five of ours before we killed them."

"The trick then, is to kill some of them before we are forced to engage in close-in combat. At a distance, you have a distinct advantage. Up close, that shifts to them. For every one of them we can kill at a distance, we are likely saving four to five of your men."

Alex tapped his fingers on the table, thinking.

"Is there any way to get above them and cause a rock slide onto them?"

"We have looked at that from every angle. The cliffs are truly impassable."

Alex nodded, accepting that.

"Do you have the ability to see over the tops of the walls?"

"We do, but if we put our riflemen there, they simply move back out of our range and wait us out there."

"True," Alex answered. "But if you have not been using that strategy, they will not be expecting it. You should be able to take a few of them out before they are able to move out of range. It's a war of attrition. Every one of their men we put out of action will save your own soldiers when it comes time to fight face to face."

Alex, Kimda, and the other commanders spent the next several hours discussing different strategies, each one designed to take out a number of Northmen before being forced to face them up close.

They broke up the meeting in the conference room and went outside, where they could plan the specifics of their attack.

Alex's idea was to place gunmen on the roofs of all buildings that faced the wall, with two men per position. One man would fire while the other loaded. His idea was to allow the gate to open partially, but block it from opening completely. That would slow the rush of Northmen into the palace grounds, where they would fall under the aim of the riflemen. That should take out a good number of the enemy.

A last resort was the infantry, which Alex recommended be armed with pistols and swords and not rifles. A pistol blast to the face of an onrushing fighter will put them down no matter how crazed they are. If any of the Northmen survived all that, the Drakana soldiers would be at a strong disadvantage.

Alex and Kimda's hope was that the combination of killing them as they ran into the palace and Alex pushing them from behind would allow for the Northmen to be vanquished.

It was not a certainty, but certainty did not exist in war.

Chapter Fifty
The Return

Alex made a few more strategic plans with Kimda, including how they would announce it was time for the pincer action to commence.

One question Alex didn't answer was how he had arrived in the Summer Palace and how he was going to escape it without going through the Northmen. He had promised the monks that he would keep their shaft a secret and he had been as good as his word.

The monks aided him in that by spreading a rumor through their sources that Alex had some mystical powers that included being able to evaporate in one place and reappear in another. When it was monks spreading the rumor, it made it easier for it to take hold.

Alex spent five days with Kimda, helping him plan out how the Drakana would fight their end when the moment arrived. On the fifth night, Alex turned into bed. He had not come close to recovering from his ordeal on the pole and was becoming concerned that his shoulders and joints would not recover sufficiently to allow him to make the climb back down the shaft. He did stretches every day, but it was still difficult for him to raise his hands above his head.

On the fifth night after being released from the chains, Alex prepared for bed. He did his normal stretching routine, then lay down on the mattress to try to figure out how he was going to get back to his army.

He heard the door to his room swish open. Alex jumped to his feet and fell naturally into his self-defense position.

It was the gray-haired woman who had brought him the hot drink his first morning in the room.

"Lie down," she said, pointing to the bed.

Alex held his hands out in front of him, unsure of what she was about.

"No, no, that's all right. Whatever it is—"

"Lie down on your stomach," she said, still pointing to his bed.

Alex was hesitant, but there was something about her expression that made him do as she said.

She knelt beside the low mattress and pressed iron-strong fingers into a very specific spot in his back.

Alex whimpered at the electric jolt of pain, but bit his lip to stop any more pathetic sound from escaping. He turned and looked at the woman.

She cocked her head slightly and pushed his face back down into the mattress.

For the next two hours, she worked Alex over from the top of his head to the soles of his feet.

Alex had known long, lingering pain while chained to the pole. It paled in comparison to what this tiny woman with strong hands and a vast knowledge of anatomy visited on him.

When she finally stood, she said, "You had much pain left in your body. I have released it now, so you will not feel well for a few hours." She stood and stepped briefly outside the room, then returned with a pitcher of water and a cup. "Drink this entire pitcher of water in the next hour. That will help push the remaining pain out of your body."

Alex wasn't sure if he should thank her or curse her for what she had put him through, but he settled on the thanks.

She bowed slightly to him and left him alone.

Alex drank cup after cup of the water, then lay down and went to sleep.

He woke up twice from unpleasant dreams, needing to pee. Each time, he voided his bladder and fell instantly back into a slightly tormented slumber.

When he woke up hours later, he felt refreshed. It was still dark outside the window, so Alex crept out of the palace and found his way to the monastery. He expected them to be asleep, but Thelon was waiting for him.

"I thought I might see you now. I sent Hanta to you last night."

"I don't know if I should be grateful or not."

"Of course you should be grateful. She made you well."

Alex couldn't argue the point, so he managed a half-hearted smile. "It's time for me to go back down."

"I agree," Thelon said. "We must hurry, it will be light soon."

They rounded the corner where Alex had first stepped into the Summer Palace and ran into a brick wall. Thelon pushed on one side and it turned inward.

Alex contemplated asking for a torch so he wouldn't be alone in the darkness again as he climbed down, but realized that would be impossible during the climb. He stepped inside the small opening and as soon as he was inside, Thelon rotated the wall shut behind him.

Absolute pitch darkness welcomed Alex. In other circumstances, Alex might have waited for his eyes to adjust, but he knew that in the total blackness of the shaft, there was nothing to adjust to. He would be blind for the duration of the descent.

He extended his arm and found the rough-hewn wall in front of him. He followed it to the stone steps that led down to the shaft. He went slowly to ensure he didn't take one step too many and make the too-fast journey to the bottom of the shaft. When he found the edge, he felt cool air rush up from below.

He stood at the precipice and waited for the water to fall. While he waited he played as much of the climb over in his mind as he could remember. He found that much of it was only a blur, as though his mind had blocked out the unpleasantness of the ordeal.

The water fell and Alex lowered himself gently over the side and felt his way from hold to hold. He had feared that the descent would be even more difficult than the climb, but he found it was marginally easier, if perhaps even more nerve-wracking. Every time he reached down with his foot, groping for the next hold, it felt like he was losing his grip and would plummet to the stone floor below.

Hanta had managed to knead life back into his muscles and joints the night before, but the climb tested him in every way imaginable.

He faced the same time deadline as he had on the way up—the water momentarily filling the shaft at regular intervals.

At one point, Alex lost count of how many times he had ducked into one of the small alcoves. Somehow, he convinced himself that he should be at the bottom. And yet, when the water fell, he could still hear it crashing into the pool below him.

As Alex always did, he quieted the small, doubting voice in his head and continued on.

When he did finally touch bottom—real bottom—he was so surprised he stood there a moment too long and the water washed over him, knocking him down. He picked himself up, sopping wet, and tried to gather his thoughts.

He tried to reconstruct in his mind the way he had come into the shaft the week before. Until that moment, he hadn't considered how he would get back out. He felt along the wall until he identified the boulder and pushed.

Nothing happened. He leaned into it and pushed again. Still nothing.

Panic rose up inside Alex.

They wouldn't leave me in here to die just because I know the secret of the shaft, would they?

It was a paranoid thought and only occurred to Alex because of what he had been through over the previous week.

He used a breathing exercise he had taught himself many years earlier and waited for his heart rate and mind to calm down. He moved to his left and tried another spot, then another and another, with no luck.

He reminded himself that he had plenty of water to drink and if need be, he could climb back up into the Summer Palace.

As soon as he realized that, he tried one more spot and the boulder moved easily out of his way.

The sunlight outside was dazzling and Alex winced and buried his eyes in his elbow.

He shut his eyes tight and opened them one little fraction of an inch at a time, letting his eyes adjust to the fact that they were being called back to work.

Alex stepped outside onto the path and immediately moved the boulder back into place. He wanted to do everything he could to keep the monk's second entrance a secret.

He held his hand up to block the sun, but gauged that it was sometime in the late afternoon. It was warm and the sunshine immediately began to dry out his fine, new clothes, which were perhaps neither so fine or as new as they had been a few hours before.

He turned right and headed toward the city.

He was still unarmed but hoped to not run into any sort of threat on the mostly untraveled path that ran alongside the mountain cliffs.

He was just about to turn a corner when he heard heavy, thundering footsteps rushing toward him.

Chapter Fifty-One
The Battle of the Summer Palace

A lex barely had time to brace himself, but saw what had been the last thing many men before him had seen.

Monda-ak jumped from ten feet away and hit Alex in the upper torso, sending both of them pinwheeling back up the trail. Alex landed on his back and Monda-ak had a huge paw on both shoulders. He stared intently into Alex's eyes, then, as though he had confirmed what he needed, he lay down on Alex.

It was the same thing he had done as a puppy.

When he weighed only a few pounds.

Now, he tipped the scales somewhere north of three hundred pounds and was slowly squeezing the breath out of Alex.

It didn't matter. Alex wrapped both arms around Monda-ak's neck and hugged him. He spoke softly, so only the dog could hear him.

"I'm sorry I had to leave you. I hope I never will again."

Monda-ak was not a big licker, but he smeared Alex's face with kisses that threatened to drown him.

"Monda-ak, you big goof, you're killing your best friend there."

Alex strained to see around Monda-ak's bulk, but didn't need to see who it was. He would recognize Sanda's voice anywhere.

Alex managed to squirm out from under Monda-ak and stood up. Sanda and Amy stood on the trail grinning at him.

"We thought you might have decided to just stay in the Summer Palace," Amy said.

"Well, it is pretty nice up there," Alex said with a grin.

Sanda touched Alex's shirt. "Nice duds, Dad."

"As I said, it's pretty nice up there." Alex realized that Amy, Sanda, and Monda-ak were alone. "How did you know where to find me?"

"Bratan," Amy answered. "He wouldn't tell us where you were going to come out, but he told us it would be somewhere along this path."

"But how did you know when I was going to come down the path. I didn't know myself."

Sanda grinned a little mischievously. "We didn't. We've been walking your dog up and down this path every day since you left." She laid an affectionate hand on Monda-ak's head. "He's been pretty impossible to live with."

Monda-ak turned his head to the side and let his tongue loll out the left side of his mouth.

"Yes, I can see that. Impossible."

"How was the secret way into the Summer Palace? A piece of cake?"

That made Alex laugh, so he recounted his adventures up the shaft. He left out how he had been tortured while there. He thought there was no need to raise their concern.

Even leaving out those details, Amy and Sanda could see his gaunt face and knew that he had been through a difficult time.

When Alex finished his story, they changed the subject and talked about happier things. Monda-ak stuck close to Alex's side, unwilling to let him out of his sight again.

When the outline of the burned city appeared ahead of them, Alex's mind turned to the battle ahead.

"How are the preparations going here?"

"Everyone has been doing their jobs. They just assumed you would be successful in recruiting Makinta. They've been drilling the troops every day in the town square. They're nervous about facing the Northmen, but everyone is ready to do what they need to do."

"When we get back, let's bring the council together. I want to attack in the morning."

KIMDA HAD TOLD ALEX where a small stash of fireworks had been hidden that would have likely not been discovered by the Northmen. Even if they had somehow stumbled on the cache, he doubted if they would have recognized what they were.

Unlike the Winten-ah, the people of Drakana had methods for keeping track of time. That helped with a coordinated attack like they were about to launch.

Early the next morning, Alex ordered a huge burst of fireworks to be set off over the city. That was the signal that the pincer attack would commence in one hour.

The truth was that Alex had no argument with the Northmen. If they had been able to negotiate with them, he would have been glad to seek a more peaceful remedy. The fact that they ran, wild-eyed and swinging weapons at the very sight of someone made that impossible. The only way to retrieve the people of Kragdon-ah who were held inside the Summer Palace was through the Northmen.

And so, Alex spent the first few minutes after they sent the signal with his lieutenants, going over last-minute details, then he led the first wave of warriors toward the foot of the mountain.

The greatest challenge of the upcoming battle was that the road that led to the castle was so narrow. Alex would have loved to use the advantage of numerical superiority, but it was a challenge to implement that strategy when they fought on a battlefield that was only twenty-five feet across.

Alex spread his troops out across the wide-open area at the bottom of the road. He had created a plan that he hoped would put as few of his troops in danger as possible. Against an opponent like the Northmen, though, he knew that there would be casualties.

Alex positioned Nanda-eh's archers twenty-five strides away from both sides of the road at the bottom. His first wave of attackers carried heavy spears and no other weapons. The farther he could keep his troops away from the savage in-fighting of the Northmen, the better.

The bottom part of the Northmen army was only a few hundred yards up the trail, around a slight bend.

Alex, Monda-ak, and twenty of his most-accurate spear throwers jogged up the hill, spears resting easily on their throwing shoulders.

The Northmen heard them coming and came around the bend to meet them.

Alex, and his first four warriors threw the heavy spears—designed to bring down a bull elk during a hunt—at the onrushing Northmen.

Having seen it with his own eyes, he knew that this enemy could shrug off many injuries. No human could manage to shrug off a heavy spear through their torso, however.

Then Alex remembered Nakama's story about the Northman who had been pinned to the ground with a spear, pulled it out, and used it as a weapon.

He shrugged. *Nothing to do about superhumans like that.*

As soon as the first group let their spears fly, they retreated to the back of the group. Each group of four stepped up and threw, then retreated. When the first twenty spears had been thrown, fifteen Northmen already lay dead or dying on the ground.

Alex's twenty warriors turned and ran back down the trail, hoping to lead the Northmen into a trap waiting for them at the bottom.

That plan worked perhaps too well.

In Alex's mind, he saw a handful of Northmen following them down, where they could use their superior numbers and dispatch them as they had done in the town.

Instead, it was far more than a handful of the crazed warriors who chased the group of twenty down the hill. As he retreated, Alex kept his eyes ahead of him. He and his warriors arrived at the bottom of the hill only a few seconds ahead of their pursuers. They continued on past the first shield wall.

WHEN THE NORTHMEN HIT the bottom of the road, their eyes flew wide to see what awaited them, but it did not slow them down. They raised their axes, or swords, or clubs and flew toward the army.

The first wave of Northmen never got close to their new enemy. Dozens of archers rained hell down on them from their positions above.

Nanda-eh had seen the effect their arrows had when they had first engaged the Northmen on the docks, and how they had kept coming, even though shot through the chest. She had devised a different strategy this time. Her archers were told to shoot for the head and neck if possible—no one could continue to fight with an arrow in the brain. If that wasn't a likely shot because of speed or a helmet, they aimed at the legs or groin. A man shot through the testicles lost a lot of steam in a hurry.

Alex's hope was that only a few of the Northmen who were lowest on the mountain trail would follow them down to his army. He wanted to repeat the tactic, taking out a few of them with spears, then luring another group of them to their death at the bottom, all without going face to face with them.

The problem turned out to be that the Northmen on the trail were bored silly by sitting in siege at the Summer Palace. As soon as a hint of action showed, they all turned and ran toward it.

Alex had hoped for a dozen or two of the savage fighters. Instead, hundreds of the most fearsome fighters on the planet ran straight at his untested forces.

Alex ordered his front-most squads to form up into a shield wall.

Then he and Monda-ak stood in front of that shield wall and braced for the oncoming attack.

Standing on a cliff above the field of battle, Sanda saw her father step directly into the wave of onrushing barbarians. Her hand flew to her mouth and she was only able to utter one word. "Oh!"

KIMDA STOOD ON THE roof of the Summer Palace. He had seen Manta-ak's fireworks light the sky almost an hour earlier and his stomach was tight. He was in charge of not just defending the Summer Palace, but the future of Drakana itself.

Makinta had been hidden away in a bunker in the most remote corner of the compound, designed for this very purpose. If the Drakana army was overrun, it would take the Northmen a lot of time and effort to find him. With such a prize within their grasp, there was no doubt they would invest enough of both to find him.

With Makinta dead, Drakana would fall. There would be no hope of rebuilding the empire at a future date.

Kimda had a plan, though. If he saw the tide had turned irrevocably against them, he would direct his men to the very end, then throw himself into the thick of the battle. He had no illusion that he could stand against the barbarian horde. He was no longer the confident, young man he had once been. Old battle wounds haunted him and he only stood erect through sheer willpower. Even so, he much preferred a glorious death on the field of the battle to any of the other options that would be available to him at that moment.

That was all a hedge against a disaster Kimda hoped to avoid. He had found a kindred spirit in this strange Manta-ak from Kragdon-ah. In most possible scenarios, they would have met on opposing sides and tested their strategies against each other. Instead, the man had appeared and—impossibly—disappeared to put together a battle plan.

And now it was time.

Quietly, Kimda turned to his second-in-command. The man's eyes were wide, but like Kimda, he was a veteran of many such moments. "Begin," was all Kimda had to say.

The second-in-command turned to his own aide, who hustled away.

The Drakana had purposefully stayed away from their stations atop the walls. They had hoped to draw the Northmen closer and closer, so the marksmen could have a chance to diminish their numbers before the actual battle started.

As he had told Manta-ak, weapons were in great supply in the Summer Palace, so there were four rifles and one reloader assigned to each marksman. By the time they had fired all four weapons, there should be a reloaded gun ready and waiting for them.

That would cause the Northmen to back off, which would allow the gates to swing open just a few feet without them instantly pouring through it.

When the command reached the gates, eighteen riflemen who stood on a small platform that ran the length of the wall, popped their heads over. They were rewarded with exactly what they were hoping to see—a crowd of the bearded warriors just a few feet away.

The Northmen were famous for never retreating, but when they were faced with an armed opponent they could not reach, they would choose to back up and fight another day. The problem for them was, they were packed tightly in. They had carried a heavy log up from the forest the day before and had put it in a series of slings. They were just about to begin pounding it against the only gate into the palace when the gunmen appeared. As crowded as it was, it was impossible for them to move out of the way.

Like Nanda-eh, the gunmen had learned the lesson of wounding the Northmen. Instead of aiming for center mass as they had been trained, they focused on hitting them in the head. That was a difficult shot with a gun that wasn't perfectly accurate, but the first volley managed to put sixteen of them down, dead instantly.

The riflemen on the wall never took their eyes off their prey below. They handed the spent gun to a loader on the right and reached to their left for their second weapon. The shots rang out so quickly, it sounded like there were several repeating guns firing instead of the single-shot rifles they possessed.

The first part of the strategy could not have worked better. The leader of the Northmen, who stood tall and fearless in the face of the guns, turned his back, and ordered those behind him to back up. One of the riflemen on the wall recognized him for who he was and aimed at the back of his head. He fired, but the shot was not true. It hit the leader just below his bull-neck. The man didn't seem to notice.

By the time the Northmen had backed up out of range, more than fifty of them lay bleeding at the entrance to the palace.

According to Kimda's own math, that opening salvo saved two hundred of his own men when the hand-to-hand fighting began.

Strong poles had been buried in the ground just behind the gate so that it would only open a crack. Enough for one or possibly two men to come through at a time, but no more. The men tasked with guarding that gate began the complicated maneuver of unlocking and removing the barricades so it could be opened.

Over their heads, the riflemen continued to fire shots at the crowd of Northmen. They knew they were too far away to do any damage, but they wanted to hold them at bay while the gate opened so the men below would have a chance to get to safety.

When the gate opened as much as it would, one single Drakana soldier stepped through it. The Northmen were perhaps fifty strides away, which was closer than anyone would want to be to them when their bloodlust was high.

Nonetheless, this man turned his back, dropped his trousers, and waved his ass at them. He had painted a design that looked like the Northmen's face paint on his butt cheeks.

At that moment, the Northmen wouldn't have cared if there had been machine gun nests facing them. They roared their hatred and sprinted toward the gate.

Mission accomplished, the man pulled up his pants and stepped carefully on a preplanned route to escape.

The soldiers on the wall had a choice to make. They could either leave their position and retreat to a safer spot to engage, or they could stay and inflict more damage as the Northmen attacked.

To a man, they chose to stay, including those who were no more than loaders. They continued to fire, injuring or killing more and more of the Northmen before the Drakana had suffered a single casualty.

From his spot on the roof of the palace, Kimda watched the gate. He knew this could be a turning point in the battle.

The incensed Northmen squirmed through the gate as quickly as possible, looking for an enemy to kill. That enemy stood in formation fifty strides away. The first ten Northmen sprinted toward them. In their all-consuming fury, they did not notice that a section of the cobblestone had been replaced with carpets. They sprinted over it and plummeted down into the pit that the Drakana had dug. They fell onto dozens of sharp wooden spikes. For the most part, that did not kill them, but it certainly immobilized them.

Overhead, the riflemen continued to fire at the endless river of Northmen that tried to squeeze into the small opening of the gate. They no longer aimed for headshots, but just fired as rapidly into the crowd as they could.

The next group of Northmen saw the trap that had been laid for them and managed to leap over the pit and ran with weapons raised toward the infantry arrayed directly in front of them.

Chapter Fifty-Two
The Battle of the Summer Palace Redux

Alex had a small shield in his left hand and a new two-bladed ax in his right. He did not wait for the Northmen to approach, but strode toward them, ax raised to striking level. Behind him, the shield wall moved forward one step at a time.

In a moment, Alex was swallowed by the rushing horde of Northmen. He hacked with his ax, cleaving a man's arm off at the elbow. A crimson arc sprayed in front of him. He raised his shield and blocked a sword attack, then spun and buried his ax in another man's neck.

He never saw the blow that felled him. It came from a swing of an ax that hit him broadside. It did not slice his head completely off, as it would if it had hit him blade-first, but it did knock him to the ground, bleeding badly.

Alex Hawk crumpled to the ground face first as the battle roared around him.

Monda-ak jumped over him and placed two paws on either side of Alex's prone body. The huge dog prepared to give his life to protect Alex's body. Each time a new warrior approached that spot in the battle, Monda-ak bared his teeth and lunged ferociously, but did not leave Alex's fallen form.

The main body of the onrushing Northmen clashed into the shield wall and the real battle began. The invaders from the north slammed into the shield and drove them back until they forced the men behind the shields to back up.

From above, Nanda-eh and her archers continued to pick key targets and fire.

Sanda had eyes for only one thing—her father, lying face-first on the bloody ground. A Northman with an expression almost as fierce as Monda-ak's, approached the dog. He raised a massive sword and took a running step, but got no further. An arrow from Sanda's bow hit him just below the nose, driving him backwards.

The largest of all fighters, Torana, took long, purposeful strides toward Alex. He put a knee against Monda-ak's side and pushed him out of the way. He picked up Alex and put his head against his chest, then protected as much of him as he could with his left hand. With his right, he swung a giant hammer in a huge arc, moving any and everyone who didn't want a crushed skull out of his way. Behind him, Monda-ak slowly backed up, still keeping a vigilant lookout for anyone who might harm Alex or the hulking giant who carried him.

Torana carried Alex behind the squads that had formed up into shield walls. Men rushed forward with a litter and hauled him back out of the raging battle. Monda-ak stayed with him, shadowing his every movement.

In Alex's absence, each of his lieutenants stepped up and deployed their squads the best way they could. Allowing the Northmen to fight one-on-one was an invitation to disaster, so they did their best to surround them.

More and more of the wild-eyed warriors streamed down from the mountain and soon the area at the bottom of the road became one massive gathering of swinging weapons, screams, clanging of metal on metal, and fallen bodies.

IN THE SUMMER PALACE, the anticipated battle with the Northmen turned out to be an anticlimax. Alex's plan to draw off a portion of the army had worked too well. More than three-quarters of the Northmen had headed down the hill before they knew there was a second battle started at the palace.

The early strategy, designed to take out as many Northmen before the battle was engaged, worked perfectly. The riflemen on the buildings that surrounded the courtyard were able to keep up with the influx of fighters, thanks to the fact that they had to squeeze through the gate.

The Northmen tried to fix this by stopping their entry into the palace for a time. They picked up the log they were going to use to batter the gate and used it to try to push it completely open. They took four runs against it, but the buried pillars the Drakana had used to block it held.

Finally, they abandoned the log and went back to squeezing through the gate, their bloodlust so high that they didn't care if they were walking into an ambush or not.

The lull in attackers had allowed the marksmen on the roofline to finish off the attackers who were wounded but still struggling to stand.

When the next wave of Northmen came through the gate, they had to avoid the pit with spikes and the rapidly growing mound of the bodies of their countrymen.

In the end, it was a slaughter, barely worthy of being called a battle. The only casualties the Drakana suffered were those soldiers who had bravely stood their ground on the wall to inflict further damage on the charging invaders. They had done so, but had paid a price, as the Northmen climbed up the ladders and killed them all.

From his perch on the roof of the palace, Kimda saw that it was a rout and hurried down. He was pleased that the strategy had worked, that Drakana and Makinta were saved, but he also knew something was amiss.

Only a few hundred Northmen had come through the gate to the slaughter. That meant that Manta-ak and his warriors were absorbing the brunt of the Northmen attack. He knew they were on an open plain at the foot of the path and had no narrow opening they could use to drip the attackers through.

"Come!" he shouted to his retinue, even as the Drakana army mopped up the last of the Northmen who had come through the gate. "Gather the troops and follow me!"

ALEX HAWK'S EYES FLUTTERED. His first thought was, *What is that smell?* When he managed to open his eyes, he saw the answer. Monda-ak was inches away from his face, breathing his fetid breath directly into Alex's nose in some odd form of dog CPR.

His second thought was, *Oh, my head.*

He attempted to lift his head off the ground, then dizziness overcame him. He turned on his side and retched. As always, he had been too nervous to eat before the battle, so all that came up were thin threads of vomit. Out of the corner of his eye, he saw Monda-ak's ears prick up, interested.

"Don't you dare," he managed.

Versa-eh hurried to him. They did not have enough healers to begin to deal with the injured from this battle, so anyone that wanted to volunteer as a nurse had been enlisted.

"You're alive," she said simply. "We thought you were dead."

"Just *mostly* dead," Alex said, making a joke that no one in this world other than his daughters would understand.

Alex reached up and touched the bandage that had been wrapped around his skull. It protruded in a two-inch egg just over his left ear, and there was still a steady flow of blood from below it.

He sat up, waited to see if the nausea would subside. When it did, he looked around him. He was in a tent away from the battlefield. All around him, warriors were screaming or clenching their teeth together, trying not to scream.

A shadow fell across his eyes. It was the human eclipse, Torana, who was carrying two more wounded men. He stopped for a moment to verify that Alex was indeed sitting up and not being prepared for burial, then turned back toward the battlefield. He seemed to have appointed himself as the field ambulance, and there was more than enough work for him.

Alex turned over onto his knees, waited for the next wave of dizziness to pass, then used Monda-ak as a brace to stand. He leaned against the dog for a long moment, then found his balance and turned in the direction he had seen Torana go.

Versa-eh watched him go and did not try to stop him.

Alex had no idea how long he had been out, but guessed it hadn't been long. The battle still raged. He saw that the Northmen had pushed his army back fifty hard-fought yards. The initial surge had subsided, but it was obvious that even though his army still held the numbers advantage, the sheer ferocity of the attack put the outcome in doubt.

He looked up in time to see that Sanda had abandoned her spot on the hillside and had run toward him.

"Dad! I was so worried!"

"I'm fine, don't worry."

Gently, she touched the bandage and looked skeptical.

Alex saw Torana carrying more wounded and spoke to him in Drakana. He was unable to answer, but he could understand what was said to him. "When you drop those men off, come back here to me."

Torana hurried away at double-speed, apparently tireless.

"Still got arrows?"

"I'm out," Sanda said, showing her empty quiver. "We've got a stash here, though. I'll be right back."

Sanda and Torana returned to Alex at the same time.

"Sanda, climb up on his shoulders. Torana, circle around the battlefield in the direction Sanda tells you. That should give you a better angle to fire down on them. Try to put the arrows through their ears. That'll slow them down."

Torana dropped to one knee and without a question, Sanda hopped onto his shoulders. They headed toward the battle.

If I had twenty Toranas, I could win this battle right now.

Alex turned back to the battle. On the outer fringe, he saw Hawthorne fire his pistol point blank at a Northman who charged him. He hit him in the throat—a likely mortal blow—but it did not immediately stop the man. He stumbled forward with his huge sword in front of him.

Hawthorne tried to parry the blow, but the man was too large, had too much momentum.

His sword ran Hawthorne through, then he collapsed on him, dead.

Alex sprinted toward him. As the battle raged around them, he dragged the dead Northman off, withdrew the sword, which made a terrible sucking sound, and picked Hawthorne up. He stumbled under the weight of both the man and his injury, but he made it away from the fight.

He carried Hawthorne to the same tent he had been in and laid him gently on the ground.

His first instinct was to yell *Medic!* But realized that was wrong. Instead, he focused and called out "Healer!" in the universal language.

Hawthorne's eyes were open but unfocused. Alex did what he could to make him comfortable. He found a nearby roll of cloth and held it over the wound to staunch the bleeding.

Hawthorne focused on Alex for the first time. "Damn you, Hawk. I wish you hadn't made me promise not to tell you what happened when we met." Blood poured from one corner of his mouth as he spoke.

"It's all right," Alex said. "I'll release you from the promise when you're healed."

"We both know that's not going to happen." Hawthorne's eyes rolled up in his head. A moment later, his labored breathing stopped.

Alex did not go through the motions of trying to revive him. His wound was too terrible.

Alex hung his head for a moment, then pushed himself to his feet. It was war. Friends die. He had learned to accept that long ago.

He returned to the battlefield empty-handed. His ax had fallen from his grip when he had been knocked out. It was a battlefield with hundreds of dead, though, so weapons were not hard to find. He circled around the action and found a longsword lying in the bloody muck that had been pristine grass at the beginning of the day.

He heard a commotion coming from the path that led to the Summer Palace and he whirled around, fearing he would see more of the Northmen rushing to reinforce those who were already winning.

It was not more Northmen. It was the Drakana army, led by ten soldiers on their mighty warhorses. They came down at a steady gallop. Each rider had a rifle to their shoulder and fired as they approached. They didn't even wait to see the result of their shot, but dropped their rifle down into a holster, drew their swords and spurred their mounts on toward the melee.

If the battlefield had been a form of bedlam before, it became chaotic mayhem with the arrival of the great horses. The Drakana soldiers rode straight into the backline of the Northmen. The warhorses, outfitted in heavy armor, tramped straight through them, scattering the invaders, knocking them to the ground and stomping

on them. Those Northmen not knocked over in the initial rush, were
run through by the riders as they went past.

THE WARHORSES ARRIVED first, but the infantry, marching
at double time, weren't far behind. They didn't bother with their rifles—in the confusing mass of people writhing in front of them, guns
were useless. Instead, they also drew their swords and charged into
the rear line, following the path that the horses had cut for them.

The Northmen turned to face the new threat from behind and
that broke the line. The Drakana approached relentlessly and Alex's
forces were revitalized at the thought the battle could be ending.

Tinta-ak, oozing blood from more cuts than could be easily counted, roared a fresh battle cry, and led the troops forward.

The true power of a pincer action put the Northmen into an indefensible position. Even their endless fury, swinging swords and clanging axes could not overcome being surrounded.

Finally, all Northmen but one had fallen. That final man stood in the mass of enemy, a bitter scowl on his face and hurled curses at those who surrounded him. He swung his huge ax in such an arc that it was impossible for anyone to get close to him.

It was obvious there was no glimmer of hope of victory, but equally obvious there was never any thought of surrender. Instead, the Northman picked out a likely victim and charged at him.

Werda-ak the Younger was the unfortunate person in his path. He was not much more than a boy, but stood on the battlefield of men and paid the price men do. The Northman swung his ax with all his strength and brought it straight down on Werda-ak's head, splitting it open clear to his breastbone.

Sanda had run out of arrows again, so Torana dropped her to the ground. He picked up a fallen Northman ax that was so large and heavy it had been a two-handed weapon. Torana plucked it up in his right hand and pushed people away until he faced the final Northman in a tight circle.

While the man tried to free his ax from Werda-ak, he looked up and saw the looming shadow of the giant. The man's eyes grew wide, but still showed no fear.

The Northman smiled, glad to have such an opponent. He finally freed his ax and stepped toward Torana. He raised his ax over his head, ready to deliver a killing blow. He never got close enough to deliver it.

Torana swung his own ax with such force that it sliced the Northman from his left shoulder, through his chest and separated the man into two piles of spurting, twitching meat.

It was later said that the Northman's lips still uttered curses, but it was hard to find anyone who had actually seen that.

Chapter Fifty-Three
Aftermath

The battle was over.

Alex's forces had worked with the Drakana army to achieve victory.

There was no delirious whooping, no war cries or victory dances.

Alex's men were exhausted, hundreds were lying dead on the battlefield and almost everyone who had fought was slashed, hammered, and exhausted.

Add into that the fact that Alex and the Drakana had only become allies when the situation forced them into it and an odd, disjointed feeling permeated the field of the slaughtered. The smell of blood, and the feeling of death hung heavy in the air.

He had not been in the initial charge, but Kimda had ridden down the hill with the forces. Alex had helped him devise a successful strategy and in return, he had turned the tide of the battle. It was a fair exchange.

Alex moved through the battlefield with Amy at his side, making note of the people who lay dead. Many of them had sailed from Kragdon-ah with him so long ago and their families deserved an accounting for their life.

Each time Alex saw a familiar face—Rinka-ak, or Harta-ak, or Akima—alive, his heart leapt.

Even so, there were those who were dear to him who had not survived.

Perhaps the biggest surprise among the dead was Hawthorne. It wasn't so much that he was invulnerable, but his still-unexplained appearance on *The Senta-eh* was so mysterious that Alex didn't think he would die like a mortal man. Alex had told him that this was not his battle, and he did not need to fight. Wherever he had come from, he would not be returning.

Grantan, who he had persuaded to come with him from Lakunadan, was lying on his back, still grasping at his fatal wound, sightless eyes staring at the sky.

Pictin, who had taught them so much about how to sail across the ocean, had likewise bled out on the field of battle.

Antan-ak, the healer who had saved Alex's arms when he had fought Panga, had been collateral damage. No one on either side ever purposefully targeted the healers who came into the battle to assist. They were unarmed, aside from their bags of bandages. But in a bloody melee like the one that had just transpired, bullets, swords, arrows, and ax blades flew randomly around. One had felled Antan-ak.

There were dozens and dozens of others. People born to a peaceful life in the caves of Winten-ah who signed up for an adventure and to protect their way of life, had died on a bloody battlefield in a place they hadn't known existed until recently. Harta-ak, Versa-eh, Tinta-ak and Rinka-ak likewise made note of those from their villages who would not return.

Hundreds would never leave this place.

It was an experience Alex had felt many times—a big city kid from the East Coast or a Nebraska farm boy bleeding out in some locale he could barely pronounce. He was familiar with it, but had never learned to accept it.

Alex Hawk vowed that this battle was his last. He would never again lead troops into an uncertain future.

Kimda saw Alex turning bodies over and taking an inventory of those who had died. He laid a hand on his shoulder and said, "They will never be forgotten. We will sing songs of their bravery for generations. I am sure Makinta will erect a garden and statues here to show how well your people fought."

Alex was so exhausted he could not stand. He dropped to one knee. "I don't know how much comfort that will be to their families."

"Such is the way of war," Kimda said. "I must return to the Summer Palace now and report to Makinta."

Alex peered up at Kimda. "He will honor his terms with us?"

Kimda's glaze turned steely. "I believe so."

Alex did not like the uncertainty of that. At that moment, there was nothing more he could do to ensure the success of his mission.

He forced himself to stand and raised his voice to carry as far as possible. "We will camp here for a few days. We have too many wounded to move."

"When we return to the palace, I will send people down with supplies to feed and help you care for your wounded."

"Can you have our own people bring them? They are no longer slaves and they belong with us."

Kimda gave Alex the Drakana salute, which was a quick flip of the thumb of the right hand across the forehead. He mounted his horse, gathered his troops, and moved back up the mountain path.

Torana came and stood next to Alex. Monda-ak, the giant, Amy and Sanda and all his lieutenants gathered in a circle around him, waiting for orders.

"There is still work to be done. We have come so far, but still have a few things left before we can return home. First we have wounded to attend to." Alex looked around the battlefield. "Mourning to do." His eyes fell on Harta-ak and Versa-eh. Harta-ak was bleeding from a deep gash running down his left thigh, but virtually everyone was injured in one way or another. "Versa-eh, will you take charge of setting up a place where we can treat our wounded?"

She put two fingers to her forehead in agreement.

"Harta-ak, you will need treatment, but will you organize a large team to dig a burial pit? We will bury the dead in the style of Kragdon-ah." Alex pointed to the headless corpse of the last Northman who had died. "These men were not truly our enemies, except by circumstance. They fought bravely and deserve to be buried with our own fallen."

Fredon stepped forward and said, "That is kind, Manta-ak, but the Northmen would feel they were being punished by burying them. They prefer that the bodies of their dead be burned. That way they can cross into the next life in a blaze."

"Fair enough," Alex said. "You are in charge of that. Let's separate the bodies. Torana, will you help dig a fire pit big enough to consume their bodies?"

The giant did not answer but simply turned and went to work.

Harta-ak took one limping step forward and started picking those who were the least-wounded to begin digging the burial pit for everyone else. "Use the battle axes to break the ground, then dig with hands and sticks if we need to," he ordered.

"Amy, Sanda, We are going to need to set up a way to feed everyone. Can you form a team to go back to the city and return with cooking pots, utensils, bowls, everything we need to set up a large kitchen?"

"I will do that," Amy said. Looking at Sanda, she said, "Maybe you are big enough to get him to lie down before he falls down."

Sanda put a gentle arm around Alex and led him to a spot where he could do just that.

A good leader commands those who are under him to do what they should. A great leader creates more leaders to see what needs to be done and make that happen even in the absence of the leader.

As it turned out, Alex Hawk was a great leader.

Even as he finally allowed himself to close his eyes and sleep, his lieutenants took his place and began the long process of recovery.

WHAT REMAINED OF ALEX'S army stayed where the battle took place for two weeks. With the city burned out, he could not see a reason to go back there.

Alex did not have any kind of accurate count of how many members of Kragdon-ah tribes had been put on the boats and brought to Drakana. Only a few hundred came down the hill from the Summer Palace, though.

Alex was surprised to see that he recognized the face of one of the men who had come to him at his hour of greatest need when he was chained to the pole.

"Gunta, friend," Alex said, hailing him.

"Gunta, Manta-ak. You look stronger than the last time I saw you," the tall man said.

Alex's fingers unconsciously went to the knot that still protruded from the left side of his head. "I am getting there. Can you tell me where the others are?"

"What others?" the man asked, puzzled.

"The other people the Drakana took from Kragdon-ah. There were many more than this."

"There were. Many of us were dropped off to work as slave labor at different places. This was all of us who were still on the ships when we arrived in Drakana."

Alex put two fingers to his forehead. That made sense, but added another thing to the list of things he needed to accomplish before he could return home.

Many of those in Alex's army had suffered injuries so catastrophic they would never heal completely. Many were missing various body parts and despite the best efforts of the healers, another fifty fighters were lost after the battle was over.

At that point, Alex realized that those who would need months to recuperate would have to do it onboard the ships heading back to Kragdon-ah. He didn't feel like they could camp out where they were forever.

As always, winter was coming.

He had just one more task to accomplish in Drakana.

Chapter Fifty-Four
Palace Intrigue

Alex and his small band walked up the hill to the Summer Palace. It was obvious that with the city below in need of a complete rebuild, Makinta would stay in the palace for the foreseeable future.

That fit into Alex's plans just fine.

Alex only brought his most-trustworthy people with him. This was the task that had worried him more than the battle with the Northmen, and he felt it was just as risky. As he did so often, having won a great victory, he gambled everything he had won for a bigger prize yet.

Alex, Harta-ak, Versa-eh, Amy, Rinka-ak, Akima, Monda-ak, and a soldier who walked with a cane and whose head was covered in a still-bloody bandage walked up to the front gate.

The barriers that had kept the gate from swinging wide had been removed and it stood open. With no threat left in Drakana, there was no reason to keep it closed and Makinta had a constant thread of people hiking back and forth to the city to retrieve one thing or another. Even so, there was a military presence standing guard, as there was at any entrance to a city.

Alex raised his hand in greeting and said, "Is Kimda available? I would like to speak to him."

The guards were not unfriendly. All Drakana people knew what a terrible position they had been in before this Manta-ak had miraculously appeared with his plan.

"Gunta, Manta-ak," the guard said, and Alex immediately knew that he had been one of the Drakana who had been to Kragdon-ah and had picked up a few words of their language. Switching to Drakana, the guard said, "Come through. You can wait by the fountain. I have sent a runner for Kimda."

Inside the gate, it was impossible for Alex to tell a battle had ever been fought. The white gravel was not bloodstained. The fountains and gardens were undisturbed. There was no sign that the Northmen had ever made it inside the courtyard.

Harta-ak looked around in wonder. He had been just a teenager when he had rescued Alex, Monda-ak, and Versa-eh from the gator and bug-infested island. Now he and Versa-eh were in late middle age. A beautiful couple with two children they had left behind in Danta-ah in order to come on this mission.

"I suppose I could build you something like this when we get home," Harta-ak observed.

Versa-eh laid her head against his shoulder and said, "I don't need any of this. I do long for our own home and our children, though."

"That is coming up. I will get you there," Alex promised.

A soldier in a crisp uniform approached and said, "Manta-ak, Commander Kimda will see you now." He looked down at Alex's group and said, "He authorized me to set you up in a house of your own for the night if you would like to stay."

"Thank you," Alex said. "Can you have someone show my friends to where that is?"

"I will do it myself." He looked at the scarred and wounded people and said, "I will be back for you."

The soldier led Alex into the palace where he had once met Makinta and had been threatened with death. They did not go into the throne room, but instead turned into a smaller room appointed with a window that looked out onto gardens and yet another fountain.

Kimda was already there, with plans spread out on the table in front of him.

Alex stood beside him and looked down at what was obviously a map of the destroyed city. "Rebuilding will take time."

"Time and resources, yes," Kimda answered. "We cannot stay here, however, no matter that Makinta may want to do so."

"He is old," Alex observed. "Perhaps ready to reincarnate in his son."

"Yes, perhaps," Kimda observed. There was something about the way that he said it that made Alex think that the commander didn't buy the constant reincarnations of the Makintas any more than he did.

"What would you do if you were in Makinta's place?"

"About what?" Kimda asked.

"About everything. Your empire is stretched very thin. Too thin, obviously. It's possible, isn't it, that the Northmen will raise another army and return stronger than before? If they find you in such a weakened state, you will be wiped out."

Kimda drummed his fingers against the table. "If it were up to me, I would spend my time reinforcing what we have here. I presented Makinta with the plans to build a wall all along our northern border. I don't know if it would have held the Northmen out, but it would have been easier for us to defend. As it was, they marched all the way to our capital city with almost no resistance."

"What else?"

"We built our empire on force. The strategy was to take our army, conquer a nation, enforce our will on them. Then we recruited all their own army into ours and used that strength to conquer the next nation and the next. The problem with that strategy is, it makes you big, but it also gives you many weak spots where you can be attacked." He looked dourly at Alex. "As you yourself discovered when you conquered Lakunadan with such a small force. One ship and a few hundred men. They should have been easily able to repel you. But the only people who put up any kind of fight were the real Drakana soldiers. The rest of the population was probably wanting you to succeed."

Alex didn't have the heart to tell him that even the Drakana soldiers hadn't put up much of a fight.

"What would you do instead?" Alex asked. "Pull back to within your own borders?"

"Somewhat. If we took all of our true Drakana soldiers and brought them home, no one could ever invade us again. Let the Northmen come, they would find their match here."

Alex wasn't sure if that was true, but saw no percentage in arguing with the commander.

"What about those territories that have been Drakana? What happens to them?"

"I would prefer to give them a voice. If they want to stay with us—and there are many advantages to being part of Drakana—then let them stay, but make them pull their own weight. If they want to leave, I would let them go. Make their own way in the world. I do not see the same benefit in having so many nations under our thumb that Makinta does."

"When I asked you if Makinta would keep his treaties with us, you said you believed he would," Alex said.

It was a statement, but there was a question wrapped up in it.

"I believe he will. I would if I was in his place."

"But there is no way for you to be in his place."

"Of course not."

Alex leaned forward, lowered his voice, and said, "I have a plan."

ALEX AND HIS ENTOURAGE left early the next morning. It was the same group who had walked up the path the day before with one exception. The man with the bandaged face who had walked with a cane the day before seemed to be unconscious and Harta-ak pushed him in a borrowed wheelbarrow down the hill. Also, there was one man missing from the group—Akima, the large and kind man who had helped rescue Alex from Shipwreck Isle, elected to stay behind at the Summer Palace.

Alex greeted the men who were guarding the palace gate with a wave.

They waved the famous Manta-ak through. One guard pointed at the man in the wheelbarrow. "Too much mead?"

"You have only the finest mead here in Drakana," Alex agreed with a laugh. He couldn't help himself, but whistled a jaunty tune as they pushed through the gate and down the hill.

The most difficult part of the journey was not letting the wheelbarrow get away from them, as it seemed to have a mind of its own.

When they reached the bottom, Alex was pleased to see that most of the camp had already left for the city.

A small group, which included Torana, stood waiting for them.

When they got close, Alex said, "Torana, can you carry this man to the boat?"

Torana stepped close, but Alex held up one hand. "Just a moment. He might wake up on the trip. I'd rather he slept until we were on the ship and underway." He took a waterbag out and tipped the bandaged man's head back. He poured a little of the foul-smelling liquid down his throat until it ran down both sides of his face. "There. That will do."

Torana picked the man up as though he was a rag doll and cradled him gently.

"Take good care of him," Alex said with a smile. "He is the god of all he surveys, after all."

"I will miss Nakama and Akima," Amy said. "They are good people."

"They are," Alex agreed. "But they will do so much more good for the world as Makinta and advisor than they ever would on Rontan."

"Do I even want to ask how you managed to pull this off?"

Alex shrugged. "Once we had Kimda on our side, everything was easy. He put two of his most loyal men at the guard post outside Makinta's room and they were told to let me pass. Nakama and I entered the bedchamber. Nakama stayed, and the man who was once Makinta left with me. Now he is here."

"What about his nephew? He was in line to be the next Makinta, wasn't he?" Amy asked. "I can't imagine he would accept this situation."

"You might be surprised. He was given a choice—to go headfirst down the shaft, or to play along. At least for now, he has agreed to play along. From this point on, it will be up to Nakama as to how he deals with him."

Amy looked down at the sleeping man. "He doesn't look so much like a god now," she observed.

"We so rarely do when we are knocked unconscious and drooling," Alex observed.

"I'm glad we didn't have to kill him, but where are we taking him now?"

"Napoleon had Elba. Makinta will have Rontan. Did you know that while Napoleon was exiled, he made substantial improvements to the infrastructure on the island?"

"Do you think Makinta will do the same?"

Alex laughed again, relieved that the hardest parts of the mission were behind them. "No. I think he will complain and rail against the people who keep him there until the day he dies. I don't think he will have much luck in converting the people of Rontan to his side, though. They have lived for his overthrow for too long, even if someone did believe him."

Amy sighed. "I can't believe it's all over," she said.

"Well, let's not go that far. We still have to find the rest of the people of Kragdon-ah. I didn't promise to bring back some of them, or most of them. I said I would bring back all of them. That means we have a lot of stops to make on the way."

"A tour of the modern world, then," Sanda added. "I like the sound of that."

"Join the army, see the world," Alex agreed.

NOTHING IS EVER AS easy as it seems. There were trials and tribulations and many, many stops on the itinerary of the return trip.

When compared to the trip from Kragdon-ah to Drakana, though, it was not bad at all. There was no giant squid that attacked them, no warship attacked and sank their vessels, marooning them on a barren island. No squalls hit them and rocked their world, and perhaps even better, they weren't left to drift for weeks without wind in the doldrums.

Also, there was no mysterious fogbank that moved toward them when there was no wind to do so.

Alex was frustrated about that fog. He had believed that once the battle of Drakana had passed, Hawthorne would tell him what had happened. How they were gone so long they had almost starved, yet had no memory of it.

Then Hawthorne died in the battle against the Northmen. The only remaining person who might have a clue about what had transpired was Quintan, the monk. Of course, Quintan was apparently mute and Alex never saw him after the great battle, so they were all equally lost as to what had transpired.

Minor annoyances like losing a year or two of their lives aside, the trip home was quite enjoyable.

Their first stop was at Rontan, where they dropped off many of the warriors who had fought alongside them. And the man who had once been Makinta. Akima had come up with the cover story before they left Drakana and Alex had been unable to come up with anything better.

When they arrived in Rontan, they gave Makinta a modest house and a housekeeper to care for him. It wasn't the standard of luxury he was accustomed to, of course, but he was fed and kept safe.

People immediately recognized that the man looked remarkably like Nakama and the official story was that he was indeed a relative of that great man. A relative who had lost his faculties over time, and who now thought he was the godhead Makinta, instead of the poor fisherman he actually was.

Alex asked that people humor this obvious falsehood, but not to worry about it.

Makinta, who had once been a god, spent his final years wandering the streets of Rontan, telling anyone who would listen who he really was and asking for their help in reclaiming what was rightfully his. People seemed to look forward to these conversations and were amused at how sincere the old man seemed to be.

As to Nakama's absence, it was explained that he simply chose to stay in Drakana, where things were much improved.

The small fleet that Alex had sailed out of Drakana grew slightly at each stop. He sailed into each territory under the flag of peace and explained to each Drakana commander what had happened. He brought a signed and stamped order from Nakama-who-was-now-Makinta that ordered them home. To a man, they seemed happy to no longer be an occupying force and to return to Drakana.

All Alex asked from them at each stop was that the enslaved people from Kragdon-ah be returned to him and that he be given a Drakana ship big enough to carry them.

It took a year and a half for Alex and his fleet to make it from Drakana to Kragdon-ah.

At first, it seemed like a vacation after all the stress they had endured for so long.

The closer they got, the stronger the longing from every native-born citizen of Kragdon-ah.

Alex enjoyed walking on the deck, stopping any random group of people and saying, "Where is your home?"

Instantly, their arms shot up, all pointing in the same direction.

Finally, Alex noticed that when he asked, they were pointing in slightly different directions.

They were getting close to home.

Chapter Fifty-Five
Kragdon-ah

Sanda was once again the first to spot land. From the crow's nest, she shouted down, "Land ahead!"

It wasn't just land, however. She had spotted the bluff that Alex had once laid on and observed the apparently unstoppable force of the Drakana as they whisked the people of Kragdon-ah away into slavery.

Where Alex had once said, "I have a plan," when what he really meant was, *I cannot let this injustice stand. I believe I will eventually have a plan.*

And he did. Eventually.

There were so many places that plan could have gone awry. In fact, there were a great many places and times when his plan *did* go awry.

All of that was behind him, though. He and his most-trusted friends, who had put their lives and future in his hands, were reward-ed with the sweetest sight they could imagine: Kragdon-ah.

Almost everyone on board hurried to the bow of the boat and scanned the horizon, greedily drinking the vision of home in.

Alex retreated to the stern. He looked behind the ship and saw a smooth trailing wake. It had taken them some time, but they had become sailors.

Alex jumped up to the wheelhouse and found Harta-ak manning the wheel.

"What do you say, my friend?" Alex asked. "Once you get back to Danta-ah, are you ever going to want to leave again?"

Harta-ak looked off into the distance, as though he was already able to see his home.

"Danta-ah will look very good," he admitted. "But I will also miss the spray of the ocean and the feel of the wind in my face. Sometimes I stop and wonder—what would have happened if I had been a tiny bit earlier or later that day that I plucked you from that island? Where would I be? My life would not be the adventure it has been."

Alex laughed. "And my own life might have ended in the jaws of one of those horrific creatures that saw me as nothing but a snack."

"Do you have a plan for when we anchor?"

Alex squinted one eye at Harta-ak, looking to see if he was joking. Alex always had a plan for everything, and they had been sailing a long time.

Harta-ak stared straight ahead, then gave up the straight face and smiled.

"I considered segregating the ships so that people from one region or tribe were together, but I chose not to do that. Instead, everyone is intermingled. I hope that will serve us well when we are home. It is easy to think of another village as an enemy. But when you have spent long hours together, sharing stories, talking about what you hope to accomplish, that makes it much more difficult. I'm hoping that will stay with people when they return home."

"You are a wise man, Manta-ak."

"Those are words I would never apply to myself. I've just been around long enough to see the mistakes we all make. I am going to continue with the intermingling while we unload. Our transport ships are small, so it will take us a few days to unload everyone. As soon as they hit the beach, everyone is free to go their own way, but my hope is that everyone will stay until all the ships are unloaded. Then we can travel together. There is always safety in numbers."

"What of the ships? Will the Drakana come and claim them?"

"I worked that out with Kimda and the new Makinta. Having Drakana not attack us is not enough. I want there to be a friendship between our nations and all the nations between here and there. So, when they have rebuilt their city, they are going to start a trade route. They have many things that will be useful to us, that we cannot make."

"Stama? How will that settle with Sekun-ak?"

The mention of his old friend's name made Alex suddenly anxious to see him. He hoped he and the Winten-ah had done well in the years they were gone.

"No stama," Alex said. "I would never do that to him. But, we have seen what great builders the Drakana are. Look at the bridge they built between you and Rinta-ah. I hope that one of the things they will trade with us will be their skills and tools. What about you? Are you happy to go to Danta-ah, put your feet up, and enjoy your old age?"

"He's not *that* old yet," Versa-eh said, slipping behind Harta-ak and laying a hand on his hip. "I've still got uses for him."

"I do have one surprise for you two. I can never repay you for everything you've done for me, but I do have a gift."

The couple looked at Alex with wide eyes. Neither could imagine what gift he could have for them.

"As long as you don't change the name, this ship is yours."

"No one would ever dare to change the name," Versa-eh said. "This will always be *The Senta-eh II*. But doesn't this ship belong to the Drakana, along with the rest?"

"I don't know why I did it, but I negotiated with Kimda for this ship. Sentimental reasons, I suppose. I have no use for her, though.

If she belonged to me, she would just stay anchored in the bay here. She's yours, so you can do as you will with her."

Harta-ak and Versa-eh shared a knowing look. "Thank you, Manta-ak," Versa-eh said. "This gift will mean more to us than you know. We will go to Danta-ah and collect our children, but then we will put a crew together and set sail. We've seen a large part of this world, but we would love to see more."

"Good enough," Alex said, glad he had made the correct guess. "As long as you stop by the cliffside when you pass that way."

"What will you do?" Harta-ak asked. "Sit in the rocking chair at the top of the cliff and watch the sun rise and set?"

"After these past few years, that sounds pretty good to me. I know Sekun-ak will never abandon the caves, but I am going to build a simple home for myself and another for Amy and Sanda, if they wish it."

"You're staying, then? Is there nothing in your other home you wish to return to?"

"The only things in Oregon I cared about are with me now." He glanced up and looked at Sanda, her long hair blowing behind her as she leaned out of the crow's nest.

Monda-ak had been following the conversation carefully and woofed softly once.

"Yes, you know that means you, too."

Chapter Fifty-Six
Home

Alex and Monda-ak led the caravan as it reversed its route from several years earlier. He hadn't managed to bring every Kragdon-ah person home, but he believed he had found all those who had survived the journey.

Soon, they would begin to split off into smaller companies that traveled together toward similar destinations.

When they trekked through the valley that led to the open plain, Alex encouraged everyone to make as much noise as they could. He wanted to let the ronit-ta know they were coming in great numbers, so they would stay out of the way.

It worked, as he never saw so much as a single silver back poking up among the tall grass.

When they came within sight of the tree line, Alex heard the sound of horns blasting the news of their arrival back to Winten-ah. The lookouts were not supposed to leave their position in the trees, but almost immediately, Alex saw one of them running toward him.

"Why does that make me nervous?" he asked Sanda, who was walking at the front of the caravan with him.

The lookout sprinted straight toward Alex, shouting, "Gunta, Manta-ak, Gunta!"

"Is everything all right?" Alex asked when the man drew closer and slowed to a walk.

"Of course it is all right! You have brought our brothers and sisters home!"

"Not all of them, unfortunately," Alex said, feeling the weight of those he had lost.

"But all of them who are alive are with us," Sanda said, to clarify.

"Long ago, Sekun-ak told us that when we see you, we are to report to him immediately. Do you have a message for him?"

"That I will see him for dinner, and he might want to put a bigger stew pot on. We might have a few guests tonight."

Alex took a deep breath and let it out as he walked. He had been afraid that he would return to find that Sekun-ak no longer lived, or that some other catastrophe had struck while he was away. Instead, it seemed that life at the cliffs had gone on as it always had.

When the caravan finally reached the trees, Alex halted. This was where he said goodbye to Harta-ak, Versa-eh, Rinka-ak, and all the tribes who had joined in the fight from the east and north.

"Gunta, friends, we never could have accomplished what we did without you."

"Now that we have traveled the world," Rinka-ak said, "the distance between Rinta-ah and Winten-ah seems small. We will see you soon. But first, we must go and check on how our son the chieftain has done in our absence."

One group continued on east, while the rest turned south with Alex. As they passed each guard post, one of the two lookouts dropped down and joined them.

"We drew lots to see who had to stay behind and keep watch," one of them said, obviously happy that he had won. "Now I will accompany you home."

The whole thing took on the feeling of a parade, as more guards joined them, then a wave of young people and children ran toward them from the open field.

The children jumped excitedly around Alex, Monda-ak—everyone, really—as though they were returning from the candy store with pockets full of goodies.

Alex pushed on into the field and finally saw Sekun-ak. He strode toward him and laid a hand on his shoulder in the Winten-ah greeting, then abandoned that and hugged him.

Sekun-ak accepted the embrace with good humor. When Alex finally stood away from him, he saw tears in his old friend's eyes.

"Gunta," Alex said, because everything else he had thought to say to Sekun-ak had fled from his head.

"Dad, look," Sanda said, pointing toward the cliffs. The waterfall, which had been destroyed years before, flowed again, splashing down into a pool beside Torana's house.

"Did you think I would just be sitting here doing nothing while you were off on your adventure?" Sekun-ak asked.

"Did you find the door?" Alex asked.

"It is there, but we did not go through it. I do not like the sound of the time you came from, Manta-ak."

Alex glanced at Sanda, knowing that they would have to make the decision about whether to return to Oregon or not. The idea had occurred to him that he could spend part of his life there and part of it in Kragdon-ah. There was something about having a foot in both worlds that did not appeal to him, however, unless Amy chose one world and Sanda the other. In the end, he knew much of his decision would come down to what his daughters wanted to do.

Alex turned and saw Tinta-ak beside him with the remainder of those he had brought from his own tribe.

"Will you stay with us here tonight?"

Tinta-ak put his hand to his throat to signal no. "We are so close after being so far away, my people want to continue on until we reach home."

Alex noticed the way he said that—*my people want to continue on*. Tinta-ak himself looked a little lost. Alex believed that although he had mourned the loss of Fantem-eh in the great unknown of the other side of the fog, as long as there was a task at hand, he had been able to distract himself. Now, with home so close, her loss was hitting him afresh.

Alex stared into the eyes of the big man who had been beside him through so many battles. "Do not stay away too long this time, my friend."

Tinta-ak raised a hand in goodbye and he and his people trudged away to the southeast.

Alex looked around and saw that many different reunions were going on. When they had left for Drakana, it was uncertain if any of them would ever return. Now that they were back, there would be a celebration.

Perhaps the strangest reunion was when Sista-eh came flying across the field and jumped into the arms of the kneeling Torana. It had been necessary to keep children at home in the dangerous conditions they faced, but that only made many of the reunions that much sweeter.

Torana immediately plucked her up and put her on her normal spot on his left shoulder. Sista-eh had grown in the years they had been gone, but she still resembled a tiny doll sitting on the giant's shoulder.

A voice carried from up on the cliffside. "Alex Hawk!"

Alex's head snapped up and he saw Reggie, known in Kragdon-ah as Untrin-ak, hurrying down the path. Like Alex, there was gray in his hair and beard now and he wasn't quite so nimble coming down the ladders and switchbacks.

"That's Monta-ak to you, Untrin-ak," Alex said with a smile. "Still living off your good looks and charm?"

"More or less. Tinka-eh and I have been settled down here for a few seasons. Sekun-ak has been kind enough to let us stay. We were a little worried about you and wanted to be here when you got back."

"No party in Kragdon-ah can be complete without the famous Untrin-ak," Alex exclaimed. When Reggie drew closer, Alex hugged him. "You didn't have to give up your life on the road just for me."

Reggie made a dismissive gesture with his hand. "Ah, it wasn't just you. Tinka-eh is pretty sweet on one of these young Winten-ah hunters. She didn't want to leave him, and I didn't want to leave her, so here we've been."

Alex had been in charge of everything and everyone for so long that he was more than pleased to let the mantle of responsibility fall from him. He, Amy, and Sanda sat on a log in the field and watched the celebrations and preparations going on around them.

A firepit was built in the middle of the field and cooks busied themselves at making a feast.

Reggie stood on the lowest level of the caves and gave an impromptu concert, with his daughter Tinka-eh harmonizing along with him. Alex couldn't be sure in the flickering light of the fire and torches, but he thought he saw a pronounced baby bump under Tinka-eh's shirt.

I think you might be grounded, Reggie.

Sanda laid her head on one of her father's shoulders, Amy on the other, and Alex let himself relax—fully relax—for the first time since they had left for Drakana.

Chapter Fifty-Seven
To Stay or Go

Alex spent that night deep in conversation with Sekun-ak, though it was mostly one-sided, with Alex giving long answers to Sekun-ak's questions.

Finally, after hearing about all the tribulations of the voyage and the battles and why Alex believed they were safe now from any further attacks from Drakana, Sekun-ak asked Alex the question he really wanted to know.

"Now that everything is good here, where are you going to live? You are Winten-ah. If you want to stay here, we will hold the ceremony and make Sanda-eh and Amy-eh Winten-ah, too. They have more than earned that."

By then, Alex and Sekun-ak were sitting around a fire in one of the small caves. It was late into the night then and many people had taken their loved ones and gone to bed.

Alex glanced at Amy, Sanda, and Monda-ak. The dog had given up on anything more interesting happening—like a sudden delivery of food—and was sound asleep. His snores echoed loudly off the walls of the cave.

Alex reached an arm out and hugged his daughters, pulling them close to him. He looked at Amy closely and saw how she had changed since she and Sanda had impetuously jumped through the door. Her fair skin was deeply tanned now. Her dark curls were sun-kissed. She had never been heavy, but now there was a leanness about her face that highlighted her bottle-green eyes. More than anything, she looked happy and content.

Sanda had never wandered far from her Winten-ah roots, even with twenty years spent in Oregon.

"I want to stay here," Alex said, "but I am worried that someone else will find the portal and come through. We saw with Doug-ak and Makinta what can happen when someone who seeks power steps through. The problem is, I can't think of a way to stop anyone else from finding their way through."

Amy, who had never met a puzzle she didn't love to solve, put her brain to the challenge. "We could go back and rebuild the wall, make it even more secure, but that would leave one of us on the wrong side." She squinted her left eye and twitched her mouth left and right as she did when solving a problem. "We could move the wall further out, so we could finish it from the inside, then step back through."

"That's the best idea I've come up with, too," Alex admitted. "But it's still not perfect. I found the door after Mr. Hadaller built the wall because it made the outer wall a few inches too short. If we leave enough room to finish the wall from the inside, that will be even more noticeable."

"Is there anyone you trust enough to seal it up after you?"

Alex ran through his mental list of old friends from his Army days. Finally, he shook his head. "I've been out of touch with them for too long. I think eventually, all of them would want to come through and have a peek at what's on the other side."

"Just like you did," Amy observed.

"Just like I did," he agreed.

"Could we hire somebody to just fill the whole basement with concrete?" Sanda asked.

As tired as he was, that made Alex smile. "Maybe we could, but I'd like to find something more permanent."

"More permanent than concrete?" Sanda asked.

"Well, the concrete would be pretty permanent, but here's what I see. We own the house free and clear, but there are still taxes to be paid every year. Even if I paid a few years in advance, eventually it would go under the gavel for back taxes. *Someone* would buy it, even with a basement full of cement. I think they'd just tear the whole place down and destroy the concrete. When they did that, it would be obvious where the door is. Whoever bought it might keep it for themselves, or worse, they might tell the authorities about it. Either way wouldn't be good. I don't want to think about what will happen if the US of A government starts sending armed troops into Kragdon-ah. That won't be as easy to fix as stopping the Drakana."

Amy and Sanda looked at each other and shrugged. "You've got us, Dad. We don't have an answer either."

"Are you sure you want to stay here? Don't you miss the twenty-first century?"

The two women looked at each other then back at Alex. Neither spoke, but they shook their heads emphatically.

"There's something about being here that we would miss forever if we had to go back."

At that moment, Nanda-eh wandered into the room and grinned at Sanda, then extended her hand. Sanda went to her, took her hand and they left together.

"Besides," Amy said, "I think one of us has found love."

"I think so, too," Alex agreed.

Alex turned back to Sekun-ak and said, "I'm thinking of making a few more buildings. What would you think of that?"

"I think our caves are best. But if you want to build something to live in, that is fine. We will welcome you back into the caves when the zisla-ta come back." His eyes sparkled a little at this last.

"God, I hope they never return. I was thinking of building a small house for Amy and I and a larger one where the archers can all stay together. They have their own special sisterhood and they would like that."

"Hey, I might find someone someday, too," Amy reminded him.

"And when you do, I will build you a house for the two of you if you want."

"We will always have a place in the caves for you, Amy-eh," Sekun-ak said. "Your father is trying to make you soft, but the caves will offer protection from anything."

ALEX FELL BACK INTO the Winten-ah routine with ease. It was late summer by the time they arrived back and winter was coming. That meant he, Monda-ak and the hunters went out every few days.

In between, he did as he said he would and built houses. There were already two of them built in Winten-ah—the tall one for Torana, and a more normal-sized house for Reggie. Alex built a slightly bigger house for himself and Amy to share. The good spots on the lower edge of the cliff were already taken, so Alex built this house below them. Not so great for defense, but not so far away from the caves that it would take them long in an emergency.

He, Amy, and Sanda had talked repeatedly about going back to Oregon just to check and make sure everything was still fine with the house. That had been all there was to it, though—talk. When it came time to go through, one or the other of them always found something else they wanted or needed to do. They had agreed that they wouldn't ever go through the door unless all four of them—including Monda-ak—was with them. They wouldn't ever again risk being separated.

It was a peaceful winter in Winten-ah. Alex finished the house for himself and Amy before the first frost came. He had learned a few things while building tiny houses for dozens of other people in Oregon, and he applied them all to this home.

He took a horse and cart and he, Amy, Sanda, and Monda-ak walked to Prata-ah. He hadn't been back since he had returned to Kragdon-ah, but he wanted to show them where Lanta-eh was buried.

When they came to the bottom of the hill, Alex told them about how he had faced the king of the godat-ta in that spot and how he and Monda-ak had almost died. They left the horse and cart at the bottom of Prata-ah and hiked up to the small enclosure where Lanta-eh had communicated with the people who came back and saved the human race from extinction.

They spent the day hauling some of the river rocks that hadn't been used in building the structure down the hill. By the time the sun dipped low in the sky, the three of them were exhausted. Monda-ak, who had spent his time chasing rabbits and foxes, then napping, felt fine.

On their last trip to the top, Alex knelt beside the statue of Lanta-eh that the visitor named Emily had made. It was a perfect likeness and he felt the same surge of emotions he had when he had first seen it.

Alex was not a man who felt like he had a clue as to what happened after life's final curtain, but he knew that he felt the spirit of the young girl who died so humanity could go on.

When they returned to Winten-ah, Alex used those rocks to build a river rock fireplace for the new house. They passed the winter in relative comfort, though there were still some improvements Alex planned to make in the spring.

Spring arrived early that year, and the Winten-ah broke ground and planted their krinta—the corn-like plant that had become a staple of their diet. They hoped that if the weather didn't turn cold enough to freeze the seedlings, they might be able to squeeze a second harvest out of the summer.

Alex was taking his turn at the hoe, breaking up the hardy weeds that took over the ground each winter. He was reflecting on how he had been doing this same task on the day Senta-eh admitted she was pregnant. In other circumstances, that would have been ecstatic news. In Kragdon-ah, during the time of the plague that killed mothers who gave birth, it had been a death sentence.

He stood to wipe the sweat from his forehead and saw a passing strange sight. A man had emerged from the forest path, but the lookouts hadn't blown the horns to announce his imminent arrival.

He was dressed strangely, but in a way that Alex could almost—not quite—place. The man looked familiar too. Just tickling the edge of Alex's memory.

The man walked confidently, with no obvious weapons. The children who had been playing in the field ran to the stranger to see what they could see.

As Alex grew closer, he saw the man was about the same height and age as Alex himself. He had salt-and-pepper hair and a longish beard that had gone mostly to white.

Alex put the hoe over his shoulder and was the first adult to reach the man. "Gunta," Alex said, half-expecting the word to go unrecognized. There was something *foreign* about this man.

Instead, the man said, "Gunta, Manta-ak," in a voice that crackled oddly.

That was all it took for Alex to place him, though he couldn't remember the man's name.

"You're one of the visitors, aren't you? The disciples of Janus?"

"I suppose that is a fair way of looking at things. I am Pandrick Masten. I have come to close the portal."

Alex Hawk felt a bit lost.

"I thought you all went home?"

"Those who wanted to go home, did so," Pandrick said. "I chose to stay." He looked closely at Alex. "Apparently, I made the same choice you did, so you should understand."

"Are they coming back for you?"

"Oh, no," the man said with a small laugh. "I have made myself a permanent castaway in this strange world. Bisla was going to close the door after you returned home, but since I decided to stay here, he left it up to me. With the technology I carry, there's very little risk of me being eaten by a huge animal or killed by an attacker. He trusted that I would return and seal the portal eventually."

"So you've just been wandering around Kragdon-ah for more than twenty years?"

"Indeed," Pandrick said. "Twenty very happy years. No matter what anyone said, the life I came from always seemed a little too easy. This world is so organic, I fell in love with it."

Alex was still trying to process the fact that he was looking at this man, who he had been certain he would never see again. "Doesn't all the technology you brought with you need batteries? I'd hate to have whatever you use to keep yourself safe run low on power just about the time a godat-ta gets a look at you."

"You are thinking like a twenty-first century man, which is understandable, as that is what you are," Pandrick said. "We made many technological improvements in the intervening centuries."

By then, others had come from the caves, including Sekun-ak, Amy, Sanda, and Nanda-eh.

"Gunta," Pandrick said in greeting. "I am just passing through. I hope you do not object to my presence here."

That spiel had the sound of a rehearsed speech, and Alex wondered how many times he had repeated it in similar circumstances.

"I remember you," Sekun-ak said. "You brought the end to the curse which plagued us. You are always welcome here."

Alex glanced at Sekun-ak. He may have seen a few more solstices than Alex, but his memory was sharp.

Pandrick turned back to Alex. "In truth, I did not expect to see you here again. Once you went through, I thought it was permanent."

"That makes two of us. It is a long story. I will tell it to you over a campfire in good time if you want," Alex said with a rueful grin, then grew serious. "I am glad to hear you have returned to close the door. It has been worrying me."

"I'll give you time to say goodbye to everyone here, then I will permanently deactivate it."

"Instead of that, can you give me a day to go through and get a few things in order, then return before you deactivate it?"

The man cocked his head slightly to the right, a very human gesture that had obviously survived the centuries. "You wish to be here when I turn the portal off? Do you understand that it will never be turned back on?"

"I returned to the twenty-first century last time because I needed to be with both my daughters. Going back to Oregon was the only way." He pointed to both Amy and Sanda, and Pandrick bowed slightly to each of them. "But they are here with me now, and they are going to stay."

"There is something about this world that pulls like a magnet, isn't there?"

Alex looked around. Spring sunshine poured down on them. The air was still a little cool, but was so pristine he never wanted to breathe the exhaust of another vehicle. Everyone he really cared about was here.

"Why would I ever want to be anywhere else?"

Pandrick agreed to stay in Winten-ah for a few days. There were things he wanted to do in the area anyway, and he said he had no real schedule in mind.

Alex made plans for him, Sanda, Amy, and Monda-ak to go back through the door that afternoon and return the next day, assuming everything was copacetic on the other side of the door.

There really weren't many plans to be made to step through the door again, though Alex wanted to put some time into anything he might want to bring back from Oregon. Knowing this would be the last time gave it extra weight.

The sun had long-since set when Alex and the others were ready to step through.

"It's gonna be dark when we get there, isn't it?"

"Probably," Alex said, "but it's our own house. I think I can find my way around."

As he had when he had crossed back to the twenty-first century decades earlier, he decided to tie all of them together. Pandrick laughed at the precaution and told him there was no way they could be separated inside the portal. Alex knew that humans had created the thing, which meant that mistakes were not just possible, but likely. He also believed that the worse the consequences of something going wrong, the more effort he would take to avoid those consequences.

He couldn't imagine anything worse than stepping through the door in Oregon and finding that one of the four of them had not made it there.

Thus, the rope, which he tied around his, Amy's, and Sanda's waists. He looped the final end around Monda-ak's wide shoulders and used it like a halter.

The people of Winten-ah gathered around as Alex prepared to step through the door, which was once again hidden behind the rebuilt waterfall.

Alex laid a hand on Sekun-ak's shoulder, said, "We'll be back tomorrow," then grabbed both ends of the rope and, one after another, they stepped through the door.

Chapter Fifty-Eight
The Door, for the Final Time

There was the same sense of slight nausea and disorientation they had felt before when they stepped through.

The door opened into a pitch-black basement.

It was Sanda who recovered the quickest. Her eyes adjusted first, and she said, "Oh, Dad."

Alex blinked, forced down the rising bile that often accompanied a trip across the centuries and waited for his eyes to adjust. "I can't see anything yet. What do you see?"

"It's trashed, Dad. The place looks like a bombed-out building."

"What, like World War III happened in the few years we were gone and Central Oregon was ground zero?"

"No, not really. More like a bunch of squatters have been living here," Amy said.

"And the smell," Sanda added. "It's like they lived here—or are still living here—without the benefit of running water."

Alex stumbled to his workbench, which still stood, though there were piles of debris all around it. He switched on the small lamp he kept there, but there was no electricity.

"Okay, let's everyone stand still while our eyes adjust. I don't want anyone falling down and hurting themselves."

"*We* can see just fine, old man," Sanda teased. "And by *we*, I include Monda-ak. Tell me we don't have to go back to calling him that ridiculous name, Mondak, while we're back."

Alex reached out his hand and Monda-ak came right to him. "No, he will always be Monda-ak now. If I put my hand on your shoulder, can you lead me to the stairs?"

Sanda reached out and placed Alex's hand on her arm and picked her way across a debris field of broken bricks, garbage, and human waste.

"Wait," Amy said. "If someone has broken in and been squatting here, that meant they had open access to the door. Why didn't we ever see anyone try to come through?"

"Maybe they did," Alex said. "It smells wet, too, like there's been mud and water down here. Maybe they tried the door and ran into nothing but the back end of the debris field or the waterfall. For all I know, they're still in that middle part of the door, wandering around." That thought raised gooseflesh on his arm and he said, "Come on, get me upstairs."

Upstairs was a little better, but not much. There wasn't evidence of mud, but it didn't feel like their home any more. Furniture was broken or overturned and it looked like some of it was broken up and burned in the fireplace.

Alex paused at the top of the stairs, alert for any threat. He was still armed in Kragdon-ah fashion, as were Amy and Sanda. If there was some potential boogeyman hiding in the dark on this night, they would soon learn they had picked the wrong house to squat in.

It was a little easier to see on the main floor, as the windows let in crossbeams of light from the streetlamps outside.

The windows hadn't been broken out, but it looked like the front door had been kicked in at one time and someone had put a sheet of plywood across it.

"I guess this is what happens when you step out for a few years and forget to even lock the doors."

"I'm sorry, Dad," Amy said. "I know you loved this house."

"I did. I do," Alex said. "My first instinct is to start cleaning up this mess. Maybe I should start by writing a letter of apology to the neighborhood, though. I'm sure this house is bringing all their property values down."

"Or maybe we should just get what we came for, if it's still here, and go back home," Sanda said. "If we ever needed a sign that this is no longer where we belong, I'd say this is it."

"If we had more time, I could do something with the house, though. Deed it to someone or something. Donate it to charity."

"This is our old life," Amy said. "Does any of it matter once we step through that door? Like you said, eventually the state will foreclose for non-payment of taxes, then it will go up for auction. Someone will either buy it and fix it up, or tear it to the ground and start over. Either way, it's not really any business of ours, is it?"

Alex opened and closed his fists, at war with himself. Finally, he let his shoulders sag. "You're right. You're both right. Get what we came for, then we can go back home."

Alex walked through the kitchen, which wasn't as bad as the rest of the house. The cupboard doors were all open and any food that had been there was gone, except for a lonely can of hominy in one corner.

"Nobody likes hominy, I guess," Alex said.

The back door wasn't broken down or boarded up, so Alex opened it and stepped into the back yard.

He had kept that yard manicured and perfect. Now it was a jungle. The grass came up above his knees and weeds grew up around the walkway and steps, almost obscuring them.

Monda-ak bounded down the steps and began the task of re-marking his territory.

It was a clear night and between the streetlamps and the three-quarter moon, Alex had good visibility. He walked around the corner of the house, expecting to find his pickup truck, but the driveway was empty.

"Guess somebody helped themselves to that, too."

He stepped back into the shadows. He didn't really want to run into any of his old neighbors and have to explain where he had been for the previous three or four years, and what he was doing back now.

Inside, he found Amy and Sanda in their room. It wasn't pristine, and neither of them could imagine sleeping on the bare mattresses that were there, but it wasn't completely trashed.

Amy had unpinned a map of the world from the wall and was rolling it up.

Sanda was digging around the bottom of their closet and found a stash of art supplies that had been neglected—drawing-paper, packets of pens and pencils, and a ream of typing paper.

"Thanks," Amy said, shoving much of it in the bag she had brought with her. "That'll be perfect. I've been thinking I want to create an alphabet for the universal language. It will make everyone feel a little more connected, I think, if we can communicate in writing with everyone."

"I was going to go to the store and buy some things to take back with us," Alex said, "but I don't know how to swing that now."

"Why?" Amy and Sanda asked together.

"The truck's gone, and I didn't see that little Mazda you guys shared anywhere either."

"We can walk to town and get anything we want, right?" Amy said.

"With what? I didn't even have my wallet with me when I came after you. It's long gone, so I don't have my debit card or credit cards. I don't even have my driver's license any more to get money out of the bank." He smiled at the thought of it. "Do you think if I walked in and said I am the famous Manta-ak that would do any good?"

"It's almost like we've already been erased from this world," Amy said.

"And that's okay, right?" Sanda agreed. "That's what we want."

"I don't want to stay here tonight," Alex said. "Let's gather up what we need and go home. Take your time, though. No rush. This is a one-way trip, now."

They wandered through the house, looking for anything they thought they couldn't leave behind.

Sanda found a few tea candles and a half-used pack of matches on the floor and that made searching easier.

Beyond the few art supplies and a few hand tools that hadn't been stolen by the squatters, they couldn't find much. They gathered in the basement, then Amy snapped her fingers.

"Damn, I almost forgot. Be right back."

She sprinted up the stairs and came back down with a photo album and a framed picture of Mindy, her mom.

"That's it," she said. "That's all I need of modern civilization, I think."

Alex, ever-cautious, tied them all together again and led them single-file through the door.

They had spent less than two hours back in twenty-first century Oregon, but it was long enough.

They came through with no problem and not too much nausea.

Alex stepped around the waterfall and took a deep breath of air. After the fetid stink of their former home, it was divine.

From a few feet away in the darkness, a deep voice said, "Gunta, brother and sisters."

Alex was not surprised. It was Sekun-ak, standing guard.

"I thought you would be gone to your old home longer," he observed drily.

"That's not our home anymore," Alex answered.

"I am glad you have returned," Sekun-ak said with a wave of his hand as he walked away. All was right in his world and all his charges were home.

Alex reached down and untied the knots around Monda-ak.

"I'm a little too keyed-up to sleep, I think. I'm going to go up and sit on top of the cliffside and look at the moon for a few minutes."

Amy and Sanda looked at each other and said, "Me too," with one voice.

They carried their bags to the first cave and set them down, then made the short climb up to the top of the cliffs.

As he had done years earlier with Senta-eh, then again with Lanta-eh, Alex sat and dangled his legs over the side.

It was a cloudless night and the only sounds came from the insects of the field and the birds of the night. The stars spread across the sky like a billion brilliant diamonds.

Monda-ak lay behind them with a small grunt, then leaned his weight against Alex's back.

Alex put one arm around each of his daughters and felt the cares and responsibilities of life slip away from him.

Hours later, Amy and Sanda had fallen asleep, still leaning against him. His back was stiff, but he didn't want to move—didn't want to disturb this perfect moment.

He watched the sun rise over Kragdon-ah.

Over his home.

Author's Note

We need to talk about that fog, don't we? Of course we do. And we will. But first a quick bit of business.

If you have enjoyed the Alex Hawk books, you might like to know when I publish something new. I have just the thing: my *New Release Newsletter*. You can join at that link, and as a thank you for joining, I'll send you a free ebook copy of *Rock 'n Roll Heaven*—the story of Jimmy 'Guitar' Velvet, who ends up exploring the titular location and meeting the titans of rock 'n roll. It's a fun read and it's yours free for joining my list.

If you'd like to contact me, you can reach me on Facebook at http://Facebook.com/shawninmonwriter. I post something on there most days and you can always leave me a message there.

I also have a website—http://shawn-inmon.com. There's lots of good stuff on there, including a library of books that have influenced me, and a way to order signed paperbacks for only $10. You can also email me .

Okay, about that fog.

Theoretically, this was going to be the last book in the Alex Hawk Time Travel Adventure series. As I was writing the book, though, that made me a little sad. I have really loved writing these five Alex Hawk books over the past year. I didn't want to leave the world behind.

Since I am a discovery writer—which just means that I don't plot my story in advance, I thought there was a real chance that Alex would die at the end of this book. I even had a death scene and a real tear-jerker ending. As it turned out, when I got to the end—as you have just seen—Alex lived.

But, in the middle of the book, when I was feeling bummed out in thinking that I might be writing the last Alex Hawk story ever, I put a little escape hatch in.

The fog.

It would, of course, be unfair to place such a giant mystery in the middle of the story and then never resolve it. I will definitely write the story of what happened to Alex and company in the fog. I will answer all the questions about it. In fact, it will be a book of its own. I can't be sure it will be published in 2021—my production schedule is already pretty full for the year—but I think I might sneak it in before the end of the year.

The Prince of Kragdon-ah is a great stopping point if you don't want to go on though, I think. There I go breaking another author rule: never tell your readers they can stop reading.

After I finished the original trilogy in this series, I thought I might be done. Then I realized that it was inevitable—as sure as the world turns—that someone would try to colonize someone else. Kragdon-ah was the obvious target. They weren't organized, they hated technology, and they were spread out. All factors that would make them easy to overwhelm and colonize.

My predicament when I had the Drakana invade Kragdon-ah in the fourth book was that I truly had no idea how Alex would find a way to overcome them in this book. The Drakana had so many advantages that I was really worried I couldn't find out a way for him to emerge victorious in a realistic way.

I think I got there, though.

I didn't know the Northmen would be invading Drakana—or that the Drakana and Alex would become allies until I got there.

All along, I thought the big battle would be between Alex and the Drakana. It turned out to be Alex and the Northmen.

As is so often the case in my series, my effort at tying up the series with a neat bow didn't work out. I love my characters and the worlds I create and it's very difficult for me to leave them behind.

Now that we know Alex is still alive at the end of this book, I could even write more books that pick up at this point and move the story forward. For that to happen, I'll need another good idea like someone attacking the Kragdon-ah, though. So far, it hasn't dropped into my head, but I'll never say never.

Before I forget, I need to mention what song I listened to while writing this book. I try to remember in every Author's Note, but my memory is not great. When I forget, I get emails and Facebook messages inquiring, so I'm glad I remembered this time.

For *Prince of Kragdon-ah*, I listened to one of my favorite songs over and over again—*The End* by The Doors. Apocalypse Now has always been near my mind as I was writing these books, so it just felt right to use The Doors' epic song for the ostensible last book in the series.

If you enjoyed the Alex Hawk books (and I'm assuming you did, or you wouldn't be likely to be reading the Author's Note at the end of Book Five in the series) I would like to ask you to consider giving my next series a try.

It's another fish-out-of-water portal fiction series. The first book is called *Kradak the Champion* and it is available at that link.

The idea for this book came to me in the flash of a single line: *Galaxy Quest meets Conan*. What if a movie star who makes Conan-like movies got kidnapped by someone from another world because they thought he was really the hero he played on the screen? And what if the fate of both worlds hung on his ability to actually become that hero?

Like the Alex Hawk series, there will be a lot of adventure, some humor, and I hope, great characters.

All five books in this series featured artwork from my lifetime best friend Jerry Weible. Jerry and I have been friends for more than fifty years and working with him on the drawings for this book has been among my greatest pleasures. By the way, that drawing of Alex at the end of the book is based on a self-portrait Jerry did.

Melissa Prideaux handled the editing on this book, as she did for *Warrior of Kragdon-ah*. She catches so many confusing bits and outright mistakes before the book ever sees the light of day that she makes me look like a much better writer than I am. I owe her a debt of gratitude.

Mark Sturgill was my graphics person again. That's such a simple sentence, but it hides a story. Mark had surgery on his shoulder on the same day I got the artwork from Jerry. He still managed to process and clean up all the drawings and prepare them for insertion into the book while in a great deal of pain. Mark also serves as one of my long-term proofreaders.

I have a group of proofreaders. Why? Because I make a lot of mistakes! Gremlins seem to sneak in and add new typos and problems while I sleep. Debra Galvan has been my first line of defense against those gremlins for at least the last twenty books and I can't imagine publishing without her. I added a new proofreader in my ongoing battle against inaccuracy—Kim O'Hara, who is an incredibly thorough reader and makes me question so many things! Marta Rubin is my first line reader—she actually reads and proofs while I am still writing the book. This helps me in so many ways—including being able to deliver a much cleaner book to the other proofreaders.

Lynn Weible and Dan Hilton also provided a valuable set of eyes for me. As I say, I make a lot of mistakes!

My next release will be *Kradak the Champion*[1]. I hope you'll join me on that adventure, too.

For now, I'll just say thank you for coming along on this adventure with Alex, Monda-ak, and everyone in Kragdon-ah.

Shawn Inmon
Tumwater, WA
March 2020

---

1.   *https://amzn.to/3b7wxQN*

Other Books by Shawn Inmon

The Middle Falls Time Travel Series
The Unusual Second Life of Thomas Weaver[1]
The Redemption of Michael Hollister[2]
The Life and Death of Dominick Davidner[3]
The Final Life of Nathaniel Moon[4]
The Emancipation of Veronica McAllister[5]
The Changing Lives of Joe Hart[6]
The Vigilante Life of Scott McKenzie[7]
The Reset Life of Cassandra Collins[8]
The Tribulations of Ned Summers[9]
The Empathetic Life of Rebecca Wright[10]
The Successful Life of Jack Rybicki[11]
The Many Short Lives of Charles Waters[12]

---

1. http://amzn.to/2aNgrdV

2. http://amzn.to/2wyUfCH

3. http://amzn.to/2yTgHnk

4. http://amzn.to/2z8seyk

5. http://amzn.to/2HkHegL

6. https://amzn.to/2rYBqVh

7. https://amzn.to/2LgxmLq

8. https://amzn.to/2D39mYG

9. https://amzn.to/2SxlzHK

10. https://amzn.to/2Ivx6Yi

11. https://amzn.to/2LBAQZx

Made in the USA
Las Vegas, NV
18 October 2021

32584969R00236